DAUGHTERS OF EDEN

At the outbreak of the Second World War, four very different young women are facing an uncertain future. Marjorie, left at a boarding school by her emigrating mother; plain Poppy, pushed into marriage with a mean-spirited aristocrat; Kate, despised by her father, but determined to prove herself; and man-mad Lily, who turns out to be the bravest of them all.

That all of them are chosen to work undercover for an espionage unit is a surprise, not least to them. At Eden Park they not only meet each other, but become involved with three unusual young men - Eugene, the seemingly feckless Irishman; Robert, Kate's brother; and dashing Scott, the undisputed favourite of the unit. While there is hardly time for romance before each is sent out into the field, there is just enough for passionate new relationships to form. Only Jack Ward, the mysterious spymaster, manages to remain aloof as he guides their destinies. The fact that they will look back on this time as having made them feel more exquisitely alive than ever before is not something they will know until much later.

DAUGHTERS OF EDEN

Charlotte Bingham

WINDSOR
PARAGON

First published 2004
by
Transworld
This Large Print edition published 2004
by
BBC Audiobooks Ltd
by arrangement with
Transworld Publishers Limited

ISBN 0 7540 9569 X (Windsor Hardcover)
ISBN 0 7540 9584 3   (Paragon Softcover)

British Library Cataloguing in Publication Data available

Printed and bound in Great Britain by
Antony Rowe Ltd., Chippenham, Wiltshire

In memory of 'Jack Ward'—patriot and gentleman.

'This other Eden . . .
This precious stone set in the silver sea'
Richard II
(Shakespeare)

To dream of Eden is to dream of a quiet wooded valley where nothing but birdsong is heard, where the clean, clear waters of a river undulate in a peaceful ribbon on either side of which the grass is grown and cut for the simple pleasure of walking. Trees have been planted so that it takes only a gentle breeze to bend them forward to see their leafy reflections in the water below. And there is a house palely lit in early morning light, its window casements long and graceful, its classical Corinthian columns guarding shallow steps that lead up to vast, carved double doors.

Around the garden are grouped buildings of the same stone as the house, lodges and cottages, an icehouse, a gazebo for lakeside picnics. Further on a stable yard houses a clock with gold painted numerals, and a cobbled stone yard that once rang to the sound of thoroughbred hooves.

But no one lives at this other Eden now, no one that was born there that is. No one that once ran about its lawns, or pushed the old ridge-bottomed wooden boat on to its lake, or sat above the aqueduct listening to the waters rushing through below, now haunts its follies. There are no beautifully dressed women to be seen, gloved hands resting on the perfectly tailored sleeves of the men accompanying them, all of them laughing and talking, wondering at the beauty of some new day. Now all that can be heard are secrets being plotted in and around the walls of the old house, secrets that will shape lives and change the world, and Eden, for ever.

Part One

ENGLAND IN THE LATE NINETEEN THIRTIES

CHAPTER ONE

Mrs Beaumont sighed with satisfaction as she put down *The Times*, for there in the engagement column was the announcement of her darling daughter Poppy's forthcoming marriage. She patted the side of her hair, and then picked up the newspaper again.

Mr and Mrs Spencer Tynant Beaumont are pleased to announce the engagement of their beloved daughter Poppy Elizabeth to Arthur Basil Hetchett Tetherington, fourth Baron Tetherington.

Despite the announcement's having been made some months before, and the wedding's being about to take place—Westminster, the Savoy and all the usual trimmings—Oralia Beaumont still loved to start off the day by once again reading that announcement in the now yellowing copy of the Thunderer. It was the knowledge of the apoplexy with which the rival mothers of other debutantes would have greeted thc announcement that gave her such particular pleasure. She could hear them moaning to each other on their telephones, or from under their hats over lunch at the Savoy.

'Poppy Beaumont *of all people*. I mean, of all the girls out this Season, you would never think that *she* would be snapped up by a baron. And not just any baron—not some ropy old Irish peer—but a rich English baron. Owner of a vast estate, a house in Eaton Square, everything you could wish for—and she as plain as a pikestaff, and wears

3

spectacles.'

Oralia stared with quiet pride around her bedroom as the maid came in to take away her breakfast tray. Poppy might not be a beauty, but she obviously must have something special to attract such a handsome, amusing, and elegant man as Basil Tetherington. For why else would he have snapped Poppy up after only three balls and a luncheon?

He was so generous, too. Nothing would do but he must buy her a new motor car, which Poppy hoped one day to be able to drive, but in which he now drove her. With all the talk of war, by necessity it had been a whirlwind romance, but a romance it most certainly was, for Mrs Beaumont was sure that Poppy was quite as happy to marry Basil as he was to marry her.

'Ah, there you are, my dear. Out again, do I see?'

Poppy peered round the door at her mother, who was now preening herself in front of a silver hand mirror. The ostrich feather trimming of her bedjacket caused Poppy to sneeze suddenly and vehemently as she drew close.

'Yes, Mother. I am just going out, to meet Mary Jane Ogilvy for lunch.'

Oralia replaced her hand mirror on the pink satin quilt.

'I expect her mother is spitting nails, isn't she, my dear?'

Poppy pushed her spectacles further up her nose and stared at her beautiful, elegant Southern Belle parent with a puzzled expression.

'I am sorry, Mother?'

Mrs Beaumont stared back at her daughter with barely concealed impatience.

4

'I mean, about your engagement, Poppy darlin',' she said slowly. 'Since Mary Jane is not engaged to anyone at all, and you are engaged to Lord Tetherington, one imagines she will be spitting nails.'

Poppy sighed inwardly. She simply did not understand her mother's competitive nature. She herself had never felt competitive with anyone, and with good reason. Born with what her dear old Irish nurse always called a *stigmata* in her left eye, Poppy had unfortunately been forced to wear glasses—or spectacles, as her mother insisted on calling them—from a very early age.

Sure and she'll never marry now, Nanny Beaumont had used to say with some satisfaction to the other nannies when Poppy was walked in the Park. *Gentlemen are simply not attracted to girls who wear spectacles, as everyone well knows.*

Even at children's parties little boys would make it quite obvious that they couldn't wait to leave her side and sit beside some other little girl, who did not wear pale pink spectacles whose wire ends pulled her ears forward, making them stick through her hair.

Fortunately she had been educated at home, so her mother and father had been only too happy to leave her to her own devices, as well as to the kindly if sporadic attentions of the servants, so that Poppy grew up with her books as friends, and her dogs for company. As long as she had books and dogs, however, she was happy, and would have remained so, living an oddly solitary existence on the upper floors of her parents' town and country houses, if her mother had not suddenly decided it might be fun for *her*—if not for Poppy—if Poppy were to do the Season as a debutante.

For Poppy it was of course the very opposite of fun—it was agony. Every single moment of her Season was torture, from the fitting of the coats and skirts, the day frocks and the evening gowns, to the trying on of the hats. Hat after hat after hat she had to try, all of them making her look more and more ludicrous, on account of her round, plastic-framed spectacles. At least they were now a sombre black rather than the vivid pink of her childhood, but inevitably, of course, as was only to be expected, it was Poppy's beautiful mother rather than her plain daughter who attracted all the attention from both people and press.

The beautiful Oralia Beaumont again stunned the assembled company in a two-piece by Lablanc, all topped off by a chapeau de chapeaux—a hat of such elegance that no one could match it. If mothers of debutantes could win prizes for the Season, then Mrs Beaumont would surely win the Gold Cup.

As her mother flourished, so Poppy wilted, as poppies so often do when plucked out of their natural environment. Seated on the side, dance after dance after dance, she became inured to feeling isolated and ridiculous. Sometimes it seemed to her that the wretched Season—with its endless banal chatter covering up none too successfully her fellow debutantes' obsessive pursuit of a diamond engagement ring—would never end. It actually threatened to last for ever, just as sitting out dance after dance on some wobbly gilt Gunter's ball chair was also a perpetual hell, until with Ascot Week finally over—and only two or three balls to endure—she realised with ever increasing relief that the end was actually coming into sight.

One particular evening she was sitting in her usual state of abandonment on the sidelines of the ballroom, watching as her mother was whirled past her in the arms of an admiring young man, when a masculine voice interrupted her bored thoughts.

'I wonder if you would do me the honour of having this dance?'

Poppy looked up in undisguised surprise at the speaker.

'I am sorry,' she stammered in confusion. 'But what did you say?'

The man looking down at her was extremely handsome, with fair hair, bright blue eyes, and a surprisingly serious expression.

'I said I wonder if you would do me the honour of having this dance?'

Poppy stared up at him, still unable to quite believe her ears.

'You do mean me?' she said, putting a hand on the bodice of her dowdy ball dress to indicate herself.

'Since all the other chairs either side of you are empty, I really think I must.'

Poppy stood up.

'Sorry,' she muttered, putting out a hand to introduce herself, only to find it being firmly taken in her unknown admirer's left hand and herself being led out on the dance floor.

'I'm—I'm Poppy Beaumont,' she stammered, already being waltzed around the floor.

'I know. And I'm Basil Tetherington.'

7

'How do you do?'

'Rather bored as it happens. Up until now. How about you?'

'Yes. Yes, I was a bit—um—a bit, well, yes, bored as well, as it happens,' Poppy admitted.

After a few more turns of the ballroom, Poppy danced so close to her mother that she could not help noticing the look in her eyes, a mixture of shock and obvious irritation. Poppy smiled at her, realising that the first thing that must have crossed her mother's mind was the fact that someone had actually asked her to dance, and not just someone, but someone extremely handsome. As she waltzed on she saw the shock was so great that her mother had actually stopped dancing altogether, staring in some amazement at the sight of her plain daughter being danced around the ballroom by one of the catches of the Season. As Poppy passed by her yet again, she leaned forward as if to ask her something, but Poppy was gone before she could begin to say anything.

'Why don't we go on the balcony,' Basil suggested. 'And perhaps cause a scandal—if we can, that is.'

Poppy nodded, only too happy to leave the oppressive atmosphere of the ballroom where everything was noted and commented upon. It was as if she were a pet poodle and she had suddenly escaped her lead. She allowed herself to be led by the hand off to one of the many balconies that overlooked the Park outside.

'God,' Basil sighed, leaning back against the stone parapet, casually lighting a cigarette. 'I hope you hate these affairs as much as I do?'

'Good heavens yes. And, you know, with pretty

good reason too.'

'The reason being?' Basil raised his elegant eyebrows and looked at her.

'Because—well, I suppose because I'm not exactly a huge success at these things. In fact I'm a complete flop.'

Poppy pushed her glasses nervously back up on to the bridge of her nose as Basil continued to stare at her.

'What was that?'

'I said I was—you know—not exactly a huge success. Sorry—why?'

'I'm sure no one as honest as you can be accounted to be a flop, Miss Beaumont.'

'I don't mind being a flop, as it happens. It's not as if I set out to be a raging success. So you don't have to feel sorry on my account. I mean, that wasn't why I said it. Said what I did, I mean. If you see what I mean.'

'I see perfectly what you mean.'

'My mother—and my aunt, for instance,' Poppy continued, now taking off her glasses and holding them up, checking their cleanliness to cover her shyness. 'Both my aunt and my mother are much more successful with the young men than I am. But I really don't mind. I don't mind sitting it out. Sometimes I actually prefer it. Sometimes it can actually be quite interesting—sometimes. Although most times to be *absolutely* honest—most other times I'd much rather be home in bed with my dogs and a book.'

'You are not enamoured of the social life, obviously.'

'I think books are usually more interesting than most people I meet. Particularly at things like this.

9

Except that was rather rude—I really didn't mean to be rude.'

'You weren't being rude at all—particularly as I happen to agree with you. I far prefer a good book any time to having to endure the appalling boredom of events such as this, but I always come to London for the Season, as did my father, and my grandfather, and his father, and his father, and so on.'

Basil smiled at her. It was neither a very big smile nor a very warm one, but—as Poppy concluded—it was a smile none the less. Most men, on the rare occasions any had danced with her, returned her to the sidelines without so much as another look in her direction.

'My family look on me as being too bookish,' Poppy admitted, with ruthless candour. 'In fact my father's forever saying what with my looks and my reading I'm bound to end up living in someone's attic, a spinster with a parrot. It wouldn't actually be a parrot—it'd be a dog, actually, in my case. And as long as I had a dog I really don't think I'd mind.'

Poppy carefully replaced her glasses, hooking the wire ends securely behind her ears before staring up at the man staring down at her, running out of idle chat and now waiting for him to finish smoking his cigarette. She knew that the only reason he had taken a turn with her on the floor was so that he could quickly steer her on to a balcony in order to smoke a cigarette. It had happened to her several times during the Season, various young men taking her out on to the balcony just so they could have a smoke. She really didn't mind that much either. At least it made a change

10

from sitting on a gold chair, like some sort of abandoned dolly.

'Isn't that the last waltz?' she wondered, barely able to contain her sense of relief.

'I think it is,' he replied, stubbing his cigarette out underfoot. 'I do so hope we meet again, and soon. Are you going to be at the Jardines' masked ball tomorrow night by any chance?'

'Afraid so,' Poppy nodded. 'That's the trouble with the Season, isn't it? No sort of escaping it. Imagine what fun I'm going to have—in a mask and spectacles.'

To her surprise this made her escort laugh out loud and genuinely so. He stopped, turned and looked at her, and this time she saw the smile on his face was much broader although not a whole lot warmer.

'Tell you what,' he said, still smiling at her. 'Wear your spectacles outside your mask, eh? Put them on the outside—that'll really cause a stir— and keep the first five dances for me.'

Poppy nodded, the way she normally nodded whenever someone was wishing her a half-hearted goodnight plus the usual litany of excuses, only to frown suddenly when she realised what it was that had just been said to her.

'I don't know whether I dare,' she admitted, pulling a shy face.

'Be a sport,' Basil pressed. 'Liven things up considerably. And keep the first five dances for me.'

*   *   *

That was the bit Poppy really remembered as later

11

she clambered wearily into her bed, patting the counterpane on one side in order to encourage her dachshund, George, to jump up—smuggled upstairs as always once she knew her parents were asleep: the fact that this tall, handsome and considerably older stranger had seemingly asked her to save a number of dances just for him. Whether or not he was serious she did not know, but at this moment in time neither did she care. What was enjoyable was the idea that a good-looking man should want to dance with her in the first place. It would be ridiculous not to admit such a thing. And now, of course, it appeared that he wanted to have several of the first dances at the Jardines' ball with her, and her alone. Fondling the silken ears of her beloved little dog, she sighed, and for once in her young life went happily to sleep, relishing the possibility, although not quite believing in it.

Yet the odd thing was that no sooner had the band struck up for the first dance at the Jardines' masked ball the following evening than Poppy did indeed find the tall, elegant figure of Basil Tetherington at her side, requesting the pleasure. He was wearing a Venetian mask, and dressed in the dress coat of the Blues and Royals, a superbly tailored frock coat that made him look as dashing as was perfectly possible. Poppy had waited until she had arrived at the Jardines' grand house before slipping away as promised to put her spectacles on over her own Columbine mask, and now she popped up, peering up at him behind her double disguise. Basil burst into genuine laughter, and whisked her on to the dance floor and into an immaculately led quickstep.

12

His dancing actually took Poppy's breath away. Oddly enough, given her deep dislike of the social round, Poppy herself was a very good dancer. She had been taught at home in a sketchy fashion by a horse-mad woman who used the money paid to her to subsidise her hunting. But after she had finally given up, Poppy had devoted many long and otherwise dreary winter afternoons to chalking out the steps from a Victor Sylvester dancing manual on the attic floor and learning all the moves from dance records played on her old nanny's gramophone. She discovered that, having a seemingly natural sense of rhythm, ballroom dancing came naturally to her, and in no time at all she was waltzing, tangoing, two-stepping and fox-trotting happily round the huge attic room with her enormous teddy bear as her partner.

No one had ever danced with her the way that Basil Tetherington danced with her, not even her teddy bear whom she had once considered to be the absolutely perfect partner. Basil seemed more than happy to dance with Poppy in return, for not only did he have the first five dances with her as promised, he asked for the next five as well, before Poppy's mother interrupted, and dragged him off to dance with her. In spite of this, Basil promptly returned after only one dance and led Poppy back to the dance floor as if he had not been away for a minute.

'I rather think I'm going to have to marry you, Miss Beaumont,' he said to her a week later as they were walking in the sunshine in Green Park with their dogs. The day was fine and warm, and for once Poppy felt as light-hearted as the scene in front of them, as well she might, since the Season

13

was at long last over and now she could look forward to returning to the country full time, and forgetting all about the trivia that had been obsessing the rest of London for the past three months.

But now the man strolling beside her had well and truly thrown a spanner in the works. She glanced round at him quickly and shyly to see if he was smiling that slow, teasing smile he often delighted in tormenting her with, as once again he waited to see if she would rise to his bait. To her supreme consternation she found he was looking at her with perfect seriousness, having now walked in front of her, stopped, and turned as if to bar her way until she answered him.

'You've gone very silent, Miss Beaumont,' he observed. 'Did you not hear what I said?'

'No—I mean yes!' Poppy corrected herself hurriedly. 'I mean yes—yes of course I heard what you said. At least I think I heard what you said. You did say—didn't you—'

'Either you heard me, Poppy, or you didn't hear me. Make up your dear little mind. If you heard me, as you say you heard me, then you heard what I said, so there's no need to remind yourself. Or for me to remind you.'

'Well,' Poppy returned, taking a deep breath. 'If you meant it—then I don't think so, Basil—not really. I don't think that's an on idea at all. Do you? Really?'

Basil just laughed and shook his head, before turning once more and walking on beside her.

'I wonder why it's not on?' he remarked. 'I wonder why you think my idea's not an on idea at all?'

14

'Well.' Poppy began again. 'Because I don't, I suppose. We might like dancing, and that sort of thing—and walking our dogs in the Park. But I don't think that necessarily makes all that good a reason for us to get married. Or even to think about getting married.'

'Most of the married couples I know don't even have that much in common,' Basil assured her. 'And actually, if you ask me, any two people who enjoy dancing as much as we do, and enjoy walking our dogs, have a duty to get married, particularly since there is a war coming.'

'I suppose that might be true. But you see, that's it, really, with this war about to start, and what with my being American—and we don't look as if we're going to be joining it—that sort of—you know—that sort of cancels all that out, because I shall probably go back to the States. At least that's what my parents seem to think. Not that I've ever spent much time in America, my father being in the diplomatic, and all that. You know how it is. What are you laughing at now?'

'I didn't know you were American!' he said, stopping once again in front of her to look her full in the face. 'I had simply no idea! American and an only child,' he finished, looking thoughtful.

'It's my parents who are American really. I'm just—I mean, I've spent just about all my life in Europe, and the last few years here, so I'm really a European–American. Just as one of my friends is a Sino–American, having spent most of her life in the East. It happens in the diplomatic, the children sort of take on the shade of the country where they spend most time.'

'So that makes you—'

15

'European born, of American parents,' Poppy interposed. 'At least that's what my father always insists on saying. I was actually born in the embassy in Rome.' She looked at him, trying to read his expression. 'Has that put you off? I mean has it made you change your mind?'

'No, of course not.'

'Winston Churchill is half American, isn't he?'

'Families like the Churchills, they all married American girls for their *money*!' Basil teased, but this time with a perfectly straight face, the only indication of his humour being one raised eyebrow.

'There are worse things to marry people for, I suppose,' Poppy replied candidly, after a short pause. 'I mean, people who marry people just for their looks—I don't think those marriages last longer than the looks, do they?'

Basil said nothing. He just eyed her, put his head on one side, raised his eyebrows again but this time quizzically, nodded to himself then cleared his throat.

'Don't you want to get married?'

'I have never even thought about such a thing.'

'I take it you're refusing my offer?'

'No,' Poppy said evenly. 'No, I'm not doing anything—one way or the other. But as far as *wanting* to get married—well no. I suppose the answer's no. Married people don't seem to be interested in anything except being married to each other, which I always find rather dull.'

'I'm not like that,' Basil told her quietly. 'Not like that at all.'

'I'm sure you're not,' Poppy returned hastily, thinking she had offended him. 'I wasn't thinking of you, really. I was thinking of some of my parents'

16

friends—who seem to be intent on doing nothing except bore each other to death.'

'So if I got you to understand that when I asked you earlier—I was being perfectly serious?'

'No, no, I realise that,' Poppy agreed hastily, feeling as if she was already in some sort of emotional cul de sac.

'I don't want to be turned down, Poppy. I don't want to be made a fool of. That is not something that a man like me could tolerate.'

'No,' Poppy agreed quietly, suddenly worried by the change in his tone, but also finding herself oddly excited by it, by the sudden menace in his voice, and the implicit threat of passion and power that went with it. 'No, I see that, Basil. Of course.'

'I wouldn't want to be turned down by you, and then have everyone hear about it.' He smiled slowly at her. 'You do see that—Poppy?'

'Yes. Yes, I think I do, Basil.'

'Good.'

He took one of her hands. Poppy hoped it was still dry and not hot and damp from the panic she was feeling inside. His eyes held hers determinedly, but she found it hard to maintain the look, despite knowing that if she didn't he would realise she wasn't sincere, that she didn't care about him and was indeed about to turn down his proposal. So in order to try to hide her confusion, she did what she had seen an actress do in a film recently. She tilted her head back and smiled.

'So, Miss Poppy Beaumont, once again, will you marry me?'

Poppy leaned forward slightly, frowning, anxious to check once more on Basil's expression.

'Are you really serious? I mean, you are serious,

17

are you?'

'Why shouldn't I be? I think you'd be ideal for me. You love dogs and you hate the social life, while you appear to quite like me too. Am I not right?'

Poppy stared at him all the while.

'Yes,' she replied slowly, adjusting her glasses with the tip of one finger, pushing them back up on to the bridge of her nose yet again. 'But then I have to say I also quite like London and Paris—and Rome. I have to say I actually like going to art galleries, and looking at people too. If that doesn't sound too—well—strange. I really don't think I could take being in the country sort of—you know—full stop. *Burying oneself* in the country does sound rather like being a bit dead.'

Once again, Basil simply raised one perfectly formed eyebrow and smiled. Had Poppy later been asked to describe the smile, possibly she would have settled on 'sardonic'. But at the actual moment, she found she was just happy to see him keep smiling at her. Very few men in her existence had smiled at her even for the shortest of spells, and her father only ever out of sarcasm at his own jokes about her.

'I feel quite the same,' Basil replied finally. 'Everyone does—that is everyone who is honest does. So, if you have no further objection?'

Poppy frowned, wanting to interrupt, to wonder exactly to what she was meant to be objecting.

'I shall call on your father later today at his convenience and address myself to him,' Basil continued, no longer smiling, and quite failing to add that he had already made an appointment with Spencer Beaumont, having foreseen no possibility

18

of having a proposal from someone like himself turned down by Miss Poppy Beaumont. 'One more thing, perhaps,' he added, a smile softening his features once more, only this time the smile was the sort of shy grin young boys often give on their first date. 'Do you think you could possibly find it in yourself to love me?'

This disconcerted Poppy, as it was meant to do. She found it faintly ridiculous to be asked by someone as dashing, handsome and socially desirable as Basil Tetherington if someone as plain, awkward and socially undesirable as she could possibly find it in herself to love him. However, she also found herself short of a suitable answer.

'Of course,' she muttered, aware that she was blushing. 'I'm quite sure I could—you know. Whatever you said.'

'I have a feeling that you love me a little already,' Basil added carefully, brushing one of her cheeks with the back of his hand. 'Am I right? Or am I wrong?'

'I don't know,' Poppy replied in haste. 'Sorry— that must sound a little rude—and I didn't mean it to. It's just—well. It's just that everything's galloping along headfast. I can't quite keep up. Sorry.'

'I quite understand,' Basil said, with what Poppy found herself considering a certain smugness, but then he was older. 'How about if we go and choose a ring? Would that make you feel a little better?'

Now that she felt she was being patronised, Poppy also felt resentful. One of the few things she had enjoyed during the Season was her private amusement at how the other debutantes seemed only interested in procuring, by fair means or foul, the inevitable engagement ring. If she had a shred of honesty and integrity left, Poppy decided, she should cut and run, which she was in fact just about to do when she remembered her father's conviction that she would die an old maid, a prediction which, now she came to examine it as compared with living a life of luxury in the fourth Baron Tetherington's stately home, had all of a sudden lost all its appeal. So, considering life could surely only get better in a marriage to such an apparently eligible and socially enviable man as the one currently holding her hand in his and kissing her fingertips, Poppy smiled, withdrew her hand from his to slip it through one of his arms, and happily agreed to allow herself to be escorted on the proposed shopping trip down Old Bond Street.

'Excellent,' Basil murmured, walking her slowly out of Green Park. 'Now shall we buy something very vulgar, or just plain ostentatious?'

'I'd say plain ostentatious will be just fine,' Poppy agreed, feeling suddenly and ridiculously happy.

*   *   *

'It's rather large, isn't it?' Mary Jane wondered, leaning across the lunch table to take a closer look at the ring.

'He likes emeralds, and diamonds,' Poppy explained. 'And he says it will go with his emerald and diamond cuff links. He says we can be vulgar and flash together. In fact he says those are to be our nicknames.'

'Vulgar and Flash?' Mary Jane sniffed. 'But someone like Basil Tetherington can't be vulgar or flash, surely? He's the very opposite of flash.'

'It was meant as a joke, Mary Jane. That's his English sense of humour.' Poppy laughed as if to show she was well in on the jest, but Mary Jane remained solemn, choosing instead to stare in defiant wonder at the plain, bespectacled girl sitting opposite her who had ended what had been an otherwise disastrous Season for herself not only engaged, but engaged to what Mary Jane's own mother called an '*extremely* titled gentleman'.

Like everyone else in her circle, Mary Jane found it utterly unbelievable that the plain little American girl at whom they had secretly laughed behind their fans all summer should have collared one of the catches of the Season. She gave a deep sigh of discontent, returned Poppy her beringed hand, and shook her head in almost open disbelief.

'You can't have believed it when he proposed,' Mary Jane said, barely concealing her spite. 'Surely.'

'I know,' Poppy agreed. 'I was taken aback a bit, as you may imagine. You know, me of all people.'

'You must have thought it another of his jokes.'

'Why, Mary Jane? Why would I think that?'

Poppy smiled innocently at her friend. She knew exactly what she meant, of course, but teasing Mary Jane was a lot easier than falling into self-examination as to why exactly Basil Tetherington had in fact chosen her out of all the debutantes to be the future Lady Tetherington. It was the sort of reflection into which, in actual fact, Poppy had found herself constantly falling since the day of her engagement.

'What I meant was did you really think he was going to propose?' Mary Jane replied, adjusting her last remark. 'And when he did, did you think he was serious? Because you said a moment ago—'

'Never mind what I might or might not have said a moment ago, Mary Jane,' Poppy interrupted, removing her spectacles and putting them beside her on the table. She hated wearing them, but since her mother had been warning her since she was small that without their aid her lazy eye would slip into the corner of its socket, turning her into a sort of comic turn, she clung to them as a drowning person to the side of a boat. 'I didn't say I thought he was joking when he proposed. I simply wondered whether or not he was really serious.'

'I can quite see why, too,' Mary Jane replied tightly. 'It's not as if you've been exactly overwhelmed with attention during the summer. So I can imagine how you felt when you found the handsome and dashing Basil Hetherington—'

'Tetherington—'

'With his famous house in Yorkshire and *fairly* ancient title proposing marriage—yes, I can quite imagine your consternation.'

Mary Jane pulled a small, sarcastic face, lit a cigarette and turned to gaze out of the restaurant window at nothing in particular, unable to carry on any further conversation about Poppy's incredible engagement, an engagement that she had to admit was the talk of the town, an engagement for which she herself would have willingly sacrificed her right hand.

She could not, however, resist making one last unsolicited observation.

'Actually,' she drawled, tapping her cigarette rhythmically on the edge of the glass ashtray. 'I have to say that when I was younger I did think one

22

had to be quite head over heels in order to get married.' She glanced quickly but—she hoped—tellingly at her lunching companion. 'But then Mummy told me that love was for servants, and not for our class. Love—she said—never puts diamond rings on fingers, or tiaras on heads. So it's probably a much better thing that he does at least amuse you, Poppy. Especially moving up to Yorkshire. And particularly with a war coming. You will need to be amused.'

It was Poppy's turn to stare out of the window, wondering to herself, for perhaps the fiftieth time, quite what her reasons were for accepting Basil Tetherington's proposal of marriage. Was she marrying him for herself? Or because she wanted to please her parents? It seemed she had made her mother overjoyed by agreeing to be the next Lady Tetherington, and her father had been made to eat his words by his jubilant wife. Much to her surprise even Basil had seemed very pleased at the prospect of Poppy's becoming his wife, so much so that Poppy thought she could not possibly be doing the wrong thing, not if she was making so many people so happy.

However, the love quotient did worry her.

She had no idea whether love was for servants, as Mary Jane's mother was apparently convinced, or for anyone else for that matter, but she was finding that she was quite definitely feeling *something* for Basil, although what it was exactly she had no idea. Yet something stirred in her when she thought of her handsome husband-to-be. He was after all an intelligent, urbane, suave mannered gentleman, a man always so beautifully dressed and groomed he could have been a regency buck, a man who it seemed could converse on any subject with anybody, but appeared to also like to laugh, and to tease, and be teased in return, who did not take life too seriously.

It was only since accepting his proposal that Poppy had come to realise that for her to find someone like Basil was actually, as her mother kept saying, 'akin to a miracle.' All of which thoughts led her to suppose that perhaps the strange emotions that ran through her every time she thought of Basil, let alone saw him, constituted this mysterious thing called love. The feelings were very sure and very deep, varying between extreme thrill and an odd though not altogether unpleasant fear, emotions so strong that sometimes when she was lying in bed dreaming of their future together she would suddenly sit up, her heart beating too fast.

So convinced had she become that this must most surely be love, she had come to accept that recognising this mysterious emotion must be as difficult as recognising happiness before it was too late; and since as a child she had never been shown any affection, never been hugged or kissed—not even by her nanny—it was surely only to be expected, she told her dog in the darkness of the night, that she should feel a little muddled. Up until now she had considered herself as being nothing more than a dreary appendage to her parents' peripatetic European lives, someone to stem her mother's boredom when no one else was around, or about whom her father loved to joke— *Here comes poor old Popsicle! Here comes the future parrot keeper!* being one of his favourite greetings. Now he would have to change his tune.

She turned away from this thought to another.

Love. In reality Poppy had little or no knowledge about the physical side of marriage. She knew there was a physical side to it, because she had heard the servants making jokes in the kitchens. She had also learned enough from books to know that marriage was not just holding hands, although so far her physical relationship with Basil had actually only consisted of briefly holding hands the evening after he had been interviewed by her father, and since then exchanging a few light kisses on the cheek on parting. Basil had never tried to kiss her properly, which while disappointing left Poppy to reason that like all good things It—whatever It might indeed actually be—was obviously worth waiting for, although she remembered hearing some disparaging remarks made by her mother on the hideous nature of physical love, and some vague advice that when It happened it was best just to close your eyes and think of shopping in Bond Street, or the Rue de Rivoli.

'Are you actually going to live at Mellerfont?' Mary Jane was now asking, breaking into Poppy's private reverie. 'It's utterly miles from anywhere, they say, and absolutely vast. Huge, in fact.'

'Some of the time, I suppose, yes,' Poppy agreed. 'Basil has a town house as well, but I imagine we shall spend a certain amount of time in Yorkshire.'

'You know there's no summer at all in Yorkshire, do you? At least not according to Mummy. She says summer starts on June the first and ends on the thirtieth. Most of the time it's dark. And wet.'

'I think that's an exaggeration.' Poppy laughed, cleaning her glasses on her table napkin. 'I've seen photographs and it looks rather sort of splendid. As for Mellerfont—Basil says he has quite a lot of

25

people working for him—in the house, and on the estate.'

'Where are you going for your gown?' Mary Jane took one last draw on her slim Turkish cigarette before stubbing it out, her eyes now back on Poppy, because she didn't like to think of Poppy's being surrounded by servants. 'The sort of wedding you're going to have, I should imagine a trip to Worth is on the cards, wouldn't you?'

Poppy put her spectacles on again, wondering as always why she did so since they seemed to make little difference to her sight, but grateful as always to hide behind them.

'I don't know where I'm going for my gown as it happens,' she replied with perfect truth. 'Basil and my mother have rather sort of taken over. I'm rather glad actually. They've both got much better taste than I have.'

Mary Jane snapped her handbag shut and prepared to leave. It was really getting far too much altogether. She could not see why Poppy Beaumont, of all people, should ever deserve such good fortune. The strange thing was, nor could Poppy.

CHAPTER TWO

In the event Poppy's wedding dress was not made at Worth. After a brief battle of wills between Basil and Poppy's mother, and despite the fact that the older generation kept murmuring about war, Poppy went to Paris with her mother but not, as was duly reported in both *Vogue* and the *Tatler*, to visit the

House of Worth.

Following the splendour of the Coronation, most brides must feel that they cannot possibly compete, but Miss Poppy Beaumont's late summer wedding to Lord Tetherington was a more than adequate reply to that most impressive of ceremonies. The bride wore a gown designed and made for her in Paris by Madame Gres, and a more chic dress could not be imagined. The dictates of the heart might be infinitely various, but those of fashion could not surely have produced a more feminine gown. Wide-skirted and flowing, made of Lyons silk, with embroidered silk veiling, it had all the style and tailoring so often lacking in more romantic designs, yet fulfilled every demand for this most special of days. The new Lady Tetherington looked everything that the bridegroom might have desired, but of which most could surely only possibly have dreamed.

Because of the now very real threat of war, Basil had recommended they spend the first night of their honeymoon at a friend's house on the way to Mellerfont. The drive took well over two hours, but as soon as Basil turned his dark green convertible Bentley through the huge ornamental gates, past the lodge that guarded the entrance to his friend's house, and up the long winding carriage drive through heavily wooded grounds before reaching the park proper, Poppy's spirits rose in spite of her fatigue. She began to feel altogether better about the prospect of sharing her life with the stranger sitting beside her in the driving seat, particularly when his car swept round a long bend in the drive to give Poppy her first proper view of his friend's house sitting in the late sunshine of a very late summer evening.

Thanks to her family's travels around Europe, Poppy had stayed in fine châteaux that had belonged to rich French diplomats and large ornate villas that were the family homes of Italian politicians, not to mention the beautiful Bavarian castles used for hunting and shooting by the German aristocracy, so she knew at a glance when she saw a jewel, and the estate into which they had driven was indeed a jewel. Early eighteenth century, and built of a pale stone, it had the welcoming feeling of a house that has no real pretensions, and so sits as comfortably as any charming personality within its gardens and grounds.

A large fire had been laid in the chintz-festooned drawing room, a luxury Poppy found most welcoming after the fatigue of a wedding and a long reception. Furthermore drinks and canapés had been laid out in advance on a butler's tray placed in front of the log fire, and Basil served them both a fine French champagne that had been left cooling in an old silver ice bucket.

'Well, Lady Tetherington, I confess I was a little nervous today, and I dare say you were too?'

'I suppose so,' Poppy admitted. 'But then it's sort of natural, wouldn't you say? I mean—you know . . . neither of us has exactly been married before.'

'Not exactly?' Basil queried as he handed her a glass of wine. 'Not *exactly*? I wonder what you can mean by that.'

'Just that people are sort of bound to get a little

28

nervous when they're doing something they haven't done before, I suppose.'

'By exactly,' Basil continued to wonder, 'does this suppose that one might have done this sort of thing *roughly* before?'

Poppy frowned and looked up at the fine paintings on the wall. She supposed this was some kind of patrician tease, and so she let her gaze wander round the room before replying.

'I know that was a stupid thing to say, Basil, but I wasn't actually thinking. And no, and I'm not really nervous now, as it happens, just a bit tired, which you must be too, do admit.'

'I admit nothing.' Basil smiled now, much more like the Basil whom Poppy hoped she knew. 'And you are a little—a little shy perhaps?'

'Perhaps.'

'Then that is all to the good. Women should never be too confident, it's most unappealing.' Basil raised his wine glass. 'To the future. To *our* future.'

'Absolutely,' Poppy agreed, raising her own glass gratefully. 'To the future.'

'Although God alone knows quite what sort of future that's going to be,' Basil added. 'The way this country is heading, we can only shudder to think of the future. Even so, we don't want to talk of politics now, do we? I say, I was wondering, do you think you're going to be able to manage all right, without a maid? I can find someone to help you dress, if you want.'

Poppy shook her head, and once again looked down. She knew this was a mark against her. All Society brides were expected to honeymoon with a personal maid in attendance.

'We were a bit short of people at home,' she explained. 'I did say I might need a maid, but my mother wouldn't lend me hers. As I say we're a bit short of servants, as everyone is. What with so many girls going off to work in factories now that war seems to be so terribly unavoidable.'

'That so?' Basil replied, without a great deal of interest. 'Never realised.' He looked momentarily bored at the mention of domestic arrangements, and fingered his signet ring. 'Don't usually talk about servants, you know.'

'No, well, no. You wouldn't. I dare say you don't have that sort of problem at Mellerfont.'

Basil's eyebrows went up as he examined the question. He shrugged.

'Hasn't occurred so far—far as I know,' he said, turning round to consult the clock above the fireplace. 'Nearly time to change, so if you're quite sure you can cope, I think we should go up in a few minutes.'

Poppy nodded in return, and sipped her champagne. Silence fell, relieved only by the crackling and popping noises from the logs in the fireplace.

'Is it all right, Basil, if George sleeps in the bedroom?' Poppy suddenly wondered, as her beloved dachshund shifted his position and sat fair and square on her foot.

'Of course. Dogs in the bedroom are de rigueur at Mellerfont. My parents, when they were alive, made the rule. Dogs in bedrooms, cats in the garden or the stables, never indoors. Might as well start as we mean to go on, wouldn't you say? I'm sure Douglas feels the same here.'

Basil lit a cigarette, glanced once more at the

30

clock then stood smoking with his back to the fire.

'So no news then,' Poppy said in an effort to break the new silence. 'That is, no talk about the news then.'

'I always think it's bad form to talk about the news, unless it directly concerns oneself.'

'Yes, of course.'

There was another silence, as Poppy tried desperately to think of another suitable topic, but due to Basil's apparent indifference to small talk her mind remained horribly blank. In hope of inspiration she turned to examine the books on the table beside her chair.

'Douglas McKinlock obviously likes poetry?' she remarked, referring to Basil's friend, the owner of the house. She tried not to register surprise as she examined the anthology she was holding.

'You seem to find that surprising.'

'No,' Poppy replied hurriedly. 'No, not a bit. I didn't mean it that way. I meant it like—as in—I've only met him once but he doesn't seem the type.'

Basil's eyebrows were raised once again as he looked down at her, his lips pursing.

'I see,' he said, after a moment. 'Yes, I believe Douglas does like poetry. And so do I, as a matter of fact. Does that surprise you?'

'I too have always liked poetry.'

'*All* poetry? You like all poetry?'

'I haven't read *all* the poetry that there is, no, Basil,' Poppy replied carefully. 'No, I don't like all poetry. You're quite right. I like a lot of the poetry that I have read. What sort of poetry do *you* like?'

'Epic mostly, if you're interested. I like poems that tell a story. That have a narrative.'

'I see. At the moment I'm reading the French

poets, Verlaine in particular. My French is just about good enough to read him in the original.'

Basil looked round at her, his expression deliberately blank.

'I don't really think I want you reading Verlaine,' he said, after a small pause during which he obviously considered the point most carefully.

'Oh, but I do so love him. He's so deliberately and horribly cynical, don't you find?'

'Cynicism is not a suitable viewpoint for you, Lady Tetherington—' Basil stopped himself from sounding irritated just in time. 'Let me put it this way,' he continued, on a different tack. 'I do not consider Verlaine to be suitable reading for my *wife*. Along with various other poets—whom I would also rather you did not read—he does not have what I would call a proper morality. Do I make myself clear?'

'I don't understand.' Poppy stopped, frowned, and began again. 'Are you—you know—are you being serious?'

'What else would I be being?'

'You don't want me reading—Verlaine?'

'That's what I said. One must know what one's wife is reading.'

'I see. Gracious. I never—I never thought of reading like that, Basil, as being something that came under a husband's jurisdiction.'

'You should have done. I really don't want you filling your head with a lot of seditious nonsense. Do you understand?'

'Yes. Yes of course, Basil.' Poppy's gaze once more took in the paintings round the room, to distract from the cold expression in Basil's blue eyes, and his immutable expression.

32

'If you are at all confused,' Basil added, 'just cast your mind back to the marriage service. What did you do? You promised to obey me, did you not?'

'Yes, Basil.'

'That being so, one of my requirements is that you regard marriage as a supremely serious state, most particularly your moral values—the way we look on life.'

Poppy nerved herself to look at her husband's face once again, and as she did so her heart sank. Whereas before Basil's blue eyes had seemed intelligent and questioning, amused and mocking, now they seemed cold. She had never really taken much notice of the difference in their ages, her eighteen years to his thirty-five, but now, as she saw him staring down at her in the way her father so often had done, the age difference seemed suddenly to be not a thin strip of years, but an insurmountable chasm.

'It is time to change for dinner,' Basil announced thankfully, having once again consulted the mahogany clock on the chimney piece whose patient tick seemed now to Poppy to have become almost as loud as that of Big Ben. 'Perhaps you would like to follow me.'

Tossing his now finished smoke into the fire behind him, Basil walked out of the room ahead of his wife. Poppy was dying to finish her champagne so that she could top up her Dutch courage, but seeing Basil waiting for her in the hall she put her still half full glass down on a table and dutifully left the room. Followed closely by her dog, and Basil, she walked all the way up the wide eighteenth-century staircase to the next floor where Basil leaned past her and opened a door at the end of the landing.

'This is your room,' he said. 'Mine is three doors down.'

'Thank you,' Poppy replied, seeing his servant had already unpacked for her. 'What a lovely room.'

Basil stared at her briefly.

'In England it's bad form to comment on people's possessions, Lady Tetherington.' He paused. 'However. If you want anything, there's a bell by the fireplace. Dinner is in forty minutes.'

He nodded and left her. At her feet her little long-haired dachshund shook himself, reminding her of his presence.

'It's all right, George,' she said, picking him up. 'We won't be at all lonely. We've got each other.'

Even so, as she sat on the edge of the bed—with George beside her—and stared round, Poppy could not help wondering at the change in Basil. He seemed so different. She pulled the dog closer to her and prayed that, like her, he was just tired.

*   *   *

Despite the awkwardness that had permeated their drinks together, Poppy could not help feeling excited as she dressed for dinner. Her choice of dress was stunning. Made of over fifteen yards of white printed satin, it had a high neck, a straight front and a draped back, one half of which overlapped the other to fall to the floor in a long train, but it was not just the cut that made the gown so arresting. It was the fact that the white satin was printed with bright red poppies.

When she entered the drawing room once more,

Basil simply stared at Poppy, his startling blue eyes fixed on the abundance of red blooms scattered over the marvellous white satin. However, since he said nothing at first, Poppy at once sensed failure.

'Whose idea was this, pray?' he finally wondered, having taken a full tour round Poppy's stationary figure. 'Your own or your mother's?'

'We both chose it as it happens,' Poppy said, feeling herself begin to tremble at the edge in her husband's voice. 'We both liked it not just because it's—well—so pretty, but because we thought it was—fun. Don't you find it fun, Basil?'

'You buy clothes for fun?'

'Not always—no. But for me, this is fun.'

'I really fail to see the humour, alas. Red is so common. I find red common. As I imagine will the servants.' Basil sighed heavily before going to the drinks table and helping himself to a large gin. 'However, I'm quite sure Douglas's servants will have a good laugh behind your back, Lady Tetherington, but behave themselves in front of you.'

'I'll go and change. I have other gowns I can wear.'

'It's too late, I'm afraid. I dine at eight sharp—not a minute after. I have to think of the servants.'

He drank his drink with his back to her, staring out through the floor-length windows across the lawns and down to the lake, smoking a cigarette carefully between sips. When he had finished, he simply turned and, ushering her in front of him with an impatient wave of his hand, headed for the dining room and a quite obviously more than welcome dinner.

During what seemed to be an endless meal,

Poppy once again tried a variety of subjects about which she had made up her mind in advance to talk, only to find each attempt met with a blanket of silence. Basil did glance down the long table at her occasionally when she spoke, but for the most part he ignored her, concentrating his interest on what was in his wine glass. Each new wine was examined first in the glass, then up against the light, before being tested on his nose and palate. Having tasted the wine he would say nothing, but simply nod to the butler to fill his glass to the full. It was a procedure that Poppy found less than interesting to watch.

Dinner being at last at an end, Basil informed Poppy she could be excused, so Poppy thankfully upped and left to powder her nose and check the rest of her appearance while Basil remained at the table smoking and drinking a glass of port. When he finally joined Poppy once more in the drawing room, he suggested they take a stroll down to the lake before retiring, ordering the butler to fetch a shawl for Poppy and a coat for him. Finally, suitably muffled against the evening chill, the newly weds took a silent amble down to the water's edge.

Basil lit another cigarette as soon as they reached the lake, while Poppy turned back to look at the house behind her.

'I think this house is really rather pretty. It's my favourite period for English architecture—about 1780, would you say? And the fact that it has always been lived in by the same family. It gives a place such a settled feel, don't you think?'

'Mellerfont was once a house like this, but my grandfather knocked it down to build something larger, and grander.'

'Are you glad for that, Basil?'

Basil stared at her, then inhaled deeply from his cigarette.

'I'm not sure,' he drawled. 'All I know is that Mellerfont is to be our home. Otherwise I don't really consider the past very much. There is too much to think about now.'

'Won't we—well . . . rattle a little, Basil? It does look exceptionally large from the photographs.'

'It is a large house, certainly,' Basil agreed, tapping ash into the edge of the lake as if it were a giant ashtray. 'But I cannot imagine you were expecting anything small.'

'Perhaps it has a dower house we could live in to start with, so we can get used to each other? Dower houses are always so pretty and cosy, don't you think?'

'You cannot live in the dower house yet. You may live in one as long as you like once I am dead, but really not before. That is the purpose of a dower house, as I am quite sure you know. Shall we walk on a little? I hope you're not getting cold.'

Since Poppy was wrapped only in the thin shawl the butler had brought her down she was in fact beginning to feel the cold, but she refused to admit it lest Basil consider it another mark against her. Instead she walked on beside him in silence, racking her brains for something to say. The quiet of the night, punctuated only by the distant hooting of owls and the splash of some large fish rising late in the lake, covered the increasing sense of distance between them.

'Do you think we might have made a mistake?' she found herself saying quite out of the blue, unable to imagine what had prompted such an outburst. Basil was even more surprised than she, stopping in his tracks and wheeling round to stare at her in the twilight.

'I am not in the habit of making mistakes, Poppy,' he informed her, once more fixing her with his bright blue eyes.

'I'm sure you're not, Basil. But I am. At least I'm always getting things wrong—and I just hope this isn't something else I've—you know—I've got wrong.'

'Isn't it a little late now for you to be drawing such conclusions? Besides, what makes you think such a thing? I find it altogether astounding.'

'Because it hasn't been altogether a runaway success so far, I suppose,' Poppy continued, determined now to see it through. 'You obviously hated my dress, you disapprove of what I read, we hardly spoke a word to each other over dinner, and now—well, we can't find much to say to each other at all. In spite of its being such a beautiful night. And being in such a beautiful place.'

'You had quite a lot to say for yourself at dinner, I assure you. I found your account of being such a flop at Ascot really quite amusing.'

'You don't think we've made a mistake then?'

'I think possibly you need to give things a little time. You can't expect marriage to be like some old overcoat that can just be put on and you expect to feel comfortable, just like that.'

'As long as you don't think we've made a mistake that's all right then,' Poppy concluded miserably, glad that the cloud passing over the moon hid her doleful expression. Further along the bank George barked at some small creature he had disturbed before running back to his mistress in some dismay,

38

his long tail dropped between his legs.

Poppy picked him up and cuddled him, ever grateful for his unconditional love.

'Time for bed, I'd say,' Basil said, almost reprovingly, as he watched Poppy cuddling the little dog. 'Before you get too cold.'

Without waiting, he turned and strode back towards the house at the top of the lawns. Poppy, still carrying George, hurried after him, but by the time she caught up with him in the drawing room, where the newly stacked fire was burning even more brightly, he had already poured himself a nightcap and lit another cigarette.

'He who aspires to be a hero,' he said. 'Or, in your case, she who aspires.'

'Yes?' Poppy queried, at a momentary loss. 'Meaning?'

'He who aspires to be a hero must drink brandy.' Basil nodded once at her, holding out the glass as if it were medicine she must take.

Outside owls still hooted hauntingly and somewhere a vixen shrieked, alarming George, whose ears shot up vertically.

'I have to say,' Basil said, eyeing her, 'you look very good tonight. In spite of the dress.'

'Thank you, Basil,' Poppy said, looking down at her dog who was now sitting on her lap. 'And I'm sorry about the dress.'

'It's a dress.' Basil shrugged. 'It's not as if the wretched flowers are tattooed on to you.'

They drank their brandies in silence, a quiet broken only by Basil, occasionally humming some unrecognisable tune while tapping his foot in time. Finally, once he had finished his drink and pointedly waited for Poppy to finish hers, he opened the door of the drawing room, this time standing by it to let Poppy go through. She preceded him up the long flight of stairs, George clasped in her arms, while Basil followed on behind, now whistling the same unrecognisable tune.

When they reached the landing Poppy hesitated, wondering into which room she was expected to go. As if to make her mind up for her, Basil stepped forward and opened her bedroom door.

'Thank you.'

Poppy entered her room, stopping when she got inside and turning back, uncertain as to what was to happen next. She saw Basil watching her from the doorway in the same way she had observed him looking at items in shop windows, head slightly to one side, lips a little pursed.

'Hmm,' he said, then fell to a short silence. 'Hmmm,' he repeated finally, with a little more decision now. 'No. No I don't think so, no, not after all.' He bestowed a small impersonal smile on her. 'Goodnight. We shall meet again at breakfast. Sleep well, Lady Tetherington.'

Before Poppy had time to say anything, Basil had closed the door and was gone. Poppy frowned, pushing her spectacles up on to the bridge of her nose before going back to the door, about to open it again. Then, knowing it was pointless, she sat down on the bed, staring ahead of her in bewilderment, before once more lifting George on to her beautiful satin skirt.

'I think I'd quite like to go home, George,' she whispered in his ear. 'But I don't think that's going to be allowed tonight, do you?'

George turned a pair of large melancholy eyes

on her and licked her nose. Poppy hugged him to her, tightly.

'No, George,' she sighed quietly, thinking of her parents who had packed up before the wedding and were about to leave for America on the *Queen Mary*. 'I think we're going to have to sit this one out, until such time as we can think of a plan.'

She sighed, her throat constricting as she realised her isolation, the loneliness of her situation, the stupidity of it all. She had married someone she did not know, and now it was perfectly apparent might never be able to even like.

*   *   *

The next day they completed the final stage of their journey to Mellerfont, arriving there as dusk was falling in and around the large Gothic house with its towers and turrets, its pushy, artificial grandeur looking to Poppy as unappealing as Douglas McKinlock's house had looked inviting. The red light from the setting sun was reflected in its many windows, giving it a glow that seemed more baleful than radiant, as if the windows were red-eyed from watching for their owner.

The servants gathered, as was the tradition, on the steps in front of the house to greet Poppy. All were in country livery, which was a little frayed, a little too worn, as were their expressions as they stared at the new mistress of Mellerfont. Despite her English patina Poppy felt that they must know that she was a foreigner, must realise she was much younger than her new husband, and therefore bound to be ignorant. The look in their eyes, it seemed to her own tired ones, was therefore not so much welcoming as warning, as if they were saying, *You can come here, you can be here, but just don't try asking for anything.*

'I will have supper in my room, if you don't mind, Basil.'

Poppy turned in the hall to find Basil all at once deep in conversation with his butler, and the rest of the servants gone.

'Of course, my dear, supper in your room. Barley water and water biscuits will do, won't it?'

Poppy looked across at him and knew at once there was a veiled threat behind his words. She also knew that he was punishing her for something, although quite what she didn't know.

'Yes, of course that will be perfect,' she agreed with no outward sign of emotion, adding, 'just two water biscuits, not more, please, Liddle.'

She had carefully memorised the names of the servants even as Basil had introduced them. Liddle the butler, Craddock the under-butler, Norman the boot boy, Mary, Beattie, and Sorrel, the maids— and at long last she could see a look of surprise in Basil's eyes. She also saw that he had registered that by ordering only two water biscuits she was throwing down a gauntlet. If he was choosing to send her to bed with a supper fit only for a naughty child, she would make sure that it was truly only fit for a very naughty child.

'Now, Liddle.' She turned at the bottom of the stairs. 'Show me to my suite, please, and goodnight, my lord. I will hope to see you in the morning.'

*   *   *

When Poppy awoke the next morning all signs of

summer had disappeared, and there were only thunder clouds to be seen beyond her bedroom window, and the sound of heavy rain hurling itself against the thin, old-fashioned glass window panes. The grounds looked very uninviting in the inclement weather, the trees already drooping with the weight of the waters that were pouring out of the skies, while the surface of the great lake looked as though it was being perforated from below by hundreds and thousands of tiny drills. In search of easy pickings a bevy of wild ducks waddled across the flooding lawns, while in the huge flowerbeds a couple of waterproofed gardeners were doing their best to go about their work.

As she made her way downstairs Poppy noticed that rain was pouring in at one corner of the ceiling high above the hall, to be caught in a strategically placed zinc bucket below, while the wind seemed determined to rattle ill-fitting windows everywhere, cross-draughts blowing up and down the staircase and across the fireless hall below where an elderly bald servant sat on a visitor's chair reading the newspaper. Feeling the chill of the house wrapping itself around her like a damp garment, Poppy at once hurried back to her bedroom in search of warmer clothes, changing quickly out of her light dress and into a wool twin set and a sensible tweed skirt.

Later, crossing the hallway once more, she observed the ancient retainer finally galvanising himself to light the fire, which smoked slowly as it attempted to catch, its fumes escaping the chimney to drift in a faint fog across the large, cold room. The old man took no notice of Poppy other than to nod slightly in response to her polite greeting,

43

standing in his well-stained white jacket and shiny black trousers flapping at the recalcitrant flames with a fanned-out newspaper. Looking about her in dismay as she hurried towards the dining room with her cardigan pulled tightly around her, Poppy found herself wondering how on earth she could ever have imagined Mellerfont would have any charm.

Basil had finished his breakfast by the time Poppy arrived at the table. He barely looked up to greet her, just nodding once at her while turning the pages of the *Daily Telegraph*.

'We shall be moving your luggage to a new suite today,' he informed her. 'I have had them open it up for a few days to give it an airing. Craddock will help you move your things across.'

'Craddock will be moving me?' Poppy wondered as she helped herself to some nearly cold scrambled eggs from under one of the silver-covered dishes on the sideboard. 'Is that quite suitable?'

'The maids are all busy with other things. He's the man lighting the fires.'

'I do now know who Craddock is, Basil.'

'You don't have much, do you? So it won't take you too long. There are people coming here for luncheon today on business. You will not be required. From today you will be in the west wing. I will be in the east, where I also have my offices. There's a primitive sort of intercom, but if you really want something, better by far to send someone like Craddock. He's very handy, you'll find.'

With that Basil rose and left the breakfast table, whistling yet another of his unrecognisable tunes.

Poppy promptly put her plate of unappetisingly cold scrambled eggs on the floor for George, contenting herself with a sequence of cups of black coffee from the pot on the table that was only marginally warmer than her breakfast dish.

Mid-morning she finally finished packing up her clothes once again, preparatory to moving to the west wing. With Craddock pushing her luggage in an old wheelbarrow, Poppy sheltered herself as best she could under a broken umbrella, doing her utmost to avoid the huge puddles of rainwater that had formed everywhere. If she had thought the main house to be in a state of decrepitude, it was as nothing compared to the west wing. The general smell of mustiness that filled her nostrils the moment she entered indicated to Poppy that the wing could not have been properly lived in for an age, and as she surveyed the general state of decoration she quickly came to wonder why her husband should wish her to live in it now, before any of the obviously necessary repairs had been carried out. At least in the east wing the areas of damp were smaller and the damage more contained; even in her slender experience Poppy imagined, given the state of what she had seen of the house, Mellerfont as a whole must be at best a lost cause, at worst, with its ancient pipes and plumbing, an ideal harbour for typhoid to fester.

As she climbed the creaking uneven stairs to her suite behind the stooped figure of the wordless Craddock, Poppy's heart sank deeper than it had ever sunk before. She wondered yet again what she could possibly have been thinking to accept the marriage proposal of a man who was all but a perfect stranger. On top of which it seemed even more ludicrous that neither of her parents had thought to enquire about the state of Mellerfont from anyone in the know—relying instead on the belief that any large aristocratic house must be an enviable place to live.

'One or other of us should have known better,' Poppy thought, as she was shown into a vast, dusty and dismal suite of rooms. 'One of us—my father, my mother, or myself—should have realised that, however plain, as an only child, and heiress to my parents' money, I was bound to be a catch for the wrong kind of man.'

Even George began to look dismal as the two of them inspected and then surveyed what was to be their living quarters for a future that seemed all of a sudden unforeseeable. The furniture, although obviously once fine, was in bad repair, as were the frayed curtains and carpets, while the bed all but toppled and gave way under her as she sat on it gingerly to try it out. The glass in the windows was cracked and filthy, the huge frames hardly fitting their casements anywhere, while the plumbing in the adjacent bathroom appeared not to have been updated since the last century, and only a few threadbare towels hanging on a radiator, and a pair of rusty scissors on the porcelain, gave any indication that it was actually meant for human use.

Depression overwhelmed Poppy as she sank into a large, vaguely damp armchair in the corner of the bedroom. She couldn't stay long, and she knew it. On one of the damp days that were undoubtedly to come, she must make good her escape.

With that thought firmly in her mind, it seemed to her that it might be as well to unpack only as many clothes as she would need over a period of a week at most, for the truth was that she had little intention of staying any longer than was necessary at Mellerfont, particularly now that winter was only just around the corner. For if this was what the great house was like at the end of summer, Poppy could not begin to imagine the conditions in the dark days of winter.

As she began to put away a few carefully chosen articles of clothing in the vast Victorian wardrobes and chests of drawers she began to wonder why Basil had married her in the first place. There could be only one answer—her money. The one thing everyone knew about Poppy was that her family, being American, was presumed to be wealthy. There had always been money on her father's side, the first family fortune being made in slaving, and then enhanced by astute investment in shipping, so that by the time her father had moved into diplomatic circles he was able to use every contact he had to gather information about possible further ventures and subsequently put it to shrewd use.

Oralia Beaumont too had money, although unlike Poppy's father, she liked to spend it.

'Ours not to reason why. Ours just to up and spend it,' she would say happily, while ordering yet another set of gowns from Paris.

It was difficult not to see the reason for Poppy's whirlwind courtship. She had only to glance around the once great house of Mellerfont, take in its appalling state, the vague smell of drains, and Poppy thought she could well understand Basil's need for marriage. The feeling was only underlined when on returning downstairs she found him in conference with a tall, gaunt man in morning clothes carrying a large architectural notepad and attended by two minions.

'I wonder who all these people are?' she said to Basil, sounding lightly sarcastic even to herself, when she managed to prise Basil away from his party. 'They appear to be builders. Surely not? Most people are boarding up the windows of their country houses and preparing for war, aren't they?'

'There are certain things that need to be done straight away,' Basil replied, with the semblance of a smile, before taking her by the arm and steering her into a room that, judging from the old desk propped up with pieces of cardboard, and the few shelves, had once been some sort of study. 'We'd better not beat about the bush, don't you think?' he enquired, closing the door tightly shut behind them. 'Even if the house is requisitioned, which it might well be, by the army or some such, it would be better if the walls were not crumbling. And since this is to be our home—and most importantly your home—a place where you will, I trust, make a reputation for yourself as a notable hostess—then it is imperative now we are married that we put this great house of ours in order. Would you not agree?'

'I'm not entirely certain,' Poppy began. 'I mean—what I mean to say, Basil, is that I think just from looking at it—I would say it might be impossible for anyone, even a builder, to know where to begin. It does seem to smell dreadfully at points—just like old turnips. I wonder that anyone would want to come and shoot here, except perhaps themselves,' she added, attempting a joke.

'They come for the sport, not for satin

eiderdowns, my dear.'

'It would seem, from the little I have seen, that this house—the main house—'

'Yes, yes?'

'It would seem it needs a great deal more than just a bit of redecoration, Basil.'

'You know about these things, do you?'

'Well—anyone can see how bad a state a place is in when there's water pouring in through the roof, when the windows don't fit anywhere, when there's mould on all the walls, and—'

'A large part of Mellerfont hasn't been lived in recently,' Basil interrupted, failing to keep the obvious irritation out of his voice. 'It simply needs living in, warming up, a few repairs. I have, as a bachelor, I do admit, tended to stay in my wing, which is perfectly comfortable for my needs.'

'I see,' Poppy replied calmly. 'And where do I come in? Do you want me to choose the paint colours and some suitable wall hangings, perhaps? Or do you want my father to write you yet another cheque?'

Basil was for once silenced, and Poppy could see that she had at long last managed to disconcert someone who obviously prided himself on being imperturbable.

'Perhaps this is something we should discuss over dinner this evening,' Basil suggested easily, his tone changing. 'Seeing as we shall be alone—the guests will be gone by then.'

'Why don't we talk about it now, Basil?'

Again her husband looked at her in surprise.

'Well?' Poppy looked up at him, all fear of him disappearing as she saw how easily she had managed to disconcert him. 'It's obviously something that is preoccupying you.'

'It can wait until this evening, my dear,' he replied, and left the room to return to his visitors.

*   *   *

In spite of her feelings of misery and resentment, Poppy still made an effort to look chic for dinner, dressing herself in a white crêpe jacket embroidered with clusters of gold beads and a contrasting black crêpe skirt. Basil was as ever correctly attired for the occasion of dining alone with his wife, wearing evening jacket and velvet slippers. Unfortunately his servants were not entirely in keeping with his and Poppy's immaculate image. The maids slopped the soup over the sides of china that was visibly chipped, the main dish of lamb arrived cold and in a parcel of grease, the potatoes were lukewarm and undercooked in contrast with the rest of the vegetables, which were so overdone they fell to pieces while being served. Poppy found it hard to believe that only two evenings before they had eaten a perfectly tolerable meal on the first night of their marriage (after all, since they had slept in separate rooms, no one could call it a honeymoon) and not only that but one that was decently cooked and properly served, yet here they were both eating food that would have been more in keeping with a gaol regime, served by as sullen a bunch of servants as it was possible to imagine.

Halfway through the all but inedible main course Poppy felt a lump rising in her throat. Suddenly she longed with all her might for London and for her home, her overbearing mother notwithstanding. She longed for the kindness of the servants at their comfortable Eaton Square house, now closed up. She even missed Mary Jane Ogilvy and the other girls with whom she had done the Season, such was the depth of her despair. In desperation she sat with her eyes closed for fully a minute, hoping that when she opened them again she would find she had been dreaming.

She enjoyed no such good fortune. When she opened her eyes, she saw Basil staring down the table at her as if she were mad, before slowly turning his gaze up to the decrepit ceiling high above them while placing both his elbows on the table and then carefully connecting the tips of both sets of fingers.

'It's a question of expenditure really,' he announced out of the blue. 'Now we are married, what is mine is yours and what is yours is mine, so when it comes down to restoring this wonderful home of *ours*, this place you have in a way *inherited* . . .' he paused to look back down at Poppy and engage her eyes, 'then it is only proper you should—since you will obviously care to do so—share in the costs.'

'I thought that might be coming,' Poppy said, wiping her mouth carefully on her napkin and putting her knife and fork to one side of her plate.

'Good. Then it is no surprise.'

'I didn't say that, Basil. I simply said I thought that was coming.'

'I do not want to do this, Poppy, but I must remind you of your place.'

'Yes?'

'You are my wife now. You are Lady Tetherington. You are the new mistress of Mellerfont. It is your duty to help restore what is regarded locally as somewhat of a treasure to its former glory. You are extremely well placed to do so, because you can well afford it.'

'Yes, Basil. I know. But affording it is not actually the same thing as wanting to do something, is it?'

'Are you defying me?'

'I don't know, really.' Poppy shook her head and stared back at him. 'What would happen to me if I did defy you? Would you take a horsewhip to me, as your Victorian forebears did to their disobedient wives? Or wall me up in a tower?'

'I will not have you defy me, Poppy,' Basil said. 'I wish to make that perfectly clear.'

'And I will not have you bully me, Basil,' Poppy replied. 'I hope I have made *that* perfectly clear. Now if you will excuse me . . .' She rose from her place.

'Where do you think you are going exactly?'

'To my room. That dreadful meal has made me feel unwell.'

'You will do no such thing.'

'I'm afraid I must, Basil. I feel really sick— actually. Not very British I know, but true.'

Basil stared at her, then throwing his napkin on the table pushed his chair to one side, lighting up a cigarette and ignoring his wife's premature departure from dinner.

Upstairs in the dreaded west wing the maid had tried to light the fire in Poppy's bedroom but had not met with much success. Poppy huddled herself in front of it, with George sitting on her knee, and prodded the miserably smoking logs with a poker but could not get it to go any better. Outside the storm had worsened into what now sounded like a

52

hurricane, the rain lashing the rattling windows and what seemed like great tongues of draught licking round the dark, shabby curtains and making the bedroom almost unbearably cold. Her so-called marriage, her husband, the awfulness of the house, everything was a sham. Her marriage unconsummated, her husband a dictator, it was all such a laugh, really. She clung to George, imagining telling Mary Jane the whole terrible tale, imagining her friend trying not to look gleeful, imagining her hurrying back to her mother to tell her. At least they would be able to laugh about it, most particularly about Poppy still not knowing about It. Giving in finally to her misery, Poppy wrapped herself in a blanket over her dressing gown and huddled herself into bed, where she did her best to finish the note she had been writing to await her mother's arrival in America.

Mellerfont is huge, horrid and freezing, the servants bad-tempered and impolite, and the food revolting. I keep thinking I am in a nightmare, and wonder what on earth I am doing here and if it were at all possible I would go home this instant—except I know Eaton Square is locked up for the duration, and you in America hoping that I have made a splendid match, which of course I have. A splendid miserable match. Please write to me. I can't tell you how lonely I am. George sends lots of licks and I send all my love, your Poppy. PS Basil hated the poppy dress . . . thinks it's vulgar, you know? PPS He and I sleep in separate rooms.

The next morning she asked a small ginger-

53

haired boy dressed in a much patched country tweed livery to take her letter to the post, but he refused, saying that he was only allowed into the village on Sundays for church and 'nowt else' as he put it. He explained there was a post box in the main house where her ladyship could leave her letter to be taken to the village later. Since the post box was dust-ridden and looked remarkably unused, Poppy decided instead to walk to the village herself. She was about to set off when her husband appeared to manifest himself in the hall, staring first from her hand to her face, and then to the post box.

'You do not walk to the village to post a letter,' he said, eyeing her walking shoes. 'It would not be proper.'

'Now the rain has stopped, I rather wanted to explore my new surroundings,' Poppy returned, taking her letter back, Basil having confiscated it. 'Would that be terribly improper, do you think?'

'You can explore them to your heart's content,' Basil replied. 'But from the back of a motor car. Leon will drive you.'

'Who's Leon?'

'My chauffeur. Come with me—he'll be round in the mews.'

Poppy followed Basil as he strode round the house, finally to disappear under a stone arch into a yard where Poppy discovered a row of garages, mostly closed but some with open doors revealing various types of cars within. There was no one about other than a small, bald-headed thickset man polishing the vast chrome headlamps of a dark red motor car, one of which, as Poppy could already see, was broken. Basil had arrived well ahead of

54

her and was already engaged in conversation with the man, who Poppy immediately assumed must be Basil's chauffeur. He now glanced briefly round at her approaching figure, before jumping hurriedly into the driver's seat to back the car into the depths of the garage immediately behind.

'Leon will drive you down to the village,' Basil announced to Poppy. 'He'll take the Austin—since you're to be the only passenger. Anywhere you want to go in future, Leon will take you. I wouldn't bother trying to engage him in any of your small talk, he prefers silence.'

'Gracious, Basil, you certainly do have expensive tastes in motor cars.'

Poppy peered in and out of the garage doors at the assembled immaculate machinery.

Basil looked at her coolly.

'Yes,' he stated, almost proudly. 'I do, don't I? Yes, I like good motor cars.'

'More than warm rooms, obviously.'

'My dear, shoring up an old house takes years. Besides, my business interests take care of my passion for motor cars.'

He patted one of the shining bonnets as if it might be the nose of a horse as Leon reappeared, squeezing his bullet-shaped head into an ill-fitting chauffeur's cap, nodded at Poppy and opened up a garage further down the row. Poppy waited for the car to be backed into the mews, then lifted George up in her arms and climbed into the back seat as Leon held the door open for her. He quickly closed it again and joined Basil once more. They engaged in yet more dialogue, the chauffeur turning every now and then to look at Poppy in the stationary car, and then he jumped into the front seat and drove at high speed down the winding drive towards the road that led to the village.

'Excuse me!' Poppy called from the back, leaning forward to tap the driver on the shoulder. 'I'd rather you didn't drive so fast, please!'

A pair of dark close-set eyes regarded her in the driving mirror, the expression in them one of dull hostility, until, after Poppy once more called for him to slow down, he did so. After that nothing was said.

The village of Mellerfont proved to be as pretty as Mellerfont the house was not, but perhaps because it was a tied village the prevailing atmosphere was in direct contrast to the neat, cloistered appeal of the place, its inhabitants apparently disheartened and downtrodden, as if ruled by some sort of unenviable feudal system. The car that Poppy was being driven in was an altogether more modest model than most in Basil's garages, but it still bore the Tetherington coat of arms on the driver's door. This meant that even if Poppy had wished to disown any association with the big house, she could not. It also meant that her arrival elicited sullen stares.

Stopping the car by the post office as requested, Leon remained firmly at the wheel, ever silent, dumb insolence obviously being his stock in trade, which meant that Poppy was forced to let herself out of the back. Biting back any comment that might have sprung to mind, she walked into the post office with George at her heels.

'No dogs in 'ere, if you please,' a sharp voice called from the gloom behind the high counter. 'Particularly Kraut dogs.'

The two women gossiping in the main body of

the shop looked startled when they saw Poppy and heard the remark of the unseen postmistress. There was an immediate exchange of whispers, prompting the appearance of a large, heavily whiskered woman behind the post office grille. She stared furiously at Poppy and finally, raising herself by her hands on the edge of the counter, peered down at the floor.

'I said no dogs,' she repeated. 'P'rhaps your ladyship din't hear me?'

'There's no notice on the door.'

There was a silence while all three women in the shop exchanged looks.

'With respect,' the postmistress said, without showing the least sign of it, 'we are all but at war wi' 'em.' She nodded at the dachshund.

'George is a dog, not a German.'

' 'E's a German make a'right,' the postmistress asserted. 'Dachshund's certainly no British dog. If it were it were called dachs*hound*.'

'He was born here and he lives here, and that makes him British. Might I have stamps for America, please?'

The whiskered woman glared at Poppy before easing herself down from her vantage point behind the counter and opening the large stamp book on her desk.

'Ah should imagine thy little dog's more than at 'ome up there,' she muttered, tearing the stamps off the sheet. 'Ah'd imagine that'd be just the 'ome for 'im.'

'My husband likes dogs, certainly,' Poppy agreed, once more uncertain as to what the woman was getting at. 'We both like dogs.'

'German dogs. Lord Tetherington's partial like

57

thyself to German dogs. They say 'e 'as two or more of them Alsatians an' all.'

'I haven't seen any Alsatians.' Poppy paused. 'But then we have only just arrived up here.'

'Aye,' the post mistress agreed. 'Aye, you did an' all.'

Having paid for her stamps and posted the letter to her mother in the box outside the post office, attracted by the smell of fresh baking Poppy decided to stroll down the little high street in search of the bakery, which she soon found a few doors down. There were not a great number of people about on the street, but she made sure to smile at those she did pass. In return the women nodded and the men raised their flat caps, but no one returned the smiles. Even the woman in the bakery who was laughing and chatting to her customers as Poppy entered fell silent, and while she served her without the insolence Poppy had met in the post office, she nevertheless volunteered nothing more than the price of the buns she bought.

Despite knowing that what she was about to do would be considered improper by her husband, Poppy was so hungry that by the time she was seated once again in the back of her car she could not have minded less if anyone saw her eating the delicious currant bun she had purchased in the shop. She was also well aware that Leon was watching her via his driving mirror and would doubtless report back to his master, but the food at both dinner and breakfast having been inedible she had no compunction in satisfying her hunger pangs. In fact, when she had finished her snack, her only regret was that she had not bought a lardy cake

58

as well.

*   *   *

Life got no better during the next few weeks, and since she had received no letter from either of her parents her spirits sank to a new low, imagining that they must be travelling around America, visiting relatives, or had not received her missive. She rarely saw Basil other than at dinner, when despite her initial great efforts to interest him in conversation the meal finally always passed in silence. Basil was invariably down to breakfast at an early hour, so happily they rarely saw each other in the morning at all, and lunch was usually a solo affair since Basil was almost always busy with the estate or coping with visiting shooting parties. In the beginning he had tried, in a vague sort of way, to interest Poppy in picking up the dead birds after the guns, but seemed only too relieved when she had refused.

On this particular morning there was a note waiting for her at the breakfast table. In it Basil informed her that he was entertaining a large shooting party that weekend, and that since it was an all male affair, perhaps she would be good enough to confine herself to her wing whenever possible, taking her meals in the small downstairs dining room. Poppy was only too happy to agree. It might mean worse food, but it could not mean worse company. She could listen to the wireless while she ate with George tucked up beside her on the chair. George, as always, being infinitely better company than Basil.

In actual fact she was more than grateful to put

59

distance between herself and Basil's sporting friends, for on the only occasion when she had been forced to play hostess to them Poppy had ended up feeling less sorry for herself than for the poor women to whom they were married. It was, as she subsequently discovered, wasted pity. The women, despite becoming quite candid about their unhappiness, were, it appeared, content to put up with their husbands, just so long as there was still plenty of money in the bank.

'You'll feel just the same,' one of her guests had remarked to Poppy as they sat crouched around the smoking fire in the drawing room, trying to keep warm, while waiting for their drunken husbands to rejoin them. 'At first one feels quite neglected. Then one day one wakes up and realises just what sort of an oaf one has married, and one feels quite different. One lets them behave exactly as they want, always provided they give one exactly what *one* wants—namely two or three nice houses, a big bank balance and a large box of jewels, not to mention clothes, and a yacht, in the south of France if possible. Long as they do that, they can do whatever they please behind closed doors. At least if they get tight it puts paid to having to sleep with them.'

But the shooting party this particular week was very different from the previous one. For a start they seemed an oddly sober and serious lot, even once they had returned from the moors. Whereas before all the men started drinking the moment they came in, this party of very disparate souls retired en masse quietly to the library from where it was possible to hear none of the usual boisterous laughter and noisy banter, but instead the sound of

60

a single voice, or at most two, as if there was some sort of committee meeting in progress behind the heavy double doors. Partly from boredom, and partly from curiosity, Poppy found herself sneaking back when she knew they had finished dinner to hide herself in the large closet to the side of the library, whither Basil's guests had once more adjourned. Feeling like a naughty child she watched with interest as Liddle and Craddock took in trays of coffee and drinks, but once again instead of the sounds of drunken exchanges she could hear only the murmur of male voices, none of them raised, none of them excited, all of them in seeming agreement.

Poppy pulled the closet door as wide as she dared, just in time to see Leon, the chauffeur, engaged in conversation while crossing the hall with Liddle, Leon looking around him all the time they were talking, as if he might be being followed, or—worse—looking for someone.

'You are sure?' Poppy heard him saying as she carefully pulled the door back almost tight shut. 'You are quite sure she's not in the west wing?'

'Not been there all evening, according to Craddock, who was ordered to take her up her supper. It was the little dog yapping that brought it to his attention. He was yapping and scratching to get out and look for her.'

'Then we had better find her.'

The butler disappeared into the small sitting room that was sometimes used as the ladies' retirement room, while Leon headed straight for the closet where Poppy was hiding. He was half a dozen steps from the door when Basil emerged from the library, and seeing Leon called him over.

61

Leon hesitated, prompting Basil to insist that he join the party in the inner sanctum, until the butler reappeared. Leon muttered something to him, which Poppy guessed might be an order to continue the interrupted search, before accompanying his master into the library, leaving Poppy to wonder first why someone like that should be required to join the shooting party in their post-prandial entertainment, and second whether or not she was now about to be discovered if not by the chauffeur then by the butler.

She need not have worried. The butler, obviously tiring of the whole idea, turned on his heel and crossed the hall towards the pass door, lighting a cigarette from the packet he produced from his back pocket as he went.

After a moment, and breathing a deep sigh of relief, Poppy cautiously pulled the closet door towards her, intent on making a bid for freedom, only to run straight into a well-built gentleman who had obviously just come out of the library.

'Gracious!' Poppy exclaimed. 'I mean I'm so sorry—you sort of startled me.'

'You sort of startled me too,' the man said in a deep, mellifluous voice, regarding her steadily from behind a pair of thick dark-rimmed spectacles. 'Is it—Lady Tetherington?'

'I'm afraid so. But please—don't say anything to anyone. I don't really think I'm meant to be here.'

'No,' the man replied evenly. 'I don't suppose you are.'

'My husband—my husband thinks, hopes actually, that I'm fast asleep in the west wing.'

'Your secret is quite safe with me, Lady Tetherington. Don't worry. And if I'm not mistaken the gentlemen's cloakroom is the next door along?'

'Yes.' Poppy nodded. 'Yes, I think it is.'

'Good show,' the man replied, and walked slowly off down the side corridor.

With a sigh of heartfelt relief Poppy turned on her heel and hurried back to her room.

*   *   *

The next day followed the same pattern, the shooting party disappearing for the day in a convoy of estate vehicles led by a truck driven by Leon with his master beside him in the front seat and a pack of dogs in a cage that sat on the open back of the vehicle. In the evening, after drinks and baths, another dinner party was held—like the previous one a strangely muted affair—and extended once again into a meeting in the library behind tightly closed doors. Since she had been unable to hear anything from the closet Poppy decided that if she timed a foray to follow the butler's visit to the library to serve the first round of drinks, and his subsequent disappearance back to the servants' quarters to have his usual smoke, she might be able to eavesdrop directly at the library doors, although looking back afterwards she could hardly have said why she wanted to take such a risk a second time.

Having made as sure as was possible that there were no other sentries posted anywhere in the shadows of the hall she tiptoed over to the doors and pressed herself as close as she dared against them. The first voice she heard was that of her husband, who seemed to be addressing the gathering quite formally.

63

'Which is why I am proposing that a select number of us make the journey next week in order to attend the rally,' he was saying. 'I have assurances of safe conduct and a personal invitation for six of us to enjoy the hospitality of the same host who entertained us on our last visit. I think it is essential that we attend in person as a delegation in order to show our continued solidarity, as well as to express our loyalty to the person whom we all hope and trust may one day lead us with the same vision and purpose and dynamism with which he is leading his own country.'

He then paused and continued in German.

Poppy straightened up. German, as even she knew, was really the first language of the English court. No one who moved in royal circles was completely ignorant of it. It just so happened that she understood not a word of it. She straightened up, frowning to herself, as she tried to work out the implications of the gathering in the library. As she did so she heard footsteps approaching the library doors, and voices becoming louder. It took hardly more than a few seconds, and she was once more back in her original hiding place, her heart in her mouth.

Her viewpoint from the cupboard was less than perfect, but she nevertheless was quite able to see several men milling about the hallway, led by Basil, and the chauffeur Leon, who had somehow materialised from nowhere. The group stood about chatting quietly in a mix of languages until one of the men eventually detached himself from the others, seeming to be heading towards her hiding place. With relief Poppy saw it was the bespectacled gentleman whom she had directed to the cloakroom the previous evening, and so pushing herself back tightly into the corner of the large cupboard she closed her eyes and said a very silent prayer.

'No!' she heard the man's distinctive tones call back to the rest of the party. 'There's no brandy in here! Only brooms. Brooms and soda, anyone! Ah, here we are . . .' He had obviously moved on to the next cupboard.

Poppy heard all this being greeted with a murmur of laughter, followed by a clink of glasses, and a toast which she couldn't quite make out.

She had just breathed a sigh of relief when a low voice said, 'Just stay right where you are and don't move until I tell you.'

To her horror Poppy heard the key being turned in the door. Left alone in a darkness that now seemed suffocating, Poppy began to panic. It took all her strength of mind not to go at once and hammer on the door and beg to be let out. She managed to control her claustrophobia by closing her eyes and breathing in slowly and deeply. A quarter of an hour later, just as she was wondering whether she might be about to asphyxiate, she heard the key turn in the lock.

Her unlikely rescuer stood in the frame of the doorway, squinting through his heavy-framed spectacles as he tried to adjust to the dark inside.

'Gracious heavens, I thought you'd forgotten me. Or that you weren't coming back.'

'Neither of those things, my dear Lady Tetherington,' the man assured her calmly. 'You're not the sort of young woman who is easily forgotten, and there was no chance of my not returning.'

'I wasn't to know that,' Poppy whispered, peering out of the cupboard, and looking round the hall to make sure the coast was clear.

'They've all retired,' the man assured her. 'Including your husband.'

'Thank you. Might I ask to what I owe this pleasure?'

'You might. But you'd be far better advised to be off to your room.'

He glanced at her briefly while producing a small briar pipe from his pocket, which he then proceeded to fill from an oilskin pouch.

'Yes,' Poppy agreed, abashed. 'Well. Anyway. Thank you again.'

'Just one more thing.'

When she turned back she saw he was holding a small scrap of paper out to her. She took it and saw a telephone number written on it.

'Victoria three nine four? Mr Jack Ward?' Poppy read out.

'You might need to call me sometime. You never know. When you reach your bedroom, learn it, and then burn it.'

Poppy went to say something, but the mysterious Mr Ward had gone, walking steadily off down the corridors to disappear into the darkness.

CHAPTER THREE

Marjorie had long grown used to Mrs Reid's School for the Children of Gentlefolk, when Billy arrived.

'This is a dump.' Billy stared at Marjorie. 'You know why it's a dump? 'Cos people dump you here, that's why. That's why this place is a dump.'

Marjorie frowned at the white-faced boy who was sitting on the floor cross-legged beside her.

'Isn't anyone coming back for you?' she asked him. 'Your mum or dad, they'll come back for you, won't they? Soon as they've finished doing whatever it is they're doing. Most people's do come back, you know.'

'No, he won't.' Billy's face set. 'My dad, he won't come back. Uncle Mikey told me. No, he won't come back because he's left me here, he's paid for me to stay here, see? So he won't come back and fetch me, not ever. I ain't got no parents now.'

Mrs Reid's School for the Children of Gentlefolk was a boarding school for boys and girls from five to eighteen—that at least Marjorie knew. She had managed to read the words on the sign by the door when she herself had arrived. In fact it was less of a school than a place for negligent parents to dump their children, for few of the pupils ever went home to see relatives, even if they knew where they were, and so holidays and term times all merged together. The Dump, as Billy continued to call it, was nothing less than a large, badly maintained and rundown Victorian house, managed by a woman who liked to call herself Pet and her partner, the self-styled 'Uncle Mikey'.

Marjorie had no idea why she herself had been dumped at Mrs Reid's except that her mother had been intent on going to Australia to marry someone she'd just met in London, and couldn't afford to take Marjorie. She also knew, young as she was, that the acrid smell of blackened toast

67

would always and ever prompt the memory of that bleak place with its rows of broken desks, and dirty walls.

'You can't have no parents,' Marjorie had stated, to reassure Billy. 'You just can't. Everyone has parents, even me, really. No, you've got parents all right, Billy, but where they is, I wouldn't like to say.'

She took him about with her after that, but their conversation always returned to the same place. Billy had no parents. He knew he had no parents now. If he stated this once he stated it a hundred times, so that even Marjorie finally accepted this version of his life, and left it at that. Billy had no parents.

'*I* heard Pet and Uncle Mikey *were* your parents,' someone on the other side of the dormitory murmured one night, evoking general laughter from the other occupants.

'They're not, they're not!' Billy protested.

But the idea appealed to the other children as being so awfully funny that they kept repeating it to each other, until Billy began to cry. He cried all that night, and was still crying the next morning. Even a beating with Uncle Mikey's belt failed to stem his tears, which seemed to surprise the perpetrator.

'It usually works,' he told Pet, shrugging his shoulders, before going off to the pub.

After that Pet and Uncle Mikey left him alone, much as owners might abandon a barking dog to its kennel, perhaps because they had never seen anyone cry with such anguish before. As it happened neither had Marjorie. She had seen other little girls crying themselves to sleep at night in their narrow rickety iron beds with only a much-darned sheet and two thin grey blankets for warmth, but Billy's tears were different. At first they terrified her, then they upset her, and finally they moved her to comfort him. Finding him alone and crying in the garden she held him carefully in her young arms and rocked him backwards and fowards, until, at long last, his tears stopped.

For a moment Marjorie, feeling vaguely astonished, looked down at Billy's pinched white face with its startlingly red eyes, wondering if he might have died of exhaustion, or expired from sorrow. He seemed to feel the same.

'I want to die.'

'No you don't, Billy.'

'I do—'

'No, you don't—'

'Yes, I do—I know I do. I want to die.'

'No, you don't.'

'Why?'

' 'Cos there's no talking when you're dead, that's why.'

'I don't want to talk to anyone.'

'Yes, you do. And you don't want to die, not even I do.'

Actually Marjorie was lying. Her first few months at the school she had certainly wanted to die. She had prayed to die. Finally she stopped praying, giving up on God, and wondering whether she might be able to finish her life for herself instead. She tried holding a pillow over her face, holding her breath for what seemed like minutes, before finally attempting to drown herself in the bath, where they were never allowed to draw more than three inches of water—water that was duly measured by the ever smiling Uncle Mikey, who used a six-inch ruler to check the depth while the children sat two to a tub with their arms folded tightly across their little chests in an effort to keep warm.

Marjorie would wait till her companion had finally scrambled out of the bath, as soon as the last ounce of heat had evaporated, before turning herself back to front and lying face down in the shallow water. But as soon as she did, inevitably panic overcame her, and she would grab the side of the slippery bath before climbing out shivering and blue with the cold.

After many such futile attempts she gave up further thoughts of ending her life, and went back to praying for some sort of salvation to arrive.

'You're always sick, aren't you?' Pet would enquire, bending over the bed in which Marjorie languished in what passed for a sanatorium. 'You're for ever sick, though search me as to what's so wrong with you. It's not as if you're running much of a fever.'

'Told you we shouldn't have taken this one on, Pet.' Uncle Mikey smiled, standing upright to light a fresh cigarette. 'She's really not worth the keep.'

'If you were running a fever, dear,' Pet said, leaning ever closer to Marjorie until the tip of her long, narrow nose was almost touching Marjorie's face, 'then I might think about calling Dr Peterson. But since you're hardly running what *I'd* call a temperature we'll keep you as is—in the sanatorium, on sick rations, with the window wide open just in case it's something nasty.'

'She looks positively consumptive to me all right,' Uncle Mikey announced, his red face aglow with the pleasure of the thought. 'I'd say a frail little thing such as her hasn't got a lot of time in this world. Wouldn't you, Pet?'

'Not for me to say, Uncle Mikey,' Pet sighed, standing up, inhaling dramatically and smoothing down her long tartan skirt. 'The good Lord gives, and the good Lord taketh away.'

After which pious thoughts she left Marjorie and retired to her sitting room to drink whisky and do the accounts.

Marjorie stared up at the ceiling, willing it somehow to descend on her and asphyxiate her.

Sometimes when the going was safe, and no one about, Marjorie would watch the world from the sanatorium window, high up on the east side of the house. From here she could just catch sight of the end of the drive and part of the sweep where visiting cars parked. There were not many visitors; sometimes a whole month would go by and the only vehicles that trundled up the drive were the trade vans that passed directly under her window in order to reach the service entrance round the back. Sometimes one of the errand boys on a bicycle would catch sight of her at the window and wave, but normally she was ignored, out of sight to the van drivers, and of little interest to the likely lads with their cycling caps set at jaunty angles and their sleeves rolled up high to reveal firmly muscled upper arms.

Very occasionally there would be a flurry of visitors, and the drive would be full of motor cars, and Marjorie would catch distant glimpses of women in smartly feathered hats and fox stoles and men in double-breasted pinstripe suits. They would leave with at least one excited child attached to them, sometimes two; or even on occasion a party of three or four inmates, jumping up and down on the gravelled driveway, would follow the couple in question. Unable to control their glee, the children would scramble into the backs of the waiting cars to be whisked away for what Marjorie always imagined would be some indescribably delicious treat.

It seemed these visitors were not parents but relatives, and sometimes not even that. A large number of them, although nominal uncles, aunts or cousins, were not actual relatives, but friends or acquaintances of the missing parents, who called out of pure pity for the abandoned children. Once, Marjorie was included in such an invitation from a jolly couple called Sidebottom, pronounced—much to the glee of the children—*Siddbothome*, only to have the trip cancelled by Pet, because Uncle Mikey had heard her coughing over breakfast and suspected she was 'going down with something'.

Eventually Marjorie grew inured to the idea that she would never be fetched, perhaps never be taken out, that her life was, and always would be, Mrs Reid's School for the Children of Gentlefolk.

Things were not much different for Maisie Appleyard. Her parents' interest in her had ceased once her brother arrived and Maisie's father was posted to India, as a consequence of which Maisie was left at Mrs Reid's by her mother, en route to Southampton docks. Although she cried for days her parents never returned for her, and Uncle Mikey, having given up on trying to beat children into happiness, left her to cry quite alone, which was how Marjorie found her, in the dormitory, although at last stilled by her misery.

'Don't worry. You'll get used to it, we all do. I've been here years and years, and I don't cry any more.'

'Where are your parents? Have they left you?'

'I don't know.'

'You don't *know*?' Maisie, red-eyed, stared at Marjorie. 'Don't they ever write to you or anything? Mummy says she's going to write to me from India.'

Marjorie didn't like to tell Maisie that her own mother had promised to write to her from Australia, but she never heard from her except occasionally, out of the blue, at Christmas.

'It's so long since she saw me they've forgotten when my birthday is. Or perhaps she lost the address, do you think?'

'When I have children I shall remember all their birthdays, and I won't send them to places like this.'

Billy, who had joined them in the dormitory, and was now listening with some interest, sighed.

'What I'm going to do when I've grown up is— I'm going to burn this place down.'

The girls started to laugh, shocked and pleased at the notion.

'We'll help you do it . . .'

'Then I'm going to give all the children everything they ever wanted, and no one will ever be beaten.'

Although they felt like cheering such a brave sentiment, both Marjorie and Maisie fell silent. A school without beatings sounded unimaginable. Thankfully Uncle Mikey seemed to have lost interest in Billy, and turned instead to a fresh arrival, making him his new whipping boy, mocking

73

him so relentlessly that he finally jumped out of an upper storey window, breaking both his legs. Although the police were called, no charges were brought, but Uncle Mikey was a great deal more silent after that, perhaps not wanting to repeat the episode, or perhaps, for once, somewhat awestruck at the outcome of his cruelty.

One morning mid-week in the summer term of Marjorie's eighth long year at Mrs Reid's School for the Children of Gentlefolk, Pet's pale, long-nosed face peered slowly round her classroom door followed by what seemed to be a long thin index finger that pointed directly at Marjorie before curling backwards to summon the child to her.

'You've a caller, Marjorie,' she said, the dead expression in her eyes for once strangely alive. 'So you'd better come along.'

Marjorie stood up but didn't follow her, unable to believe the unbelievable, imagining that Pet must have returned to playing some sadistic game.

'Come on, child.'

As she shut the door on the gloomy classroom with its half-broken desks and benches, its smell of disinfectant, and its piles of old books leaning drunkenly against each other on sloping shelves, Pet took hold of Marjorie by her upper arm, pinching it.

'Hurry along with you—you haven't got all day.'

'Who is it?'

'Whatever happened to *please*, I wonder?'

'It can't be anyone I know, so who can it be?'

For a moment from the curiously sadistic look in Pet's eyes Marjorie imagined it might at last be the doctor come to take her to hospital, something with which she had often been threatened when she was growing up.

'This visitor, she's your aunt—she wants you to go and live with her. It seems the matter has been settled with your mother, which must be a matter of amazement to everyone. It appears to be cut and dried and there's an end to it. And good riddance to you, because Uncle Mikey and I will certainly not be sorry to see the back of *you*. It has to be said that the bits and bobs of money that *occasionally* dribble in from your mother in Australia wouldn't keep a rabbit in a hutch. As far as we're concerned, the sooner you've left our hands, the better. So in you go.'

The hand in Marjorie's back started to push her through the dirty cream-painted study door where visitors were always received. Marjorie resisted, turning instead on her tormentor.

'What do you mean, my mother?' she enquired. 'I thought it was my stepfather who sent the money for the fees?'

'Your *fees*?' Pet sneered. 'We kept you on here out of the kindness of our hearts. The money sent for you from Australia would hardly cover your tuition, let alone your board and keep. And your mother sent it, not your stepfather. Believe me, I know, because it barely covered your food and laundry.'

Marjorie looked at Pet, realising suddenly why, when she wasn't sick, she and a few of the other children had been employed to make up and change beds, and help with the washing up in the kitchen.

A sense of complete bewilderment settled over her like a suffocating blanket, as yet again she came to realise how little she knew about her parents. Why hadn't her mother sent enough money to cover her schooling? She hadn't even the slightest notion as to why she had been sent to Mrs Reid's in the first place, other than to hope it had only been a temporary measure and that her mother would return to collect her—please, please, *please* God—very soon. She had lived in that hope, even though it became ever fainter with each passing long and miserable year, clinging finally to the idea that the reason she still remained at Mrs Reid's school was due to some terrible mistake, an accident of fate that would be made good by the sudden, joyful and unexpected arrival of her mother and her new husband. She had always imagined that her mother could not have known how terrible the school really was, or she wouldn't have left her there.

The brief time spent following Pet to her study was perfectly enough for Marjorie to imagine how her aunt might look. She pictured a pleasant-faced woman, with her hair perhaps piled high on her head, and topped off with a little hat. She imagined that she might be wearing a lavender-coloured twin set with a pretty necklace and matching brooch, like the kindly aunt in the book she had just finished reading. Hardly had she succumbed to this warm image when she came face to face with a tall, thin-faced woman wearing a rust-coloured mackintosh tightly belted at the waist in a knot and a dark brown felt hat with a single pheasant feather stuck in the band. On knees well hidden by a thick tweed skirt she clutched a large handbag in one hand while her other hand gripped the top of a black furled umbrella. Marjorie took an instant dislike to her.

'You Marjorie, are you?'

Marjorie nodded at the middle-aged woman standing in front of her.

'I'm your Aunt Hester. Your mother's sister. Hester Hendry.'

'How do you do?'

'Quite well, thank you.'

There was a long pause as Marjorie's aunt stared at the pale-faced, slender girl in front of her, and then smiled, as if having inspected her she had finally passed her.

'You have quite a look of our family, I will say,' she said in approving tones.

'Very nice to meet you, I'm sure,' Marjorie replied, stepping forward and extending a hand. 'How do you do?' she said again.

'I told you, I'm quite well, as you can see.' She nodded. 'How long will she take to pack?' she asked Pet, who was standing by the window with her back to them, lighting a cigarette. 'I have a train to catch.'

'Not long,' Pet replied without looking round, blowing a plume of smoke directly at the net-curtained window. 'She doesn't exactly have very much to take. Your sister's never shown much interest in her, as you know.'

Marjorie packed her few belongings as slowly as possible, hoping that by doing so she could make time to say goodbye to Billy and Maisie. Finally, hearing the unmistakable sound of Pet's tread on the stairs outside her dormitory, Marjorie slammed the lid shut on the school suitcase that had been given to her on temporary loan, and rushed to the door to try to escape the clutches of the hated figure she now saw emerging round the corner of the stairwell. She had to go and say goodbye to Billy, and Maisie. She just had to.

'Taking your time, aren't you, dear?' Pet sighed through the cigarette that was clenched between her small, discoloured teeth. 'And you know your aunt has a train to catch.'

'I have to go and say goodbye to someone,' Marjorie said defiantly, thinking now that there was nothing Pet could really do to stop her, until one long and bony hand grabbed her by the back of her collar as she tried to make off in the opposite direction.

'No you don't, dear.' Pet laughed, screwing the material of Marjorie's collar around in her hand so that her grasp was even tighter. 'I want you out of here, and I want you out now.'

'Please.' Marjorie tried to turn. 'Please, I must go and say goodbye to Billy. Please.'

'That's what you say, dear. But I say differently. I say you're on your way, and what I say still goes.' Still with a hold on Marjorie's collar she pushed her down the stairs in front of her. 'Least it does while you still have one foot in my house,' she finished triumphantly. 'Dear.'

Pet let go of Marjorie while they were still on the stairs, pushing her even harder so that she would have fallen down the rest of the flight had she not quickly grabbed the handrail with her left hand. But the violence of the shove made the cheap suitcase bang against the wall, causing it to fly open and spill Marjorie's few poor belongings on the hall floorboards.

Aunt Hester appeared as if on cue to find Marjorie crawling round on her hands and knees repacking her case.

78

'You'll need to keep an eye on this one, Mrs Hendry.' Pet smiled. 'She's both clumsy and wilful. You'll really need to keep a weather eye on her, I'm afraid.'

CHAPTER FOUR

Marjorie and Aunt Hester both kept an eye on each other, through a long and mostly silent train journey up to London. Marjorie had never been to London, about which she had only the haziest of notions. At first she found the journey exciting, only once having been on a steam train before. For half an hour she watched the countryside rushing past the window of their Ladies Only compartment while Aunt Hester sat reading an old copy of the *Church Times*, glancing up every now and then to note various landmarks as they passed them. But then the landscape began to change, turning from pastoral dignity to dingy urban, a seemingly unending sequence of the backyards of all but identical terraced houses, bisected only by regular level crossings where motor traffic waited for the London-bound train to pass. So did errand boys on their bicycles, cheerily patient as, elbows propped on handlebars, cigarettes stuck in mouths and caps turned backwards on tousled heads, they waved lazily to the train and its passengers as they passed.

From her seat facing the engine Marjorie watched everything, her heart sinking as she realised that London spelt dirt and grime, crowds and noise. Once she had alighted, she could hardly believe the bustle, smoke and cacophony that greeted her as she stepped on to the platform at Victoria Station. In all her short life she had truly never realised there were this many people in the world, so huge were the crowds surging and hurrying in all directions as trains pulled in at other platforms, dropping people, picking up others. Her newfound aunt strode on ahead of her, umbrella used both as a walking stick and a sort of lance to cut a swath through the disorderly crowd. Despite the chaos Marjorie hurried quickly behind, ever anxious not to lose her.

From the main station they took something that Aunt Hester called 'the underground'. Buried in the bowels of the city, its curved walls seeming to propel Marjorie towards its tracks, it seemed a hellish kind of place, filled with dour-faced individuals who sat staring straight ahead of them, like the living dead. As the train swayed and bumped its way in and out of tunnels, Marjorie found herself longing to ask her aunt how far below ground they might actually be. But it seemed her hatchet-faced relative was too immersed in the same old copy of the *Church Times* to pay any attention to her niece, other than to check now and then that she was still seated beside her.

The train swayed and clattered through the dark, sooty tunnels, stopping without warning between stations, arriving at places with strange names. In the tunnels Marjorie sat upright in the dark staring around her, but since no one she could see seemed to be showing any sign of panic she remained seated, silent and afraid.

At last they arrived at another main station, and after a thankfully brief journey they climbed out of a station taxi to confront a narrow, redbrick terraced house in a row of almost identical narrow, redbrick houses. The street was so lacking in any sign of human life that it seemed to Marjorie that even the sound of Aunt Hester putting her key in the front door lock reverberated in the silence of the late afternoon. Only the sight of a cat moving slowly down the street, hugging the low, red-bricked walls, was witness to any kind of life, while not a leaf on the trimmed trees moved, not daring to disturb the suburban stillness, as if frightened that by doing so they might offend the unseen beings that lived behind the net-curtained windows.

Inside, the house was narrower than suggested by its exterior, with three rooms downstairs, a living room, a dining room and a kitchen, a short staircase with a shaky cream-painted balustrade leading up to two bedrooms and a bathroom, and yet another staircase that led up to two tiny rooms in the attic, one of which it seemed had now been designated as Marjorie's bedroom.

Marjorie set down her case and, tired out from the journey, looked around her with dismay. Her new bedroom, although neat as a pin, was little more than a boxroom, with only a small window and a truckle bed that had to be let down from a rickety old cupboard. Standing properly upright was only possible in the middle of the tiny space, all other areas requiring whoever was in the room to stoop to avoid banging their heads on the rafters.

'I understand you do at least know how to wash up—and cook, up to a point, at least so Mrs Reid told me,' Aunt Hester said, when Marjorie reappeared downstairs on her first evening.

Marjorie nodded, her large, dark-circled eyes fixing themselves on her relative's face. It was so odd hearing Pet called 'Mrs Reid', for a moment she hadn't know whom Aunt Hester might be talking about.

'Yes, Aunt Hester. I can wash up, and I can cook.'

'Well, cooking is as cooking does. We'll soon see if you're as good as your boast. Now what you need to know is the geography. Where the aunts are, and so on. There's one in the first floor bathroom, and one out in the yard at the back. Baths are twice a week, Tuesday and Friday nights only. The geyser won't run to more than half a bath without causing a problem, so we'll soon know whether you're being obedient, because if you aren't you'll be blown clean out of the bathroom. Now follow me through to the kitchen and I'll show you what is what, and how I want everything kept.'

Mrs Hendry wanted everything kept perfectly. Nothing was allowed out of place. The tea towels must be hung up just so, the lines on them touching exactly, so that when you stood back and looked at them they looked as if they were for sale in a shop. The soap for washing up was cut into cubes and kept in a tin. Toilet paper was handed out in rationed amounts, as was toothpaste, which was kept locked in the bathroom cabinet. Also supplied in measured doses was the soap for Monday washday, the supply of digestive biscuits for teatime, and the Sunday cake that was put away in a Coronation tin after a slice measuring no more than a few inches had been cut. By the end of her first full week at Number 32 Castle Gardens, Marjorie found she was missing not just Billy and Maisie, but Mrs Reid's school, and more than she could ever have imagined.

Monday was the worst day, because it was the start of another week that was bound to end in another ghastly Sunday, a day when there was nothing to do, once church was over for the day. Indeed Aunt Hester was so religious that even after attending church on a Sunday she would sit and read the Bible after lunch.

The rest of the day was spent in silence, the radio being forbidden, as were board games of any sort. There wasn't even a good lunch to look forward to, Aunt Hester's idea of a weekend treat being to put custard on the apple pie. Faced with such unending boredom, Marjorie soon learned to use her imagination, and would spend most of Sunday inventing a totally secret life for herself, finding out on the way that the better she got at doing this, the more quickly Sunday would pass by and turn into Monday.

At least on Monday there was something to do. First she had to heat the water up for the enormous zinc bucket which held the wash, boiling it up in kettle load after kettle load, all of which was poured into the bucket which was left simmering on the stove. Once there was enough water, the soap was added and stirred in with a long wooden spoon until completely melted, after which the first batch of sheets, towels and other whites was added, prodded well into the foaming suds until completely submerged. The wash was then agitated with a long thick stick with a brass end used to pummel the laundry. As it was summertime, the laundry was pegged out on lines slung across the narrow back yard where it soon dried in the sunshine. At Mrs Reid's school, where in fine weather Pet was only too relieved to chase her charges out of doors and leave them to their own devices, laundry had been done by a service. Now all Marjorie wanted was an escape from the heat that followed her everywhere, from her tiny little boxroom in the roof of the house to the sweltering kitchen with its boiling laundry, to the Turkish bath that was the scullery where Marjorie laboured to get as much of the ironing done as she could while it was still damp. At the end of a Monday Marjorie was exhausted, ready only for her truckle bed.

'When should I be going to school, Aunt Hester?' Marjorie dared to venture, as the long, hot summer was finally drawing to a close.

'If your mother sent me money perhaps you *could* go to school,' Aunt Hester replied, giving her a skein of wool to hold, 'but I can't be expected to keep you as well as educate you.'

'There's that school down the road. The one everyone goes to round here.'

'Out of the question. I'm not sending you to a school like that, free or not. The pupils when not setting fire to each other's uniforms are only too happy to be fighting each other behind the bicycle sheds. No, you can put that out of your mind, young lady. There's only two things that girls from that school become, and neither of them would be what we want for you.'

'Can I ask you about my parents—'

'I've told you everything you need to know, Marjorie,' her aunt interrupted, beginning quickly and skilfully to wind the thick red wool into a ball. 'Your father was gassed in the war and died when you were a year old. And your mother went to Australia with a gentleman who is now her husband.'

'Do you have a picture of them anywhere?'

Aunt Hester glanced up at her for a moment, before continuing to wind her wool.

'I'll see what I can find. I can't promise anything, mind. But I'll see what I can find. Hold the wool up higher, dear, please.'

'I'd quite like to go to school.'

'You're fifteen. There's no real need for you to go to school any more. There are enough books in the house that aren't getting read. And what you think you can't find, I can always get from the library.'

'At Mrs Reid's we used to play out of doors—'

'Much more of your complaining and you'll find yourself *back* at Mrs Reid's, my girl. Girls like you should learn the domestic arts—cooking and sewing and so on—practical things, but in the meantime, you can read. And after all, if you can read, you can learn. Reading is learning.'

Later, Marjorie took down some of the books from the shelves in the sitting room and examined them. They were books by old-fashioned authors she knew nothing about, with handwritten dedications on the flyleaves to people whom she imagined must have been long dead, but since she never knew when to expect Aunt Hester she would quickly return the book to its place, fearing that her aunt would take exception to seeing her reading instead of doing something more practical. The truth was that she had little time to herself either to read or to sew, or any other thing, except on the days, and sometimes evenings, when Aunt Hester went out.

'Business' was what Aunt Hester called it.

'I'm out on business tonight, Marjorie,' she

would say, before she left the house. 'Don't expect me back for a few hours, will you?'

Sometimes she went out at night, sometimes in the morning, sometimes, quite suddenly, at late teatime. As a consequence Marjorie never really knew when it was safe to do whatever she wished, without a mind to her aunt's possible disapproval.

Once or twice, thankfully, Aunt Hester announced that she wouldn't be back until after half past ten at night, so Marjorie was able not just to listen to a comedy show on the radio, but to sit in the living room wearing her best clothes, a floral dress and the pink cardigan her aunt had purchased for her birthday, along with a pair of new sandals and knee socks, her hair washed and dried in front of the electric fire, with a book on her lap and the radio playing in the background.

Sometimes she would imagine she was having a visitor, and would conduct a make-believe tea party with her invisible guest seated opposite her at the dining table under the front window. On one occasion so well did the party go that Marjorie and her invisible guest ended up dancing to Jack Payne and his orchestra, remembering only just in time Aunt Hester's imminent return.

Occasionally Aunt Hester would have visitors of her own, sometimes to play whist, more usually for a cup of tea. The most frequent was Mavis Arnold, a small, rounded woman who wore a permanently cheerful expression, despite the fact that she was a piano teacher.

'It would be nice if she had some young company, don't you think, Hester dear?' Mavis would wonder on each successive visit, with an increasingly wistful look at Marjorie. 'Company of her own age, you know what I mean?'

'I hardly think it's necessary, Mavis.' Mrs Hendry's eyes would narrow in return as she stared at her friend over the top of her teacup. 'And I don't hear her grumbling.'

'Every child needs company their age, Hester. It's only right.'

'She's fifteen years of age, she has no need of school.'

'It's not the education, dear, it's the company, girls of her own age. Least you should do, dear, is send the girl to school.'

'There isn't the money, Mavis dear, really there isn't. We've been into this over and over. If I can't afford a fee-paying school, then school is out of the question, and there's an end to it. I'm not having her dragged downhill at St Mark's. Not a girl her age. Those girls at that school. I think we know how they're all going to end up, without a doubt, don't we?'

Whenever she visited, Mavis rarely let the subject alone, returning to it with a persistence that alarmed Marjorie, making her suppose that there must be some reason for their neighbour to want her out of the house. Her suspicions were alerted even further when one day, after Aunt Hester had disappeared into the kitchen to make a fresh pot of tea, Mavis moved over to sit at the table where Marjorie was reading. For a few seconds she said nothing, staring out of the window beyond them, and then she spoke.

'Been into the spare room yet, dear? The room next to your aunt's, that is?'

Marjorie stopped reading and stared at the round face staring into hers.

87

'It's kept locked. It's always locked.'

'You've tried to go in then, have you, dear?' Mavis smiled, one eye now on the door. 'But of course it always is locked. Always has been. Ever since—' She looked round fully at the door now, hearing Hester returning. 'The key's in the old cocoa tin. If you ever feel so inclined,' she quickly finished, before sliding her ample frame off the chair and back into her own by the fireside.

*   *   *

It was wrong to go prying into a room that was kept locked, which of course made it somehow irresistible. Now, her aunt out on business, Marjorie found herself standing on a chair in the kitchen, inevitably reaching up to the cocoa tin. She stared at the key and, replacing the top on the tin, made her way out of the kitchen before beginning to climb slowly and quietly up the narrow staircase to the locked room. A few seconds later, having taken one deep breath, she put the key in the door, and opened it.

The room was curtained and dark, so dark that at first Marjorie was unable to make out anything at all, except where thin slits of light filtered from a shuttered window that looked out on to the narrow, suburban front garden. Making her way across the room she banged her shin on something hard and wooden before reaching the heavy metal clasp that held the shutters together. Pulling them back seemed to suddenly create a cloud of fine dust, as the autumn sunlight flooded the room, and she slowly turned to see what she had uncovered.

It was evident straight away that it was a boy's

room, and to judge from the school photographs of cricket and football teams he had been a sporting youngster, and one of whom his school thought a great deal. Besides the usual mementoes of scarves and caps, there was also a notice announcing that Richard Hendry had been elected to the captaincy of the Cricket XI. It was all strangely, quietly sad, with some objects so carefully placed that they made you stare. A cricket bat that had been left resting against a bed whose pillow was embellished with a much worn teddy bear. A small wardrobe in the corner containing clothes that were few in number but immaculately laundered and pressed, as well as three pairs of shoes, one pair of whitened cricket boots and a pair of football boots.

But what took Marjorie's eye most of all was the photograph hanging directly above the bedhead. It was of a happy teenage boy with his mother, and it was to the image of her aunt that Marjorie's attention was drawn. Instead of the gaunt, unsmiling, drably dressed person with whom Marjorie now spent most of her days, there, with her son standing beside her in his best suit, was a woman who was beautiful in her happiness, her hair thick and glossy, her eyes calm as she gazed out at the photographer, her hands not knitting frantically, or winding wool as if her life depended on it, but resting calmly in her lap.

After a few seconds Marjorie hastened to the shutters, fastening them quickly, blacking out the room once more, unable to contain her sense of shock at the changed person that she knew as 'Aunt Hester'. More than that, to her shame, she realised she felt jealous of the boy who stood in his grey flannel suit and white shirt behind his seated mother, a loving protective hand resting on her shoulder. He had loved his mother, and Aunt Hester had loved him. It was something that Marjorie realised with an aching heart she had never known, and probably never would.

*   *   *

That afternoon Marjorie had tea ready for her aunt's return, the kettle simmering, waiting to be poured on the leaves in the already warmed pot, the two slices of bread lying on the rack of the grill waiting to be toasted.

Aunt Hester nodded at her niece through the open kitchen door as she hung her coat up on the stand in the hall. Seeing her, Marjorie quickly set about her teatime duties, hurrying, eager to please, in a way she had not been before entering the locked room.

'There's no need to do that for me, Marjorie,' Mrs Hendry remarked as Marjorie spread her hot toast for her. 'You always use far too much butter.'

'I just thought I'd do it while the toast was still hot, Aunt Hester. Did you have a nice afternoon?'

'Please don't use the word "nice". Use any word but that. I had a very *uninteresting* afternoon, thank you.'

Marjorie found herself at a loss for words without quite knowing why. Her aunt had said nothing accusatory, and yet there was already a distinct atmosphere as they settled down to their usual teatime ritual, her aunt watching her carefully, as she always did, making sure that she poured the tea correctly, that the lump sugar was offered, with the tongs, that the paper doily that

90

was placed under the biscuits to set off their charms was clean and perfect, that the jam spoon was set beside the jam, that the hot water jug was polished to the point where she could see the reflection of her hand as she reached for it. And yet all the time Marjorie knew that today was different, although she could not for the life of her say why.

'If you're interested, Marjorie,' Aunt Hester stated, finally, without a trace of emotion, putting her teacup carefully down on her saucer, 'Richard was run down on his way back from the shops. It wasn't his fault. He had just come out of the corner shop when a lorry lost control and mounted the pavement. It killed Richard outright, so they told me, and the poor boy he was with.'

There was a long silence as Marjorie realised that Aunt Hester knew she'd been into the spare room without permission.

'I'm sorry, Aunt Hester,' she said quietly, staring down at the embroidered flowers on the tablecloth. 'I really am.'

'That Richard was killed? Or that you couldn't resist going to his room and prying? All you had to do was ask me, you know. I keep the room locked not to stop people going in, but to prevent anything getting out.'

Marjorie looked up in surprise. Her aunt's tone was so changed. It was as if something had been released in her, as if by catching Marjorie out she was actually feeling some sort of relief, as if she had been waiting to tell her niece about the room, about the tragedy, but had not quite dared. Marjorie stared at her, feeling that her aunt was no longer aware of her, but staring instead back into the past, to unimaginable pain.

'I really am sorry, Aunt Hester,' she said eventually.

'Of course you're sorry,' her aunt agreed. 'You're sorry that I found out, but not so sorry that you went in.' She leaned across the table, looking more calm than Marjorie. 'More than that. You are curious as to how I found out that you went in without going upstairs.'

'Well—'

'Of course you are. Why shouldn't you be? I would be.' She paused, and smiled suddenly. 'You see, I always leave the cocoa tin in the same position. I have done so, as a matter of habit, for years. That way I can tell if anyone's moved it the moment I come in. I can tell from the position of the letters. As I said, it isn't locked to keep people out, but to keep my Richard in, as he was, his memory always there. That's why the door is kept locked.'

'But it was wrong—'

'Mavis told you where the key was.' Aunt Hester looked at her, her mouth twisted into a sort of half smile. 'I should have known. That would be old Mavis all over.'

'I'm still sorry. I mean I'm sorry not because it's wrong—'

'What then?'

'Because I wish you'd told me before, I suppose.'

For the first time she could remember Marjorie saw her aunt looking surprised.

'You'd have preferred that, would you?' she finally asked. 'I see. In that case I'm the one who's sorry.'

'No. No, you don't have to be sorry, Aunt

92

Hester. I mean not on my account. Although I suppose—'

Marjorie petered out, realising in the nick of time that she might be heading for waters out of her depth.

'I can't be sorry, Marjorie. Not any more,' Aunt Hester said, pouring herself more tea. 'Rather I shouldn't be. I was sorry all right. I was sorry right up to—well. All I can say is I'm not going to be sorry any more. Life's too short, and besides, quite frankly, I've used up most of my ration of sorrow. What I must be, what I am, is proud. Yes, that's the word—I'm proud. That's what I am. I'm proud I had a boy like Richard, but I will not go on feeling sorry for myself because he's not here with me. It is a waste of time. Of course I will always miss him, but I will not feel sorry for myself. I will know that I was lucky to have him with me when I did. Now, let us have some more tea.'

Marjorie wanted to take Aunt Hester's hand, to hug her, to do something to show her that she was feeling love for her, but since her aunt wasn't even looking at her any more she decided the best course was to do just as she was told and put on more toast.

When she turned back from the stove she saw her aunt was on her feet reaching up to the top shelf of the dresser for the cocoa tin. She sat back down at the table, unscrewed the top and took out the key.

'After we've had our tea, Marjorie,' she said, 'you and I will go upstairs and open up Richard's room. And we'll leave it open. And the key in the lock. So that's that.'

But beside the door being unlocked, everything

93

in their lives remained the same, despite Marjorie's hoping that her aunt would change, and somehow turn back into the beautiful, radiant woman she had seen in the photograph. Not surprisingly, the return to the status quo made Marjorie vaguely resentful, as if she had opened a beautifully wrapped gift, only to find nothing inside—until the day she received a letter.

* * *

Marjorie had often written to Billy, but never received a reply. In her letters Marjorie always made sure to explain why she hadn't been able to say goodbye to him and Maisie, and continued to do so each time she wrote. Perhaps in some desperation, she finally took the bull by the horns and, without reference to Aunt Hester, invited Billy to spend Christmas with them.

'Letter for you,' Aunt Hester announced one morning at breakfast, a meal always eaten in silence while Aunt Hester concentrated on her copy of the *Daily Sketch*. 'Not like you to be getting letters.'

Noting the spidery writing on the front as well as the postmark, Marjorie found her hands trembling as she opened it.

'Are you going to tell me who it's from then? Or am I going to have to read it for myself? When you're at the shops.'

Marjorie looked up from her reading, not sure whether this was intended as a rebuke, or light sarcasm.

'It's from the boy I told you about, Aunt Hester,' Marjorie replied. 'Billy at the Dump, or rather Mrs

Reid's school—' she corrected herself quickly, but Aunt Hester was on to her at once.

'I do wish you wouldn't call it that, Marjorie dear. It conjures up the most horrible picture.'

'It wasn't my word for it, it was Billy's, actually.'

'IImm. So what's this Billy want then? Not a handout, I hope, because I'm a poor woman, Marjorie.'

'No, no, nothing like that, Aunt Hester,' Marjorie said hurriedly.

She folded Billy's letter, excitedly accepting the invitation to come and spend Christmas with them, and carefully replaced it in the envelope before slipping it into her pocket. Her aunt said nothing more about it, and the letter remained in the pocket of Marjorie's skirt for the rest of the morning before being put in the little desk her aunt had recently installed in her tiny bedroom.

The next day Marjorie sat down and wrote to Billy to say that she was afraid she couldn't ask him for Christmas after all. She gave the letter to her aunt to be posted, and heard nothing more back from Billy, which as usual came as no surprise.

＊　　　　＊　　　　＊

In spite of this, Marjorie found herself looking forward to Christmas. All the previous Christmases she could remember had been at the boarding school. Since Pet and Uncle Mikey hadn't liked children, there had been no attempt to include those left in their care over the holidays in their own celebrations. The only glimpses their charges had of Christmas was a sight of their tree when they distributed the children's token gifts, a tangerine or a small bag of nuts wrapped in brown paper.

As Christmas drew nearer Marjorie became increasingly excited at the lengths her aunt appeared to be going to in her arrangements. It was not just the purchase of a proper tree to place in the sitting room, it was the jaunt to Woolworth's to buy tinsel and a box of glinting silver glass ornaments for the tree, a small fairy with a wand for the top and two of the most glamorous decorations Marjorie had ever seen—paper bells that when opened out revealed themselves to be made of bright yellow, blue, red and green quarters. These were hung in solemn state on either side of the fireplace.

There was one slight difficulty that Marjorie still had to overcome and that was how to afford the gift she had in mind for Aunt Hester. The day before Christmas Eve she faced the proprietor of the shop with her dilemma.

'I thought if I gave you what I'd saved out of my pocket money so far—which is five shillings and sixpence—I could then give you sixpence a week for the next fourteen weeks. If that would be all right?'

'No it would not be all right, young lady, and even if I was to let you break the law in that way, you'd have to pay me back a lot more than fourteen sixpences. You'd be looking to pay me back more like *forty* sixpences. What's called interest, see?'

'Why should that be of interest?'

'Not *of* interest,' the proprietor said curtly. '*Interest*. The money you are required to pay on top of the asking price in deals such as the one you're suggesting. You borrow money—you pay for it.'

He put out a hand to ruffle Marjorie's hair, but she quickly stepped back from him.

'But like I just said,' he continued, 'you're not old enough, so it's cash up front or nothing at all, Christmas or no Christmas.'

Marjorie eyed the object of her desire, the delicately wrought bracelet studded with brilliant mauve stones, and wished there was something she could sell or do to earn the extra seven shillings that she needed.

'I nearly forgot,' Aunt Hester announced at breakfast the next morning. 'I don't know what I can have been thinking. Must be all this rushing about for Christmas, I suppose. I was going through my desk and found this.'

A hand appeared across the table, having taken something from a pocket. The postal order was waved at her while Aunt Hester continued to read her morning paper. Marjorie took the order and carefully unfolded it. The middle line promised to pay the bearer the sum of ten shillings. It was unsigned.

'I don't understand,' Marjorie said carefully. 'Who's the bearer? Who does this belong to?'

Aunt Hester lowered her paper.

'When your mother agreed to my having you here, she sent me a few pounds. Not much, but enough to help get you some clothes and things. She also asked me to keep back ten shillings so that you could have something at Christmas. It's nothing to do with me, so you can stop staring.'

Marjorie frowned at the money in her hand.

'But if it's a present, shouldn't it be under the tree?'

'Suppose so, except a present is no sort of

97

present at all if it's just money. Much better for you to go out and buy something you'd like. Much more the thing.' She smiled suddenly.

Marjorie returned to the shop and excitedly presented the postal order to the proprietor.

'It's gone up, now it's nearly Christmas.'

'How much exactly?'

'All the way up to fifteen shillings.'

Marjorie took her purse from her coat pocket and unclipped it. 'Do you like Christmas, Mr Gingold?' she asked him suddenly, after a short pause.

'I love Christmas! Shall I tell you why I love Christmas? Because I make a lot more money!'

Marjorie stepped forward and counted out the sum they had originally agreed.

'That's what I'm paying, and not a penny more. Now if you wouldn't mind wrapping it.'

The shopkeeper stared at her and then snapped the case shut, after which he stared hard at Marjorie.

'You're quite a little card, you know that?' he said, as Marjorie moved out of range of his extending hand. 'It's all right. I don't really bite. And you can have the bracelet for what we originally agreed.'

'Two pounds five shillings and sixpence wasn't it?' Marjorie asked, deadpan. 'With the interest?'

'Twelve and six, to be precise,' he said, fetching some tissue paper to wrap the dark blue leather case. 'And that includes the wrapping.'

'Thank you.'

'There,' he said, having wrapped it in gold paper and stuck a small piece of imitation holly in its ribbon. 'That'll look all right under the tree, won't it?'

'Very nice. But before I go, mind if I ask you why you let me have it cheaper?'

' 'Cos like I said, you're a right little card—and I likes right little cards, the cheekier the better. That surprise you, does it?'

'Yes, it does, rather,' Marjorie agreed, carefully taking her gift-wrapped package and slipping it into her shopping bag. 'Happy Christmas.'

'You too, young lady. You too.'

The shop bell seemed to be ringing with a triumphant note as Marjorie closed the door behind her.

Aunt Hester was out when Marjorie returned, which was unusual because it was not one of her business days, and lately she seemed to have tired of whist. But then, seeing as Christmas was all but upon them, Marjorie imagined a few changes in their routine were only to be expected. Having hung her coat up on the stand in the hall, she went into the living room, wrote a card for her aunt and carefully placed her gift under the tree. There weren't many presents to accompany it, only a couple wrapped in brown paper, and tied with red ribbon.

Seeing Mavis Arnold and her husband from Number 30 next door had been invited for Christmas lunch, she imagined the gifts under the tree were probably for them, which meant there was nothing for her. What she always called *the wishbone*, not a lump, started to constrict her throat as she struggled with threatening tears, and then taking a deep breath she shook her head hard. No more wishbones, no more lumps in the throat, from now on she would be as she had been with the man in the jewellery shop—strong as she could be.

It seemed only a moment later that the door flew open and her aunt reappeared, still in her hat and coat, and, for her, unusually red in the face. At first Marjorie suspected that she might have been drinking, just as Pet and Uncle Mikey always took to doing as soon as they saw Christmas heave into view, but as she began to talk Marjorie sensed her excitement was rooted in something quite different.

'Marjorie dear!' she exclaimed. 'Ah, there you are! Now, let me see. Ah yes, I want you to pop upstairs for me and find—and bring me down my flat shoes, there's a good girl.' She cleared her throat, and looked at her feet. 'Ah yes, my poor feet are killing me with all the walking I've done today. Go along now—and hurry. They're probably under my bed!' she called after her as Marjorie hurried from the room. 'If not, try the wardrobe!'

As Marjorie reached the landing she heard the front door opening again, although the bell had not sounded. She found herself feeling suddenly excited. Perhaps it had something to do with her aunt's odd manner, her usual brusqueness mixed with a sense of excitement.

'Ah, there you are,' her aunt said from her armchair by the fire when Marjorie finally returned with her flat shoes. 'Thought you'd gone to Timbuctoo, I did really. Shoes. Must be hard to find, shoes, eh?'

'Your shoes weren't by your bed, and they weren't in your wardrobe. They were under your chair, right at the back.'

'Fancy that.'

'Anyway, here they are.'

100

'Fancy,' Aunt Hester sighed. 'Must be losing my marbles.'

'I'll go and put the kettle on, shall I?'

'In a minute, in a minute. I need to talk to you first.' She stared up at Marjorie. 'I expect you've spotted there isn't anything under the tree with your name on it, eh?' She laughed. 'And I expect you've been thinking mean old Auntie, that's what you've been thinking, I dare say.'

Marjorie shook her head.

'No, really not, Aunt Hester. You've done more than enough for me, really you have.'

'Oh dear.' Aunt Hester sighed over-dramatically. 'Sometimes you're a little *too* good to be true, aren't you?' She looked at her niece with her head on one side, while Marjorie stood looking at her own feet.

'You didn't think I'd let Christmas go by without you having a present, did you? Your present, dear, is behind my chair.'

'Behind your chair, Aunt Hester?'

'Behind my chair. What's the matter? Not been washing our ears out?'

'I meant shouldn't it be under the tree?'

'Don't think it'll keep till then, dear,' Aunt Hester murmured. 'Think you'd best have it now.'

Realising that was as much information as she was going to get from her relative, Marjorie approached Aunt Hester's chair, and looked behind it.

'Billy? *Billy!*'

A much taller and even thinner boy than she remembered uncoiled himself from behind Aunt Hester's chair.

'Happy Christmas, Marjorie dear!' Aunt Hester

101

beamed at them both.

Billy was standing in front of her now, looking more like a lost sheep than ever before. He had grown so much in the last six months that the clothes that had been a size too big for him when last seen by Marjorie were already far too small. He was paler and more straggly-haired than ever, if it were possible, but his dark eyes were as affecting as they had always been, as was his slow shy smile. Marjorie wanted to hug him to her. Instead, she took one of his hands, smiled at him and led him over to the table where she sat him down while she finished laying tea.

It being Christmas Eve, Aunt Hester had laid on a special tea, with scones, strawberry jam, fruit cake and a big jug of orangeade. Although Marjorie was accustomed to having cake or scone treats at least once a week now, she was nevertheless hardly able to take in such a spread, while Billy, who could only ever have dreamed of such heavenly delights, was reduced to a stupefied silence, particularly when he was encouraged by his hostess to drink his orange squash through two coloured straws.

'In case you're wondering, Marjorie,' her aunt said, pouring herself some tea, 'Billy's sleeping in Richard's old room. I cleared it out and made up the bed when you were out shopping the other day.'

'Is that all right?'

'Is that all right indeed. Would I have done it if it wasn't "all right"?'

Marjorie took Billy upstairs after tea to help him settle in and unpack his small suitcase. Aunt Hester certainly had done it out all right. The room was hardly recognisable, at least not in its furnishings.

Gone were all her son's belongings, his sporting equipment, his photographs, and his clothes, and in their place were a few ordinary sporting prints and photographs of contemporary sportsmen.

'Mr Arnold,' Marjorie suddenly exclaimed, looking closely at one of the photographs. 'Of course, these are his.'

Seeing Billy looking at her in some bewilderment, she shrugged her shoulders.

'Mr Arnold is a friend of Aunt Hester's, and these were his. I saw them one day in his house.'

Unsurprisingly Billy had as few things to his name as Marjorie had when she arrived so just at first he seemed too embarrassed to unpack his suitcase. While he dallied, Marjorie pulled open the top drawers of the chest. To her amazement there were still clothes in the chest, boys' clothes, but not the clothes she'd seen there before. There was a whole new set, everything from simple shirts and sweaters to socks and warm underwear.

She looked across at Billy who was finally taking his few belongings out of his case and putting them away, and noticed the present wrapped in shiny bright blue paper on his bed, with a card with one robin redbreast in the corner that announced *Happy Christmas, William, from all at Number 32.*

'We'll put that under the tree,' she said, picking up the package. 'With the rest of the presents.' She stared at him. 'Actually, I suppose I really should wrap *you* up and put you under the tree tomorrow.'

'I couldn't believe it when Pet come and said I been called for,' Billy announced, sitting himself down on the edge of the bed. 'Pet come and said *Billy—you been called for*, and honest—I couldn't believe it. I thought it was one of their stupid jokes.'

'Didn't you get my letters, Billy?'

'Yeah—course I did. Why?'

'I was wondering, that's all. 'Cos I never heard from you, I suppose.'

'What?' Billy turned to her, as she sat down beside him. 'But I wrote straight back to you. Honest. Every time you wrote, I did. And I gave them to Pet to post as usual. Couldn't do other, could I?'

'Oh, I suppose she never posted them, the old meanie.'

'Look what I got, Marjorie.' Billy opened his small suitcase and sure enough there were all the letters she'd written to him, done up tight with a piece of brown string. 'See?'

'You got the one there that said you couldn't come for Christmas?'

'No.' Billy shook his head and frowned. 'But I got a letter from Mrs Hendry saying as I *could*—but that I was to keep me mouth shut.'

Marjorie laughed, and putting her arm round Billy's shoulder gave him a quick hug.

'I won't ever forget this, Marjie,' he said, quietly, not looking at her. 'Not never.'

They sat like that for a little longer, Marjorie with her arm round him, Billy staring straight ahead, before Marjorie jumped up and started to tickle him to distract him from realising that being with her and Aunt Hester at Christmas couldn't go on for ever.

*　　　*　　　*

On Christmas Day Aunt Hester wore an old, faded

but still glamorous full-length red velvet dress while Marjorie wore a white organza dress with a taffeta underskirt that Aunt Hester had found for her in a second-hand shop. It was too long for her, but they sewed up the hem and after that it fitted as if it had been made for her. Billy wore the clothes that he had found in his room, put there especially by Aunt Hester.

'Even though they're not new, William, they're quality, and it's quality that counts. Don't you ever forget that. Quality clothing makes you feel like quality, while cheap makes you feel just that. Flannel's quality suiting, young man, and I'll warrant you'll look just the thing when we see you in these tomorrow.'

Billy did indeed look quite the thing in his grey flannel suit, white shirt and new blue tie.

'You scrub up something lovely,' Marjorie teased him when he came downstairs wearing the solemn expression of a boy who had never worn such a smart suit before, after which they all opened their presents. Dinky toys for Billy from everyone—'so they make up a set, Billy dear,' Aunt Hester kept saying. A beautiful pale blue cardigan and a pair of silvered shoes, placed under the tree after she had gone to bed, were Marjorie's surprises, and last of all Aunt Hester's bracelet—*with love from Majorie AND Billy*—was taken out of its box. Billy had added the *AND* as well as his name, underlined two or three times, as if anxious for Aunt Hester to remember who he was exactly.

'Oh, dears, this is so sweet of you.'

Aunt Hester held out her wrist and Marjorie did the bracelet up for her, realising as she did so that Aunt Hester was more than a bit moved by its prettiness, so quite grateful for the distraction of Mr Arnold and Mavis's oohing and aahing, and opening their own small gifts, which were teaspoons with place names on them for Mavis, and a pair of thick wool socks for Mr Arnold.

Christmas lunch was a golden roast and stuffed chicken, succulent butcher's sausages, roast potatoes and bread sauce, the whole served up with a thick golden gravy poured liberally over everything. Billy was so transported he never said a word, other than to leap up when offered a second helping.

Mavis and her husband had arrived a little later than asked, flushed and happy, and they seemed to laugh inordinately at things that neither Marjorie nor Billy could understand, helped no doubt by pre-lunch sherry and the bottles of beer they consumed with their meal. Home-made plum pudding with a thick yellow custard followed, after which they all pulled their crackers, put on their paper hats and generally behaved as people always do when they have enjoyed a Christmas lunch that was as happily memorable as it was delicious.

After lunch and listening with reverence to the King's speech, Aunt Hester produced a gramophone from under the stairs and a stack of records. Still full of joyous energy, she wound up the gramophone and put on Myra Hess playing 'Jesu Joy of Man's Desiring' half a dozen times, followed by an Irish tenor singing 'Bless This House', a record that also got more than one airing, and then they all sat down and played Happy Families with a deck of engagingly illustrated cards. Later Mr Arnold fetched a bottle of port wine from his house which he offered to

106

both the ladies, who tried to refuse but then accepted with alacrity, and the next thing Marjorie knew the carpet was being rolled back, and what with Billy Cotton's Band playing on the gramophone it wasn't long before everyone was dancing.

Marjorie and Billy didn't know how to dance properly, but by watching the grown-ups they started to learn, and after a great deal of giggling, not to mention clumsy, left-footed efforts, were soon aping their elders to the sound of a singer called Alan Breeze crooning the tender lyrics of the latest popular songs. It was the most perfect day of both of their young lives, although as they finally climbed the stairs to bed Billy very nearly spoiled everything.

'I suppose I'll be going back soon, won't I?' he asked, as they reached the landing.

'Don't ask me, I don't know, really I don't, just don't ask me.'

'No, I know,' Billy agreed, combing his straggly hair with his fingers. 'I just wondered, that's all.'

'Why don't you just keep to wondering then? Long as you keep your wondering to yourself. And happy Christmas one last time. Night night, Billy, don't let the fleas bite, eh?'

Marjorie sighed as she sat on the edge of her truckle bed, unbuckling her shoes and beginning to get undressed. Of course Christmas couldn't last for ever, which was why she'd found herself getting tetchy with young Billy, because of course, Billy being Billy, he'd have to ask the question that was on both of their minds. It had been kind of Aunt Hester to invite him, but they couldn't expect any more of her, and they both knew it.

But as the time passed from Boxing Day to the day after Boxing Day, to the day after the day after Boxing Day, Marjorie began to regret her decision to be patient. She found it increasingly difficult to enjoy Billy's visit as much as she wanted to, feeling that at any moment it could be ended as abruptly as it had begun.

As days passed Marjorie began to see that the question hung so heavily over the house that despite Marjorie and Aunt Hester's home cooking, Billy could barely swallow his food. They both started to delay going to bed for as long as was reasonable, sitting at the table doing a jigsaw or playing highly competitive games of Snap or Pelmanism, while Aunt Hester sat by the fire knitting yet another of her endless supply of garments which were despatched from the house almost the moment she cast them off her needles.

Still nothing was said. When they both came to say their goodnights each evening, two pairs of eyes begged Aunt Hester to give them the news, but even if she was aware of the pleading she paid no attention to it, allowing both children to kiss her cheek lightly while she rummaged in her knitting bag for fresh balls of wool or a new pattern, before sending them off upstairs.

New Year had come and gone, and the shops were doing a brisk trade in everything from bootlaces to blackout material, when Aunt Hester made an announcement.

'Billy,' she began, not looking up from her knitting. 'I should have mentioned this earlier, but it wasn't possible.' She looked up at him.

'Yes, Aunt Hester?' Marjorie promptly answered for Billy.

'Dear me, I didn't know your name was Billy, Marjorie dear,' Aunt Hester said with a smile, putting her knitting down. 'No, it's about Billy's being fostered.'

'What's fostering?' Marjorie enquired.

'It means coming to live here. As part of the family. It's not possible to adopt you, not yet anyway, what with me being a widow and that, but it would give you and me a better chance of becoming acquainted, if I fostered you, and then we can see whether or not you might want to make the arrangement more permanent. That would be entirely up to you, do you see?'

She was no longer looking at him, holding up the back of the dark red garment she was making in front of her as if to examine it for flaws, giving Billy and Marjorie the chance to exchange looks.

'Are you saying, Aunt Hester,' Marjorie began carefully, 'you're not saying, are you, that Billy doesn't have to go back to Mrs Reid's, are you?'

'I'm not *saying* anything, Marjorie. That's entirely up to this young man here. It's for him to say, Marjorie dear.'

There was a long, uncertain sort of silence, not just because of the continued uncertainty as to the precise definition of fostering, but because neither Marjorie nor Billy could quite believe what they thought they were hearing.

'I don't want to go back to the Dum—to Mrs Reid's, Mrs Hendry,' Billy said finally. 'Not never.'

'Ever, dear,' Aunt Hester corrected him. 'Not ever.'

'Exactly, Mrs Hendry. I really don't.'

'Then—neither shall you.'

Once again the knitting was held up for

inspection as once again the two youngsters exchanged looks, this time of unabashed glee.

'This mean I been *called for* by you, Mrs Hendry?' Billy asked, struggling to keep looking grown up and able to cope while his face lost all colour. ''Cos if it does, I don't know what to say. Really I don't.'

'I hope maybe you'll say yes, young man,' Aunt Hester replied. 'And if you do, you can stop calling me Mrs Hendry, and begin by calling me Aunt Hester.'

'Yes, Mrs Hendry.'

Billy stared at her, the import of what she had just said gradually sinking in, but Aunt Hester only continued her knitting, frowning slightly at her fingers as the needles clicked and clacked.

'Now if that's all done and dusted,' she said, finally, 'I suggest you both take yourselves off to bed.'

'Aunt Hester—' Marjorie began.

'Bed.'

'I just wondered—'

'Tomorrow, Marjorie. I promised I'd finish this pullover last Saturday.'

'Couldn't we just know a bit?'

Aunt Hester sighed and put down her knitting.

'Well, if you really want to know, Billy's father did a bunk, quite a few years back. I'm sorry, Billy—very sorry I'm the one to tell you, but there it is.'

'It's all right, Mrs Hendry. I mean Aunt Hester,' Billy replied, glancing down shyly at his feet.

'He left enough money in the bank for you to stay at the boarding school, may God help you, till now. Till you're fourteen or so, I think it was. Any old how, since the people that run the Dump, as you like to call it, since all they're interested in is being paid, any offer to take a hungry boy off their hands is more than welcomed. Far as fostering goes, the people in charge couldn't have been more helpful, which says something, although what I'm not sure. Now—off to bed.'

'Blimey,' Billy said as Marjorie and he climbed the stairs. 'Blimey.'

'You shouldn't say that, you know,' Marjorie said from behind him. 'It means God blind me.'

'Strewth, then.' Billy stood stock still as he reached the landing. 'It means strewth, I don't have to go back to the Dump. Not never.'

'Not ever.'

'Not *ever*!'

CHAPTER FIVE

Knowing her father had now returned home, Kate kept resolutely out of his way, remaining outside on the lawn tennis court with Robert, her elder brother, playing a less one-sided game than was customary. In fact much to Robert's astonishment he found himself two sets all and two one up in the final set, having broken his sister's first service game.

'You're not concentrating, Kate!' he called from the back of the court, collecting the balls for the next game. 'Wake up, woman!'

Kate gave yet another nervous glance up to the house.

'Quite frankly, it's a wonder it's this close,

knowing what's going on in there,' she murmured in her oddly deep voice, as her long, slender bronzed legs in their white tennis shoes moved easily towards her brother.

They both came to the net to collect the three or four balls that were lying there.

'It can't take him that long to read the blasted thing,' Robert groaned, sharply tapping one of the grounded tennis balls with his racket so that it bounced up into his hand.

'It's not the reading that's taking the time, Bobby. It'll be the endless arguing about what's in it. Worse than anything.'

'At least Mother's on your side.'

'Mother doesn't pay the fees, in case you haven't noticed, poor old darling. She just runs the house.'

'Come on,' Robert urged over-cheerfully. 'Half a crown says I'll beat you.'

'Hardly surprising if you do,' Kate returned, banging the gut of her racket against her forehead as she returned to the baseline. 'The way I'm playing.'

'OK—so let's have five bob on it, shall we? Make it a bit more interesting?'

'You're on.' She stared at something in the distance. 'After all, if I'm going to have to do a bunk, I shall need every penny that comes my way.'

Robert glanced up at her, delaying his first service, wondering whether or not his sister was teasing. Realising she wasn't, he shook his head, and prepared to serve. Poor old Kate, she was always in hot water.

His first serve cut back from left to right as it sped over the net and kicked up the chalk deep on the centre line. But now the money was down, it wasn't good enough to beat his sister. She was in position before the ball had swung back on to the line, despite its keeping very low. Astonishingly she had even found the time to go round on her forehand and pick up the shot, half-volleying it across the court, well out of her older brother's reach.

'Shot!' he called, tossing his blond fringe out of his eyes. 'We'll see you at Wimbledon yet, Kate Maddox!'

*   *   *

'This is just as I expected,' Professor Maddox said quietly, taking his glasses off and folding them up precisely before placing them on the still immaculate small chamois strip that lay on the bottom of the plum-coloured spectacles case. 'These nuns are stupid. They encourage girls in such a way as to turn them into nothing more and nothing less than a bunch of suffragettes. Bad enough that Kate has the voice of a boy, and the figure of one too, but now they're encouraging her to strike out in a way that will mean she never snares a husband. Men simply don't like educated women. Nuns, really, I ask you—what do they know about the world or anything in it?'

Helen Maddox nervously adjusted the hair to one side of her neck and wondered as she so often did whether she was expected to agree with her husband's remark, or simply make some sort of sympathetic noise. Harold was a brilliant man, but he was also a very difficult and demanding one, sides to his character that had become particularly apparent once it had become all too obvious that

113

not just one but both of his children might be going to be at least as gifted as himself.

'In all fairness to the nuns, Harold,' Helen said quietly, as she began to clear some of the papers from the table in order to make ready for dinner, 'to be perfectly fair, Kate's results are just as good as Robert's. In fact in some instances they're considerably better—'

'Attend to the point, Helen,' her husband interrupted, without looking up from the list of notes he was making. 'Robert needs to be bright, while Kate has no such need.' He looked across at his wife with unconcealed despite. 'And while we're on the subject of our children, perhaps a little less emphasis on them when we entertain? Or are being entertained? As far as your small talk goes, Helen, sometimes I feel I do not even exist.'

'That isn't very fair, Harold. Friends ask after one's children, just as we do after theirs. It's only natural.'

'Yes, yes,' Harold said dismissively, as if what his wife had to say was really of no importance. 'To return to the problem of Kate.'

'I didn't realise there was a problem. Not with a report as glowing as that, surely?'

'You don't seem to understand, Helen. But then why should I find that so unusual?' Harold looked at his wife and shook his head slowly, sighing before he continued. 'I am really not interested in her intellectual growth simply because it is a waste of money educating a girl any further. I keep telling you this, and you keep ignoring this remonstrance. What's the result of your ignoring me? Reverend Mother, some over-educated religious crank who has never properly tasted life in the outside world,

114

is trying to convince us to send Kate to *Oxford*.'

'And you think there isn't any point.'

'None whatsoever. Whatever her teachers may say—or may think.'

'I don't think perhaps you're being very fair, Harold.'

'There is no point in sending girls to university, Helen, because what do girls do when they leave university? They get married. And there's no point in arguing. There is no point in your trying to tell me otherwise—for instance that Kate will prove to be the exception to the rule—because I maintain otherwise. It would be akin to pouring money into a drain to send Kate to Oxford. She would skitter through academe, playing tennis and going to dances, the way all girls do at university—and we simply cannot afford to burn money in such a fashion. And there's an end to it.'

'I think we should at least go and discuss the matter with her teachers. And with Reverend Mother, surely?'

'There is absolutely no point, Helen. I intend to take Kate away from the convent. I have already written to Reverend Mother to signal my intentions.'

'You have *what*?' Helen returned, unable to keep her voice from rising and earning a look of stern disapproval from her husband.

'There is no need to *shout*, Helen, I assure you,' he scolded. 'There is absolutely no need at all.'

Helen felt like telling him there was all the need in the world, but she fell silent for a moment or two instead, knowing that if she started taking issue with Harold the person to suffer finally would be Kate.

'I'm sorry. I can't really believe you have made this decision without consulting me. I don't see how you could,' she said, finally.

'Then I'll tell you how I could, as you put it. I have made this decision because I pay the fees. For your information I am not wasting my hard-earned income sending a girl to university on the whim of a bunch of nuns. Kate will leave the convent school when term ends and she will then go to be trained for some suitable job that will tide her over and help her keep herself, until such time as she gets married—which will not I pray be too long in coming.'

'This is a waste of Kate's ability, and you know it.'

'I'll pretend I didn't hear that,' Harold replied, his mouth tightening. 'It's going to be hard enough having to pay for a wedding in this day and age, so just imagine—if you can—how stretched our somewhat limited finances would be were we to have wasted the little money we have in the bank on a university education, only then to have to spend out even more on a wedding. It simply does not bear thinking about.'

Helen turned away to look out of the window for a moment at her two children playing tennis on the grass court laid at the end of the garden. Kate was so elegant and talented. She knew just from watching them that Robert must be losing heavily by now. The longer she observed them, the more her heart sank at the thought that Kate was about to be deprived of an interesting future, purely because of her father's meanness of spirit.

She also knew that there was nothing she could do about it. Because of the way their marriage was,

116

because of the way she had let life go, Helen knew that whatever she wanted for her children and however much she wanted it, Harold would simply go his own not so awfully sweet way.

'Do you know what her school means to Kate, Harold?' she wondered, still looking out of the window, vastly preferring the sight of her handsome, athletic children to that of the back of her husband's now fast balding head. 'Kate's been so happy there. She's made such friends. And she's done so well there—'

'And now it's over,' Harold interrupted abruptly, rolling up the newspaper he had been reading and tapping it against his knee for punctuation. 'The sooner she leaves that place and starts earning some sort of a living the better.'

'I'm sorry, Harold,' Helen sighed. 'But I don't think this is making much sense. Kate's only seventeen. She doesn't really know any boys, so she's hardly going to run off and get married at the drop of a hat.'

'Helen. That is quite enough.' Harold rose, still tapping the rolled-up newspaper against one leg as he prepared to leave the room.

'Harold—very few girls have the kind of gifts that our Kate has. Shouldn't we be thinking that it's a good thing rather than a bad thing to be so gifted? And that eventually, having obtained a degree—which she is bound to do—she will be so much better qualified, be able to get a better job. Rather than just something menial such as secretarial work? If you don't mind my saying—'

'I mind you saying it very much indeed, as it happens. I'm all for women having a certain amount of knowledge so they can at least converse with their husbands, but nothing will change my view that a woman's place is finally in the home—looking after her husband, who after all is the bread winner, and bringing up his children. That is the way it has always been. Blue stockings do not look good on a woman.'

'I know how you feel, Harold, but things are changing, I'm sure they are. Things always do.'

'Thank God you never thought of becoming a teacher, Helen. The rubbish you would have filled your pupils' heads with . . .' He shook his head, before going on. 'Change is all fine and large, and greatly to be encouraged, as long as everything finally remains in place.' Harold smiled appreciatively to himself at his *bon mot*, before looking to his wife to see if she had enjoyed it as much as he had, which unfortunately was not the case. 'I said,' he began again, only to be once more interrupted by his wife.

'Kate has considerable sporting gifts, as you know,' Helen said, raising her voice enough to make sure she was going to be heard. 'Besides her academic qualities, her tennis coach thinks that she could really go far.'

'I am simply not interested in what some failed ex-club player has to say about my daughter's so-called sporting abilities, Helen. Heaven knows Robert's education hasn't come cheap, but he is my son. I am not spending any more on our daughter's education and that is an end to it.'

When Kate and Robert finally appeared for dinner, Harold ignored Kate, talking only to Robert about the latest news, digesting the contents of his newspaper reading so that he could then discuss the increasing severity of the world situation.

Kate tried to draw her mother aside to see what had been said about her school report, but the moment she did her father interrupted, sending Helen out to the kitchen to fetch in the dinner, while making sure that Kate remained listening to him in respectful silence.

Nor was anything said over dinner.

When Harold had finally withdrawn to his study, Kate and Robert turned to quiz their mother.

'Well, Kate darling . . .' Her mother looked away. 'It's not up to me, but I really don't think it's fair.'

'What isn't, Mum?' Kate asked, looking to Robert once she had noticed the despair in her mother's eyes.

'What is it, Mother?' Robert wondered, coming and sitting on the arm of her chair. 'What isn't fair?'

'Everything, Robert. Absolutely everything.'

She walked out of the room, closing the door quietly behind her.

'I thought so,' Kate said quietly. 'I bet you anything Father's going to take me away.'

*   *   *

Kate knew she was right, long before her mother confirmed as much. Kate also knew there would be no further debate on the matter, since whenever her father made up his mind about something, whatever it was, it became a *fait accompli*. Kate was to leave the convent of St Augustine at the end of term in order to go to a local secretarial training college and follow the path ordained for her by her father.

'Ridiculous,' Robert announced once their father had left for work the next morning. 'Ridiculous, and unfair.'

'You know your father, Robert,' Helen said, stacking the sideboard with a pile of freshly ironed and folded table linen. 'He doesn't exactly deal in fairness.'

'No point in us having another word with him, I suppose?'

'Since when has your father ever listened to me?'

'Even if Mother did have a go, Bobby, it would be pointless,' Kate said, walking to the window to stare out over the garden. 'Once Father's mind is made up, that's it.'

'That's defeatist talk,' Robert remarked. 'We're going to need a bit more backbone than that in the coming months, aren't we?' he added, looking quizzical.

'It's different for you—being a boy. You know what Father's always said—girls don't count.'

Kate hurried out of the kitchen through the back door, and into the garden. Helen shook her head at Robert and indicated he should go after her. When Robert caught up with her, Kate finally confessed that it wasn't anything that her brother had said about her education that had particularly upset her, but the mention of the coming war.

'Actually,' Robert said quietly as they sat on the garden bench to one side of the tennis court, 'if things go on as they are I'm thinking of volunteering for the Navy anyway, rather than waiting for hostilities to break out. I'd rather be prepared for what I'm going to do than join up in a panic and be taught in a rush. It's only sensible when you think about it. Joining up now doesn't

120

make it any more risky. Besides, I know it's something Father wants.'

'I should have thought that's enough to make you go for the army.'

Kate laughed her deep gurgling laugh, tossing her head back as she did so.

'Oh, I know!' Robert agreed, joining in the laughter. He turned and looked at his sister. 'But it is a bit odd, don't you think? The way Father treats us? Like—like we're sort of—what's the word . . . appendages.'

'Appendages,' Kate echoed, mock impressed. 'Appendages no less.'

'Well, he doesn't really treat us as humans, does he? It's a bit different for you, because you're only his daughter—'

'I know, not his son. Not heir to the vast Maddox fortunes.'

'Girls don't count—not to Father. You know that. He's forever saying—quoting Grandfather who was forever saying *girls don't count*. But even with you he has this—this reserve. As if he's afraid.'

'You're too smart for me. *Expliquez-vous.*'

'Seriously. Bobby—just be serious for a moment. What I reckon is Father had us, or rather Mother had us and Father said fine—got the two children, the pigeon pair, fine. That's what married people do, they get married, make a home and have their pigeon pair. And then he suddenly realised—and you know how jealous and competitive Father can be—'

'Try playing Canasta with him.'

'I did, for my sins. He threw the cards in the fire when I won. And that's my point. It was just about all right when we were small—I was something

121

Mother looked after, and you were a bright, sporty boy at school—and he was still cock of the walk. The brilliant Professor Maddox. One of the great brains of his time.'

'As he keeps telling us.'

'Then not only did you start getting better and better school reports, with all your teachers saying you were university material both academically and psychologically—but I developed a brain and started getting good reports as well.'

'Good reports?' Robert widened his eyes at her. 'You started getting extraordinary reports.'

'That's my point, you see. I think Father became afraid. I think he thought he was going to be outgrown by his children. I think he thought we were going to outstrip him and that suddenly the great and famous Professor Maddox would be no more.'

'Which is an absolute nonsense, of course.'

'Yes—to us—but not to Father. And that explains the way he treats us. How he's quite happy to steer you into the Navy and keep me out of Oxford. In other words, get shot of us.'

Robert blew out a plume of tobacco smoke and turned to look hard at his sister.

'You know what you're saying, don't you?'

'I'm sorry,' Kate said, dropping her eyes and looking at the ground. 'But you know what I mean. Tigers like their cubs as long as they're cubs. But when they grow into tigers . . .'

'I'd still want to go for the Navy, Father or no Father.'

'Of course you would, Bobby.' Kate looked up now, putting a hand on one of her brother's. 'I know that. It doesn't make any difference to your resolution. But it does make sense of what's happened to us.'

Robert nodded, took a last draw on his smoke, and trod the butt out under one foot.

'Don't worry. If there was a choice, I'd rather be going up to Oxford than into the Navy, but that's the times we live in.'

'So would I. But since I'm now not going to be, I'm starting to see this war—if it's going to happen—'

'Which it will—'

'I'm beginning to look on it all quite differently.'

'In what way exactly?'

'As a way of escape, I suppose. As representing some sort of a chance.'

'Yes,' Robert said, glancing over his shoulder back towards their home. 'Yes, I think I see what you mean. In fact I know I do.'

'So. Roll on the war I say.'

Robert stared at his sister, half appalled, half admiring.

'That's you all over, Kate Maddox,' he grinned finally. 'You always go that bridge too far.'

*   *   *

Five days after term ended Kate found herself enrolled at Mr Martin's Academy for Clerical and Secretarial Education, an institution housed in an ugly Victorian redbrick house on the edge of the town, the purpose being for her to receive a bookkeeping and secretarial training up to Diploma level. A week later Robert signed on for the Royal Navy and then returned home to await his call to arms.

Professor Maddox seized the opportunity to take down and lock away the tennis net from their court. To Kate it seemed to be a calculated move, as if to symbolise the end of any freedom childhood had afforded her, and to signal a time when she was to fall into line and lead what her father delighted in describing as a *quiet ordinary existence*, the sort enjoyed by decent folk. The silver lining in this particular dark cloud was the fact that no sooner had he locked the tennis net away and dismantled the perimeter than he was called away to replace another lecturer on a two-week tour.

The professor's family used this heavenly gift of freedom to do all the things they were usually forbidden from doing when the head of the household was in residence: eating meals at the kitchen table without napkins, playing noisy card games, listening to the Light Programme rather than the Home Service on the wireless and flopping around the house in dressing gowns and pyjamas at the weekend. All of a sudden they found themselves creating a childhood that they had never really experienced, and most of all they were left alone with their mother at a time in their lives when they could all fully relate to each other.

It was the happiest of times, a holiday at home, despite Kate's having begun her secretarial course at an institution she described as being so dry it could self-ignite, and even though her fellow students were to a person unexciting, and notwithstanding the fact that Robert was waiting for his official summons to join whatever ship on which he was to serve.

Finally when their little holiday came to an end, and the professor returned, Kate, finding herself at a loose end, went for a long walk that somehow ended up in the grounds of the convent.

It being the holidays, it seemed there was no one about at all, other than a distant figure cutting the lawns. Before she knew it, Kate found herself standing on the number one tennis court, imagining she was playing a vital match as in fact she had done so often. She got so caught up in her fantasy that she began to hit imaginary shots with an imaginary racket, chasing imaginary balls over the court and even leaping up to smash back what she knew was a certain winner.

'Good shot, Kate!' a familiar voice called from behind her. 'Wish we still had you on the team.'

Kate turned to greet her old coach, feeling a little foolish.

'Hallo, Mr Wilkinson.' She smiled. 'I was just replaying some of the old matches.'

'You certainly look as if you haven't lost your touch, young Kate.'

Kate cleared her throat and looked at the ground, before deciding to come clean.

'I've been banned,' she said. 'I'm not allowed to play any more.'

'Not allowed to play? Who says so?'

'My father. He says if I'm to go on playing I have to continue with my lessons—and since he can't afford to pay for the lessons, and neither can I—' Kate stopped and shrugged hopelessly. 'My father's a firm believer in if a thing is worth doing it is only worth doing properly.'

'That isn't the real reason, Kate, is it?' Mr Wilkinson put down the tennis equipment he was carrying on the court chair, and took his jacket off. 'He just doesn't want you to go on with the sport.'

125

He looked at her, then handed her one of the two rackets he had brought with him.

'From what I remember of your father, he doesn't think much of women in sport.'

'Well, there is that.'

'Come on, enough of that. Let's have a game.'

Kate looked down at her feet.

'I haven't brought my tennis things, just came by for old times' sake—'

'Never mind, sandals will do.'

As they began knocking up, Kate got that old heady feeling of the power skill imbues. She had only been off court for a matter of a couple of weeks, but the knowledge that her father had forbidden her to play made it feel infinitely longer. In fact only the night before she had begun to wonder whether she still had any real ability left, which was possibly why her subconscious had directed her up to the grounds of the convent.

They played, and as they did so it became even more apparent that Kate was right at the top of her game. Mr Wilkinson, no mean player himself, found himself at full stretch to reach and cope with the fusillade of volleys, smashes and aces that flew at him, and as Kate extended her lead by two games, then three, then four to win the first set 6–2 he found himself smiling.

'Right,' he said, collapsing on the chair by the net and towelling himself off. 'Reckon it's time I started trying.'

'Me too.' Kate grinned back at him. 'If I'm to give you any sort of game.'

Kate had hardly broken sweat in the first set. She stood by the net, swinging her racket in practice, eyeing the imaginary balls and self-correcting any possible faults she thought she might have made. Mr Wilkinson cast an approving look at his former pupil, witnessing yet again her natural athleticism. Tall without being gangly or awkward, which so many tall girls were, Kate was also deceptively strong and able to move lightning fast. Most importantly she had the right mental attitude. If the game started to go against her, she never seemed to tighten up. She simply moved up a gear, stepped up the pace and attacked the net, taking the game to her opponent rather than seeking safety in the base line.

Realising Kate Maddox was not only going to beat him but beat him in straight sets Mr Wilkinson began to play as if his life depended on it. He played as if he were qualifying for the last available place at Wimbledon, putting the fact that he was playing a seventeen-year-old girl out of his head.

It wasn't enough. In spite of winning the second set 9–7, he not only lost the deciding set but found himself drubbed, going down 6–3. 'Come on, Kate,' he sighed, collapsing with exhaustion on the bank of the lawns that rose above the grass court. 'Out with it—because I no longer believe a word you say. You haven't been not playing—the way you're playing I'd say you've been taking lessons from Dan Maskell.'

'As a matter of fact, Mr Wilkinson, I'm not sure where all that came from. Maybe that game came from not being able to play.'

She gave him back his racket.

'I think I'd better go home now,' she said quietly in her deep voice, at the same time untying her hair and letting it fall.

'Maybe I should have a word with your father,'

Mr Wilkinson decided, getting up and following Kate off the court.

'I'd rather you didn't, if you don't mind,' Kate said politely, but Mr Wilkinson had already caught sight of the look in her eyes which was quite at odds with her quiet manner. 'It's very kind of you, but there wouldn't be any point.'

'You could go all the way, Kate,' Mr Wilkinson insisted. 'There aren't many young women players of your calibre.'

'That's really very kind,' Kate replied carefully. 'But I'm being sent to secretarial college, to learn typing and shorthand.'

'Typing and shorthand?' Mr Wilkinson stared at her in sheer disbelief. 'No. No, that is just ridiculous.'

'It might be, but that's what I'm doing. Now I really must go. Thank you so much for the game.'

Before he could say another word, Kate turned and hurried away from the courts. Peter Wilkinson watched her go, shook his head, then in a fit of uncharacteristic pique kicked the slatted wooden chair by the net.

Kate ran home, fearful now that she was going to be too late to bathe and change after her unexpected exertions. As she ran she could not help thinking that if war broke out tomorrow she would not sigh, or cry. Her young life had already ended in a cul-de-sac. She knew now there was only one way to go, and that was forward, although to what exactly she could not have said.

CHAPTER SIX

While Marjorie had become so unconcerned by the whereabouts of her mother that had she received news of her death she would have found herself only mildly interested, she had become more intrigued by her aunt's so-called business days, the three days a week she left the house for a still unspecified purpose, disappearing after breakfast and sometimes not returning till late in the evening. The reason for Marjorie's fascination lay not only in the unnamed nature of her work, but also in the irregularity of the hours she kept.

'If she was working in a shop, or an office, Billy,' she would remind them both over and over again as they tried to puzzle it out, 'she'd go out at the same time and come home at the same time.'

'Which she don't,' Billy would always add, his eyes running round the ceiling as he tried to visualise what it was that Aunt Hester did exactly. 'Maybe we should follow her one day and see for ourselves, Marjorie.'

'She's too smart for that, Billy. She'd be on to us by the end of the road, and then where would we be? I can just see us trying to explain to Aunt H what we thought we were doing.'

'Maybe she got one of those—what they call 'em?' Billy scratched his head. 'Part-time job things. You know, helping out with something, somewhere that's not *necessarily* some shop nor office.'

The dilemma stayed with them. Sometimes they'd pick it up and chew it over when Marjorie went to collect Billy from the school he was now attending. The pair of them would amble back to Number 32, Billy kicking stones in the gutter or chasing pigeons while pretending to be a fighter aeroplane, his copy of the *Magnet* firmly tucked under his arm, while Marjorie would amble along the pavement trying to imagine herself plucking up the courage to ask Aunt Hester the Tuesday, Thursday and Friday question.

'She could be a spy!' Billy suggested one afternoon as he finished circling Marjorie with his arms spread out wide like an aircraft. 'She could be, though, couldn't she? We was all talking in class the other day just about that. About how we all got to be dead careful of who we say anything to and all. 'Cos the teacher said there's spies everywhere! That's what Aunt H could be, Marjorie! She could be a *spy*!'

'Don't be daft,' Marjorie replied, completely unable to entertain the idea of her aunt's being a foreign agent. 'If she was a spy she'd have to be a German spy, wouldn't she? And I can't imagine Aunt Hester being any such thing. I mean there are Coronation mugs everywhere on her dresser. And cake tins. Coronation cake tins I mean. And a picture of the new King and Queen, so I really can't see Aunt Hester being some sort of German spy. It doesn't make sense.'

'That's what she is!' Billy insisted, still circling and buzzing Marjorie. 'She's nothing but an old spy.'

'Aunt Hester isn't old, Billy,' Marjorie interrupted.

'She's very old for a woman—as old as her teeth.'

'She's not old. And stop buzzing me. It's making me fed up.'

'Sorry.' Billy stopped being an aircraft, falling into step beside Marjorie, one foot on the pavement and one in the gutter. 'You don't usually mind.'

'Course I don't mind,' Marjorie reassured him. 'Not usually. But I also don't mind a bit of a rest now and then. While I think. I can't think with you buzz-bombing and sky-diving me, can I?'

Billy shrugged and continued with his mock limp, one foot on the pavement, the other in the gutter. Marjorie glanced at him. He was such a twerp, really. Mind you, he'd settled so easily into Number 32, it now seemed as if there never was a time he'd not been resident there, just as there never seemed to have been a time when she had not known the white-faced, lead-hearted, melancholy boy, abandoned by his father, who quite obviously could see no real point in existing. Now, he was a quite changed child, his reflective moments seemingly not as introspective as they used to be. Sometimes she would catch him sitting at the kitchen window looking out to where the birds he had tempted with breadcrumbs and bacon rind had come down to eat, arriving at last to feast at the bird table he and Marjorie had made one weekend.

He would watch their flight with a dreamy smile on his face and a look of longing in his eyes as if he wanted to join them, as if their very flight suggested a freedom he could only imagine. At other times Marjorie would find him looking at her when she was making scones for their tea, or a jelly covered with his favourite hundreds and thousands for

131

Sunday lunch, that same indefinable, far-way look in his eyes. Just as quickly he would change into one hundred per cent boy, tearing after rabbits on the nearby common, playing aeroplanes on the way home from school, trying to wrestle Marjorie in the yard behind Aunt Hester's back.

'If Aunt Hester *is* a spy,' Billy suggested as they discussed their favourite topic yet again on the way back from Billy's school, 'she will be shot when there's a war, 'cos the postman told me all spies are shot in war.'

'In that case, if you're so sure, Billy—ask her, for heaven's sake. Ask her at teatime. I dare you.'

'Can't. I'm too frightened.'

'I dare you.'

'Please, Marjorie—you do.'

'If you don't I'll—I'll send you back to the Dump.'

'You don't mean that, Marjorie, do you?' Billy asked, suddenly stricken. ' 'Cos I wouldn't like that. I promise I won't be a pest any more, Marjorie. Promise.'

'Course you're not a pest, you twerp.' Marjorie laughed. 'You just go on like one, that's all.'

'So do you.'

'You do treble double with knobs on!' Marjorie laughed, grabbing him and tickling him.

'Stop!' Billy yelled helplessly. 'Please stop! Please! Please, I'll do anything! Anything, I promise, just please stop, Marjorie!'

'You'll do anything?'

'Anything! Anything, I promise! Cross me heart and hope to die!'

'Right.' Marjorie stopped tickling him, getting hold of him playfully by one ear. 'You can ask Aunt

132

Hester what she does then, can't you?'

*   *   *

At teatime that afternoon Marjorie gave Billy a nudge with her knee under the table, prompting him to take up her challenge.

'Aunt Hester?' Billy began very quietly, hoping that he wouldn't be heard. 'Aunt Hester—Marjorie wants to know what you do when you go out.'

'No I do not!' Marjorie protested. 'I never asked such a thing.'

'Gracious heavens, if ever there was a pair of nosy buggins it's you two.'

There was a short silence, while Aunt Hester carefully cut them all a slice of home-made sponge cake before pouring herself more tea.

'So what do you do, Aunt Hester?' Billy tried again, quickly responding to a tap on his shins under the table from Marjorie.

'What do you think I do, Billy?'

'Go on buses.'

'What do you think I do, Marjorie?'

'She thinks you're a spy,' Billy said, smart as new paint and quickly moving his legs out of the way of the expected forthcoming kick.

'A spy,' Aunt Hester mused, narrowing her eyes and turning to look at Marjorie, who was now looking quite at sea. 'What sort of a spy, Marjorie dear?'

'It's not me who thinks you're a spy, Aunt Hester,' Marjorie replied. 'It's Billy what thinks—'

'That thinks—'

'That thinks you're a spy. I don't.'

As Aunt Hester turned away to put the cake

133

back on the tea trolley, Marjorie took the opportunity to pull a face at Billy.

'Any more of that, Marjorie, and the wind will change, and you'll be stuck with that face.'

'So what do you do . . .' Billy swung his legs to and fro under the table.

'I do government business. I do a bit of work for the government, which means running a few errands here and there. Mostly here but sometimes there. Now does that answer my nosy parkers' questions?'

Billy thought about it for a moment, but since he had little idea of what constituted a government, let alone what sort of business it did, he could only conclude that it must be dull, because every time he heard Aunt Hester discussing the government she always referred to it as boring. So he nodded and returned to the much more satisfying task of eating the delicious sponge sandwich Marjorie had made for their tea.

'Now, more to the point,' Aunt Hester said, as they finished. 'The way things are, I propose to take you both for a little break, to the seaside.'

They both stared at her, neither of them wanting to admit that they'd never been before, although Marjorie did her best to hide it behind a new veil of sophistication by saying, 'What a jolly idea.'

'We'll go in my car,' Aunt Hester went on, airily, and this time not even Marjorie could hide her astonishment.

'You don't have a car, Aunt Hester! I mean, not unless you've just gone out and bought one.'

'You two really think you know everything,' Aunt Hester replied, clearing the table with Marjorie's help. 'And don't think you can just sit there, young man. You know what your job is.'

Billy was on his feet in a second, fetching the small soft-haired crumbs brush and tray from the dresser and sweeping the table clean. Wide-eyed he caught Marjorie's eye, and she stared back at him in like fashion, as if to say *what is going on*?

'A friend of mine has a little cottage by the sea. Overlooking Foyle Sands. Lovely spot right by a little beach. I thought it might be a bit of a treat for us all.'

'Do you really have a car, Aunt H?' Billy asked carefully, having deposited the crumbs from the little tray carefully in the dustbin.

'What do you think this is, young buggins?'

Aunt Hester took him to the front door and opened it. Outside parked at the kerb was a plum-coloured, well-polished Austin 10. Billy stared at it in silence.

'Cor,' he whispered at last. 'Smashing.'

'It's hardly a Rolls-Royce, young man.'

'It's smashing, Aunt H. Can I sit in the front?'

'If you behave I might let you. But you'll have to take it in turns with Marjorie otherwise it wouldn't be fair.'

'I don't mind, Aunt Hester,' Marjorie assured her. 'I shall be just as happy in the back.'

'How long have you had it?' Billy said, swallowing with excitement as they went back inside. 'And where do you keep it?'

'I have had it for over two years, and I keep it in a garage in a friend's house.'

'And you really can drive, Aunt H?'

'No,' Aunt Hester said, with a mock glare. 'Normally I just push it. But tomorrow I'm going to have a chauffeur.'

'A chauffeur?' Billy could not open his eyes any wider if he tried. 'Who?'

'You,' Aunt Hester said, aiming a pretend clip at his head. 'Now get inside the pair of you and wash up the tea things.'

*　　　*　　　*

They left before dawn, when not even the milk pony had started his patient round, staring around him with blinking eyes as the bottles clanked, and the milkman swayed through suburban gates with his carrier. Billy had been so excited he would not stop talking and asking questions. Aunt Hester, concentrating on the road ahead of her, did her best to ignore him, sitting bolt upright at the steering wheel which she gripped with white-knuckled hands, only ever letting go with one hand when she had to change gear. This was an operation which she somehow managed despite the screams of protest from the gearbox. At long last, after negotiating what seemed to be endless suburban avenues and small streets, they found themselves on the open road, and as the sun rose and the road to the coast unfolded in front of them Marjorie and Billy played I-Spy, Marjorie inventing the most ridiculous objects to keep Billy's interest, until such time as Aunt Hester decided to stop for lunch at a prettily fronted hotel complete with roses growing up the walls, and dogs lazily wagging tails at the front door. For once Marjorie and Billy were completely quietened, overcome by the white linen cloths and napkins, by the swift waitress service, but most of all by the delicious hot pies and home-made ice creams.

136

By teatime Aunt Hester had turned into the little lane that led up to Seagull Watch, a white-painted, thatched cottage that stood last in line in splendid isolation, separated from the beach by a quarter of an acre of beautifully maintained walled gardens. There were three bedrooms, a sunny living room that directly overlooked the sea, and a kitchen large enough to cook and eat in quite comfortably. As soon as the tired trio tumbled out of the car and breathed in the sea air, admiring the view of miles of sunlit sand, the fatigue of the journey seemed to vanish at once, and exhilaration took its place.

Billy and Marjorie were given permission to explore once the car had been unloaded and their cases unpacked, so as Aunt Hester pottered happily around the cottage, while the kettle boiled for tea, Marjorie took Billy to the beach and together they stood at the edge of the receding sea. Calm as a millpond at low tide, it only added to the sense that the recent threat of war that had been hanging over everyone had not only been left behind, but had somehow altogether vanished, as if the quarrelling world they had left behind was a figment of all their imaginations.

'First time I seen the sea,' Billy said after a while. 'Other than pictures, course. Big, in't it, Marjorie, the sea?'

'This isn't the only sea, dopey,' Marjorie explained. 'There are lots of seas.'

'Don't stop it from being huge, Marjorie. You don't get that in school. The size of it. It just goes on and on and on. Blimey.'

'This actually is only a channel. The English Channel. And it's not all that big. I mean Germany

137

and France—'

Billy picked up a handful of pebbles off the beach and started hurling them into the sea.

'France is only a matter of a few miles away,' Marjorie continued, more to herself as Billy continued to hurl his pebbles. 'Only about twenty miles away, that's all. Not far, is it?'

Billy was too preoccupied to have picked up the question, or notice the look of sudden anxiety in Marjorie's eyes as she visualised an armada of enemy ships steaming towards her island home.

'Come in, Billy,' she said suddenly. 'It's getting cold. I want to go in.'

All the time they were by the sea Aunt Hester, like Marjorie, seemed worry-free, so much so that it seemed to Marjorie she had never seen her aunt so relaxed and happy, determined to teach Billy not just how to swim but how to build proper sandcastles. Her sand building was certainly better than her swimming tuition, to judge from the yells and splutters and watery thrashing that went on every time Billy was led to the waterside in yet another attempt to get him afloat. But such is the power of the sea, and such its buoyancy, that in spite of all his initial resistance within three days Billy found that not only could he float, but while he floated he could also swim a couple of strokes without plunging to the bottom. Exhilarated and convinced he was now a fully fledged swimmer, the next morning he discarded his swimming ring and plunged into the glinting sea, only to be knocked down by an enthusiastic incoming wave. Marjorie went to his rescue, pulling him spluttering out of the sea and handing him back his lifebelt.

'You know what they say about walking and

running? Well, the same goes for swimming and floating, young man.'

But Billy was back in the water within minutes, determined to come to terms with this new sport. As he floated, arms out in front of him, holding tight to his lifebelt, legs thrashing behind him, he left Aunt Hester behind on the beach, planning her massively complicated castle in the sands while Marjorie ran between the two, always arriving too late to be of much help to either.

Aunt Hester did not just build sandcastles, she built ramparts, moats, towers, drawbridges, and outer fortifications with defences so strong that as the incoming tide first tried to overrun them it seemed she had actually managed to build the first sandcastle capable of withstanding its traditional enemy. But then the waters gathered and the tide strengthened, and away went the towers and ramparts, the drawbridges and the moats, washed back to sand. This only seemed to delight Aunt Hester who would sit back on her heels watching attentively, as if determined to learn from this newest invasion. The next day, undaunted, she was back out with buckets and spades to start building again with renewed determination.

And when she wasn't building she was catching shrimps in rock pools, swimming out to sea for miles, climbing rock faces and even fishing from the beach with a rod she found under the stairs in the cottage.

She seemed to be champion at everything to do with the seaside, and if her two adopted children hadn't loved her already, they surely would have done by now. Quite apart from anything else the holiday was as unlike their normal life as was perfectly possible. There was none of their usual preoccupation with the pending war, the news bulletins, the fearful talk of Hitler and gas attacks, not to mention the threat of invasion. All that seemed to be a thing of the past until the evening they had visitors.

The first was a serious, square set, heavily bespectacled man in his early forties, dressed in a light suit. The second was a tall, young, handsome Frenchman. They both appeared, as if out of the blue, one early evening at the door of Seagull Watch.

'These are friends of mine,' Aunt Hester told Marjorie, who, dressed in her best summer cotton frock, pink cardigan, white socks and sandals, had opened the door to them and was finding it difficult not to stare at the young Frenchman who had just finished kissing Aunt Hester's hand. 'They've come over for a drink—and a talk . . .'

Aunt Hester stopped to give a look at the older of the two men who nodded affably, but said nothing in return.

'It's purely a social call—so if you and Billy popped off to bed a little early, would you mind? You can play a game of cards together upstairs, and then perhaps an early night might be indicated?' Aunt Hester looked both vague and apologetic at the same time. 'You can take my new book, if you like,' she added, knowing that if she was asking Marjorie to sacrifice their nightly card game, a bribe would not go amiss.

Marjorie looked appreciatively at the spine of the book that was being offered to her. The idea of missing their card game saddened her, but on the other hand she certainly didn't mind making

140

herself scarce to read the latest novel by Georgette Heyer.

'*Bonne nuit, mademoiselle*,' the young Frenchman called out to her, smiling.

Marjorie paused and turned as she went up the stairs, and as she did so she found herself looking down into a pair of beautiful dark eyes, for now that he had removed his beret, and was standing in the simply furnished living room of the cottage, it became quite clear that the young Frenchman was as good-looking as anyone could wish, well over six feet tall with thick dark hair and large dark eyes. He towered over her aunt, his stature making her look frail and suddenly, strangely old.

'Say *bonne nuit*, Marjorie dear,' Hester called up, gently prompting Marjorie.

'*Bonne nuit, monsieur*. Goodnight.'

Marjorie was promptly rewarded with a charming smile from the Frenchman, while his companion lit a pipe and nodded at nothing in particular. With a shy smile at the foreigner, Marjorie finally disappeared upstairs, closely followed by a reluctant Billy. It was the first time she had really noticed a man, and since the Frenchman was handsome, and young—and his visit so mysterious, since Marjorie reckoned that her aunt must always have known of their coming, but had said nothing—Billy was two hands of whist up on her before Marjorie finally came back to earth. But as she lay in bed that night the memory of the handsome dark-eyed young man stayed with her, as if he himself was determined to haunt her.

The next morning no reference was made by Aunt Hester to her visitors, and since it was, all too soon, the last day of their holiday they said nothing, only hurried through breakfast so that they could have more time on the beach, returning to the cottage at lunchtime to help with the packing up, before starting the long journey home.

'It's been—well, I don't know, just like a dream,' Marjorie said after she had finished sweeping the kitchen and hall free of sand. 'Billy and I are trying to think of how to say thank you—'

'If you can't think,' Aunt Hester said, tongue firmly in cheek, 'I shouldn't bother.'

'It's been the best time of our lives. Billy thinks so, too,' she added quickly, nudging Billy.

'Couldn't agree more, dear. Now don't forget your piece of seaweed, or we'll be sunk when we want to prognosticate the weather when we get back.'

'Progwhaticake?' Billy wondered, stumbling by with a bulging suitcase.

'Forecast, Billy. Prognosticate means to tell in advance. And you don't need all those sea shells, surely?'

'I don't need 'em, Aunt H,' Billy replied. 'But I'd still like to take 'em.'

'Shan't be able to sleep with the sound of all that sea in your ears,' Aunt Hester murmured. 'Go on—run along and put the cases in the car, while I lock up.'

Marjorie and her aunt went round the little cottage one last time to make sure that everything was in order and that they hadn't left anything behind.

'Some of our neighbours,' Aunt Hester told her as they were doing the final lock-up. 'They thought I was off my hinges—particularly Number 30. Taking us all away for a seaside holiday just when

142

war's about to break out—but that's the whole point really. It's because there's going to be a war that I brought us all away. We'll always have this memory to share, you and Billy and me—I wanted us all to be able to remember this time, being happy the way people should be happy, without a care in the world. Since there's nothing much we can do about what's coming, I don't see the harm. For once we've been happy and carefree. Nice word, that. I've always liked that word—carefree. Because really so little of life is ever carefree, so when you get a bit, grab it. That's what I say.'

She gave one last look round the cottage sitting room before ushering Marjorie outside. She then locked the front door behind them, blew the place a kiss, and taking her niece's arm walked off to the car.

*   *   *

By the time Billy had returned to school it seemed there was nothing else to talk about other than the preparations that had to be made for the forthcoming conflict. It actually seemed to be affecting Billy rather more than either Marjorie or Aunt Hester, probably because they found themselves so preoccupied with the business of shrouding lamps and making blackout blinds and curtains, while Billy sat silently at the table under the front window toying with his homework, pencil stuck in mouth, always wondering, trying to think how *war* might be. The word seemed to be echoing through his head. War, war, *war*.

'Are we going to be bombed do you think, Marjorie?' he asked one night as Marjorie sorted

143

out the matches she had been splitting in half into boxes. 'The nearest shelter's miles away—and if there's a sudden air raid, we mightn't make it.'

'Why should they bomb Castle Gardens, Billy?' Marjorie laughed, trying to lighten the atmosphere. 'They're hardly going to waste their precious bombs on our bit of town.'

'What about gas? Everyone at school says they're going to attack us with gas.'

'Which is why we've been doing our gas mask practice, dopey. Long as you're carrying your gas mask you won't die, will you now?'

Billy pushed his homework to one side and began tapping the table with his pencil.

'Wish I was old enough to join up.'

'Don't be daft, Billy. You'll wish your life away if you're not careful.'

'I don't want to just sit here doing nothing. I want to kill Hitler.'

'Never mind killing Hitler, first you must learn to knit,' Marjorie joked. 'Like Aunt Hester and me. Help us knit mufflers and socks for the soldiers, and then you can kill Hitler with your knitting needles, poke his eyes out with them, that's what you can do.'

'How old do you actually have to be?' Billy wondered, ignoring Marjorie's tease. 'I'm sure if they really want soldiers, if they really need them, they might take me, don't you think?'

'No I don't, Billy. And I don't want to—and I wish you'd stop thinking like that, too. All right?'

'I could learn to shoot.'

'You haven't got a gun, muggins.'

'I could join the rifle club.'

'You're too young.'

144

'No I'm not. George Perry goes shooting there. With his dad. He's the same age as what I am.'

'That you are—that I am.'

Marjorie looked at him and sighed inwardly, remembering the pale-faced, first weeping then almost silent young boy she had befriended, whereas now all she could see was a boy determined to learn to kill. Seeing the look in his eyes and realising the change that was coming over him, Marjorie felt a momentary despair. Despite their parents' abandonment, the rough treatment they'd had at the boarding school—despite everything that had happened to them, in some strange way, she realised, they had actually remained innocent, until the war clouds started to gather, blocking out the blue skies they'd only just begun to enjoy.

Marjorie sat down opposite Billy at the table, turning his homework round to her and pretending to study it. She couldn't stand the thought of Billy with a gun, or in a uniform, but she knew that one day she had to stand it. It was just how it was.

*   *   *

Oddly enough, the following day when she turned out to help fill sandbags she found the atmosphere in the street was one of considerable gaiety, as if people were relieved to be out of their houses and doing something positive rather than just sitting inside wondering when all hell was going to break loose.

'You still going to them anti-gas lectures?' Mrs Watling from Number 31 asked, as they found themselves standing next to each other in the queue for sacks. ' 'Cos if you are, I wouldn't mind coming with you.'

Marjorie turned and stared at her in barely disguised indignation.

'When we asked you last month if you were interested in coming, Mrs Watling, you called Aunt Hester and me warmongers, if you care to remember.'

Mrs Watling blushed, and turned away for a second.

'Yes—well I dare say I did,' she excused herself. 'But then I dare say I was wrong, too, see?'

'It's six thirty at the school, if you want to know. If you knock on our door we can all go along together.'

'Just don't tell Mr Watling, mind. He still thinks it's a lot of fuss about nothing. That it don't affect us—says it's no business of ours what Hitler does. That foreigners are nothing but trouble and they're nothing to do with us no how, no way.'

'Mr Watling won't think it's nonsense when he has to go to work wearing his gas mask, Mrs Watling,' Marjorie retorted. 'And the whole town's on fire, and there's Nazis delivering censored letters, and putting him in prison, he won't think it's nonsense then.'

'Mr Watling doesn't think much of gas masks neither.'

'He's going to have to. Aunt Hester says they'll soon be compulsory, by law—and no one will be allowed to go anywhere without one.'

'That so? No doubt I'll hear all about it tonight when we go to this 'ere class.'

*   *   *

146

Marjorie couldn't help feeling astonished when she saw just how many people had come to the class. The first couple of lectures had been attended by only a couple of retired army officers, half a dozen dutiful housewives and a bored teenager who'd been sent along to get him out from under his mother's feet for the evening. Aunt Hester insisted that both Marjorie and Billy went, for in her opinion there was too much ridicule about anti-gas lectures, not to mention Air Raid Precautions. Not to attend was not only short-sighted and impractical, but unpatriotic. Her stance was belittled not just by the neighbours but by people in the local shops. Now it seemed she was suddenly not alone, for the small schoolroom dedicated to these civil defence lectures was packed to the door.

'If you ask me it's this Munich business,' a large, moon-faced woman announced loudly as she settled her ample girth on one of the school benches. 'Ever since we let Hitler march all over those poor Czechs even my old man's started to think we should stop sitting on the fence and stand up and fight.'

'Quite right too,' Mrs Watling agreed, leaning across Marjorie to tap the other woman on her arm. 'We got to go to it and fight, or sure as eggs we'll all be dead before we know it. Just wish I could get my old man to see it, that's all, but see it he can't—or do I mean won't?'

'Mine's just volunteered for the Auxiliary Fire Service,' the large woman replied. 'He's that serious about training he don't even go to darts evenings at the Hero of Inkerman no more—and for my George that's quite something, believe you

147

me.'

'Where's your aunt, Marjorie?' Mrs Watling leaned forward to attract Marjorie's attention. 'Thought she never missed a meeting?'

'Aunt Hester's out sticking up posters and distributing pamphlets for people to come to meetings of the ARP. She says it's getting so serious we need air raid wardens more than ever. We're going to First Aid tomorrow, Billy and me. Aunt Hester says nobody's too young to learn about dealing with the kind of injuries that will be coming our way.'

'That's nice,' the large woman said, folding her arms across her ample bosom. 'That's just what I come out to hear.'

*   *   *

'Mustard gas blisters on limbs,' the uniformed lecturer who had just walked in began, without any announcement, pointing to a particularly graphic illustration he had just hung up over the blackboard. 'That's our kicking off point this evening—the effects of mustard gas on life and limb.'

At this, Mrs Watling carefully withdrew a large coloured handkerchief from her handbag and held it over her mouth, breathing out loudly as she did so.

Despite Mrs Watling's dramatic reaction the lecturer began a detailed examination of the precise effects of gas attacks on troops in the previous world war, accompanied by increasingly bloody illustrations of severed arteries, burnt flesh and fractured bones protruding from open wounds.

Billy, his eyes out on stalks, followed every word, quite obviously riveted, while Marjorie managed to pretend to take it all in while secretly reciting a poem. It was finally too much for Mrs Watling, who after five minutes of hiding her face behind her large handkerchief suddenly excused herself and was not seen for the rest of the evening.

'I say.' Billy was once more an aeroplane as they made their way slowly home in the dark. 'That was really good, wasn't it?' He sighed with some satisfaction before strategically bombing an imagined Nazi division.

*   *   *

'You quite sure you're up to going to First Aid class with Marjorie, Billy?' Aunt Hester enquired.

'If you'd seen him at the gas mask lecture, Aunt Hester,' Marjorie replied, 'you wouldn't be bothering to ask. He can't get enough of blood and guts.'

Billy was silent. Much as he had put on a brave face at the lecture on the fearful effects of gases on the human body, he had actually, finally, found it more than a little frightening, although he would be the last to admit it. Despite this he was determined to attend the First Aid classes, because not to would be thought wet, and that just couldn't happen.

'You don't have to go, Billy,' Aunt Hester said, turning the boy to her and straightening his school tie. 'You say if you don't want to go.'

'I'm fine, Aunt H,' Billy said as firmly as he could. 'I got to learn to do me bit.'

'Please yourself, dear. Probably best with a war,

eh? Bit like swimming—best to jump in with both feet. I shan't forget the sight of you and your ring in the briny in a hurry.'

She ruffled his hair affectionately, and then began to collect her belongings prior to going out.

'Think we'll be sent to the country, Aunt H?' Billy wondered, trying to smooth his hair back down with both hands. 'They said all the kids are going to be sent to the country. I don't want to go.'

'Don't think what you want's going to have anything to do with it, Billy.' Aunt Hester checked her appearance in the mirror, and then searched for her car keys. 'Anyway—won't be until well after Christmas, if at all. We've all got that to look forward to, haven't we?'

'Where are you going tonight, Aunt Hester?' Marjorie asked.

'Ambulance Service. Driving in the dark in a gas mask, God help me. Just hope I don't crash the blooming ambulance trailer, that's all. It was a close run thing the other night.'

She smiled at them both, then all of a sudden hugged first Marjorie and then Billy.

'You're not too big for a hug. Yet.' She cuffed him affectionately.

'Aunt Hester?' Marjorie asked as she opened the front door. 'Could I learn to drive an ambulance trailer? I could, couldn't I? Be much more useful than just sitting at home.'

'Yeah? And what would I do? Knit?' asked Billy.

'You could go next door. You'd be all right,' she replied.

'You're a bit young, dear,' Aunt Hester replied, pulling on her gloves. 'It's this night-time driving. It isn't easy.'

150

'I could learn.'

'Needs must, I know, Marjorie. But let's wait until the devil takes the wheel. I'll think about it. I'll ask our instructor.' Aunt Hester added, about to leave. 'Heaven knows you'd probably make a much better driver than me, dear. We're in the forest tonight, for our sins.'

Marjorie and Billy stood at the door and watched Aunt Hester drive off into the dusk, delaying the moment when they would have to shut the door and go back inside the house alone. Even though war had not yet been declared, every time she left the house it felt as if she was going off to fight.

*   *   *

For some reason when she woke up in the early hours of the following morning, Marjorie knew instinctively that her aunt wasn't home. Seeing her bed not slept in, and not finding her downstairs, she turned on the electric fire in the sitting room, and watched the dawn coming up on the quiet suburban avenue as she tried not to worry.

She had fallen into a half sleep when the doorbell rang at last. Normally she would have hurried to the front door, imagining that Aunt Hester had lost her front door key, or left it behind, but remembering her aunt's warnings about not letting in strangers, and always leaving the chain across the door, Marjorie went first to the window to see who it might be. Outside the narrow suburban house there was a black Wolseley parked in the road, and a policeman on the doorstep. Marjorie at once hurried to the door.

151

'Miss Hendry?' the policeman enquired politely, taking off his hat. 'Sergeant Holmes. Might I come in, please?' As Marjorie nodded he added, 'Thank you.'

He walked by her into the living room, followed by Marjorie who at once turned on the light, shielding her eyes with one hand.

'You all alone here, miss?'

'No—Billy's here as well. He's asleep. Billy's my aunt's foster child, like a sort of brother for me, really.'

'I see.'

'There's something wrong, isn't there?'

Marjorie pulled her dressing gown cord tighter around her. She was still standing in only her thin night things, which now seemed inappropriate beside the policeman in his heavy serge uniform.

'Will you excuse me for a moment please?' she asked, and hurried out to the hall, fetching her coat from the hat stand and putting it on over her nightgown.

'What is it?' she asked the policeman on her return. 'Has something happened to my aunt? Is that why you're here?'

'Afraid so, miss. I'm sorry to say your aunt—I'm sorry to report Mrs Hendry has met with a bad accident—'

'Was it in the forest?' Marjorie interrupted. 'I know she was out doing ambulance practice.'

'I don't know anything about that, miss,' the policeman answered, looking surprised. 'When would that have been?'

'Last night,' Marjorie replied. 'She had ambulance driving practice in Bardham Forest all evening.'

152

'Not to my knowledge, miss,' the policeman replied. 'That was cancelled two days ago. Anyway, your aunt was nowhere near the forest when the accident happened. She was fifteen miles away up on the London road, headed south. As if she was coming home.'

Marjorie stared at him. 'I don't understand. What happened?'

'According to a witness to the accident, a large Jaguar ran her off the road, just below Stileman's Corner.'

'It can't have been an accident if someone tried to run her off the road, can it?'

'I see what you mean, miss. Perhaps not. We will have to see. She's in Gateley Hospital. I'm afraid your aunt's condition is a cause for concern.'

Marjorie turned, knowing Billy was behind her, just as she had known Aunt Hester hadn't come home.

'It's Aunt H, isn't it, Marjorie?' Billy asked quietly. 'I knew it. I had this dream, see? I knew it. I just *knew* it.'

*   *   *

Billy would keep asking to go to the hospital to visit Aunt Hester, but Marjorie dissuaded him with the excuse that the doctors didn't advise it until Aunt Hester regained consciousness. Billy grew gloomy and suspicious at Marjorie's delaying tactics, but since he was still too young to make the journey to the hospital alone he was forced to rely on Marjorie to tell him how his newly adopted mother was getting on.

In an effort to protect him, Marjorie lied. She

153

told him that Aunt Hester was unconscious, but having recovered from her injuries was expected to regain consciousness soon, while knowing all the time that even if Aunt Hester did recover consciousness she would be so badly disabled her life would be intolerable.

'It's hard to say, Miss Hendry,' the doctor at the hospital had finally admitted to Marjorie. 'I don't mean it's hard to say what will happen to your dear aunt for I know that well enough. What I mean is it's hard to say what I'm going to have to say to you, lassie, isn't it? No—sorry, I really must get out of the habit of calling every young woman lassie. My wife gives me terrible stick about it.'

He indicated a chair in the waiting room before sitting down beside Marjorie, and knitting his thick, sandy eyebrows together so tightly that for a second Marjorie found herself wondering if they would ever part again.

'Fact is, Miss Hendry, and it's a hard fact, but it's a fact—due to the severe injuries your aunt sustained not only to her chest but also to her head, and given how long she has been in a coma, I have to be quite honest—it might be better if your aunt failed to make a recovery.'

'How do you know?'

'Being a doctor helps, I suppose.'

'You can't be certain, can you? I mean you're not her, are you?'

'The best we can do now—in fact all we can do now—is pray. Pray that your aunt has a merciful delivery from her suffering.'

'Suppose she does come round? Suppose she does recover consciousness?'

'It's hard for you to understand this—but it

154

would be a far better thing if she does not.'

Marjorie finally managed to find it in herself to be grateful to the doctor for his frankness. But for him she would have lived in false hope, a hope she all too soon realised she had been careless enough to hold out to Billy.

* * *

'You—you should have told me!' Billy punched the side of a chair. 'You should have, you oughta have!' Billy gripped his hands together and struggled against his emotions, turning first white then red in his efforts to control himself.

Watching him Marjorie felt helpless, realising quite soon that seeing Billy not crying was actually worse than seeing Billy crying, his courage so touching that it brought the wretched wishbone back to her throat.

'I want to see Aunt Hester,' he finally announced. 'Don't tell me I can't because I want to. I didn't see her in hospital, and I understand why, so that don't matter—but I want to see her now. Say goodbye, and that.'

At the hospital Billy leaned over and carefully kissed his dead benefactor farewell on one cheek.

'She looks all right,' he said, standing back. 'Not really done in at all, not really.'

Taking courage from Billy, Marjorie did the same. Aunt Hester's cheek was cold but surprisingly firm. After she had kissed her goodbye and stood back up, she half expected to see her aunt move, as if the love they felt for her might awaken her, or because perhaps it had all been a mistake and she wasn't dead after all, just sleeping.

155

'She's all right, now, you know,' Billy assured her as they waited for the bus to take them home. 'She's dead—yeah, I know. But she in't gone, 'cos we got her right here, in our memory. She's not dead to us. Never will be. Not ever. And you know—she'll always be Aunt Hester, won't she?'

'Wonder what's going to happen to us,' Marjorie said, preparing to get into the Green Line bus that was now drawing up at their stop. 'With Aunt Hester gone now, do you ever wonder what's going to happen to us?'

'Why should anything happen?' Billy wondered, hopping on the bus and grabbing the front seat. 'We can manage.' He stared ahead of him, his expression resolute.

'I know we can manage, Billy, it's more a question of how.'

It was no good trying to turn to Marjorie's mother and stepfather for help. She had received a card on her seventeenth birthday, postmarked Canberra, Australia but with no address, and merely the words *still travelling around, love from Mummy and Jo* scrawled on it. Billy she knew must be an orphan, if not literally, certainly in practice, because he had been well and truly dumped, yet even so Marjorie suspected that she would have quite a struggle on her hands to try to stop them from being separated again. When it emerged that Aunt Hester had neglected to update her will, Marjorie knew that there were storm clouds ahead, and not just because of the impending war.

The question of their future hung over them both until a Mr Anthony introduced himself to her at the funeral tea.

'Miss Hendry?' As Marjorie nodded he pushed

156

his face closer to her, while at the same time carefully wiping the end of his long, reddened nose with a clean white handkerchief. 'Since your aunt's death you have possibly been made aware that she died without making any alteration to her Last Will and Testament, which means neither you nor your adopted brother nor indeed your mother, her sister, have been included.'

For some reason this caused him to smile.

'I don't mind,' Marjorie asserted, stepping back from him. 'It really doesn't matter. Billy and I don't mind, really. We wouldn't expect her to think of us.'

'Well, I think perhaps the matter of the house may be of interest, Miss Hendry, since this is your present abode. It seems Mrs Hendry long ago bequeathed the house and its contents to her other sister—Miss Roberts. The lady seated in the corner there.' Mr Anthony indicated with a small nod of his odd-shaped head. 'Although the two ladies had become somewhat estranged by circumstances over the last few years, Mrs Hendry made no alteration to her will and so the inheritance stands. This will mean, naturally, that you will have to vacate the premises and find yourself some other place of—of abode.'

'I don't mind,' Marjorie maintained, as stoutly as she could. 'I'm not sure I would want to go on living here without my aunt. Not want to go on living in this—abode.'

'Miss Roberts wants you to understand that when you go, you are not to leave here with anything that is not in your direct ownership. She wishes to avoid any controversies concerning items that might be claimed possibly to have been gifted

157

when in fact they were no such thing. Shall we say anything loaned to you by your late aunt shall have to be returned to its new rightful owner? Miss Roberts informs me that for instance her sister is said to have lent you quite a large amount of clothing, which naturally must be returned.'

Marjorie was about to protest that Aunt Hester had bought her the clothes in her wardrobe when she felt a tug on her skirt from behind.

'Come on,' Billy whispered to her. 'Someone wants to say goodbye to us—in the kitchen.'

Excusing herself from Mr Anthony's company, Marjorie went out to the kitchen. Billy followed her and shut the door behind him.

'That woman in the corner just told me. She says we gotta move out. 'Cos she's goin' to sell the place. So what are we goin' to do, Marge? What's goin' to happen to us?'

'Nothing's going to happen to us, Billy,' Marjorie replied, watching him pick up a plate of fresh food. 'Least not for a while.'

'What about what they're saying? About what Aunt Hester gave us really belongin' to them?'

'It doesn't. Everything Aunt Hester gave us is ours. They're just trying to bully us, Billy—and I'm not going to let them. So stop your worrying, *and* stuffing your face. That food's meant for our visitors.'

'Yeah,' Billy said with a look into the living room. 'And you'd better go look after Mrs Watling 'cos it looks as though she's about to fall over.'

Marjorie followed Billy's glance and saw how right he was. Mrs Watling had been happily helping herself to an abundance of sherry wine, and was now standing holding on to the lintel of the door with one hand and beckoning to Marjorie with the other.

'You all right, Mrs Watling?' Marjorie wondered, hurrying to her side.

'Me? I am fine, dear. Absolutely fine. I just wanted to say how fond of your auntie I was, Marjorie, how very fond,' she said, nodding seriously to underline her point. 'I wanted to say also how very fond I am of you as well, dear. Very, very fond, and of little Billy too—who's really not so little any more, is he?' She nodded over to where Billy was standing watching and smiled crookedly at him. 'Furthermore,' she continued slowly. 'Furthermore I want you to know that whatever I can do for you two little orphans I shall do, and more than that I *will* do. My door is open for the two of you, always. Open. Always. Your aunt was a very lovely lady. A very lovely lady indeed.'

'Thank you, Mrs Watling,' Marjorie said, even though she had carefully noted that Mrs Watling had as yet not made any definite offer.

'It's the very least I can do,' Mrs Watling assured her. 'We may not be able to offer much in the line of home, you know, but what we do comes from the heart. My heart. And at least you would both have a roof over your heads, dear. If needs be. So you just keep me in the picture, won't you? There's a good girl.'

'Are you—are you inviting Billy and me to come and stay with you?'

'You young people.' Mrs Watling smiled. 'Only got half an ear for everything, haven't you? That's what I said, didn't I? At least I'm sure I did. Didn't I? Anyway. Anyway, at the risk of repeating myself,

159

you and Billy are more than welcome to put up with us for just as long as it takes you to find something better. It will be our pleasure, dear. Least Mr Watling and me can do in your hour of need. Least we can do.'

Mrs Watling nodded at her once again, put her hand suddenly to her chest to try to stifle a hiccough and then with one final nod left, but not before walking into the front door and apologising to it.

Once she had seen her neighbour safely out of the door Marjorie went in search of Billy to tell him the news, only to find herself intercepted and sidetracked by another guest, this time someone not immediately known to her.

The fact that she failed to recognise him immediately was not surprising since she had only seen him once before, and then only very briefly. It was a moment or two before she remembered who he was—one of the two mysterious gentlemen who had called on her aunt when they were on holiday, the quiet pipe-smoking middle-aged gentleman in thick horn-rimmed spectacles who had arrived at the cottage in the company of the dashing young Frenchman.

'Miss Hendry?' he called again, pipe out of his mouth and held in one hand while he nodded to her. 'Might I have a word? I am Mr Ward. We met very briefly at Foyle Sands. You may remember?'

'I remember,' Marjorie said, looking straight into a pair of very resolute eyes, and finding her hand held in greeting in an equally resolute grasp, while the pipe stayed in his left hand. 'You called at the cottage.'

'I'd like a quiet word.' Mr Ward looked round the small crowded room. 'Is there somewhere more private?'

'Only outside,' Marjorie replied.

'It won't take a minute. Lead the way—if you'd be so kind.'

There was something in the way he said that last phrase that sounded as if he was mocking his own words, but seeing the determination in his eyes she led him outside to the garden.

They stood on the stone steps outside the back door, overlooking the tiny, brave patch of lawn inset in the yard that led down to the outhouse and the privy. Mr Ward, pipe back in his mouth, nodded at Marjorie as he closed the door tightly behind him then stood in silence for a moment, drawing on his pipe and staring across the small yard at nothing in particular.

'The thing is,' he began carefully, 'the point is I knew your aunt very well. She and I worked together.'

'You worked together?' Marjorie interrupted. 'Doing what? I often wondered what Aunt Hester did—'

'That isn't important,' Jack Ward insisted. 'Particularly now she's gone. What matters is that we knew each other very well. She was one of my most—my most *trusted* friends. We were very fond of each other—in the way that real friends are. I wanted to make that perfectly clear.'

'I see,' Marjorie said, although nothing was at all clear to her. If anything matters were a lot less clear than they had been before she was summoned outside by her mysterious visitor.

'To come to the point,' Jack Ward continued, after examining the state of the tobacco in the bowl of his pipe, 'because of my association with your

161

aunt, and because the times we live in are becoming increasingly difficult ones, I want you to know that if you ever want anything—you must call me. From what I understand of your circumstances you don't have a lot of people to call on.'

He had a remarkably beautiful voice, low, measured, and immediately charismatic. Marjorie was so entranced by it she missed taking in what he was actually saying. As if noting her inattention, Jack Ward looked over the top of his thick spectacles and stared at her hard.

'I'm sorry to ask you this—but do I have your undivided attention, Miss Hendry?'

'I'm so sorry.' Marjorie blushed. 'It's the funeral. And all this—the tea. I've never done anything like this before.'

'Of course. I understand. Would you like me to go over what I said? Or did you catch my drift? So to speak.'

Again his voice took on that near mocking tone, although his round, unlined face betrayed no sign of any such jocularity, other than a slight softening of his dark, determined eyes.

'You must call on me if you need help,' he repeated. 'You and your young friend.'

'Billy's not my friend, he's my sort of brother.'

'It's no cliché, it's a reality—we live in dangerous times, Miss Hendry. Here's a telephone number at which you can always reach me, any time, day or night. Learn the number and then destroy the piece of paper. I mean that. Learn it, and burn it. It's been very nice making your acquaintance, and again, please accept my condolences for your loss.'

Having handed her a slip of paper on which was written a telephone number in pencil, he shook hands with Marjorie and returned inside the house, collected his hat from the back of a chair where he had left it, and disappeared from the gathering as discreetly as he had arrived.

His departure did not go entirely unnoticed, however. A man standing in one corner of the living room, dressed in nondescript fashion and smoking a cheap cigarette, had been watching the conversation between Jack Ward and Marjorie through the adjacent window while engaging another guest in desultory small talk. Seeing Jack Ward come in from the garden he turned his back on him as if he were of no interest, watching him instead in the round gold-framed diminishing mirror that hung above the fireplace as he picked up his hat and disappeared through the throng of mourners. The watcher lit another cigarette from his now finished smoke before excusing himself to collect his coat from the pile on the chair in the opposite corner of the room and putting his own hat back on, a stained grey trilby that had never left his hand. Timing his own departure to what he thought perfection, he opened the front door and slipped out of the house after his quarry. But once outside he saw there was no sign of the heavily bespectacled man in the light grey suit and fawn raincoat who seemed to have vanished into thin air. But then vanishing into thin air was one of Jack Ward's stocks in trade.

*　　*　　*

In the house Marjorie was memorising the Victoria exchange telephone number, before destroying the slip of paper as instructed. Once she was sure she had the number firmly in her mind, she folded it into a taper and set it alight with a match. As she watched the piece of paper extinguishing in the grate, it seemed to her that her future might well be as black as the charred remains of the message.

*   *   *

'I've been giving this all some thought, Marge,' Billy said to her one day as she walked him back from school.

'What's this?' Marjorie wondered, leafing through the exercise book that Billy had been carrying rolled up in a trouser pocket. 'What are all these hieroglyphics, Billy? They teaching you Greek now, or something?'

'What? Higher-o what?'

'This funny writing of yours, Billy. Looks like Greek to me.'

'That's code. If you must know,' Billy replied tightly, taking back his exercise book.

'What sort of code? You don't know any codes.'

'Want a bet?'

'You mean a made-up code?'

'What else are codes but made up, you nit.' Billy rolled his exercise book up again and stuffed it back into the pocket where it belonged. 'Friend of mine and me. We got this gang, see. And in order to keep things secret, we have a code. Like our enemies, the Black Spot mob. They got a code too, see? Except we cracked it already. Rather I did.'

Billy grinned at Marjorie and started to whistle a cocky little tune.

'That's clever, Billy,' Marjorie said admiringly. 'I mean it. I mean cracking someone's code has to be pretty clever, I'd say. How do you do it?'

Billy shrugged.

'It's easy.'

'Will you show me?'

'Yeah. Well—maybe. But you got to promise not to say. The Black Spot mob's pretty rough.'

'Mum's the word.'

'Anyway—I was going to tell you something else, wasn't I?'

'Were you?'

'Yeah. I was thinking about Aunt Hester. About the accident. Her accident. Because I mean, just suppose it wasn't an accident? Suppose someone run her off the road deliberate like?'

'And?'

'Well, we owe it to her to find out what happened, like, and then go and give whoever it was that did it what for.'

'I don't know what else they're teaching you at that school, Billy,' Marjorie sighed. 'But it certainly isn't the King's English.'

'Yeah,' Billy muttered. 'But I certainly learned how to look after meself.'

'Yes,' Marjorie agreed, remembering the black eyes and bloody noses with which the younger Billy had returned home. 'I'm glad you have too. I was getting fed up with being your nursemaid.'

'You on or in't you?' Billy demanded, walking along backwards in front of Marjorie. ' 'Cos if you don't want to find out what 'appened, I shall.'

'I'm on,' Marjorie replied. 'But I don't see us getting very far.'

'Girls,' Billy sighed with a despairing shake of his head. 'Bloomin' girls.'

CHAPTER SEVEN

Poppy had also carefully memorised Jack Ward's number but had never yet had real reason to use it. Lonely and frightened, she had been tempted several times. Once she had even gone so far as to dial the entire number before suddenly being overcome with panic, and quickly dropping the telephone back on its base as she sensed what might happen to her if Basil found out. She was alone in his vast house. She was alone in a vast county. She had to get out, somehow, but using the telephone, when she knew Craddock was bound to be hovering, was surely not the way?

Besides, what would she have said to Mr Ward? That Basil was cold and unloving? That she wished that she hadn't married him? That Basil was having her watched by Craddock at every moment of the day? He would surely think her not just strange, but mad.

So Jack Ward's number, while not forgotten, remained uncalled. None the less as her misery deepened Poppy took some comfort from the fact that he must have recognised her unhappiness. But then again, perhaps he knew more about Basil and his strange entourage than Poppy. And because of what he knew, might wish her to know that she needed protection? This was an increasingly discomforting thought, but Poppy, as happens with those who are being haunted, was only slowly coming to realise the impossibility of her position.

The more she had considered her plight the more Poppy realised that she had very little choice except to bolt from Mellerfont. The problem was how? Being as yet unable to drive she could hardly steal one of the estate cars and drive to London. Certainly it would be impossible to ask anyone to drive her to the station since everyone on the estate or in the village was, in one way or another, in Basil's pay, and the station was over fifty miles away. Besides the large amount settled on her as a dowry by her father when she married, Basil, as was the English custom, had taken over the rest of Poppy's finances, persuading her, before their marriage, to share her private income with him for what he called 'ease of management and housekeeping'. She had very little idea of the sums at her disposal, so whatever money she withdrew would have to be drawn immediately after the arrival of their bank statement, which was not due for some weeks. She considered selling her jewellery, but realised that this too might raise an eyebrow in a village that was not only owned by Basil, but boasted nothing more than bakeries and haberdasheries, greengrocers' and ironmongers' shops. It would be hard to get very far on how much they would give her for her gold watch or diamond pin.

Occasionally, but foolishly, her hopes were unaccountably raised; most particularly when Basil told her he was going to Italy for a few days. Of course as soon as he had finished his short announcement Poppy's imagination ran riot, seeing herself ordering a station taxi, her bags piled high, the ever-watchful servants somehow absent, either drunk or on holiday. For the truth was that the servants, particularly Craddock, were as much her prison wardens as was Basil.

'I shall be staying in Venice with Gloria d'Albioni,' Basil informed her. 'I shall not leave you a number because there will be no need for you to telephone me. If there is any great emergency either Liddle or Craddock knows how to get in touch with me.'

He looked across at her with his usual air of detachment as if, despite Poppy's being ever present in his house, he could never really believe that she actually was there.

'What is the purpose of your trip, Basil?' Poppy asked, knowing that the answer was bound to be only a very slight variation on its being none of her business. 'Italy? Is it pleasure? Or is it something to do with your fine arts dealings?'

'If you must know,' Basil said, admiring himself in the looking glass hanging over his study fireplace, 'it is a little of both. But then it would be impossible to go to Italy just to do business. In Italy there is always pleasure to be had—particularly in Venice.'

Poppy turned away. She knew she had to run away from Basil as soon as possible, divorce him, start a new life, no matter the scandal, no matter the fact that it would horrify her parents. She could no longer put up with anything to do with Basil, Yorkshire, or Mellerfont and its cold, its draughts, and its surly servants. With her father and mother still in America, fund-raising on the west coast for one of their myriad causes, and knowing how little they would want to hear of her troubles, Poppy felt more isolated and helpless than ever, so much so that she finally found herself ringing Jack Ward's number on the Victoria exchange.

Expecting to hear his memorable tones on the

other end of the line Poppy was disconcerted to be greeted by a cold female voice.

'Hallo?' was all the voice said, not even repeating the number that had been called. 'Yes?'

'Sorry,' Poppy found herself mumbling. 'I was wondering whether it might be possible to speak to Mr Ward, please.'

'I'm very much afraid not,' the voice replied, as if such a thing was not only out of the question now but always would be. 'Do you wish to leave a message?'

'No. No, it's nothing important.'

'Who shall I say called, please?'

'Nobody,' Poppy said quietly, the receiver already on its way back to its rest. 'It really isn't important.'

*   *   *

To her shame Kate found herself longing for war to break out. Not only would it ease the undoubted tension that everyone was feeling, it would place her in a better position to conduct her future. Not satisfied by the fact that it was coming, she wanted it to be there, so that she could become involved, so that she could pitch in, so that she could escape. It would give her the chance to do something adventurous and possibly important, rather than having to pursue some boring occupation for which her typing and shorthand course was all too quickly qualifying her.

On this particular morning her father sat down for his breakfast looking even grimmer than usual, studying the news in the paper slowly, and with ever increasing gloom.

'You should eat your bacon, Harold,' his wife Helen advised him. 'There may be none next month.'

'Kindly shut up, Helen,' her husband replied. 'You don't know what you're talking about—as usual.'

After years of insults Helen was impervious to her husband's petty cruelty. Instead of responding she cleared her throat, trying to summon up the courage to address her husband on the topic arising from the correspondence she had just read.

'There's a letter that's just come in the post, Harold,' she stated, holding it out.

'I see nothing unusual in that. Perhaps you do?' Harold replied, taking the letter without looking up from his newspaper.

'It's from the secretarial school. Where Kate is.'

'It would hardly be from a secretarial school where Kate *wasn't*, Helen. Unless you are in the habit of conducting a correspondence with such places.'

'They are very impressed with Kate's abilities—'

'So we have already gathered. However, I myself would hardly call tapping at a typewriter and learning to scratch out a set of hieroglyphics an *ability*. A capacity perhaps. A competence or indeed an aptitude. But hardly an *ability*.'

'They want to recommend Kate for this place. This place wherever it is that is advertising for girls of singular—singular aptitude. In typing and shorthand. And related skills.'

'What other skills relate to typewriting or shorthand, I wonder? Scribbling and scratching perhaps? Lifting a telephone receiver? Answering to a summons from the *boss*.'

It was at this point that Kate felt a familiar feeling of panic. It was as if she was being personally stifled by her father's sarcasm, a pillow of facetiousness weighing down on her to the point that, had she not felt so protective of her mother, she could have screamed.

'I thought, since you were so keen for Kate here to start working, you'd be pleased to hear about this, Harold.' Helen's voice was becoming more not less firm, despite the verbal onslaught. 'They're so impressed with Kate that they have given her a three star recommendation. To this place I've just mentioned.'

'And what's the top rating?' Harold wondered mock idly, pointedly keeping his place in the paper with one fingertip while he bestowed a fleeting glance on his wife. 'Fifty stars perhaps?' He returned to his reading.

'It will mean Kate having to live away from here of course,' Helen continued. 'But since you have been so anxious about towns like ours that might be bombed, it may be a good idea.'

Now her husband looked up at her altogether differently.

'How far away?' he asked. 'What is this place anyway?'

'It's somewhere called Eden Park,' Helen replied. 'I thought you might have heard of it. It's been taken over by some government department or other. And they're very short staffed—short of the right sort of staff I should say. They want girls of exceptional ability. I mean aptitude.'

Harold, teacup still in hand, looked slowly from wife to daughter then back again to his wife, for once interested in something one of them had said

171

to him.

'Where is this place?'

'Eden Park, but the location is secret.'

'Eden Park.' Harold frowned momentarily. 'Doesn't ring any bells. Eden Park, you say?'

'All the details are there—in the letter.'

'I'll read it in a minute. But it sounds like a very good idea. If they want girls like Kate, let 'em have them, I say. And the sooner the better. No, really'—Helen stared at him—'let her go. A nice dull job, countryside and so on, sounds just the thing for her.'

He once more returned to his reading, while Kate looked across the room questioningly at her mother, who indicated with a tilt of her head that Kate should follow her out of the room.

'What's all this about, Mum?' Kate whispered, joining her in the hall with some of the dirty crockery.

'You want to go away, don't you? So here's your opportunity.'

'Yes, I know. But I don't want to leave you all alone. If I go away, now that Robert's left for the Navy, you'll be on your own.'

'You should have thought of that when you decided to be so clever.' Her mother smiled at her, opening the kitchen door with her back and reversing in with her tray full of crocks. 'I'll be fine. And from what I gather the work they do at this place, at Eden Park, is pretty important stuff. It's quite near the coast, I think. So it could be interesting.'

'You sure you'll be all right?'

Helen faced her daughter with a bright, brave look.

'I'll be better knowing that you're all right. You can't stay here. Your father will have you working for some crummy solicitor. He thinks education is wasted on women—and this from a man as well educated as he is meant to be.'

'Maybe that's what education does for men, Mother, educates them to despise women,' Kate joked, with a nod towards the dining room.

Helen smiled, and began to offload the dirty crockery into the sink. Kate automatically rolled up her sleeves ready to wash up, but this morning her mother was having none of it.

'No, off you go and get yourself sorted out,' she said. 'They want you to start immediately. Now your dad's more or less said yes.'

'Immediately?'

'They suggest you take the train there as soon as possible. So off you go and pack. There's nothing more to be said.'

'Can I see the letter?' Kate wondered, seeing that her mother had rescued it from her father and brought it out to the kitchen with her on the tray.

'No!' Helen said quickly, trying to snatch the letter back.

It was too late. Kate was already reading it. When she had finished she handed it to her mother with a look of amazement.

'Supposing Father had read it?' she asked.

'He wouldn't,' her mother replied quietly. 'He never takes any notice of anything I say, let alone do. So I thought it was almost a certainty that he would never actually read the letter through. He might have opened it—and if he had he would have seen it was from the secretarial school and left it at that.'

173

'But you don't think he would have seen it was about something altogether different?' Kate continued to wonder in amazement. 'About the fact they might have to relocate because of the threat of war? Nothing to do with Eden or any other park!'

'It's worth the risk, Kate dear. I'd do anything for you. To let you have your wings.'

Kate shook her head and, after a second or two, hugged her.

'Wait a minute,' she said, holding Helen back at arm's length. 'Where did you get all that about this government place? Wanting especially able secretaries et cetera? You didn't make that up, did you?'

'As a matter of fact, no. That's what started the whole thing off. Someone I know—an old friend, that's all I can tell you—told me about Eden Park, and how they were staffing it up. How they were particularly looking for a certain type of young woman who would be the right sort for the work that goes on there. I can't tell you any more than that. He knows quite a lot about you, although you don't know him at all. But he's someone who can be absolutely trusted, I promise you.'

She stopped and looked at the door as though they might be being spied on. Wiping her hands on the front of her apron, she went silently over to check. There was no one there.

'You're never to tell,' she warned her daughter. 'You're never to say a word to anyone.'

'But—'

'No buts either. Now off you go. I said—*off you go*. In case you didn't hear the first time.'

Kate shook her head and hurried away to start packing. The rest of the world was going to war,

174

she thought as she ran up the stairs two at a time, and now, at last, so was she.

Downstairs Helen Maddox opened the kitchen door once more and went back into the dining room. Harold was still reading the newspaper with all the assiduous attention of a man who was going to be needed by the government at any minute.

She looked across at him with a sinking heart. No longer would she have Kate and Robert as fellow refugees from his sarcasm. There would be no one now with whom she could put her feet up and listen to some comedy show on the radio while Harold was off on one of his lecture tours. She glanced down at the newspaper. She might not be able to bring herself to leave Harold, but she could at least help to give Adolf Hitler a bloody nose.

'Harold.'

'What now, Helen?'

The weary glance, the tired, bored look to the eyes, worst of all the vast superiority of manner was once more focused on Helen.

'Nothing, Harold.'

At that point the telephone in the hall started to ring.

'Answer the damn thing, would you, Helen? It's sure to be some nonsense for you.'

Helen left the dining room, quietly shutting the door behind her.

'Hallo,' said a cold female voice. 'Is that Miss Appleby?'

Helen's heart missed a beat.

'Yes.'

'I have a call for you.'

There was a pause, and then a man's voice spoke.

'Be outside the cinema at eight o'clock tonight. I will be waiting for you.'

At seven thirty Helen, wearing a stylish coat and skirt, her hair brushed up into a pre-war fashionable hat, walked down the road to meet the owner of the voice.

CHAPTER EIGHT

Everything had at last been arranged. Marjorie looked at Billy critically, finally leaning forward to straighten his cap despite the fact that it did not need it.

'There's no need to look so down in the mouth, Billy,' she scolded him. 'The place we're going to—'

'I know,' Billy sighed, with an impatient click of his tongue. 'You told me. It's this place where this friend of Aunt Hester's has people who will look after us, this Mr Ward.'

'That's right. And it's lovely. You'll really like it. It's called—'

'I know. Paradise Park. You told me.'

'*Eden* Park,' Marjorie corrected him. 'The house is pretty big—huge in fact—and old as well. It's set in this great big park, miles from anywhere.'

'I still don't really understand why we're goin' there, Marge,' Billy complained, moving himself out of range of Marjorie's fussing hands. 'Other than because we can't go on livin' 'ere.'

'Course we can't—not now it's been sold,' Marjorie chided him. 'So I'd be a bit grateful, if I were you, that we've got somewhere to live at all. Somewhere nice, particularly. I told you—the man

176

who came to Aunt Hester's funeral tea—he asked me to see it, and I have, and it's really, really nice. Gardens and water, and statues and things, and a nice cottage for you and me.'

'I know,' Billy sighed. 'It was this mysterious bloke. The one who said he'd 'elp you—as if you needed 'elping, bossy-boots.'

'Stop dropping your aitches, Billy,' Marjorie said, moving in on him to try to straighten his tie. 'It's become an affectation of yours. You can speak perfectly properly when you want to.'

'I can dress meself perfectly proper too, thank you,' Billy said, keeping on the move. 'I don't need forever tidying up. All right?'

'I'm sure we're going to like it,' Marjorie assured him. 'They're letting us have this cottage because of you more than anything—and there's a good school in the village.'

'I won't have any friends.'

'You'll soon make friends. There are masses of boys like you who are having to go and live somewhere different, who are being evacuated, and they won't know anyone either. So it's not as if you're going to be the only fish in that sea.'

'And what are you going to do? You're going to work for this bloke, are you? This mystery man?'

'Not directly, no.' Marjorie picked up her coat and her bag, ready now to leave her aunt's house for the last time. 'I'm going to be working for someone called Major Folkestone. At least, he's the man in charge of operations.'

'You make it sound as if you're going to work in an 'ospital, Marge. Operations?'

'It's what they call the sort of work they do,' Marjorie said with a dismissive shrug. 'Now if we're sure we have everything—'

'I don't want to leave here. I really don't, Marge. I mean it,' Billy said, taking a good look around him.

'We have to, Billy. You know we have to. Come on—or we'll miss the bus.'

Marjorie went to the front door and opened it, waiting for Billy.

'Billy?' she called. 'Billy?'

He was sitting on the sofa when she went back into the living room, with a fixed look in his eyes.

'What's the matter, Billy?' Marjorie wondered. 'We really do have to go, you know.'

'You're not spivvin' me, are you?' Billy said quietly, looking at her with a ferocity she had not seen before. 'If you're spivvin' me about this, I won't forgive you, Marge, I'm warning you.'

'I don't know what you mean by spivving, Billy.'

'If you're tryin' to kid me into doin' somethin'. If you're tellin' me one thing but meaning somethin' altogether different—'

'Such as?'

'Such as spivvin' me this yarn about this great house and everythin', when all the time what you're really doin' is sending me back to the Dump.'

Marjorie was so entirely amazed she nearly burst out laughing. Seeing this only angered Billy, and he was on his feet in a second, standing in front of her with tightly clenched fists, eyes narrowed.

'Well, you'd better not be, Marge,' he warned her. 'You'd better be telling me the truth. ' 'Cos if you ain't, I'm tellin' you somethin', right? That the only way you'd get me to go back to that stinkin' dump is dead. You'd 'ave to kill me. I mean it.'

'Billy.' Marjorie put a hand out to him, but he

178

just shrank away from her. 'Billy, do you really think I'd do something like that to you? After all we've been through together? You really think I'd lie to you and send you back to that terrible place? What sort of person do you think I am?'

'Your mum left you at the Dump, my dad left me. Maybe my time's up—the time when you and I can be together—so all you can do is send me back there.'

'I'm not sending you anywhere, Billy Hendry. I wouldn't desert you ever. No matter what.'

'Yeah.'

'Yeah—yes. Look at you, you've got me at it now.'

Marjorie could see that Billy was on the verge of tears, and knew at once that she must be careful or he might just take off, run away, leave, in the firm belief that he was about to be returned to the Dump.

'Billy,' she said. 'You and I are friends, as well as being practically related, aren't we? And people like that are not going to let each other down, are they? I promise you, cross my heart, that you and I are going to this place called Eden Park, and we're going to live there together in the cottage just as I've described. I'd never lie to you, Billy. Never.'

Billy didn't move. He stood there as if fixed to the spot, breathing in and out deeply and slowly.

'You have to believe me, Billy,' Marjorie repeated. 'I can't make you come with me. You're too big for that. But you can't stay here. For a start there are other people coming to live here so you won't have anywhere to go.'

'They said we could go and live with them, the Watlings said we could go to them, remember?'

179

'That isn't possible now, Billy. I told you the Watlings have had to change their plans, because of relatives. You remember.'

'Changed their plans as far as we go, yeah. Soon as old Mrs Watling got sober again—'

'That isn't fair, Billy. Things are different now. Now that everyone's certain there's going to be a war. They've got to think of themselves first. They can't afford to have two more people dependent on them.'

'Well, Aunt Hester always did say Mrs Watling was a bit of a toper.'

Billy looked at Marjorie, despair still in his eyes.

'We'll be all right, Billy, I promise you,' Marjorie assured him once more. 'And we'll be together. And you'll really like the place. Wait till you see it.'

*   *   *

Kate was also on her way; although where precisely she was headed she only had the vaguest of notions. Her mother had made another of her secret arrangements, organising a friend to drive Kate to Eden Park, although for some reason this friend was not to be allowed to pick Kate up from the front of the house for fear of being spotted by Harold. Instead the arrangement was for Kate to take the train only to the next stop where she was to disembark and meet her mother's contact in the car park, from where she would be driven to her destination.

'It's all a bit cloak and dagger, isn't it?' Kate laughed. 'I mean you know best, so I suppose it is absolutely necessary?'

'You can go all the way by train if you'd prefer,

but rather you than me, given the distance and trains,' her mother replied. 'As it is, since this acquaintance also happens to be going to Eden Park I thought it would be preferable for you to travel in comfort. It also might be quite useful for you.'

'Useful?'

'Yes, useful.' Her mother smiled as she handed Kate her coat. 'And take your tennis racket. There's bound to be a court there of some sort. Most of these large estates have their own tennis courts now. Lucky people.'

'What else do you know about this place, Mum?'

'I didn't say I knew there was a tennis court. I just said there's bound to be one.'

'There's something else,' Kate insisted. 'What kind of work do they do?'

'How should I know, Kate? All I've been told is that it's government work, which is why it's probably better that you're driven there by someone in the know. You know all the rumours about spies at the moment? How they're everywhere? I read only this morning about two nuns being arrested yesterday who turned out to be spies. Nuns, I ask you. You simply don't know who you can trust and who you can't. Mr Underwood said that it was Ted Molton's boy who found the two of them walking in the woods for goodness' sake. Dressed as nuns. Having only just got out of their parachutes. The cheek of it—to think they wouldn't be arrested because they were dressed as nuns. If it had been me, I'd have taken a shotgun to them. Would have blown their heads off.'

'Oh yes?' Kate laughed. 'You who can't even swat a wasp without having to go and have a lie down to recover.'

'It's different now, Kate, very different. Once your country's under threat. It makes people behave and think quite differently, believe you me. I actually sit there now thinking of ways to kill the Nazis—if they invade us. Hiding from them and stabbing them in the eyes with my knitting needles. All sorts of things, you'd be surprised. And you may laugh—but just you wait. You'll find things exist in you that you never dreamed existed before. My parents said the same thing about the last war. How it changed them. For ever. All their friends gone, all killed in the trenches. Half the village gone. Not one of my father's class left. All those boys he grew up with in the village. Imagine.'

They both fell to silence, looking round to see if there was anything Kate had forgotten.

'I'm going to miss you, Kate. We always have such fun together.'

Helen looked suddenly wistful, and took Kate's long-fingered hands in her own more roughened ones, and held them.

'You've been gardening without your gloves, Mother.'

'I'm going to join the WVS to take my mind off things,' Helen said. 'Your father's against it. Of course. Says I'm a fool, and that they won't find anything for someone as useless as me to do, but that's not true.'

'No, it's not. Firstly you're not a fool, Mother—'

'I know that.' Helen smiled. 'And you know that. But your father doesn't.'

'Then why do you let him say you are?'

'Because it's a whole lot easier, Kate. Why do you think? Now—just one word of advice—before

182

you go. Whatever happens, I want you to promise me something, Kate dear.'

'All right,' Kate agreed cautiously, the way people do when asked in advance to vouch for something unknown. 'What do you want me to promise?'

'It's not so much of a promise—more of a recommendation. Don't be like me. Don't marry unless you're absolutely sure, and above all don't give up doing anything that matters to you for the sake of your family.'

'Is that what you did?' Kate wondered, watching her mother as she carefully folded all the clothes Kate had rejected to put them in the charity box they kept for such purposes. 'I know you've given up a lot for Robert and me—but that's not really what you mean, is it?'

Helen shook her head, closing the wardrobe doors to look round a room that all at once seemed deserted, with no dressing gown hanging up behind the door, the small bookshelf all but empty of her daughter's favourite books, the bed no longer to be slept in. Everything that identified her daughter was gone, packed away in the small light blue suitcase that lay closed on the bed.

Helen looked from the case to Kate and then sat down on the edge of the bed. The house was quiet now, with Harold gone to his work, and only some orchestral music playing on the wireless that had been left on in the sitting room.

'I was meant—to go to art school. To learn how to sculpt.'

'To sculpt?'

'Don't sound so surprised. There are quite a few lady sculptors as it happens.'

'It's not that. It's because I had no idea.'

'You wouldn't have. I never mentioned it. And your father certainly wouldn't. He's probably forgotten anyway.'

'So why didn't you go to art school?'

'Oh, because I got married instead. I got married because my parents wanted me to get married. It was all my parents wanted, particularly my father. Girls are terrible burdens to their parents if they don't get married, and by the time I was twenty-three my father was convinced I was going to be an old maid. I was an albatross around their neck. They'd survived a terrible war, somehow—and now they wanted to travel. Having me at home cost money—and so I got married. I met your father at a dance, he asked me out a couple of times, my parents were in awe of his brilliance, and the next thing I knew I found myself married. Once I was married, of course, I could say goodbye to any idea of pursuing my art. Not only would it cost money but your father considered the sort of art I was interested in absurd. As for the notion of a woman actually sculpting—you can imagine. So there you are. I buried what I wanted to do, and got on with being married to your father.'

'Why are you telling me this now, Mother? It's hard enough leaving home.'

'I'm telling you—why do you *think* I'm telling you, Kate?'

Kate simply did not know what to say. Such was the look of hopeless despair in her mother's eyes that even if she had been twenty years older she still would not have known what to say.

Her mother couldn't come with her to the station since she had to attend an interview at the

184

local Women's Voluntary Service, and although she tried to maintain her appointment wasn't that important, and she could easily change it, Kate knew better and insisted that they said their goodbyes at the house.

They stood in silence in the hall waiting for the station taxi to arrive, the grandfather clock ticking loudly behind them, and time seeming to stand quite still, until her mother became suddenly galvanised into action, deciding to run yet another full and totally unnecessary check on her daughter's luggage and belongings.

'It's all right, Mother.' Kate laughed. 'I'm only going to Gloucester, not Timbuctoo.'

'It might as well be Timbuctoo,' her mother replied, slipping another ten shilling note into Kate's purse. 'You will write as soon as you get there now, won't you?'

'Course,' Kate nodded. 'Say goodbye to Father for me. And explain to Bobby when he comes home on leave that I had to leave quickly and that I'll write to him. And be sure to send him my love.'

Helen nodded again, not quite looking at Kate, trying her best to look efficient and businesslike.

'Of course, Kate dear. Now here comes the taxi—and not before time.'

Kate smiled and kissed her mother lightly on the cheek.

'Don't *worry*. I can take care of myself. I am eighteen, you know.'

Helen followed Kate down the garden path to the waiting taxi.

'Sorry if I'm a little late for you,' George Grosvenor, the town's oldest taxi driver, said, touching his cap. 'Seems the world and his wife all want taxis today. You'd think war had broken out already.' He took Kate's suitcase and put it in the boot of his car.

'Not going to be easy when it does, George,' Helen replied, clasping her hands tightly behind her back. 'They say petrol will be the first thing to be rationed.'

'They'll be a-measuring it out in teaspoons, as soon as likely, ma'am.' George grinned, revealing a breath-catching lack of upper teeth. 'Unless you're doing war work, course.' Having shut Kate in the back of the taxi he winked at Helen. 'So guess what George here's volunteering for?'

Both women laughed at George, grateful for his cheery manner, for, given the times, it was a lot better to look on the bright side.

'You take care now, Kate,' Helen said, bending down to the window Kate had wound open. She kept a hand on the taxi until it began to move away, when she waved it frantically instead.

After a short pause during which she watched it disappear into the distance with such attention it was as if she had never seen a car before, she went back into the house and quietly closed the front door behind her. She had imagined she would be calmer in the daytime, once she had made up her mind to carry her plan through and make sure Kate flew the nest before her father ruined her life. Yet now her fears seemed to have grown worse, so much so that it was all she could do to stop herself telephoning George Grosvenor once he had arrived home, and asking him to come back for her, to take her away, anywhere—to Ireland, or the north of Scotland or the most rugged part of Wales—anywhere as long as she got away from

Harold and the ice house that their home would now become. If she remained all she could expect was misery, and that was before she had to make over her children's rooms to the myriad strangers that, rumour had it, might be billeted on them at any minute.

As she climbed the stairs to shut the door on Kate's room, the past seemed to be drifting back to her. Children's voices laughing and talking in the early morning. The feel of their arms tight around her neck when she kissed them goodnight. *Night night, sleep tight, don't let the bugs bite!* She drifted aimlessly towards her own bedroom, trying to avoid the memories, trying to pull herself together, finally collecting her diary from its hiding place on top of her wardrobe, and taking it downstairs to the kitchen where sitting at the table with a freshly made pot of tea in front of her she prepared to bring it up to date.

Said goodbye to Katherine, the second goodbye to one of my children in a week. Robert is off to the Navy, and now Kate has left us to work as some sort of secretary for some hush-hush government body housed in some great estate. JW told me about it, knowing what a bright spark Kate is— said it would be just the ticket for her and that she'd be just the ticket for them, so rather than have H go on ruining her life I worked out a plan to get her up there 'officially' as it were. Everything was fine until we came to say goodbye—but then that's how it always is with people you love (I think). But this was a little different, because with the war coming, who knows what will happen? It took all I had to let Kate go, not to give way,

187

*particularly when I saw her little face at the taxi
window, waving as the car disappeared from view.
God speed her. I hope she can call when she gets
there—if not I hope she writes as soon as she can.
I can't call her—and as yet I can't write because I
don't know the full address. I can't imagine not
being in constant touch, but then with the way
things are in the world, I might as well start as I
mean to go on—and get used to it.*

*   *   *

In the absence of her mother Kate decided to be
dashing and spurn the Ladies Only carriage,
preferring to sit in second class where she found a
seat in a compartment among service men and
women who were all chatting merrily as if they
were off to a dance rather than preparing for war.
Kate took a book out of her bag and pretended to
read, while all the time watching the faces and
listening to the banter of the men and women
barely older than herself, some of them she
guessed being precisely the same age.

Out of the window the countryside they were
passing through looked as green, pleasant and
ordered as ever, with no hint of any mayhem and
confusion to come. She tried to imagine the sky
filled with enemy planes, and the fields below with
defending artillery, but failed because it just
seemed far too unimaginable. The farms and
villages through which the stopping train chugged
looked less than real and more like the toy villages
and farms she and Robert used to create in their
garden or playroom, down to the half sleeping
cows, and the grazing sheep and horses.

The train began to slow down as it approached the next station, Short Cross Halt. As she prepared to get out, Kate's eye was caught by a headline in the newspaper hiding the passenger opposite her. PEER KILLED IN EXPLOSION. There was a picture of a fair-haired, handsome and immaculately dressed Englishman under the headline, who turned out to be a Lord Tetherington. She climbed out from the train giving no further thought to the story. Nor did it cross her mind that the man waiting to drive her to Eden Park somewhere in Gloucester was none other than her mother's lover.

*   *   *

He was reading a newspaper when Kate identified him from his car and description, half seated on one front wing with his spectacles pushed up on to his head while he digested the story. For a moment Kate hesitated before introducing herself, and during that moment Jack Ward saw her, got up, put his spectacles back on, took her suitcase and opened a rear passenger door for her to get in the car.

'I can't take you all the way,' he said once they were motoring. 'Something's come up. But don't worry, I'll see you're safely delivered.'

Kate made no comment, only staring out of the car window in some amazement. She had a very highly developed sense of direction as well as a first class knowledge of geography, the result being that after the first half hour of her journey she realised there was something radically wrong with their route.

'Excuse me,' she said to her driver from her

position in the back seat. 'Aren't we headed for Gloucester?'

'Not exactly. No.'

Kate's heart began to beat faster, but she was determined to have her say.

'I was told I was being taken to Gloucester and for the last half hour or so I have had the distinct impression we're headed south, not north.'

'I appreciate the point, Miss Maddox. The change in your arrangements is because I can only take you a certain part of the way. In fact I'm going to bail out in the next town and hand you over to a colleague.'

Her escort's polite tone soothed her for a while, until she saw they were passing into a town that had every appearance of not being in the Cotswolds.

'Dinton?' she exclaimed. 'But that's in Kent, isn't it?'

'As ever was,' her driver agreed, peering out of his side window for the required landmark.

'It certainly isn't on the way to Gloucester.'

'It most certainly is not.'

'Can you explain, please? Or am I not allowed to know?'

Having spotted the pub sign for which he was looking, Jack Ward pulled over to park at the kerb outside. He looked at Kate in the mirror for a moment before speaking.

'All I can tell you is that it is important that no one knows where you are going or indeed where you are going to be stationed in advance,' he said quietly, still looking at her in his rear view mirror. 'It's the same for everyone, have no fear. Now, here's your new driver . . .' He nodded at the man hurrying out of the pub, someone who had obviously just finished a hasty lunch, judging from the way he was wiping his mouth on his pocket handkerchief.

Jack Ward got out of the car, closed the door, had a few words of conversation with his colleague then nodded a curt goodbye to Kate, who was doing her best not to look as utterly bewildered as she felt.

'Well then, on to the next phase, eh?' her new driver greeted her. 'Home, James, and no sparing the horses, what?'

Kate said nothing. She just sat back in her seat and wondered what on earth her mother had involved her in, and more importantly—why.

CHAPTER NINE

When she received the telephone call and had digested the information given to her by some attaché at the British Embassy in Rome, Poppy sat down in a chair by the drawing room window and stared out at the winter landscape of Mellerfont Park, which was now doing its best to turn into spring. She found herself strangely uncertain as to whether to laugh or to cry at what she had just been told.

Basil was dead.

As she said it again to herself, she suddenly shivered, because it was the first death of anyone known to her, or even more important associated with her, that she had experienced. Suddenly the word *death* took on a quite different meaning, moving from something abstract that happened to other people to something positive and altogether nearer home.

Basil was dead.

Now she wanted to laugh, or at the very least smile. She had been praying each and every night for her release, for something to happen that would enable her to escape from a house she had come quickly to hate quite as much as her husband, whom upon close examination of her emotions she now found she actually abhorred.

Basil was dead.

The tears began to roll down her cheeks, slowly but remorselessly. She wiped them away carefully with a spotless white handkerchief, but still they fell, even though she knew she wasn't sad, but ecstatic. It was as if these tears that were falling were outside of her, as if they didn't belong to her but were tokens for the moment, symbols that she wasn't really the cold-hearted, insensitive, unloving young woman she had come to fear she might be.

Basil was dead.

And Basil had been her husband. She had married him to please her mother and father, she had even thought for a moment that she loved him—and perhaps she still did. Perhaps all that had been needed was for her to prompt Basil into adopting some sort of acceptable attitude towards her, or for her to help him see that she loved him so that he would stop being insufferable and cold and become the entertaining, clever, witty and shrewd person she had thought he was when she first met him and allowed him to woo her. But it was too late now.

Basil was dead.

She tried to imagine him dead. She closed her eyes and tried to see him laid out in his beautiful clothes—with his hair perfectly done as always, his skin shining with good health, the handkerchief in his pocket flopping out with just the right amount of linen showing, his handmade shoes immaculately polished and that look of sublime indifference in his eyes. Except those cold blue eyes were now for ever closed—because . . .

Basil was dead.

With a shock Poppy opened her eyes and stared across the empty drawing room. Swallowing hard, and trying to stop herself from shaking, she hurried across to the drinks tray and poured herself a very large gin and tonic, after which she took a cigarette out of the engraved silver box on a side table and lit it, choking at first on the unaccustomed smoke and then puffing at the cigarette carefully as she tried to get used to the taste. The novelty of these actions worked, for in another minute she had stopped shaking.

'Basil is dead,' she said quietly. 'And I am free. Basil is dead—and I am free.'

She remembered then what the attaché at the Embassy had told her, and when she recalled it she began to shake violently. For Basil would not be laid out perfectly dressed, with his hair immaculate and his shoes shining like leather mirrors, because Basil was not only dead, he was obliterated.

'Sadly formal identification was not possible, Lady Tetherington,' the voice had said quietly in her ear. 'Due to the nature of the incident, your late husband's car plunging off the mountain road and crashing in flames so far below, the Italian police have informed us that unfortunately the

193

body was burned beyond recognition. Identification was made from personal effects—such as your late husband's signet ring, and his watch—and of course reports from eye witnesses who saw Lord Tetherington getting into his car at the Villa Maria prior to leaving his hosts.'

'Who exactly made the identification?' Poppy had asked, curious as to who knew her husband well enough to be able to say with certainty that the ring and the watch had indeed belonged to Basil.

'The Marchesa d'Albioni,' the voice had replied. 'Who perhaps was known to you formerly as Lady Gloria Devine. Your husband had been staying at the villa belonging to the Albionis prior to the accident.'

The Marchesa d'Albioni, Poppy thought. Lady Gloria Devine. *I shall be staying in Venice with Gloria d'Albioni*. There had been rumours about Basil, tittle-tattle Poppy had overheard at the end of the Season once her engagement to Basil had become public, word that he had enjoyed the company of many glamorous and well-connected Society women, Gloria d'Albioni being often mentioned. Poppy made a private resolution to contact the Marchesa when it was appropriate. After all, Basil had told her he was going to be in Venice, yet his car had crashed on the precipitous mountain roads that ran along the Amalfi coastline. What was he doing so far south?

I shall be in Venice, was all he had said. *I shall not leave you a number because there will be no need.*

For some reason Poppy found herself frowning, as if suspecting something untoward, yet there was absolutely no reason for her to have doubts. Basil was accustomed to visiting Europe, and even

194

though travel was becoming increasingly difficult he was so well connected that papers were always easily available to him. She remembered him remarking on this fact when she had attempted to show concern about his plans.

There is absolutely no need for you to concern yourself, he had replied with just a hint of impatience. *I go where I please. I have impeccable credentials and even more impeccable connections.*

Even so, now Basil lay dead, smashed to pieces on the rocks of Amalfi and burned beyond recognition in the fire, but with his death, it had to be faced, Poppy was free.

She stood up, preparing to refresh her glass, only to find it taken from her by Craddock who had silently appeared, as always, as if from nowhere.

'Milady?' he asked, over-loudly as usual, making Poppy flinch. 'Please. Allow me.'

'How long have you been here?' Poppy said, putting a hand to her throat in her surprise.

'I am never very far away, milady, not when Liddle is on holiday,' the under-butler replied in his loud voice, before walking over to the drinks table. 'Gin and tonic, I believe, milady. I took the liberty of bringing in some fresh lemon.'

Poppy looked around the room, expecting to see an array of spy holes suddenly visible in the panelling, but other than a pass door in the corner that was still swinging slightly on its hinges there was nothing untoward to be seen.

'I have to go to London, Craddock,' she said to the under-butler's back. 'Can you please make the necessary arrangements?'

'Of course, milady,' Craddock boomed, carefully preparing the perfect drink. 'Although if I may say so, people are being discouraged from making any unnecessary journeys to the cities, London most especially.'

'This is hardly an unnecessary journey, given the circumstances,' Poppy corrected him, although wisely not going into any further details. 'So please make arrangements for me to go to London tomorrow.'

'I am sure you would prefer to be driven, milady?' Craddock boomed again, bringing Poppy her drink on a small silver tray. 'I understand the train services have deteriorated to the point of being practically unreliable. It has taken Mr Liddle a day and a half to reach Devon, I understand. I am sure Leon would be more than happy to drive you down.'

'Is there anyone else who could take me, Craddock? I wouldn't like to bother Leon— knowing how much he hates to leave the place,' Poppy added, sounding feeble even to her own ears.

'I shall enquire, milady. But I would suggest that if he is willing to do so, Leon is by far and away the best chauffeur on the estate.'

Craddock bowed politely and disappeared back through his pass door, leaving Poppy to herself. Although Craddock's booming voice got her down on occasions, he was infinitely preferable to Leon. She actually feared going south with Leon, most especially because she knew he would be difficult to shake off. Something told her that Leon was used to playing a far more complicated role than merely that of a chauffeur. Yet if she was to bolt, she would have to try to do it without alerting the staff's suspicions, and further resistance to the idea

196

of Leon's driving her might do exactly that. Basil might be dead, but his henchmen were all too alive.

She put her drink down beside her and patted her knee for George to come and sit with her. The little dog looked round from his place in front of the fire, yawned, then rolled over on to his back, as if to show he was quite happy where he was. Poppy smiled at him, and despite his resistance picked him up, stroking the top of his silky head. She had no need to be frightened, she told herself, and yet she was, perhaps even more than when Basil was alive. She felt there was something terribly wrong, something going on in the house, which was more than the usual unease brought about by sudden death.

*   *   *

George heard something long before Poppy. She awoke to his growling, a fierce sound from such a small dog. At once she put her hand on his neck to quieten him, holding his collar between two long fingers and stroking his head while she sat up in bed trying to hear whatever it was that had alerted him. She could hear nothing at all, not one sound from anywhere. The house was as quiet as she had ever heard it, yet George continued to growl as resolutely as ever. Curiosity inevitably getting the better of her common sense, Poppy slipped out of bed, pulled on a dressing gown and, with George still in her arms, tiptoed out on to the landing.

She held George firmly, while putting a hand over his muzzle with the intention of stifling any noise. He might be small, but he had a vicious set of teeth and was quick off the mark, and definitely

197

able to produce a valuable distraction. She knew she should have stayed in her room, but something was driving her forward to find out what, if anything, was going on downstairs in the dark, echoing, cold and silent house, and that something must have been the power of the Fates.

When she reached the bottom of the stairs she noticed a faint light coming from under Basil's study door. She peered through the crack in the door to see, standing by her late husband's desk, the silhouette of a man who was obviously searching for something, a torch in one hand, head bent over as with his other hand he opened drawer after drawer, putting the documents he found inside them on the desk before riffling through them.

Poppy watched in silent fascination, her hand still covering George's muzzle, while the intruder systematically rifled first the desk and then the cabinets and shelves behind him. Soon the desk was piled high with papers and files, while the man continued his search, moving more quickly as he failed to find that for which he was so obviously looking. Poppy thought she knew where it might be, in the safe hidden by the small oil painting directly behind the desk where she had often seen Basil stowing documents as she was entering the room. He had never seemed to mind, or if he did he certainly never showed it, simply locking the safe and nonchalantly closing the picture over it with a bored expression, as if to say that whatever Poppy saw him do mattered less to him than if she had been a servant.

But now the intruder had found the whereabouts of the safe and was directing the light from his torch on to it to examine the locking mechanism. Poppy at last came to her senses, standing up suddenly and realising that however much she had hated Basil she couldn't possibly just go on watching someone burgle her late husband's house without raising some sort of alarm. After all, he might well be armed and dangerous, and once he was unable to break open the safe, which Poppy felt he was bound to do, as well as failing to find anything of value in the desk or cabinets he might move into other rooms, or go in search of someone in the house who just might know where any items of value were—say Poppy herself. After all, women married to aristocrats who lived in large mansions usually had jewellery of value.

Determined now to hurry as silently as she could to the servants' quarters in order to raise Craddock and a couple of the younger male members of staff, Poppy took one last look through the crack in the door to check on the position of the intruder, at which point the man turned away from the wall safe, allowing the light from his torch momentarily to light his features. Seeing who it was, Poppy immediately slipped into the study, closing the door tightly behind her.

'Don't say a word!' She removed her hand from poor George's muzzle and put a finger to her lips.

The man looked at her, not betraying any of the surprise Poppy felt he surely must be feeling. Then he flashed his torch to check her identity before he spoke, and kept the beam shining in her eyes.

'Go back to your room,' a familiar voice advised. 'You haven't seen me.'

'I think I have the right to ask what you are doing here, Mr Ward,' Poppy replied, her voice low, but unable to keep a measure of indignation from it. 'Or would you rather I simply went and called for help?'

'I know it must look a trifle strange, but believe me it is not,' Jack replied, still holding the torch trained on Poppy. 'Now please go back to your room and forget you ever saw me.'

'And if I refuse?'

'If you refuse it's going to complicate matters.'

'All I have to do is walk out of this door and raise the alarm.'

'And all I have to do is take this gun out of my pocket and tell you that you will do no such thing.'

Poppy now found herself looking at the business end of a small revolver Jack Ward had produced from his coat pocket.

'I assure you I will shoot if I have to, Lady Tetherington,' he continued coldly. 'I won't necessarily kill you, but I will shoot all the same.'

'Who are you anyway?' Poppy said, putting her hand up to shield her eyes from the glare of the torch. 'And what the heck do you mean by threatening me? In my own house?'

'Just go back to bed, Lady Tetherington,' Jack Ward repeated. 'You and your little dog.'

'Not until you tell me what you are doing here.'

'What does it look like?'

'You're not a burglar. At least not the kind of ordinary burglar I would expect to find stealing.'

'Go back to bed.'

'What are you looking for?'

'Go back to your bed,' Jack Ward repeated slowly, as if to a child. 'Please.'

'I might be able to help you find what you are looking for.'

'I doubt that very much.'

'You know I overheard what was going on that night,' Poppy persisted. 'The night you came to my rescue. I know my husband was up to some sort of no good. And I suspect that actually you and he are not—or were not in his case—on the same side.'

There was a short silence, then Jack Ward lowered both his torch and his revolver, replacing the latter in his coat pocket.

'Your husband—' he began.

'My late husband,' Poppy corrected him.

'Your late husband had a pocket book. Leather-covered. An antique-looking thing, bound in dark red hide. I need it, urgently, for my work.'

'I saw it once or twice, yes. I know the book you mean.'

'Do you know where he kept it?'

'I saw him putting it in the safe on at least one occasion, so I imagine your suspicion is probably right—and that's where it is now.'

'But you wouldn't know the combination of this safe.'

'You're absolutely right, Mr Ward. I don't have any idea.'

'Mmm.'

Jack Ward breathed in deeply.

'I have to have this book, Lady Tetherington. So if you have any bright ideas . . .'

'Wouldn't he—I mean if this journal is important to him, wouldn't he have taken it with him?'

'My thoughts entirely. But apparently this was not the case. No—' He held up one hand. '—don't ask me how I know, because I can't tell you. All I can say is that we know the journal is still somewhere in this house.'

'We?'

'Just stick to me knowing.'

Poppy nodded but accompanied the gesture with a shrug, to indicate that she did not think all that much of what he had said.

'How many numbers is the combination?' Poppy wondered. 'Do you know? I mean can you tell?'

'Four. You know how many permutations that is?'

'I can hazard a guess. But my husband's—my husband was a bit sort of self-obsessed. So I imagine he would choose a number that related to him, rather than just any old random numbers. His middle name was Narcissus.'

'I'm open to suggestions.'

'Birthdays. Age. Lucky number? And if you're asking—'

'Which I am.'

'He was born on the seventeenth of April, he is—was thirty-five, and his lucky number was thirteen.'

'Worth a try. But don't bet on it.'

Jack Ward scribbled the permutations of those three numbers down on a sheet of paper, rose, pushed his glasses on to the top of his head, and shone the torch on the dial of the safe.

'I think this might help,' Poppy said, switching on the desk light. 'After all, I know you're here now.'

Jack Ward looked at her dolefully, raised one eyebrow in doubt, and clicked off the light.

'Never use permanent light. Always use a torch. Switches off quicker, see?'

He turned back to his work.

The first attempt to open the safe using seventeen and thirty-five failed, as did the second using seventeen and thirteen. Without holding out much hope Jack Ward dialled thirteen and thirty-five.

'No?' Poppy wondered.

'Unsurprisingly—no,' Jack Ward agreed.

'Try thirty-five thirteen.'

'I might as well start nought-nought-nought-nought and work my way up through the subsequent six million permutations.'

'Just as you might as well give it a try,' Poppy suggested, sounding impatient even to herself.

Jack Ward's expressionless face looked round at her again before he turned back to follow her recommendation. To his well-disguised amazement the tumblers clicked and fell and the safe door swung open.

'Just guesswork?' he asked, standing back and preparing to delve inside. 'Or inside information?'

Poppy shrugged.

'Knowing one's enemy, I suppose,' she replied. 'Not that I knew him that well. But the combination had to be something to do with himself, because that was Basil.'

Jack Ward withdrew a slender journal bound in dark antique leather.

'This is obviously pretty important,' Poppy remarked, wandering over to the desk. 'This book must be important for you to go to all this trouble.'

At once Jack Ward shut the book up the way one schoolboy might hide his work from another.

'That important, is it?'

'I wouldn't know,' was all Jack Ward would tell her. 'It's in code apparently.'

The next thing Poppy knew Jack Ward had a tight hold on her arm and a finger to his lips. He said nothing, his eyes behind his spectacles narrowing at her to warn her of danger, before edging her round the room towards the window. Poppy frowned back at him, as if to ask what was going on, only for Jack Ward to grimace at the door while giving a curt nod to indicate they might have company.

They were by the heavy curtains that hung in front of the study windows opening on the outside wall of the house. Pulling the drapes quickly aside, Poppy saw the windows were open, and guessed that not only must this have been the way her uninvited visitor entered, but it was also going to be his exit route—and, obviously, hers. Judging from the way she was being urged towards the open window, Poppy was fairly certain he was not going to be leaving alone. He shone his torch outside, and suddenly Poppy could see the point of his earlier remark. You certainly couldn't shine a lamp so easily.

'There's a bit of a drop.'

'Why don't you go first and catch me?'

'Hang on from the edge and drop,' Jack Ward instructed her, keeping his whispered tone reassuring.

Jack Ward's manner was enough for Poppy. She felt neither afraid nor daring, and promptly handed him her little dog and clambered nimbly up on to the stone ledge in her thinly slippered feet before turning herself round, gripping the bottom of the lintel, holding on tight and allowing herself to drop the eight or so feet into the flowerbed below. Unhurt, but now considerably muddier, she stood up, reaching skywards for George. Jack Ward promptly dropped the uncomplaining dachshund into Poppy's outstretched hands. When she had him safely under her arm, Poppy scrambled clear, suspecting rightly that Jack Ward would follow at once, which he did.

'Come on,' he whispered, grabbing her hand. 'Round the corner and out of sight, and hang on tight.'

They had barely made the corner of the building when Poppy heard voices behind them. Glancing back as Jack Ward towed her round to safety she saw two heads peering out of the study window, although she was unable to identify either. Then suddenly she saw a familiar face turn in their direction, and a hand being held up, but before she could observe anything more Jack Ward had hauled her out of sight.

'Now what?' Poppy gasped, as they stopped both to draw breath and become orientated. 'What are we supposed to do *now*?'

'Get out of here as fast as we can. Come on.'

He took hold of her arm, only for Poppy to resist.

'Mr Ward, in case you may not have noticed, I am in my *night* things.'

'I know, but I'm afraid that can't be helped. We'll find you a change soon enough, once we're out of this rather tight spot.'

He had a firm hold on her arm by now, half pushing half hurrying her away from the house, not towards the drive or the stable yard, but across the lawns and towards the woods beyond the lake.

Poppy ran along beside him imagining that he was panicking for nothing, until coming towards her, indistinctly, but nevertheless real, she heard the sound of urgent voices, and saw what looked like Leon and Craddock running around the front of the house waving torches, shouting and pointing in various directions. But Jack Ward had stolen a march on them, and not only that, he was headed in the direction it seemed no one was looking, and towards what, Poppy now prayed devoutly, their pursuers would consider to be the one place from which there was no immediate escape from Mellerfont, the densely planted woodland to the north of the lake.

When they were well inside the small forest, Jack Ward slowed to a stop and let go of Poppy's arm. Poppy, almost completely out of breath by now, her barely protected feet sore from the run across first gravel, then a cinder path and finally the rough ground lying on the verge of the woods, and poor George tucked firmly under her free arm, put the other arm out to steady herself against the rough bark of an old fir tree, and stood trying to catch her breath.

'I don't believe this is happening. I know I'm going to wake up in a moment and find I was in bed asleep all the time.'

'We can't stop, I'm afraid,' Jack told her in a low voice, coming to her side. 'They're no slouches, that lot down there. And they'll be sure to have the dogs out and after us before you can say knife. So we have to get round through the woods and up on to the lane above. It's only about a quarter of a mile. Think you can make it, Lady Tetherington?'

Poppy nodded. 'Except I do happen to be freezing. If it's of any interest.'

'I'm sorry,' Jack Ward said, taking off both his overcoat and his jacket at once. 'I should have thought.' He looked momentarily embarrassed.

206

'There wasn't exactly a lot of time for chivalry back there. Come on—we'd better get moving.'

This time they ran side by side without Jack Ward's having to drag her along. Now they were running over ground that contained sharp flints as well as fir cones and smaller pebbles; in fact the going was so bad at one point that Poppy fell, grazing both her knees. Jack Ward helped her up at once, but Poppy just shook her head, picked up George who had slipped from her arms, and ran on, if anything even faster, and without complaint.

Less than a couple of minutes later they found themselves on the lane as hoped, and thanks to Ward's excellent sense of direction less than fifty yards from a small car parked on the verge.

Jack Ward shut Poppy in the passenger seat, grabbed a travel rug off the back seat, opened the driver's door, threw Poppy the rug then jumped in himself.

'Damn,' he muttered. 'Keys. The keys are in my jacket pocket, I think. Quickly.'

Poppy dug deep into the pockets but at first could find no keys.

'Quickly!' Jack urged her. 'I can hear dogs!'

Poppy's blood ran cold as she too heard the barking and baying of Basil's guard dogs, just before she saw the flashing of lights as their pursuers closed on them.

'My coat!'

Leaning across her, Jack delved in his overcoat pockets, first the far side and then the pocket nearest to him. Finding the keys at last, he jammed one into the ignition but it wouldn't fit.

The next one he tried did.

'Now all we need is for Bessie not to start,' he

said, glancing up to see the first dog leap out of the woods and begin to run for the car. Quickly he turned the key and pressed the start button. The ignition failed to fire. Jack yanked out the choke and tried again. This time the engine coughed and mercifully fired. At once Jack engaged gear, released the handbrake and floored the throttle. The car leaped forward, just as the first Alsatian hurled itself towards them. As Jack accelerated down the road, Poppy looked back over her shoulder through the rear window to see two men jump up the bank from the woods on to the road. One of them had a rifle.

'It's Leon with a gun!'

'Duck!'

Poppy put both her hands on the back of her head and ducked as low as she could, having thrown an even more bewildered George into the foot well. Jack, with a glance in his driving mirror, first swerved the car violently then also ducked his head down, but not as low as Poppy so that he could still just about see the road ahead. He kept swerving the car from left to right in an effort to avoid the shots he knew must follow, and follow they did, just as Jack saw a right hand corner ahead and steered for the safety it would afford them.

From the sudden sound above them it seemed that the first shot must have passed overhead, but the second drilled through the back window, shattering the glass and thumping into the cloth lining of the car roof. Jack immediately swung the car to the left, and only just in time, as a third shot smashed past his wing mirror. Seconds later he had swung them right again and to safety, well out of sight round the sharp right hand bend that introduced them to the top of a very steep hill.

'You all right, Lady Tetherington?' he enquired politely.

'I've been better,' Poppy replied, sitting back up.

'At least it was only gunfire.'

'Only?'

'Yes. For a moment I was convinced we'd blown a tyre. Now that *would* have been serious.'

'This is no time for good old British humour, Mr Ward. George and I have quite lost our *sang froid*. Now what?'

'London,' he replied.

'London?' Poppy echoed in amazement. 'Dressed like this?' She stared down at herself. 'I can't go to London dressed like this. I'm American. We like clothes.'

'We'll stop off somewhere for the night, don't worry,' Jack assured her. 'We can shop for some clothes for you in the morning.'

'I think you might have to define that *we*,' Poppy said with a sigh. 'I for one am certainly not going to go shopping in one torn nightdress and an equally ruined dressing gown.'

Jack Ward looked round at her, his face expressionless as usual.

'We'll work something out,' he said. 'Don't worry.'

* * *

The drive was a long and arduous one, and certainly had they not been in headlong flight it would have been a journey both Jack and Poppy would rather not have undertaken. The ordeal was made worse by the hole in the back window, and the cold of the car had Poppy shivering, silently, and sometimes not so silently.

After several hours on the road they arrived at a small nondescript town, somewhere, Jack Ward explained, in the south midlands, where he drove slowly round the streets apparently looking for an address, until a policeman with a torch suddenly stepped out in front of the car and flagged them to a halt. Before Jack could say anything, he put his head into the driver's window to demand what they were doing out at this hour of the night driving in a suspicious manner. Jack glanced at Poppy. She had sunk even lower in her seat, desperate for the policeman not to catch sight of her state of undress as Jack stepped out of the car to explain many things, including the shattered back window.

Poppy watched intrigued as he muttered something to the policeman, taking a small leather wallet from his inside pocket as he did so. The officer's manner changed immediately, and he pointed in the opposite direction.

Turning the car round, Jack drove off in line with the directions he had just been given, until he pulled up outside a row of identical-looking semi-detached houses.

'Here we do be,' he muttered, assuming a country accent, and indicating for Poppy to disembark. 'Sorry for the unguided tour, but at night all streets are grey.'

'He seemed to be a friendly sort of policeman,' Poppy remarked in a whisper as they stood on the pavement by the car. 'Rather helpful sort in fact.'

'Yes,' Jack agreed quietly. 'Wasn't he just?'

With the help of his pocket torch Jack found the house he was looking for, took a key from his pocket and let himself in, Poppy following in answer to his beckoning gesture.

'This where you live?' she asked, once they were inside the hall.

'No, no, not at all,' Jack replied quickly, opening the door into the living room and nodding for Poppy to enter. 'Wait here, please. I won't be a minute.'

Poppy sat carefully on the edge of a square-armed easy chair, staring first at her still muddied legs and nightclothes, and then round the unlit room, wondering what on earth was happening, and into quite what her curiosity had led her. She was grateful for the warmth of the room, for its ordinariness, which seemed so welcoming after Mellerfont and its grandeur and discomforts. On the other hand, once she was thawing out a little, she could not help wondering who or what her companion was. She really knew nothing about him other than that he had somehow to be connected to some sort of political opposition to Basil and his minions, which meant he must be what Poppy would deem a good rather than a bad egg.

Her thoughts were interrupted by the return of Jack Ward, accompanied now by a sleepy-looking tousle-haired woman busily doing up her tartan dressing gown.

'This is Julia,' Jack announced. 'Julia, this is Miss Smith.'

Julia looked up from her tassel tying, shook her long hair back from her eyes and nodded at Poppy.

'Don't worry.' She smiled. 'I'm quite used to this with the Colonel here.'

'Julia has very kindly offered us a bed for the night,' Jack said, taking off the hat he had kept on despite the fact that he was only in his shirtsleeves. 'She'll also find you something to wear tomorrow.'

Both Poppy and George, exhausted by their adventures, finally slept without stirring, so much so that when they eventually awoke it was late morning. Judging from the animated conversation she could hear drifting up from downstairs, Jack and Julia had risen well in advance of them.

As soon as Poppy entered the kitchen the conversation stopped, Julia engaging her guest in small talk while Jack excused himself to go and smoke his pipe in the small back garden. After a decent and ample fried breakfast and two cups of excellent tea, Julia took Poppy upstairs and found her some suitably ordinary clothes from her wardrobe.

Jack looked up in some surprise when he saw Poppy coming downstairs dressed all but identically to Julia, in a short-sleeved blouse, a plain dark blue skirt, a black wool cardigan, stockings and a pair of wellington boots.

'Our only failure,' Poppy explained, holding her spectacles up to the light to see if they required cleaning. 'My feet are a little smaller than Julia's, and I'm afraid I floundered a bit in her shoes, so we settled for wellington boots and three pairs of socks to bulk them out.'

'You never know.' Julia smiled. 'You could start a fashion.'

Poppy laughed.

'It could catch on!' she agreed, feeling suddenly strangely free and altogether differently daring, as if she was no longer herself, as if the clothes were going to allow her to go where she pleased, without people whispering and talking behind her back,

212

which had been her experience over the last days and weeks at wretched Mellerfont.

Unsurprisingly the drive to London was considerably less eventful than their journey of the night before. Despite the fact that there were all sorts of questions Poppy wanted to ask her companion there was something about Jack Ward's manner that did not invite being quizzed. He had an inner authority that seemed to be all the more noticeable for the fact that he was not a handsome man, and this too made him seem more formidable perhaps than he truly was, but since she had put both her life and also her future, to some degree, in his hands, she was reluctant to push her luck, whatever it might be.

They talked in fits and starts all the way to London. Poppy was soon all too aware that she was being interrogated, in however gentlemanly a manner; aware too that since her life was—to a greater degree than she might wish—in her driver's hands, she must present herself in a way that would make him understand the kind of person she knew herself to be, rather than the kind of person she might wish she actually was. She was therefore careful not to portray herself as someone forced into a loveless marriage by the social ambitions of her parents, blaming only herself for her foolish mistake, explaining that she had been such a sensational flop during the Season that it had taken very little for someone as sophisticated as Basil to turn her head. She was careful also to make fun of her looks as being of the kind that did not draw queues of dancing partners.

All of this seemed to satisfy Jack Ward.

In fact, without Poppy realising it, the more time

Mr Ward spent in her company the more he was coming to realise that Lady Tetherington might prove to be most suitable for his purposes. Best of all she was still very young, and being very young would be game for anything. There was nothing braver, in his experience, than a young woman under the age of twenty-one. They were not so much reckless as joyous in the face of danger, coming to love it as much or perhaps more even than the passion of love. Danger was an aphrodisiac, as he knew only too well, and if all went as he hoped, it would only be when Lady Tetherington looked back, when she was, like him, middle-aged, that she would realise just what risks she had run, and lie awake at night wondering at the pattern her life had taken. If she lived that long.

'What are your feelings about Fascism, Lady Tetherington?' he wondered, making sure to keep his tone light. 'I ask you this for good reason, don't worry. So don't be alarmed.'

'I don't really have any,' Poppy replied. 'Other than of course what you might call the normal ones. Such as thinking Mr Hitler the most awful kind of person, and of course the same goes for all his cohorts. I'm afraid until I was married I was a bit naïve, probably because my parents are not British. Fascism seemed to be just a foreign thing— something embraced by people over in Europe rather than by us.'

'Fair enough. You could hardly say fairer than that.'

'You could actually. I mean I can now—because of what's happened. And what I sort of suspected was happening at Mellerfont.'

214

'That your late husband was in fact a Fascist?'

'I think it's pretty obvious, don't you? Well, surely you must know, don't you? Because you looked as though you were part of the inner circle. I mean you'd got yourself pretty well in, well in enough to know what was going on.'

'Not quite well in enough, as it happens,' Jack confessed. 'When we first met, I think I was about to be rumbled. It was the shooting, oddly enough. Something I just can't stomach. Everyone from my background is meant to be so keen on it, but I have never been able to muster an enthusiasm. Certainly, if you go walking on your land and you see a rabbit or a pigeon and take a shot at it, that I can understand, but not killing slow, defenceless birds reared for the purpose. It's not English. It's not sport. In England, in the old days, it would have been considered just not on.' He took a deep breath and exhaled slowly. 'Anyway. I wasn't making quite the progress I'd hoped, and thinking I was about to be rumbled I bailed out.'

'But not before you'd found out about Basil's journal, and the importance it has.'

'It has an importance all right,' Jack assured her. 'That lot of blackshirts don't convene just for the fun of it. Unfortunately all I discovered in my time in the inner sanctum was that your husband was possibly the best connected of them all, and the *soi-disant* real leader of the British Fascist party. Does that shock you?'

There was a long silence, and then Poppy nodded.

'It does rather, I have to admit. I mean what about that Mosley chap?'

'I can't say for certain, but it does seem your

215

husband was infinitely better connected than Mosley, and rather brighter. I think that's why he was more deadly. He was if you like the *éminence grise*. The power behind the throne, something which I think he greatly enjoyed. Mosley liked to swagger about the place, which is why he and his wife are pretty closely watched. Your husband on the other hand, as you know, was quite different. The point is—and it's worth making—that these people, the Fascists in our midst, are very much that. They're not just in the big homes of the rich, or floating about in idle society, they're everywhere—in newsagents, selling papers on street corners, in high office, in the armed forces, in factories and even teaching in schools. Half the fun for them is keeping their despicable beliefs secret, because like all fanatics they get a kick out of being a secret society—waiting, as it were, for their particular messiah to come, for the time when Hitler takes over this island, when they'll reveal themselves in their true colours, welcoming the invaders with flowers. Mind you, they're no fools. Don't you believe it. They know we're after them, and what's more they're trained to look out for us, knowing all the time that their hour may well come.'

'I'm sorry,' Poppy interrupted. 'But what do you mean by *us*, I wonder?'

Jack took his eyes off the road for a moment to look at her carefully.

'Hmmm,' he said, shifting his unlit pipe to the other side of his mouth. 'Whatever they might have thought about you before last night, since then you are—I'm afraid—most definitely not one of them. You fled with me. They don't actually know it was me, but sure as eggs is eggs they know about you. They know you bolted with the diary, Lady Tetherington, and they know the safe has been robbed. So they will be coming after you, I'm sorry to say.'

For the first time since her flight from Mellerfont Poppy now faced the reality of her situation. She scolded herself for being so dim as to think her adventure of the night before could simply be enjoyed in retrospect, before being brushed away under the carpet. She knew how dangerous Basil must have been, so as a consequence she should have realised that the people with whom he had involved himself were equally lethal. As a consequence of not taking Jack Ward's advice to go back to bed and forget about it all, she was now a target for their guns.

'I see,' she said quietly, after a short silence. 'Yes, of course.'

Jack glanced at her again, in an effort to read her state of mind.

'We can take you out of their sights, you know,' he said. 'We can give you a new identity, a new appearance, a new way of life, and the chances are no one will find you until after the war, when it won't matter any more. If that's what you want.'

'I don't think so,' Poppy replied. 'I don't think I'd like that at all as it happens. I could go to America, couldn't I? I could join my parents, except I wouldn't want to put them in any danger.'

'You might well. Unfortunately the way these people work is very much like the underworld everywhere, Lady Tetherington. Just when you think you're all right, strolling down the street for a newspaper, going to the beach, taking a taxi ride, they strike. They love the power of it, you must understand, the power of knowing what you don't know—in other words, the sadistic power of control. You never knowing, your mother and father never knowing, when, or if, they might strike. It is wisely said that revenge is a dish better eaten cold, and that is how they will think of what they might plan to do, as a revenge killing, as totally justified. That is what bigotry is—blind faith in what you think, blind faith in how you think the world should be ordered. But, of course . . .' He paused. 'It's a big step, and it has to be your decision, naturally.'

'That's not quite true, is it?' Poppy smiled at him. 'I mean I don't have an awful lot of say in the matter. I can't just ask you to stop the car, and get out, and go back to normal life now, can I? The dic is sort of cast, at least by my reckoning.'

They both fell to silence, Jack for once feeling regret that he had somehow involved an innocent young person in his world, a person who in a way didn't deserve to be in this position, although the other part of him, the larger part in fact, could not help but be secretly pleased that he might well have found an entirely suitable agent, someone who could be of great use, most of all because she was modest. He had always found the bigheads were useless for his particular work. All right for others perhaps, but not for him. He had also always believed that women made the best agents not just because they were modest, but because by and large they did not seem to succumb to flattery in the same way that men so often did. They seemed to always have that other voice running through their heads, the one that told them that honeyed

218

words concealed black motives, that what a man said with his lips was often belied by what his eyes were saying.

'If you know who all these people are . . .' Poppy began again, frowning at the road ahead as she tried to work everything out. 'If you know who all these people are why don't you—'

'Yes,' Jack interrupted. 'I think I know what you are about to say. Why don't we simply round 'em all up and throw them in jug? I'll tell you why. Because they're far too useful where they are. It's sometimes better to leave people like this—never losing sight of them, naturally—so as we know what they're up to—as well as the fact that we learn from 'em all the while. It's all to the good, believe me. You learn to think like them. Some have to learn to become not just like them, but actually one of their number.'

'Go underground?'

'Join their ranks, Lady Tetherington. Dangerous stuff, I assure you.'

'Yes,' Poppy said quietly. 'But *interesting*.'

Jack gave her another look. This time she caught it, and gave him a suddenly brilliant smile.

'Interesting, yes,' he agreed. 'But are *you* interested?'

'I might be,' Poppy said. 'And there again I might not be,' she countered, playing for time. She began again after a short pause which Jack Ward was careful not to fill. 'I am just thinking from your point of view I am really rather suitable, aren't I? First, strangely enough, because I am not British. I have no relations over here who will worry about my going missing, so that makes me quite suitable. Second I have parents who know I have been unhappily married, but I would imagine certainly do not want me round their necks again—and third, being an only child, and educated at home, I have made few friends in England. But, you know, despite all that, what would happen if I say no?'

'Nothing would happen.'

'Oh, I think it would, Mr Ward. I think something really might happen, for all that you say it wouldn't. I mean, looked at again from your point of view, I already know enough, first about you, and then about Julia, and then about the leather book, and all that—quite enough to make me a bit of a liability, wouldn't you say? I would, if I were you. I would say, by refusing to leave the room when you told me, I have found out too much to be altogether quite nice. No, you're not just going to let me go. You can't. I might prove to be the famous millstone around your neck, and that would never do. After all, I know when I faced you in Basil's study, you were quite prepared to shoot me. Perhaps not dead, but shoot me none the less, which shows that when faced with someone who is getting in the way, you will act quite aggressively. Because I actually find shooting someone quite aggressive.'

'Quite so. And yes I would have done, if I'd had to. If you'd tried to raise the alarm I would have shot you, but not through the heart or the head. However, that must not influence your decision. Believe me I want you to join my side, of course I do, but it must be your decision, made in cold blood.'

'I have to decide?'

'Of course. This is something that is entirely up to you. If you don't wish to join my side I can make arrangements with the authorities for you to go to Canada, or America, as you suggested earlier, but finally it's up to you.'

'Yes,' Poppy slowly agreed. 'Yes, it is, isn't it? After all, up until now, all the decisions in my life have been made for me. So now is a turning point. And that *is* interesting.'

CHAPTER TEN

Marjorie and Billy's journey to Eden Park was much easier and less eventful than the one that Marjorie had originally taken, her first trip having been as complex as those of her as yet unknown colleagues, setting off for somewhere she thought was in Gloucester, only to find herself being picked up at the railway station by none other than the mysterious guest at the funeral tea—Mr Jack Ward.

He had met her at a small and remote country station before driving her all the way to Eden Park, explaining as they went that it was a matter of security that she should not know the precise location of her future place of employment.

Marjorie was both pleased and surprised at the mention of employment, although she was careful not to say so to Mr Ward, imagining that if she showed too much enthusiasm he might change his mind.

'But if I don't know where Eden Park is,' she had wondered, 'how will I bring Billy down there—that is if everything's all right and it all goes—er—ahead?'

'Leave me to handle that,' Mr Ward told her

firmly but kindly. 'That's not your worry. I shall fix up all the transport. After all it's for everyone's good that we maintain maximum security. Until everyone is sworn in, that is.'

Marjorie had no idea of what he could possibly have meant by *sworn in*, although she was soon to find out. She was, however, amazed by the sight that greeted her when she had been driven in through the grand carriage gates that stood at the entrance of Eden Park, as obviously Billy now was, to judge from the expression on his pale face as the taxi, having taken them across country for what seemed the larger part of a day, dropped them both off at the gates, and they began their long walk up the drive.

'Blimey,' he whispered, staring at the acres of cultivated parkland that stood on either side of the long drive. 'Look—look at them deer, Marge. And them stags.'

He pointed to the herd of red deer peacefully grazing beneath huge and ancient oak trees. And it was not just the deer that took his breath away after his urban upbringing, but the sight of the river that meandered through lush meadows, and the green lawns that swept gently down from the great house.

'There's a lake, too,' Marjorie pointed out. 'With any amount of fish. I'm sure if you're good they might allow you to fish it.'

'Blimey,' Billy said. 'Stripe me pink.'

'Not a bad house either.'

Marjorie turned his attention to the building that stood bathed in warm sunshine, a gentle light that turned the colour of its mellow stone into honey.

To the far side was a smaller house with another exquisitely domed roof and more long, graceful sash windows that one could step from when raised straight on to the grass. Beyond that house stood a classic stable yard, complete with a clock, at that moment in time festooned with a host of white doves sunning themselves in the warmth of the late afternoon sun. As they finally found themselves in front of the perfect colonnaded entrance, a large loose-limbed grey horse ridden by a handsome, shaggy-haired man accompanied by a large dog that loped along beside him clattered out of the stable yard and disappeared at a sharp canter up the hill to the far side of the lake.

Billy stood staring, taking everything in, *drinking* it in, for once silenced while Marjorie thankfully put their suitcases down on the bottom of the flight of steps.

Entering the house between a set of graceful Corinthian columns at the top of the shallow steps, Marjorie, with Billy in distant tow, walked across the fine marble-floored hall, past ancient marble busts set on plinths and then to the foot of the magnificent gold and white cantilevered staircase rising in flights of twenty steps, illuminated from above by light streaming through the magnificent glass dome.

'Blimey,' Billy said yet again, turning round and round in circles to stare at all the extravagant beauty surrounding him. 'I never seen the like.'

'I should think you haven't, young man.' Marjorie laughed. 'If you had, I'd be wondering what you'd been up to. Told you that you'd like it. Now—we have to find the pass door, because this bit's nothing to do with us, alas, and I must find

Mrs Alderman the housekeeper, who's meant to be expecting us. I was told to report to her on arrival. There's a pass door somewhere round here.'

'Before you go looking for any pass door, miss,' a male voice said from behind her, 'I think it best if we first establish who we are. Pass, please? Or letter of conduct.'

Marjorie turned to see two soldiers standing in the hall, both with rifles slung over their shoulders. Taking a closer look Marjorie thought they looked friendly enough, but they were soldiers none the less.

'What are you—' Billy demanded.

'What do we look like, son? We're soldiers.'

'I know, I can see that,' Billy insisted. 'But what are you doing here? You're on our side, aren't you? You won't want to shoot us, will yer?'

The soldiers looked at each other and grinned, and then at Billy.

'I know, son,' the first one replied. 'But we're doing our job, see? We're sentries.'

'There weren't no sentries at the gate.'

'That's right, son, there weren't no sentries at the gate. That's 'cos they don't want no sentries seen at the gate, see? It would give the game away, wouldn't it? If folk walk past and see sentries at the gate they're going to get clued up, see?'

'No I don't,' Billy said stubbornly, while surreptitiously examining the rifle of his questioner. He was allowed to go no further by Marjorie, who finally took over.

'It's all right, Billy,' she said. 'They are only doing their duty. They have a perfect right to know what we're doing here.' She handed them the official letter of introduction, which Jack Ward had

224

given her.

'Thank you, miss,' the second sentry said, consulting his list. 'That's right—you're expected, miss. You too, son.' He smiled at Billy and ruffled his already tousled head. 'You want to see my rifle?'

'Yes please!'

Billy went silent, pale with excitement, as the soldier showed him the workings of his rifle.

'Is it loaded?' he finally asked.

'Course it's loaded. We're on sentry duty.'

'Blimey,' said Billy. 'Stripe me.'

He sighed with huge contentment, before following Marjorie down to the lower ground floor of the great house.

Mrs Alderman was seated at the kitchen table when Marjorie and Billy were shown in by their escorts, a small, round-figured woman with a fuzz of grey hair and wearing a long old-fashioned dress. She was holding a handkerchief to her forehead as she tried to make sense of the billeting plan she had laid out in front of her on the table.

'You're very welcome, Miss Hendry, I'm sure,' she said in her soft country burr. 'You too, young man. And I'm sure you'll both be starving and hungry after your long journey.'

The new arrivals were a pleasant distraction for Mrs Alderman, who was fast becoming bewildered by trying to find enough rooms let alone beds for the number of people she had been told were arriving within the week. Putting the kettle on the hob, she made them a plate of juicy tomato sandwiches and polished up a couple of old-fashioned green and red apples.

'You've fallen on your feet coming here.' She

225

gave a smile of some satisfaction. 'We grows so much of our produce, as well as having a large flock of sheep and a herd of good cattle. You shouldn't go short, my dears—always provided this blessed war don't go on too long, which we're all hoping, aren't we? Although if the government's got anything to do with it, Lord alone knows what will happen to us.'

Marjorie and Billy ate the sandwiches too quickly for really good manners, but Mrs Alderman didn't seem to mind, only watching them approvingly, until, much refreshed by their tea, she showed them across the stable yard to the particular cottage which had been made ready for their arrival.

'Told you it was nice, didn't I?' Marjorie nudged Billy, who had once more fallen into a stupefied silence as he stood staring around at the comfortably furnished cottage, where a small log fire had even been lit in the fireplace in readiness for their arrival.

'Nice?' Billy said, bouncing on the bed he had already decided was to be his. 'This place is bloomin' heaven, Marge. Blimey.'

'I do wish you'd stop saying that, Billy,' Marjorie said, wandering off to the room that was to be hers, with Billy traipsing behind her. 'You know what it means, and I'm sure it's the last thing you want. To go blind.'

'To go blind? I should think not!' Billy said happily, before taking in the cosy pretty bedroom where Marjorie was to sleep. 'Cor. Look at this then,' he whispered. 'Blimey.'

*   *   *

226

Jack Ward had driven Poppy to a safe house somewhere in Victoria. Once again they were greeted without any undue surprise, this time by a pleasantly mannered, soberly dressed woman in her early thirties who disappeared to make her visitors some refreshments while Jack briefed Poppy in the privacy of the small, sparsely furnished living room.

'You still have the chance to back out, Lady Tetherington,' he began. 'I assure you there will be no problem, if you decide what you hear is not for you.'

'I think we both know the answer to that, Mr Ward,' Poppy replied. 'And I think it might be easier—as well as necessary, wouldn't you say—if you were to drop the Lady Tetherington thing. And call me Poppy.'

'I was going to mention that as it happens. You'll certainly need a new name, which is something we shall work on. In the meantime perhaps it would be better, under the circumstances, if I simply called you Miss Smith. I don't think we should become any more informal than that. And by the way, most of my people, if they call me anything, call me Colonel. It's not my rank, just a nickname, really. All started a long time ago, long, long ago, with someone I knew rather well, a sort of joke really.'

His voice tailed off, but despite the light-hearted words his tone was careful, as if he was recounting an historical fact rather than a sentimental anecdote.

Poppy tried to read the look in his bespectacled eyes, but, failing, thought she had picked up something in his tone that he could not voice, but

227

at which he was nevertheless hinting—ever present danger. All of a sudden she saw the sense of his attitude. *Under the circumstances*. It would be the very opposite of sensible for them to establish any sort of intimacy such as using their first names— *under the circumstances*.

Under the circumstances she had already been shot at, and she imagined that given the task that Jack Ward might have in mind for her there would be many other occasions when Poppy might find herself in similarly dangerous circumstances.

'Yes, of course,' she replied politely. 'I quite understand, under the circumstances.'

First Jack Ward outlined what her main objective would be, then how she would be prepared for it. This involved considerable and painstaking preparation which would bring about a complete change, not just of appearance, but of personality.

When Poppy expressed some reserve, the Colonel, as she now began to think of him, explained that given her experience of Society she would be ideal, particularly after she had undergone a complete change.

'Can someone change completely, enough to deceive, do you think?'

'We are becoming very skilled at this sort of thing,' Jack assured her. 'I shall put you in the charge of one of our best people who will turn you into somebody even you yourself would not recognise.'

'I think it sounds rather fun,' Poppy replied, while actually feeling the very opposite. 'I have often become altogether fed up being me. In fact, if you really want to know, Colonel, I have become very, very fed up with being me. Not a very successful person, as you may well imagine, already a widow at eighteen, already on the run, it's not the best kind of record, is it?'

Poppy laughed, and although Jack Ward did smile, he also looked momentarily wrong-footed by her candour.

The plan was for her to be handed over first to one of Jack's contacts in London who would work on Poppy's character transformation, then to the woman who, as Jack had just assured Poppy, could be guaranteed to turn dross into gold.

'Not that that's the case in this instance,' Jack added quickly. 'In this case she will have the perfect raw material to work from.'

'I wonder why you say that,' Poppy joked, pushing her spectacles back up her nose. 'I really do.'

'I think possibly because I have seen things in you that others have not,' Jack replied carefully. 'Things I'm sure that you most certainly have not seen in yourself, until now.'

Poppy said nothing, intrigued by the compliment, but refusing to demur since it had been unsolicited.

'Now I have to ask you something,' he said, taking off his heavy spectacles. 'It's important, as it happens.'

'I have the feeling that everything you ask is important, and that if not you won't be bothered.'

Jack nodded, cleaning the thick lenses of his spectacles carefully on the immaculate white handkerchief he always carried in his top pocket.

'What exactly is wrong with your eyes?' he asked.

'Astigmatism,' Poppy replied. 'At least I think

229

that's what they call it. My old nanny said if I didn't wear glasses my eye would finally end up looking at my nose. This eye.'

Poppy tapped the relevant lens of her own spectacles.

'Might I see your glasses?'

Jack put a hand out politely. Polly shrugged slightly, carefully removed her spectacles and handed them over.

Jack cleaned them again on his handkerchief and put them to his own eyes.

'Don't make a lot of difference to me,' he said. 'But then I'm a bat.'

Now he looked at her. Without his own spectacles on, for the first time Poppy was aware of the true set of his face and found herself disconcerted. Most people who wear glasses look oddly vulnerable once they are removed. But Jack Ward, without his glasses, looked quite the opposite. He looked determined and strong and— Poppy found herself admitting—more than a little frightening.

As he stared at her she realised that he was not making any attempt to menace her. He was simply looking at her, and from what she had gathered from sight of his own glasses, she would look nothing more than a blur to him. But the look wasn't to distinguish her; it was to determine something about her, and Poppy soon guessed what it might be.

'I can see all right,' she admitted. 'Whatever is wrong with my eyes doesn't—you know, doesn't affect my actual vision. It's a condition. Astigmatism—if that's what it's called. A slight squint in other words. A slight squint that could turn into a proper one if it doesn't stay corrected. So I'm told. And as my old Irish nanny said, men just aren't interested in boss-eyed girls. "You'll never get a man now with your stigmata, Miss Poppy," she used to say.'

They both laughed.

'Nonsense,' Jack replied. 'Stuff and nonsense. Firstly men find a slight squint most attractive— and that's all you have, I'd say. Judging from the weakness of your lenses.' He put his own glasses back on to study her now without hers. 'A very slight squint in fact,' he pronounced. 'So slight that it is barely visible.'

He folded the sides of her glasses up carefully and consigned them to one of his inside pockets.

'Sorry?' Poppy said with a frown. 'Are you confiscating my spectacles?'

'Yes,' Jack replied. 'You don't need them, Miss Smith. At a guess I'd say you never have.'

Poppy frowned, and then smiled at the once more serious-faced middle-aged man in whose hands she was now placing her life. It was not a polite smile but one of sudden and infinite gratitude.

*   *   *

By now they were arriving thick and fast at Eden Park. Marjorie and Billy watched in fascination as the constant stream of cars and on a couple of occasions small single-decker buses delivered more and more people either at the gates of the park or at the house itself. Most of them seemed to be women, all apparently young, the oldest no more than in their middle twenties. They appeared to be

231

arriving in all shapes and sizes, yet they all shared one thing in common—a look of unconcealed bewilderment as they found themselves unshipped in a place of such splendour.

At the same time as the influx of new arrivals, more staff appeared as if from nowhere, most of them already resident on some part of the estate, as Marjorie and Billy later discovered, having been press-ganged into service by the undoubtedly persuasive powers of Major Folkestone, to whom it was fast becoming obvious no one could, or indeed wanted to, say no. They were put to work organising the interior of the house for the work that was to take place there, removing all the most valuable items of furniture and the more portable works of art, storing them away in the dry cellars that ran in catacombs under the great house. The most valuable, and in some cases priceless, paintings, were removed from their frames, rolled up, and transported to a secret place somewhere in the grounds, perhaps the family mausoleum, as Mrs Alderman once hinted to Billy.

After which, under cover of night, with all the secrecy that normally would be afforded to the movement of troops, large lorries rolled slowly up the long drive, loaded to the brim with ministry files, office equipment, extra beds, and utility furniture, enough to seat, sleep and occupy the houseful of immigrant workers who were still arriving, in larger or smaller groups, daily.

Daytime was spent setting all the new equipment out under the command of Major Folkestone and a Miss Browne, who had arrived shortly after Marjorie and Billy to take up her post as supervisor. She was a short woman dressed in

232

tweeds and with her bright ginger hair worn in a Windsor bob. When he first caught sight of her, Billy thought she was a man, and still remained somewhat uncertain even after he had been introduced to her. He sympathised with Marjorie at the prospect of working for such an extraordinary creature, but Marjorie shrugged her shoulders philosophically. There were bound to be some prices to pay in order to earn the right to live in a place such as Eden Park.

Finally, when all the new beds had been put in place in the rooms on the third floor, places Marjorie told Billy that in former days would have been occupied by the servants, Mrs Alderman pinned up a list of the updated sleeping arrangements on a large green-baize-covered board that had been placed on an easel in the main hall so that it could be seen by all who came and went in such swift succession that not even the amazing Major Folkestone could have said exactly who they were.

Thanks to Jack Ward the list did not affect Marjorie and Billy. Major Folkestone himself told them they were to stay in their cottage for the duration.

'Mr Ward insisted young Billy here must remain with you.'

The Hendrys watched as a crowd of young women gathered to read where they were to be sleeping, and furthermore to which section they were to be attached for their forthcoming work.

'Blimey,' Billy said, putting his hands to his ears. 'What a lot of squawking.'

'Do stop saying blimey, Billy!'

'Why they all screeching like that, Marge? Sound

like a lot of 'ens.'

'This place echoes, Billy. Bound to. Look at the size of it. It isn't their fault.'

'Never 'eard such a din. Never. I 'aven't.'

Billy kept his hands to his ears as he regarded with some trepidation the girls who were still trying to find their names on the lists pinned to the board, laughing and calling to each other as they did so.

'I think this is a case for the sentries,' Billy announced seriously. 'Maybe they could fire a couple of warning shots over their 'eads.'

Marjorie laughed and wandered over towards the back of the pack more out of curiosity than anything. So far, due to the young Hendrys' singular lodging arrangements, she hadn't come into much contact with any of the new arrivals, although she imagined that was all going to change once the work started in earnest.

The crowd was dispersing now, with everyone either committing their room and section number to memory or writing them down in notebooks or on scraps of paper. Finally the only person left in front of the notice board was a tall blonde girl, tapping her leg idly with the tennis racket she was carrying as she searched the lists for her name.

'Need a hand?' Marjorie wondered. 'There are rather a lot of names.'

'And I can't see mine anywhere,' the girl replied. 'Thanks. The name is Maddox. With an x. Kate Maddox.'

'I'm Marjorie. And this is Billy. My—well. He's my sort of stepbrother really.'

Marjorie smiled at Billy who pulled a face back at her, doing his best to hide his blushes now he was confronted with what he immediately decided was possibly the most beautiful girl he had ever seen in his whole life.

'Hello, Billy,' Kate said, putting out a hand to be shaken. 'Aren't you the lucky one? All these girls, and besides Major Folkestone and a couple of soldiers, you're the only boy here so far. I say, from your point of view it should be renamed Paradise Park!'

Billy blushed even more, frowning furiously and staring at the floor in despair.

'Come on, Billy,' Marjorie encouraged him. 'Help us find Kate's name.'

'It's not there,' Billy said, after a moment.

'Of course it is,' Marjorie scolded. 'It has to be. You haven't looked.'

'All right,' Billy shrugged. 'Don't believe me.'

The girls looked first at each other, then back at the lists, this time even more closely.

'He's right,' Kate said. 'They seem to have left me out.'

'Told you,' Billy said. 'Told you.'

'You can't possibly have seen, Billy,' Marjorie said in exasperation. 'You didn't even look. You didn't have time.'

'I told you,' Billy said, squaring up to Marjorie's irritation. 'I did look.'

He walked off, leaving Marjorie staring after him with a puzzled frown.

'What seems to be the trouble?' Mrs Alderman wondered, as she came to pin a new list to the board, one announcing the various times for the daily meals. 'You two look a bit lost. Oh, it's you, Marjorie, dear,' she said, recognising her young friend. 'What are you bothering with the billet lists for? You got your own little place, dear.'

235

'It's Miss Maddox here, Mrs Alderman. She doesn't seem to have been allocated a bed.'

'I've got my section all right,' Kate added. 'But nowhere to sleep.'

Mrs Alderman consulted both the board and the list of names in the large ledger she was carrying under her arm. She scratched her head then shook it.

'Strange,' she sighed. 'I thought I'd done everyone. What I have done is fill all available beds—'

'Oh dear, so I haven't anywhere to sleep?' Kate interrupted.

'There's a spare bed in the cottage, Mrs Alderman,' Marjorie said. 'There are two beds in my room so Miss Maddox could easily sleep there. If that's all right.'

'That's the answer then,' Mrs Alderman agreed, closing her ledger. 'Long as it's all right with you two?'

It turned out, at least from the look on Billy's face, to be very all right.

*   *   *

Later that afternoon the series of newly installed bells rang through the house, a signal for everyone to assemble once again in the main hall, where they found Major Folkestone and Miss Browne seated on a small podium awaiting them.

'Quiet, please, everyone!' Major Folkestone called over the hubbub. 'Quiet please!'

Everyone fell to silence and turned to face the major, who was placing some sheets of paper on a lectern in front of him.

'Good, thank you—good,' he began. 'First of all a formal welcome to Eden Park, and I hope you have all settled in. Now—I won't beat about the bush. This isn't a holiday camp or a hotel, so I'm not going to give you any tips about where you can swim or ride a horse or get your hair done or anything like that. Like Miss Browne and me, you are all here to undertake vital tasks, at a very important time. I don't need to remind you that we stand on the brink of war. I doubt very much if we'll go another week without a formal declaration and the commencement of hostilities.' He paused. 'This might well be the most critical phase in our island's history since the Spanish Armada. We face a very dangerous foe, and if and when war is declared we also face the very real possibility of an invasion. We've seen the invaders off before, of course, and I have no doubt we shall see this chap off as well, but—' There was an outbreak of applause. 'No—no applause, please. Very kind, I'm sure,' the major said with a nod, holding his hand up. 'But I'm not addressing troops here—I'm not trying to rally you all to the call. I'm simply trying to put you in the picture. So that you may understand why you have all been brought here at considerable trouble and expense, because if and when the balloon goes up you can put fun and games right out of your minds.'

He cleared his throat.

'You've all been hand-picked, as you know, because you're said to be good at what you do. Just as importantly, you are also deemed to be trustworthy, loyal and utterly reliable. Good qualities—admirable ones, and when you understand the nature of the work we shall all be

237

engaged upon you will see why it is so important that everyone here is trustworthy, loyal and utterly reliable. The operations in which we shall all be involved are classed as top security. You will be working for the government under the auspices of the War Office. In other words, the work we shall all be doing is classed as Top Secret. This means that each of you is required to sign the Official Secrets Act. For those of you who may be unclear as to what precisely signing the OSA involves, it simply means you are sworn to secrecy about every single facet of your work and existence here, as well as every single fact about Eden Park itself and any information that may come your way while you are engaged in the activities for which you are employed. Should you break the trust invested in you by revealing to any other person the nature of your work, the identity of your colleagues, or any information you have gathered in the course of your work, then if apprehended, charged and found guilty you will suffer the punishment that all traitors suffer.

'Now I want this firmly understood in case in the excitement or the heat of the moment you find yourself forgetting the importance of your work and its confidentiality. Loose tongues cost lives— and never more so than in this case, in the work we shall all be doing here—since we shall be dealing with the lives of agents and operatives. This place is so important it is as if you were at the Front itself.

'Finally, I have to tell you that now you are all here, now that you have accepted the work offered to you by our field officers, there is no turning back. You may only leave here once you have obtained Special Leave, but even if you do you will still be bound by the OSA in effect for life. That means that if you commit treachery thirty years after leaving here and are discovered, believe me, you could still pay the ultimate price. As far as your day-to-day existence goes, no one leaves the grounds without a Special Pass, and that pass can only be issued by myself. So I strongly recommend you keep on the right side of me, especially in the case of compassionate leave—or *passionate* leave as I understand it is more commonly known.'

When the ripple of nervous laughter had died down, Major Folkestone continued.

'You have all been assigned to a section, and each section has its Section Head to whom you are immediately answerable. But finally all roads lead to me, so if there are any special problems, tell your Head of Section, and they will tell me. Good luck to you all.'

Major Folkestone sat down to a round of applause that while respectful was more than a little muted as the assembled company looked round at each other, all of them at last facing the facts of their new existence.

'Cripes,' said Billy, when Marjorie and Kate had put him in the picture. 'Will I have to sign it as well?'

'You could do, Billy,' Marjorie replied. 'I mean you are here for the duration, aren't you?'

'Crikey,' Billy said again. 'This is exciting, at least it's *really* exciting, not just not exciting like it has been up until now.'

'Major Folkestone told me that if there is a war, he's got some special tasks earmarked for you, Billy.'

'What?' Billy asked incredulously. 'What sort

of things?'

'I don't know,' Marjorie said with a look to Kate. 'He wouldn't tell me. It's too Top Secret.'

For ever after Marjorie remembered the look in Billy's eyes when he realised that even though he was too young to carry a rifle, he was not too young to play a part in the defence of his country.

*   *   *

Three days later, on 3 September, slightly earlier than predicted by Major Folkestone, Neville Chamberlain broadcast the Declaration of War. Everyone at Eden Park heard the broadcast, and at its closing stood up for the National Anthem. In the silence that followed they listened to Major Folkestone order what was now a platoon of soldiers stationed in the house to lock all gates to the Park, and to mount constant armed sentry patrols, while from the windows of their bedrooms on the third floor of the great house its new inmates gazed out at the countryside beyond the estate walls, a land now seemingly forbidden to them, but a land whose freedom they must do everything in their power to preserve.

'One bond unites us all, to wage war until victory is won and never to surrender ourselves to servitude and shame, whatever the cost and the agony may be . . .'

Winston S. Churchill

Part Two

ENGLAND AT WAR

CHAPTER ELEVEN

The weather was cold and bleak, and Poppy Tetherington was no more. She had ceased to exist. She had vanished from the scene, leaving behind only rumour. Word was that her marriage to the late Lord Tetherington, although brief, had been such an unmitigated nightmare that on learning of his death she had upped sticks and fled from the hell that was Mellerfont, headed it was said for America, and no doubt the infinitely preferable company of her parents.

Not that anyone cared very much, the fact being that the now missing Poppy Beaumont had few friends and had attracted next to no attention in the Society in which her mother had been so anxious for her to move. As Lady Tetherington, so short and uncharismatic had been the tenure of Basil Tetherington's timid, bespectacled young wife at Mellerfont, that most who had visited the gloomy Victorian pile would barely have been able to put a face to her, let alone describe her character. The only gatherings she might have been expected to host had been the shooting parties from which Basil had largely excluded her, and as for venturing out, Poppy had attended one private dance and a couple of large dinner parties at similarly disposed houses where she had spent the time either being ignored or listening dutifully to her fellow diners' post-prandial complaints about their husbands.

Poppy's disappearance from the social calendar, therefore, went unsurprisingly completely unremarked. Besides, at this particular moment in England's history, its inhabitants had things of far greater import to occupy their minds than the fate of a dead aristocrat's unmemorable young American wife. This suited Jack Ward's game plan admirably, as well as that of Cissie Lavington, the woman to whom Jack sent Poppy to be 'turned around', as he called it.

Cissie Lavington was in her early middle age, good-looking in an even-featured handsome way, her strong face marred only by the black silk eye-patch she sported over her left eye.

'Shot in the eye by mistake while horsing around,' Jack had told Poppy in advance. 'Lucky not to have been killed as it happens. Not that she'd tell you that. She treats the whole thing as a huge joke. It just happened as the result of a bit of roughhousing.'

Happily she and Poppy took to each other at once, Poppy unaware that many of her pupils had found Miss Lavington altogether too daunting for words, thrown off balance at the outset by this tall, statuesque woman with her remarkable bone structure, lustrous auburn hair and her chain-smoking habit, the Black Russian cigarettes she so enjoyed housed in a long ivory holder, a prop she used to help describe any salient point she was intent on making.

'They certainly dressed you up well, my dear,' she had remarked when Poppy and she first were introduced. 'Wish I could afford rags like that. But on my pay all I can afford is drab.'

Poppy smiled at the obviously quite intentionally absurd comment, as the woman doing the complaining looked as though she had just stepped straight from the catwalk.

'Manners are the first thing we're going to tackle, my dear,' Cissie had continued. 'Not that one's manners aren't as good as gold, doncher know, but there's the rub, d'you see? Your manners I bet are more than a mitey *too* good, and all that. What we got to teach you, my lady, is disdain. You got to learn to look as though you have a bad smell under yer nose. Only people good enough for you are the people who are as good as you—and the Lord only knows they're few and far between, doncher know? Got it? You know the sort of beast I'm talking about. And that's the sort of beast we have to turn you into. Gawd help you. The sort of deeply horrid person that as far as I can twig poor you was married to. Yes? The sort of person who's so busy despising the rest of humanity that his woods become trees, and his trees become woods, and he wants to get rid of all those he considers to be beneath him, doncher know.'

'Quite correct,' Poppy agreed, after a short pause, because it did seem to sum up Basil really rather well.

'Does one remember why one took on and married this beast in the first place?'

'One does,' Poppy returned gravely. 'One thinks,' she went on, catching on to the game that Cissie Lavington was playing, 'one remembers, that is, that one's mother had been such a success during the Season, unlike one, that one had to end off one's months as a debutante having a wedding to make her feel she had been the great success she had undoubtedly been, most especially since she was leaving for America and all her friends in her luncheon club would have been disappointed if the whole thing hadn't ended in a titled alliance, d'you see?'

Perhaps because Poppy kept such an admirably straight face during her speech, Cissie Lavington found this unbearably funny, as she was meant to do, and dissolved into paeans of laughter, involving much spilling of ash down her silk blouse, before starting again.

'Well done! I say, you have cottoned on very quickly. I don't suppose you spent much time with that ghastly husband of yours rolling round in fits of glee, eh? Bet not. Fascists do take themselves so *very* seriously, don't they now? Added to which, the female beauties of the same inclination are too damn' busy looking after their faces to crease 'em up in smiles et cetera. So besides developing a look as if one has this most ghastly smell *sous le nez* you will have to learn to grow an iron face as well. Not a smile must pass the lips, let alone a laugh be heard. All helps with the disdain. The Colonel tells me you didn't have much to do with the other lot, that one was rushed away to one's wing whenever it was time for them to roll out the old Swastika. All helps, doncher know, if they can't remember who the hell the beast was married to—not that they'll recognise you when you're done here. No, once you are done here, the horrid little housepainter will be extending a personal invitation to you to join him at one of his ever-so-lovely rallies, that I promise you.'

Cissie smiled, stubbed out her now finished cigarette and immediately lit up a fresh one, selected from an expensive-looking gold case.

'Does one know what one's letting oneself in for?' she enquired, staring at Poppy over the flame of her lighter as she lit her smoke. 'One does know this ain't all fun and games. One's going to be mixing with a particularly nasty set, and not just mixing with them—one's going to be living amongst them. One's going to have to think like 'em, talk like 'em, and I'm sorry to say behave like 'em too. No going back, doncher know. These people worship Mr Hitty, the horrid little housepainter. Just as they worship power. It's their aphrodisiac, d'you see? They want to kill the weak, those who disagree with them, and those whom they consider not ethnically pure. Everyone is to be pure, blond, and Teutonic, preferably—and this includes everyone living in this poor old country of ours, so I'm for the high jump, and that is certain. So one's not playin' games here, doncher know. This is serious stuff.'

'I know,' Poppy had replied. 'I'm well aware— but thank you all the same. I may not know exactly what I'm letting myself in for, but I know enough.'

'Course you do. Jack will have given you a run-down. Good at that, the Colonel. One of the best in the game. Not a bad picker, either.'

Again Cissie had regarded Poppy over the end of her cigarette holder, this time with visible approval.

'First things first,' she had then said. 'If we're burying Poppy Tetherington we have to give you a whole new background. From now on you're to be Miss Diona de Donnet. Norman family doncher know. Came over with William the Conk—family stayed on in Dorset where they got given a damn' great chunk of land—and so on. It's all in here. Read, learn, inwardly digest, then burn it.'

Cissie had handed Poppy a file, which contained

everything she would need to know about her new persona.

'One last thing, my dear,' Cissie had enquired as Poppy began to look through its pages. 'One last thing before we get down to work. Why you doin' this? You doin' this for you? Or our country? For your parents? For whom? Because there's always someone one's doing it for.'

'I know I'm not doing it for me, Miss Lavington, no. At least I don't think so.'

'Good, because it won't work, you know. If one's doin' it to get back at someone. A husband say. However beastly a chap.'

'And I'm not doing it to get back at my husband. Who as it happens was a very beastly chap.'

'So why you doin' it then?'

Poppy thought for a moment.

'I think I'm doing it, Miss Lavington, because it has to be done.'

*   *   *

Madame Moisewitch, Poppy's next teacher, had not been so easy to win over. A diminutive, dark-haired woman with a tightly corseted rounded figure, her natural demeanour was one of aggression. She seemed to be waiting to pounce on anyone or anything that crossed her path, and this stance was made all the more apparent since it emanated from a pair of cat-like green eyes. Otherwise Madame's features would have been unremarkable until you noticed her hands and feet, which were most beautifully elegant.

'Young woman,' Madame had said, taking a round-the-houses tour of her new pupil, whom she now looked up and down as if she were a horse trainer inspecting a yearling with four bad legs. 'I fear you are to be my first failure. The way your head pokes forward—no good. The way you keep staring at your feet. The way your feet splay. Have you never been to ballet class? Is this what it is?'

'Sorry, Madame,' Poppy had replied. 'But no. No, I never attended ballet class, only ballroom dancing.'

Madame snorted lightly.

'Ballroom,' she said, as if it was a swear word. 'Diaghilev was not the choreographer of ballroom dancing. Nijinsky did not dance ballroom dancing. The Russian Ballet did not come to this country and change everything with a display of *ballroom dancing.*'

'I am so sorry, madame, I did not mean to upset you. I was just trying to demonstrate to you how very ignorant—'

'My dear,' Madame Moisewitch said, interrupting impatiently. 'There is very little point in being sorry, young lady. The damage has been done. And well and truly so. So what is it that happened to you? You fell downstairs, perhaps.' Madame had been round behind Poppy at this moment, which disconcerted her even more. 'You fell out of a tree, fell off your pony, missed the chair or some such. You certainly must have done something like this.'

'I fell down the nursery stairs.'

'Good. I see. That explains this perfectly ghastly posture. Had God intended us to slouch he would have given us bows for backbones, instead of the spine. Straighten up. You will never impress if you look as if you have been humping coal bags on your back. Your weight is on your left foot entirely. Your

251

back is round. Your head sticks out on its neck. We shall have to proceed at once to the *barre* where we shall start exercises. Please take these ballet shoes and wear them. We must start at once. I do not want you to be my first failure. But unless there is a large miracle, it seems this is what you are destined to become. My very *first* failure.'

Oddly enough, the lessons with Madame were the most difficult part of Poppy's transformation. She had never considered herself to be the most graceful of creatures, but conversely nor had she seen herself as the clumsy, lumbering and gauche giraffe that Madame seemed to see her as. She was duly humbled, and the lessons began.

Naturally Poppy could not help wondering why it was completely necessary to start to train as a classical ballet dancer when she had understood that her future occupation as an agent was destined to be one of infiltration—until the day she realised she had actually, physically, changed.

It was early one afternoon, as she dressed before walking back across the room containing the dreaded *barre* with its wall of mirrors, that Poppy caught sight of herself, and stopped. Never one to stand and admire her own image, none the less she could not help but be arrested by what she saw. In order to check that her eyes were not deceiving her, she walked slowly on while never taking her eyes from her mirrored image.

Gone was the old Poppy, the young woman with the terrible posture and the untutored walk, and in her place was the person she was groomed to become—Diona de Donnet—upright, poised, graceful and above all disdainful. She also appeared to have grown a good two or three inches, having worked non stop on what Cissie insisted on calling her *internals*, as well as doing her very best to improve her posture and carriage. Poppy continued to stare at herself, for the first time becoming convinced that she did indeed seem to have shed her old self and begun to put on a whole new persona. Diona de Donnet was becoming a fact, not a figment of Cissie's imagination.

To her further delight, Madame seemed inclined to agree, since when Poppy went to wish her farewell until her next lesson the older woman suddenly embraced her, putting both her hands to Poppy's cheeks and kissing her most affectionately.

'I had abandoned hope last month,' she confessed. 'I was about to wave the white towel. Then I see how hard you try and I also see suddenly there is progress. Then—look! Today! What is it that happened? The miracle we pray for. This wonderful miracle Miss Cissie, and I, Madame Moisewitch, always pray for with our pupils. Pray God that you do all of you what you can, that you make everything you have to do happen as it should, as we want, and that we will all succeed against this terrible evil.'

When Poppy saw the look in her teacher's eyes she realised the weight of the responsibility she was carrying. There was no need to ask Madame Moisewitch what she meant. They both knew.

*   *   *

Billy was living in paradise. Major Folkestone, having taken a shine to the lad, wasted no time in loading all sorts of responsibilities on to his young shoulders, the most important being fire and pane watching. There was actually little risk of fire thanks to the iron military-style discipline imposed on the occupants of Eden Park, but there was a very real risk of enemy planes passing overhead. Even with a total blackout, since the place was now a top security site there was always the chance that someone might betray its whereabouts, with the result that a surprise enemy raid could blow the whole place and its inhabitants to kingdom come.

Later there would be two heavily camouflaged ack-ack guns positioned strategically in the parklands, but at the moment the only defence came from the soldiers' rifles. So Billy took his duties very seriously indeed, and when it was his turn to go on watch up on to the roof he dashed, with notebook and pencil in one hand, and binoculars swinging from his neck. There he would sit watching the skies until, weary to the point of collapse, and hardly able to keep awake, he would stumble downstairs again to pass out in his cottage bedroom.

But Billy was quite alone in his new and exciting boy's paradise, for certainly no one else living in Eden Park, despite the resolutely cheerful faces they presented to the world, felt anything but dread when they contemplated the future. Outwardly they laughed and joked, and made light of everything, while inwardly they all felt, but never said, that while Chamberlain was in power they did not have a hope of winning. The most common phrase being heard all over England was 'we will win despite our government' until the day that Chamberlain resigned, and Winston Churchill became Prime Minister, at which point, with the warmer weather, the long, bitter winter, so filled with grey despair, seemed at last to be over.

*   *   *

It had been an especially bitter winter, despite the war's seeming to have been put on hold for the last months of the old year.

The Phoney War the newspapers had dubbed it, as if it was all some kind of practical joke, so it was only when Germany invaded Norway and Denmark, and Holland, followed by Belgium and Luxembourg, that everyone suddenly realised that the war—the real war—for which they seemed to have been preparing for so long, was well and truly upon them.

Everyone at Eden Park listened to Churchill's speeches on the radio, standing up as they did so, as if standing to sing the National Anthem.

We shall defend our island home—and outlive the menace of tyranny, Marjorie would repeat to herself as she went about her work, fortified by the power of the words and the profound confidence of the man speaking them.

'*We shall defend our island home . . .*' she would repeat out loud in the evenings as they were making ready for bed, loud enough for Billy to hear and immediately finish what was now their motto.

'*And outlive the menace of tyranny!*' the call would echo back to the room where Kate and Marjorie were climbing gratefully into their warm beds.

'Not that I know much about tyranny,' Marjorie said to Kate one night. 'At least I know a bit— having been to Mrs Reid's school. If Hitler's

255

anything like Pet and Uncle Mikey then Billy and I will be out there with every weapon we can lay our hands on if he dares try and set foot on these shores.'

'My father's a dictator,' Kate said wistfully, sitting up in her bed and pulling the bedclothes up over her knees. 'So I know a little about people like Hitler.'

'How's Robert?' Marjorie wondered, changing the subject, and she turned round the photograph of Robert that Kate kept by her bed to take another look. 'He really has got film star looks.'

'Oh yes, he's a star all right.' Kate laughed. 'He doesn't need to be in films.'

'He's even more handsome in his naval uniform.'

'Don't you think everyone looks good in uniform, though, Marjorie? Even Major Folkestone—'

'Who's not exactly the most good-looking of blokes,' Marjorie murmured. 'Kind though he might be.'

'He looks good in his uniform, though.'

'You couldn't possibly be getting a crush on Major Folkestone, Kate?' Marjorie teased. 'Isn't he a little old for you?'

'I'll tell you who I *have* got a crush on,' Kate said, dropping her voice. 'Have you seen that man who rides about the place on that big white horse?'

'Grey actually,' a solemn voice came from the doorway. 'Horses can't ever be white. They're called grey, white horses are grey.'

'Thank you, Billy.' Marjorie rolled her eyes at Kate and sighed. 'Now go back to bed.'

'I want to hear about Kate's crush.'

'Perhaps Kate doesn't want to tell you.'

'Kate?' Billy wondered, opening his big brown

eyes as wide as he could as he smiled at his beloved.

'It isn't anyone, Billy,' Kate said tactfully. 'I was only teasing. Trying to make Marjorie jealous.'

'Oh yes?'

'Yes, Billy,' Marjorie assured him. 'Now go back to your bed or you'll be too tired for your watch later.'

Billy eyed them both, torn between his loyalty to his duties and his early adolescent passion.

'All right,' he muttered. 'But I'll be listening.'

The two young women chatted about anything and everything until they guessed Billy had fallen fast asleep, before Marjorie closed their bedroom door so they could continue their gossip.

'He's gorgeous,' Kate whispered. 'I haven't spoken to him, I know nothing about him, but he is so handsome. And he rides beautifully.'

'Maybe you ought to ask him for a game of tennis this weekend. If he plays as well as he rides his horse, you could be in for a drubbing.'

'For once I wouldn't mind if I didn't win a single point.' Kate laughed her deep little laugh and seconds later was fast asleep.

'I'll believe that when I see it,' Marjorie murmured.

*　　　*　　　*

Billy got to him first the following morning. After he had finished his stint on watch, he spied the stranger riding back down the hill on the north side of the lake, headed back for the stables. By the time Billy arrived red-faced and out of breath in the yard the man was taking the tack off his

257

steaming horse.

'Who are you?' Billy challenged. 'What are you doing here anyway? This is government property.'

'I know,' the man said with a sigh. 'I know that, nipper.'

'So who are you? Who are you anyway?'

'I am Eugene anyway. I am Eugene the Brilliant, nipper—Eugene the Mighty, Eugene the *Fierce*.'

He suddenly bent towards Billy and bared his teeth.

'You don't frighten me,' Billy told him staunchly.

'I'm delighted to hear it,' Eugene replied. 'I terrify the pants off meself. Who are *you*, come to that?'

'The name's Billy. That's who I am.'

'Billy. Billy the Kid perhaps? Or Billy the Goat? Or Billy the Bull?'

Eugene looked at him, staring hard and making his blue eyes go wide then immediately narrowing them.

'Billy Hendry. And I have a right to be here. I have official tasks given me by the British Army.'

Eugene tucked his saddle over one arm and saluted Billy with his free hand.

'I have a right to be here too, soldier. My uncle owns this place.'

Billy frowned at this piece of news, which caught him well on the hop. Eugene did the thing with his eyes once more, and then sauntered off into the tack room. Billy waited for a moment, wondering how to get the best of his new adversary, then decided to follow him into his den. He found the big Irishman striking a match on the sole of his riding boot to light a thin dark cheroot he had clamped between a set of strong white teeth.

'What now, soldier?' Eugene teased. 'Come to check me tack's all clean and orderly?'

'You can't live here, even if your uncle does own it,' Billy informed him. 'The only people allowed here are those with official permission.'

'Jccze.' Eugene laughed. 'Will you listen to the nipper?' he asked the stable boy who was helping him put away his tack. 'We'll have to get him a brown shirt all his own.'

'Why should I need a brown shirt?' Billy wondered. 'I don't like brown.'

'And I don't like brownshirts,' Eugene said, over-seriously. Then he put two flattened forefingers under his nose to simulate a moustache and saluted the air. 'Heil Hitler!' he said, clicking his heels.

Billy laughed. 'Yes, I know, but really. You really shouldn't be here unless you're official. Major Folkestone wouldn't like it, really he wouldn't.'

'I'm official all right, nipper,' Eugene said, ruffling Billy's hair. 'I couldn't be more official. Ask old Major Popesnose. He'll tell you. Tell him you have been speaking to Eugene. To Eugene the Garrulous.'

Eugene smiled, and hung up his horse's bridle on a shiny hook for the groom to clean.

'What you think of me old nag?' he said. 'Like a ride one day?'

'I ain't never ridden a horse,' Billy replied.

'Ain't you just?' Eugene laughed, mocking Billy's cockney very badly. 'Well then, chief, thah's a first toime for everythink! Come on—I'll put you up on him now. I'll hold on, don't you worry.'

Next thing Billy knew he was lifted up in a pair of extremely strong arms, swung through the air, out of the tack room and up on to the horse's bare back. The horse took no notice whatsoever.

'You're such a featherweight, nipper—he doesn't even know you're up. Come on, I'll walk you round the yard. Hang on to his mane—you'll be as safe as a house.'

Billy couldn't believe how high up he was, or the lazy power that the horse exuded as he walked around the stable yard, led only on a halter by his master.

'Is this your horse, mister?'

'This is my horse, nipper.'

'But you don't live here.'

'I live here now, nipper. And where I goes, me horse goes too. I brought him over from Ireland with me. Shipped him to Welsh Wales, then put him on a train here. He'll travel in anything. Goes to sleep on the train. Lies down in the van and sleeps like a tired hooligan.'

'He's smashin',' Billy said, leaning forward to pat the horse's neck. 'I never seen such a smashin' horse.'

'Love my horse, love me.' Eugene sighed. 'We are now friends for life, you and I. And that needs celebrating.'

He lifted Billy down, let him lead the great horse into his stable, took off the halter, bolted the heavy wood and iron door and nodded to Billy to follow him.

Billy did as he was told until after a tortuous journey through a labyrinth of underground corridors they emerged into a small wood-panelled room with a fire already alight in the iron grate, three comfortable old leather chairs, a table with a deck of cards scattered all over it and a large half-open cupboard Billy could see was stacked with

260

bottles of drink.

'I imagine what you'll be wanting, nipper, is a good strong lemonade with a thick head on it. Am I your man?'

'Yeah,' Billy agreed gratefully. 'You bet.'

Eugene unstopped the marble at the neck of a fresh bottle of lemonade, half cleaned a glass on the tail of his hunting shirt, and poured Billy a foaming drink. Then he pulled the cork from a bottle of Guinness with his perfect white teeth and raised the bottle in a toast.

'To us,' he said solemnly. 'And all those like us— who are few and very far between. So long live us both.'

'Long live us both,' Billy echoed, already in awe of his new acquaintance. 'What is this place? This where you lives, mister?'

'Nope, nipper. This is not where I lives. This is where I drinks. And this is where I gambles.'

'They don't really know you're 'ere, do they?'

'Sure they don't. Not at all,' Eugene replied, his face very serious now as he tapped the side of his nose. 'And that's our secret. Is it not?'

'They must see you on your 'orse.'

'Ah, they do see me on me 'orse. They do— you're absolutely right. But they think I'm someone else.'

'Someone else? Who?'

'Me uncle. But hush it. Sure you're the only soul in the world that knows that.'

'Yeah?'

'Yeah,' Eugene replied. 'Most definitely yeah. Now away with yous,' he went on, when they'd finished their drinks. 'I have work to do and you must away. Go out that door there, across the yard,

261

in the door opposite, along the corridor and you'll be back in the kitchen of the main house. And remember—you haven't seen me.'

Eugene gave Billy a final wink, one last ruffle of his hair and shooed him out, shutting the door tight behind him.

From the house Billy made his way to the cottage to catch up on his sleep. As he entered he met Kate and Marjorie just leaving to go back to work after lunch.

'Where have you been, young man?' Marjorie asked him. 'We were looking for you. We thought you might be here asleep—but you weren't.'

'I was busy,' Billy said loftily. 'On government business.'

'What sort of government business exactly, Billy?'

'A check-up, if you must know. Just checking on certain people,' Billy replied, assuming an appropriately mysterious air, and beginning to whistle silently.

*   *   *

As everyone else was learning their designated task and settling to their work, Marjorie learned what hers was to be.

Summoned to Major Folkestone's office, which had been set up in the library on the ground floor, she found the major seated at a desk working his way through a file of papers. Without looking up he asked her to come in and sit down. Marjorie took the chair that had been put at the near side of the desk.

'You might be wondering what you're doing

here,' Major Folkestone said finally, closing the file and taking off his spectacles. 'Particularly since most of the rest of the girls are all qualified typists and stenographers and that sort of thing—while you, Miss Hendry, have no particular qualifications whatsoever. At least not pertaining to the sort of work in hand here. Correct?'

'If you say so, Major Folkestone,' Marjorie agreed. 'I was meaning to ask what I could do to help, but never got the chance. Least not so far.'

'Good,' Major Folkestone replied, getting up to stretch his legs and walking towards one of the floor-length sash windows that afforded a wonderful view of the parkland and lake beyond. 'Lucky to be here in a way, wouldn't you agree? Not a bad place to fight a war from. Anyway. Anyway the point is I have a position for you. I don't know how much you know or don't know about this sort of work—or let me put it another way.' He turned from the window to look at her directly. 'I don't know whether or not you were aware of what your late aunt did. The sort of work she did. That sort of thing?'

Marjorie shook her head.

'Other than the fact she had some sort of a job that meant she had to go out at all sorts of odd times, no,' she replied. 'I never asked because I thought it was none of my business, and Aunt Hester never told me.'

'Good. Good. I see. Good.'

'Billy thought she might be a spy.' Marjorie laughed. 'But you know Billy.'

Major Folkestone's eyes opened so wide it was comical. Marjorie bit her lip to stop herself from laughing and looked down at her lap.

263

'Did he?' the major spluttered. 'Did he, by Jove. I see. Yes. I see. Good. Well, little Billy's got no flies on him, has he?'

Marjorie looked up now and saw that Major Folkestone was smiling as well.

'That's exactly what auntie was, as a matter of fact,' he said. 'In a manner of speaking. She worked for Intelligence, and dashed good she was too. She has been working for our side for some good long time—since the Twenties, as a matter of fact—and her colleagues thought very highly of her. Very highly indeed.'

'Billy imagined that it wasn't an accident, that killed Aunt Hester I mean. Billy thought she could have been—well—killed on purpose, because of her work, perhaps.'

Marjorie knew that she was now pushing her luck, but she felt careless of any repercussions that might come from her curiosity, in a way because she liked to think of Aunt Hester as a heroine, and in another way because she had always imagined that Billy's seemingly childish suspicions might have some truth.

'Everyone has their theories,' Major Folkestone replied, clearing his throat. 'It's a free country, anyone can have their theories, whatever they might be, but sometimes it is best to keep them to yourself.'

He stopped smiling and, picking up a wooden ruler from the desk, began to walk about the room, tapping the ruler on the palm of one hand.

'Now listen up, because this is the point, you see,' he began. 'Because of his connection with your late aunt, Mr Ward wanted to make sure you would have somewhere safe to live, since my

264

understanding of the matter is that following the death of your aunt you would have been homeless. However. However, I do not believe in carrying passengers, not at a time like this, just as I am sure you want to make some sort of contribution to the war effort, and the work we are doing here in particular. So given then that you are the niece of one of Mr Ward's top people, and a highly trustworthy young woman—given all that and the fact that I am woefully short of a pair of quick hands, particularly a pair allied to a bright mind—I propose to take you on as my personal assistant, well, dogsbody, if you will. If you want to know what that involves. I have me a first class secretary, but I need an extra pair of reliable hands, so that together with Lily Ormerod, that's my secretary, I dare say we'll make a first rate team. First rate. Any questions?'

'No,' Marjorie said carefully, her mind turning over rapidly as she tried to understand what exactly being a personal assistant or dogsbody would involve, 'I don't think so, sir. I just hope I won't let you down.'

'You won't,' Major Folkestone told her, as he walked back behind his desk to resume his work. 'I'll see to it that you don't. Dismissed.'

Marjorie left the major's office, a high-ceilinged room with beautifully painted walls, gold decoration and early eighteenth-century plasterwork, feeling elated. She turned back as she closed the door behind her and saw the major staring out of the window. He looked strangely small in the room, just as his filing cabinets and desk looked strangely incongruous in the elegant, old-fashioned room. It didn't seem quite possible that soon she would be in and out of that room, helping him with his work in whatever way she was able, helping him to drop agents into France and Belgium, behind enemy lines. She shivered, not because of the war so much, but because of the risks she knew those people would take, unimaginable risks; and when she walked out into the park from the main hall, through the large doors, past the sentries, and stood for a moment on the top step of the flight of shallow stone steps looking across to what were no longer lawns, but fields of long grass, some of which had been divided up into yet more allotments for villagers without gardens to grow their vegetables, she couldn't help wondering how many of the people she could see walking about the grounds would soon be caught and shot—or worse.

*　　　*　　　*

The following weekend Kate was playing tennis with three colleagues from her section. The couple the other side of the net played good country house tennis, capable enough to keep their end up in any ordinary friendly confrontation but way out of their depth against a player of Kate's talent. Over-aware as always of her gift, Kate soft-pedalled as well as she could without looking as though she was patronising her opponents, but even so she wasn't able to bottle up her skills, and she and her partner ran out easy winners.

The victory did not pass unremarked. Most of the game was watched by the man on the huge grey horse, who, returning from a leisurely hack, pulled his mount up on the slope above the tennis court to watch, dropping his reins so that his horse might graze while he sat tall in his saddle, arms folded across his chest and a half-smoked cheroot in his mouth, as Kate turned on the tap in the last set, leading her partner and herself to a resounding victory. After the game had finished, Eugene gathered his reins and urged his horse on into a gentle canter, to finally disappear out of sight behind the screen of great beeches that lined the side of the court.

His presence did not go unnoticed, but then a handsome man on an equally handsome horse appearing on the side of a hill on a fine early spring afternoon is not exactly invisible, particularly to four young women playing tennis on a court nearby, and most particularly to Kate Maddox.

If there was a reason for Kate's sudden determination to conclude the deciding set quickly and imperiously, it was the tall, dark-haired figure on the grey horse.

'Who was *that*?' her partner wondered as they towelled off after the game was over. 'I didn't know there was a mounted section.'

'I am going to demand a transfer straight away,' one of the other girls stated, laughing. 'Even though I don't know one end of a horse from the other.'

'But you do know one end of a man from another.'

Kate said nothing. She had long since looked away from the horseman, pretending he wasn't there, a pretence she intended to keep up until Eugene could no longer bear her indifference. For whatever her father thought of her boyish figure and addiction to tennis, Kate Maddox was after all beautiful, and young, and there was a war on.

*　　　*　　　*

At the end of May, the Nosy Parkers, as the Eden Park girls had decided to jokingly nickname everyone sequestered in the great house and its parkland, learned about the worsening position in France from the bulletin boards and information circulated in their various sections—days in advance of the rest of their countrymen.

'The situation is grim,' Major Folkestone informed his section, which now included Marjorie. 'The British Expeditionary Force and the 7th and 1st French armies have to all intents and purposes been split in two on what should have been their advance into Belgium and there's every danger of their being cut off. Only way out is via Dunkirk, with Calais and Boulogne supplementing it.' He tapped a wall map of Europe with a pointer. 'But we're talking about an impossible evacuation here, as well as one that will have to be effected in a matter of days rather than weeks. On top of that, we ourselves, as you know from the board over there'—he nodded across to a board set about with markers, each one representing an undercover agent—'many of our people are behind enemy lines, some of them in extremely precarious positions, and we have to hope we can somehow get word to them so they can also bail out with the troops—if, that is, we manage to organise a successful escape. The PM has let it be known internally that the position in France is grim. General Gort is already worried that Belgium is on the point of surrender as well as expressing grave doubts as to France's being able to sustain fighting

268

power. So all in all, not a good outlook. Three hundred and fifty thousand of our troops are stranded out there, on top of which our intercepts show that in the last week the enemy appear to have made their codes denser, so that is, alas, a further headache.'

*   *   *

Mrs Alderman was quite quiet, for Mrs Alderman, until Major Folkestone, after a night spent torn between his many wartime duties, appeared suddenly at what Mrs Alderman always thought of as *her* kitchen door.

'You look like something Pussikins just brought in,' she told the major informatively.

The major looked over at the cat who was curled up in front of the old kitchen range.

'At least he's able to have a sleep, Mrs Alderman,' he remarked, looking at the picture of contentment with some envy.

'I expect you'd like your usual breakfast, would you? A soft-boiled farm egg from one of our hens, some of my home-baked bread, and some farm butter and syrup, wouldn't you? No sugar, but plenty of syrup. Want some porridge too, I dare say?'

'I will have everything you set in front of me, Mrs Alderman.'

The major sat down, steadying himself suddenly at the table as he did so. Billy was seated opposite him.

'Aren't you meant to be at school, Billy?' he asked, for want of something better to say, after suppressing a large yawn.

269

'It's half term, Major Folkestone.'

'It's always half term with you, Billy Hendry,' Mrs Alderman scolded him. 'Mind you, the amount of homework he gets given I'm surprised he's not feeling as tired as you, Major Folkestone.'

'What's up then? Too much set work? Want any help, young man?' The major squinted down at Billy's exercise books, which Billy immediately covered with the upper half of his body, laughing.

'Don't look, sir. Please!'

'Come on, Billy. What is it? Don't say you've put something I shouldn't see in your homework book, because if that's the case I'll have to have you thrown into my prison down in the dungeons here.'

'You wouldn't really, would you, sir? What a wheeze. I've never been in a dungeon, or a prison.'

At that Billy straightened up, and Major Folkestone seized his opportunity, and grabbed his homework. As soon as the major saw what was written out in the exercise book his expression changed and he turned accusing eyes on Billy.

'Billy. What are you doing here, please? What is this?'

Billy reddened to the point of feeling his face was on fire.

'It's only a joke, sir. I saw what Marjorie was helping you with last night, and, you know—I thought I'd have a go.'

'This isn't a joke, Billy. This is Top Secret, and you could get into terrible trouble. Don't you ever do this again, do you hear? I can't allow you to play about in my office with Marjorie working there on the files, if this is the kind of thing you get up to— snooping.'

'I—I—I'm awful sorry, sir. I just thought it was

some fun.'

Mrs Alderman immediately felt for Billy, who was looking as if he wished he could drop dead in front of his hero, so she quickly placed a plate of delicious-looking porridge down in front of Major Folkestone, and handed him a small jug of fresh cream.

'Let the poor lad off, sir. He doesn't mean it, really he doesn't. The truth is he is more than good at them codes, see if he isn't. He's like our father with the crosswords; he's cracking, even if he is eighty-five. No trouble for him whatsoever. The same for the young lad here. You should see some of the conclusions young Billy comes to, my dear; it fair turns your head to see him once he's off with one of those. *And* he invents his own and all, he does.'

Mrs Alderman ruffled Billy's hair for no better reason than to show that she was on his side, while Billy ducked away from her and continued to stare at the major, who had at least begun to wolf his porridge.

'Ridiculous!' he barked before filling his mouth once more. 'Quite ridiculous!'

Mrs Alderman sighed and shook her head.

'It's not ridiculous, Major Folkestone, if you don't mind my saying so. It's Billy. Some people, now . . .' She searched around for another example of extraordinary powers. 'Some people, take my uncle, well, he was like that, he could tell you the result of a horse race before it finished, some people they're like that, quick as a flash. Billy here, he can do numbers and codes and all that. I never have to time his egg of a morning, and that's the truth. Four minutes to the second he will put his

271

hand up, and by George and by jingo, Major Folkestone, four minutes it is. Instead of telling him off, my dear, why don't you *let* him off? You should let him have a go, my dear. You'd be surprised.'

Major Folkestone gave Mrs Alderman a brief look. She had never called him 'my dear' before, and he wasn't quite sure that he liked it. On the other hand, he wasn't such a fool as to think that he could tell off a cook in her own kitchen, and her food being of the kind that would melt the hearts of kings and emperors he settled for ignoring the innovation.

'Ridiculous,' he said, wiping his mouth with a napkin. 'Ridiculous.'

'It was just a thought, sir,' Mrs Alderman said. 'But in case you think I'm daft as a Somerset cider drinker, look at that, then.'

She held up another of Billy's exercise books.

'I won't look at it,' the major told her, taking it from her. 'But I will appropriate it, thank you. And don't you ever do this again, young man.'

'No, sir.'

'And where are you going now?'

'To school, sir.'

'I should think so too.'

*   *   *

Nearly a week later, on his return from school, Billy found Major Folkestone waiting for him in the kitchens of the main house. It was hardly a surprise for the major, since he knew Billy invariably headed straight there to scrounge what he could from Mrs Alderman—usually a glass of

272

home-made ginger beer and a slice of equally home-made fruit cake—but it came as a shock to Billy to discover that on this particular afternoon Major Folkestone was there before him, enjoying a slice of newly baked sponge cake as well as a welcome cup of tea.

'Good afternoon, Billy. And there's no need to back out of the kitchen just because I'm here,' the major announced, patting his mouth in his usual precise way with his napkin.

'Afternoon, sir.'

The major finished his cake and his cup of tea, watched by a silent, subdued Billy, and then, taking a sheet of paper out of an envelope, he put it on the kitchen table in front of him.

'What do you make of that then, Billy? Something? Anything? Or nothing?'

Billy hesitated, looking nervously at the major, suspecting some trick.

'Go ahead, Billy, go ahead.'

Billy picked up the piece of paper. 'It's not in English, sir, so that's easy enough.' He frowned at the paper and traced the words with one finger.

'How do you know that?'

'I dunno, sir. I just do. It ain't in English, that's all I know.'

'That's all?'

'Give us a mo, sir. I mean I've hardly had a dekko,' Billy told him with the sudden authority of someone who is really concentrating on the matter in hand.

'Very well. Take as long as you like. Just because we need to know by tomorrow morning doesn't mean that I am going to rush you.'

Billy looked up.

'Can I keep this, sir?'

'Afraid not. Top Secret, old chap.'

'Is this German?'

'You tell me.'

'Dunno what German looks like. But it certainly ain't English.'

Billy leaned on the table, his chin on his two fists while he stared at the sheet of paper.

'This could take days, sir,' he said with a sigh. 'Then I still might not be able to crack it. Are you sure I can't have it for a bit, sir? I could take it over to the cottage, and—'

'I can't do that, Billy,' the major interrupted. 'Sorry. But there it is.'

Billy looked at him sideways with sudden cunning. 'You could if you made me swear to the Act, sir.'

Major Folkestone cyed him back, and then straightened himself up.

'Give me that, lad,' he said, holding out his hand for the paper. 'And come with me.'

Billy hopped after him, bursting with excitement.

'You're too young to sign anything, but I shall read this to you, and you may read, mark and inwardly digest this, young man, and remember if you let down your country you let me down, and if you let me down, you let down Marjorie.'

The major read him the relevant clauses of the Act. Billy swallowed hard and hopped from one leg to the other in his agitation before taking the proffered envelope and legging it back to the cottage where he immediately locked himself in his bedroom and wouldn't even come out for his dinner when Marjorie and Kate called him.

'You can't come in!' he yelled. 'I'm engaged in

274

government business!'

Marjorie pulled an amazed face to Kate, who shook her head and laughed.

'Something tells me we're sharing quarters with one of England's secret weapons.'

As it turned out Kate Maddox wasn't that far off the mark, and England's secret weapon, based securely at Eden Park in Kent, was about to make quite an auspicious debut.

*　　　*　　　*

The following morning, long before breakfast, Billy staggered out of his bedroom, clutching the all-important piece of paper and one of his exercise books full of hieroglyphics.

With both the girls still sleeping he cut himself a piece of bread. Quickly spreading it with home farm butter, and some of Mrs Alderman's home-made raspberry jam, he rammed his still socked feet into his shoes and stumbled off to find Major Folkestone without even bothering to do up his laces. He tripped over them twice as he hurried across the courtyard, scuffing both his knees and the palm of one hand, but despite this he hardly seemed to find the need to pause, so set was he on finding the major and telling him what he had discovered.

When he finally arrived in the great hall of the main house he realised he hadn't an idea of where to look for the Major at such an early hour of the morning. Fortunately the soldier on sentry duty at the front door knew where his CO slept, and in answer to Billy's urgent pleading directed the boy upstairs to the major's sleeping quarters.

Major Folkestone was shaving at a hand-basin in the corner of the room, in his short-sleeved vest with his braces hanging down from his army trousers, half his face still covered with a layer of thick white shaving soap.

'Got some news, have you, lad?' the major wondered, watching Billy in his shaving mirror. 'Find anything out?'

'I found out what sort of code this is, sir,' he said, waving the envelope. 'It's a double substitution and a—I don't know what you'd call it.'

'Don't follow you, young Billy.'

The major shaved the area just under his nose carefully then rinsed off the last of the soap.

'Care to explain?' he went on, as he towelled off his face and wandered over to sit at a flimsy card table under the window that held a bowl of shrivelling fruit and a nearly empty bottle of whisky. 'Park yourself down, and tell me what you know, Billy.'

'The double substitution thing's easy. You take a letter, see? Such as G.' Billy had his exercise book open and was tapping a line of letters and figures he had written in one margin. 'But instead of making G equal I dunno—let's say you use T. Then working the alphabet from there—which would be dead easy—you takes G to equal T but then you makes T equal something else. You got to find that, course—and I mean, I think I have. I think their G equals T, then far as I can see—'cos I don't speak the lingo which is a bit of bish—T equals E. It's a double code, see? Each letter having two equals, I'd say, see?'

'Two values,' Major Folkestone said tactfully, as if Billy knew the word but had simply forgotten to

276

say it. 'Go on—this is most interesting.'

'Course it ain't as easy as that, is it?' Billy complained, scratching the side of his head with a pencil. 'The Nazis aren't going to send coded messages—least not important coded messages—in just a double-sub code that kids like me can crack. There's something else what I can't work out, sir. What I always look for, ever since I first started this at school, is the repetition thing. You know—the stuff they all think's so brilliant at school—it's dead easy, all you have to look for is shape. Little words—like *the* and *and* and *for*—and you work on those to see which is which then get the letters that way. I can't explain it very well, but that's what I do. Kids just do letter codes, but they don't code sentences. I do though. That's why they can never crack my codes,' he added, giving a proud sigh. 'Least not that I know of, anyway.'

'I don't follow,' Major Folkestone told him excitedly, buttoning up his shirt wrong. 'How do you code a sentence?'

'By sticking the short words on to long words— or a bit of a word on to the next word. That sort of thing. And I think that's what they've gone and done 'ere. 'Cept I can't work it out 'cos I don't know German.'

'Can I see that?' Major Folkestone took Billy's exercise book and examined what the boy had written out on the pages subsequent to the decoding columns. Even with his limited knowledge of German, the major could identify portions of enough words to indicate that Billy had certainly managed to get past the first two stages of the code and was all but through the third stage.

'You've done extraordinarily well, Billy,' Major

277

Folkestone said, standing up and going to fetch his tie and Sam Browne belt. 'Remarkable work, young Billy. I'll see you get mentioned in despatches.'

'Ta,' Billy said with his sudden brilliant smile. 'That is, I mean—thank you, sir.'

'Ta will do just fine, Billy.' Major Folkestone nodded solemnly. 'Don't mind ta at all. Now you're not to say anything about this, not even to Marjorie. Not until I come back to you. It's difficult to explain why—but you must understand we've got a lot of bright sparks working on this thing here, and if word gets out you're running rings round them, it's going to come over very badly.'

'Mum's the word.'

'This won't go unnoticed, Billy, I promise you that. As I said, I'll see you get mentioned in despatches.'

The major smiled approvingly at him, after which he tapped him lightly on the head with his swagger stick and hurried out of the room. Billy scratched the top of his head, and then gave a sudden, vast, relieved yawn as his tiredness finally and at last caught up with him.

Back in the cottage he curled up in his bed and fell fast asleep in his clothes. Marjorie tried to rouse him, but Billy firmly pronounced himself dead to the world, and fell back once again into a deep sleep.

'I'll send a sick note to your teacher,' Marjorie muttered, before hurrying off to work in the main house.

Two hours later, Major Folkestone had the results for which he had been hoping on his desk. Section C, the decrypting specialists, had finished the work Billy had so enthusiastically started, and decoded the message in full.

*   *   *

Although Billy was never to know it, it was a vital breakthrough. The relevant message unveiled the German plan to take advantage of the wedge they had driven between the British and Belgian troops in an area between Ypres and Menin. This critical piece of information was relayed at once to British High Command, with the result that they were able to redirect two divisions to help block the developing breach that could well have proved fatal in the event of any evacuation.

Despite this reprieve, three days later the Dunkirk perimeter was finally cut off, leaving over three hundred and fifty thousand troops and possibly an even greater number of civilians isolated on an area of only a hundred square miles.

*   *   *

'There wouldn't seem to be any way out for them now, sir,' Marjorie said to Major Folkestone as a group from his section stood surveying the updated map. 'There's only sand to the north and sea to the south.'

'And Jerry has it all covered,' Major Folkestone replied. 'Every road in the area can be commanded by enemy artillery fire, so all he has to do is keep shooting and drive us all into the sea. It all looks pretty damn' bleak. Particularly since on top of it all, there are goodness knows how many military vehicles and all important supplies on those beaches. We're looking at possible heavy losses all

279

round here.'

But since it was not the job of anyone at Eden Park to help decide strategy but just to pass on to the War Office any information they might garner that might be helpful or instructive, all everyone could do was maintain a watching brief, while working on any messages they might intercept from the enemy.

In the early hours of one morning, Kate, who was on a late shift, picked up a message that was being transmitted from behind enemy lines to a receiver somewhere in London. It was coded and so she sent it at once to Section C, who had little trouble in decrypting the information now they had successfully decoded the earlier and extremely vital message that had been passed on to them. Once she had been handed back the translated message, Kate hurried down to Major Folkestone's office. He too was working into the early hours as everyone gave their maximum effort to try to help the rapidly deteriorating situation on the French shores.

'I don't think this can really be so,' the major said after he had carefully read the message not once but three times. 'No, I really don't go for this at all.'

'I'm assured it's an absolutely correct decryption, sir,' Kate said, standing the other side of his desk.

'I don't mean that, Kate,' Major Folkestone replied. 'Of course it's bona fide—what I mean is I don't believe Herr Hitler is going to allow us to escape in the hope of our making a quick and convenient peace. At least, if he is, then he's got another think coming.'

'But why hasn't the enemy tested our defences,

sir? They only seem to have had a go at the south-western section, and not bothered with any other areas.'

'Maybe Herr Hitler believes fat Hermann when he says that his air force is so mighty it can simply wipe us all off the map there single-handed. If so, he hasn't allowed for our boys. None the less, this information must be passed on immediately, and what we must concentrate on is trying to find out to whom Jerry was broadcasting.'

'So far I understand the trace shows London definitely, and possibly a receiver somewhere in Mayfair.'

'Hmm. Someone somewhere is operating from London, some Nazi agent.'

The next day, in response to governmental urging, an armada of little ships set sail from English ports all along the southern coast in the hope of helping transport the retreating forces from the French shore to the naval ships waiting in deeper waters. They succeeded triumphantly, helping three hundred and forty thousand British, French and Belgian soldiers.

The cost was high, since two hundred and fifty of the thousand little ships that made up the rescue force were blown up and sunk with all hands. Besides this civilian and naval loss there was the terrible cost in weapons, ammunition and vehicles that had to be abandoned, fired or blown up so they would not fall into the advancing enemy hands. At the final reckoning, on the sandy shores of northern France lay the wrecks of near one hundred thousand vehicles, from tanks to motorcycles, to armoured vehicles of every kind. Two and a half thousand artillery guns, and half a million tons of ammunition, a seemingly unsustainable loss to the outnumbered and overwhelmed British Expeditionary Force and its few allies.

'The French garrison in Dunkirk has surrendered,' Major Folkestone told the Nosy Parkers at his briefing on the morning of 3 June. 'I imagine it won't be long before the whole country follows. I also imagine it won't be very long until Italy decides to get into bed with Germany, and if I'm right we're going to be standing alone. If this is the case, then rather than be downhearted we shall not redouble our efforts to prevail—we shall increase them one hundred fold. I am equally sure I express the wishes of everyone present when I say that we will probably be better going it alone, isolated as we are from the rest of Europe, and we can only thank God from the bottom of our hearts that we are an island.'

Someone shouted a *hear hear!* from the back of the great hall, an affirmation that was immediately followed by a hearty three cheers. But although everyone left the hall full of determination to work and fight ever harder, they all knew full well that, as their Prime Minister had said, while Dunkirk was a splendid deliverance, wars were not won by evacuation.

'Pretty grim, eh?' Marjorie commented to Kate as they prepared to return to work. 'If what Major Folkestone says is true—'

'Which I think it is, I'm afraid,' Kate chipped in.

'Then if ever there's a chance of us being invaded—'

'This is it.'

The two young women looked at each other, putting on their bravest faces. Both of them knew

282

that across the Channel the mighty Luftwaffe was preparing to bomb and blitz their towns and cities, paving the way for the inevitable invasion.

Sitting huddled in the lifesaving warmth of a thick blanket in the tiny cabin of one of the rescuing small craft headed back for England's shores, a young man sat silently contemplating his escape. Cut off well behind the enemy lines in the town of St Dix which he had failed to reach in time to contact Section H as hoped, he had very little idea of what was happening ahead of him, although he could see from his hiding place the massive movement of German troops headed north-east towards the coast of France. Imagining this must be the build-up to the expected invasion, he had kept low until it seemed that all troop movements had finished.

He waited another two hours buried behind bales of straw at the top of one of the farmer's huge barns near the road the Germans had been using to transport their soldiers, tanks and artillery; waited until the dust from the huge convoys had settled before making any move.

Unsure of where to go and quite what to do and without hope of another opportunity to make contact with his section, he reckoned that the only way home for him was also to head for the coast and try to find a breach in the enemy lines through which he might pass unnoticed. He knew it was only a slim chance; in fact as he began to walk through the countryside keeping the coast road to his right and a constant watch and ear out for any sight or sound of approaching traffic he knew his chances of making it home were all but non-existent—until he heard the sound of a motor bicycle approaching from behind.

Diving into the ditch and drawing his service revolver at the same time he looked back down the road to see a German despatch rider heading for the coast. He could see the messenger was alone, but moving too fast for him to be able to fire at him with any degree of success, until he heard the bike coming to a halt, and saw the rider lift a cigarette packet out of his top pocket, and start to light up. Knowing that he was being presented with a perfect piece of luck, he aimed his revolver and fired, hitting his target in the head with satisfactory accuracy.

As he dragged the dead messenger into the ditch to strip him of his uniform and papers he knew this was not just a piece of luck, it was also his only chance of salvation.

Less than half an hour later he had caught up with the last line of advancing Germans. Happily for him no one paid the slightest attention other than to wave him through in response to the evident urgency of his demeanour. Once out of sight of the advancing battalion, he turned his bike to head north-east rather than due north, guessing that since he had been specifically directed to proceed to a position west of Dunkirk, and since he had gathered from previous messages that the British Expeditionary Force was headed in that direction, his only chance of getting through the German lines was to hope that the British and their allies had a line of solid defence around that part of the coast.

Some time later he reached a gap near Nieuport just before General Brooke's II Corps closed it. Now, dressed as a German despatch rider, he feared that his luck was on the verge of being

285

reversed. Happily he was able to dump the stolen motorcycle, along with his German uniform. Without the motorbike, and dressed once more as a Frenchman, he tied a white handkerchief to a stick, and hoped to God none of the British soldiers he was facing was in the mood for indulging in some free target practice.

Captured minutes after making himself apparent, he was taken straight to the Commanding Officer who interrogated him for some minutes before becoming sufficiently convinced of his bona fide standing. Which was how he found himself just one of the thousands waiting and hoping to be rescued from the vast sandbanks lining that part of the French coast.

The next day, having survived devastating bombardment, and witnessed the annihilation of so many of the patient soldiers who waited on the beach beside him, knowing they were sitting ducks for the Luftwaffe, he found himself on board a small fishing smack that had set sail from the little port of Bexham in West Sussex.

Two hours later he was finally ashore in his homeland, filthy, exhausted and quite unable to believe his good fortune.

A further six hours later, after another debriefing, a good wash, a change of clothes and his first meal in two days, having been given final clearance, Scott Meynell headed as quickly as he could for Eden Park, where his young life was destined to take a wholly unpredictable turn.

CHAPTER TWELVE

Following the evacuation of Dunkirk, everyone's thoughts were concentrated on not just the possibility of invasion but the moment it might be due. No longer was it something to be put at the back of people's minds, a dread but a distant one, as in the days before the evacuation of the British Expeditionary Force when everyone imagined that while Hitler might wish to invade their homeland, as long as there was an army, a Navy and an air force to protect them the former Austrian housepainter would think twice before launching an all-out assault across the Channel.

But now with so much invaluable military equipment lying abandoned and burned out on the nearby French beaches, and with the Expeditionary Force returned home dispirited and all but defeated in their own minds, a feeling of inevitability settled over the nation as everyone tried to avoid the thought that it was only a matter of time before they heard the crash of jackboots on the streets, the rumble of tanks across the countryside and the sound of blitzing bombers arriving in ferocious numbers.

Every precaution was immediately taken to try to thwart, hinder and bewilder any invading force. Not a signpost anywhere was left standing in its original position, all being either taken away or falsely aligned. Every town sign was removed and every railway station name was painted out. Travelling became a nightmare, particularly by train where in blacked-out conditions, unless passengers were familiar enough with their route to be able to count their stops, many who were not so fortunate found themselves getting off at wrong stations, and trying vainly to find their way home in pitch darkness.

Yet somehow everyone kept going, supported by Churchill's ever-growing outward pugnacity.

Of course, like everyone else, the Nosy Parkers at Eden Park all lived in dread of an invasion, imagining time and again that every sound they heard in the night might be the enemy at the door.

One night Marjorie, Kate and Billy were all awoken by the sound of steady trampling on the gravel path that ran under their bedroom windows.

'Shsh!'

Kate turned the light on and stared at Marjorie.

'My God, they're here, Marjorie. They're at the door.'

Marjorie went to say something in return.

'Shsh!'

The sound was undeniable. It was most definitely that of tramping soldiers, and it seemed they were now knocking at the back door. The sound rang out loud and clear, and Marjorie lost all colour, knowing as they both did that this must be *it*.

Although their knees were turning to jelly, and their insides to water, the young women knew just what they had to do. They had to be prepared to kill, or die, or both.

Grabbing the weapons they always left ready by their beds—in Marjorie's case a bread knife and in Kate's an antique policeman's truncheon which she had found only lately in an old outhouse—they found that Billy had beaten them both to it. When

288

they collided with him downstairs they found him standing at the front door with a pitchfork in one hand, a bed-knob in the other and an impish smile on his face.

'It's only a couple of goats,' he said. 'They must have got out of their field!'

Kate and Marjorie, still trembling with the shock of thinking that they had been about to have to tackle a platoon of Nazi soldiers, followed the line of Billy's hand and saw not two but three goats happily ensconced in front of the kitchen drying rail. At the sound of Billy's voice they had turned their bearded faces towards their night-dressed visitors, to be greeted with a yell of indignation from Kate.

'Stop that!'

However, the goats busily eating the girls' underwear were most reluctant to give up their prize.

'Wonderful,' Kate exclaimed, as Marjorie opened the back door to shoo the animals out. 'They nearly gave me heart failure.'

'Me too!' Billy laughed. 'I thought sure as anythin' it was the Nazis come up the drive to murder us in our beds.'

'Wonder what we *would* have done if they had been Germans,' Marjorie said, shoving the last of their unwelcome visitors back into the night as Kate closed the kitchen door.

'Gone for 'em of course, given them what for,' Billy replied. 'I'd have run 'em through with me fork before they could say *Heil Hitler*.'

'Course you would, Billy,' Kate agreed, steering him back to his bedroom. 'They wouldn't have known what hit them.'

289

Ten minutes later Billy was back fast asleep dreaming of repelling the Hun from Eden Park single-handed, while along the corridor Kate and Marjorie lay wide awake, finding themselves quite unable to go back to sleep, both their minds full of images of war and invasion, most particularly of what might actually happen to young women like them if they ever found themselves in the hands of enemy troops.

*   *   *

Poppy meanwhile had finished what she thought of as her second coming-out, although this time the end product was altogether different from the shy and reticent debutante of the previous year. In place of the apparently timid and bespectacled wallflower, which was how she saw herself in her previous incarnation, in her looking glass Poppy now saw a haughty, disdainful, beautifully dressed and extremely poised young woman, the sort of female who could and would move easily in the ever critical ranks of Society, most particularly the sophisticated echelons to which she was being directed.

'You are all those things and more, my dear,' Cissie assured her as they lunched one day in a private first floor room in a house off Curzon Street. 'You are also, I am happy to say, extremely beautiful. You'll be turning heads the moment you walk into all their wretched, treacherous little lives, doncher know. How does one feel oneself, eh? Inside out with nerves, or just so far in it doesn't matter?'

'It still feels odd, and very strange,' Poppy said,

in her new, measured and deliberately flattened voice. 'Because deep down I'm still me—very much so—yet as soon as I concentrate, I become her at once. I mean I even find one *thinks* like her—which is really rather too much.'

'Delighted to hear, my dear,' Cissie said, lighting up a cigarette between courses as always. 'Thing you want is to start dreamin' like her. Once you start dreamin' like the wretched creature, you're home and hosed. D'you see? When one's learning a new language, which is what one is doing now, one knows one hasn't conquered it until one dreams in it, and the same with undercover work. When you're dreaming as Diona de Donnet, then you know for sure that the character has taken over your whole being, which is really what is wanted, to my mind. At least that is what I always found when out in the field.'

Cissie's occasional references of this nature served to remind Poppy that her mentor knew exactly what she was going through, and as a result they also made her feel that she was not being called on to do something that the caller hadn't done. It was mildly salutary, and as such it worked.

'When do I actually start what one might call the real work, Miss Lavington?' Poppy enquired. 'And when will I know what it is one's expected to do?'

'They're sending a chap up from the Park. He's going to be your entrée. He's a very experienced agent, just back from abroad where he's been working for the last couple of years. Soon as he's been dusted down, he'll be directed up here, one gathers, and then you're off and runnin'.'

'Good. The sooner the better as far as I'm concerned. I don't want to get rusty.'

'You won't, my dear. You won't. I shall see you won't, don't you worry.'

*　　*　　*

While Major Folkestone was questioning Scott in preparation for his next assignment, Kate was taking advantage of her half day, it being fine and sunny, to get in some tennis practice. Standing down the south end of the court and hitting services into the right hand box, she failed to notice that she was being observed from behind a light screen of trees that ran along the back of the court.

After watching Kate with some interest for a few minutes, Eugene ambled slowly round until he came into her line of vision.

'Devastating,' he called, clapping enthusiastically. 'Simply and quite utterly devastating. Wish I could hit 'em like that.'

'Thank you!' Kate called back formally.

'Quite a player you are! And that's to be sure! Yes, ma'am—quite an old player you are indeed!'

Eugene was holding on to the side netting, aware as he did so that it must give him the appearance of a monkey in a zoo.

'You'd never give us a lesson, I suppose?'

Kate stopped, showing every appearance of reluctance, until she saw he was standing swishing a tired-looking tennis racket.

'I brought me own racket,' he called. 'See? Me own racket. Just in case.'

'You knew I was here?'

'Sure the whole place is a nest of spies, is it not? There's nothing nobody doesn't know about no one here, and that's equally for sure. Of course I

292

knew you were here, Miss Kate Maddox. Why else would I be here?'

Eugene strolled on to the court. He was wearing tennis shoes, a pair of old cricket trousers tied up with a striped tie, and a cricket jumper with a V of red, black and green stripes at the neck.

'You obviously play,' Kate remarked, immediately becoming aware that it was a pretty stupid remark, but for no reason she could name the tall dark-haired man made her feel strangely shy.

'A cat may look at a king,' Eugene replied enigmatically. 'If I carried a crown would that make me royal?'

'Do you play? Is that a better way to put it?'

'I play after a fashion. Not after your fashion, madam, but after my own.'

'Do you really want a lesson, or are you just fooling around?'

'Me?' Eugene now managed a look of total outrage. 'Me—fool around? That would hardly be a gentlemanly thing to do at all now, would it?'

'First we have to establish whether or not you are a gentleman.'

'The name is Eugene *Hackett*,' he replied, giving a mock courtly bow. 'There has never been anyone in our family who was not a gentleman. Except the women, and they were all ladies, to a man.'

Kate did her best not to laugh but found it difficult, so to hide her amusement she turned round and pretended to sort out some tennis balls in the boxes on the umpire's chair.

'Very well,' she said, once she knew she had won the struggle not to show that he had won. 'If you really want a lesson—'

'I really want a lesson, madam,' he interrupted her, essaying an odd stabbing shot with his racket. 'And as I get better, here's hoping the need for lessons will lessen and lessen. On your marks!' he cried, bounding off like a foolish hare to the baseline.

Kate walked slowly back to her end and looked over the net at her pupil who was swishing away on his line as if being attacked by a horde of giant flies. Every now and then he would leap clumsily into the air as if to swat the largest of the insects attacking him, before resuming his bunny hops at the back of the court. Kate hit a ball gently at him, dropping it at just the right distance in front of him to allow him every chance of an easy return. Lining the shot up with his racket held high over his shoulder, Eugene missed it by yards, nearly toppling over with his effort.

'Oh, hard luck, Yoogie!' he called. 'Hard cheese on me, wouldn't you say?'

'Take it slower,' Kate advised, coming to the net. 'Look—take your racket back like this, dropping the head so—then come up under the ball and through. See?'

'Nope.' Eugene frowned back at her. 'Perhaps if you came round here and showed it me?'

Kate eyed him then walked round to his side of the net. She stood by his side, demonstrating first the perfect forehand and then the perfect backhand. Eugene it seemed could manage neither.

'Perhaps if you stood behind me and kind of nursed my arm through it, that might help?'

Kate nearly fell into the trap, seeing it just as she was about to wrap her arms round Eugene's waist.

294

'I think it's probably just as effective if you watch what I do,' she said primly. 'And then imitate it.'

'Very well,' Eugene sighed. 'You're the teacher, teach.'

Oncc she thought she had his forehand in some sort of shape, Kate returned to her side of the net to lob some more balls at him. This time he managed to get nearly half of them back, and after about half an hour was managing to hit some backhands as well, although not with any accuracy whatsoever.

'Do you want me to try to do anything about that serve of yours?' she asked without much hope, having seen him throw the ball up and miss on practically every occasion.

'Depends whether you can spare me the next year of your life, teach!' Eugene called back cheerfully. 'Perhaps you'd better leave me alone to work on it! Even so—just for devilment—let's have a wee game, shall we? Just to see how good your coaching is?'

Kate shrugged and knocked half a dozen balls down to him.

'You start,' she said from the net, collecting another set of balls with her feet and lobbing them over to him. 'Suppose I give you two points game start? Fair?'

'Suppose you do,' he wondered. 'Isn't that rather a lot to catch up?'

'Let that be my worry!'

Kate bounced the last remaining ball once with her racket, then crashed it down past him with a classic forehand passing shot.

'Love all—thirty love to you—first service!' she chirped.

Eugene frowned at her as if trying to focus on both her and the lines, then, changing his racket from his right hand to his left, prepared to serve.

'What are you doing?' Kate wondered, advancing off the base line towards the net. 'You're not going to play left-*handed*?'

'I am!' Eugene called back. 'Haven't you seen how useless I am with me right?'

Kate didn't even see his first service, or indeed his second. She saw very little of the ball at all in fact as Eugene romped to a 6–2, 6–1 victory.

She said nothing at all during the game, realising after the first two aces that she had been well and truly taken, concentrating instead on keeping her end up, but she was never in the game with a chance. Eugene was all over her. He had every shot in the book and a few more on top. He was agile, extremely fast and above all highly skilled, far and away the best tennis player she had ever played against. Finally, at the end of the concluding set, she sat on her chair with a towel to her face trying to get her breath back as Eugene, as cool as he was when he began, lit a cigarette and strolled about the court singing a ballad in what she could only suppose was Gaelic.

'I take it you thought that was funny,' she said from behind her towel. 'Though personally, I can't exactly see the joke.'

'It's a private thing,' Eugene said. 'And I have to say I'm enjoying it.'

'Why couldn't you just have come clean and said you can play?'

'That I can what? That I can *play*? I'll have you know, missie, you are looking at the ex-Junior Champion of All Ireland.'

'I thought you just played that game with a stick and ball.'

'And ran around saying *begob* and *begorrah*.' Eugene laughed. 'That's half the fun of it really. Playing it close to your chest. Not showing your hand.'

'Making a fool of someone.'

'Oh, come on!' Eugene looked genuinely hurt. 'I wouldn't ever make a fool of you, Kate. You're a damned good player. Sorry—I mean a *dashed* good player. I mean it—you're the best girl I've ever played, and I've played a few.'

'I'm sure.' Kate finished towelling herself dry, and pulled on her sweater.

'Ah, come *on*! No hard feelings!'

'*No hard feelings?*' Kate echoed. 'On the contrary, tons of hard feelings! And with knobs on!'

'With *knobs on* bedad!' He laughed as she walked off feeling thoroughly humiliated. 'With knobs on no less!'

'Oh, *go away*!' Kate muttered through clenched teeth, banging her racket against her legs. 'Go away and stay away. Why did you have to go and *spoil* everything?'

Behind her, abandoned on the tennis court, Eugene let the expression on his face change entirely as he watched the elegant blonde figure of Kate stride away from him, wishing from the bottom of his heart that it hadn't been necessary to make an enemy of Kate Maddox.

'But it was, Eugene old fellow,' he muttered to himself as he ambled back towards his quarters. 'It was, it was, it was—and you damn' well know it. Alas.'

The church bells woke them all. Had they just been the bells in the village church the Nosy Parkers would have taken a lot longer to be roused, but since there was a private chapel in the grounds with its own set of bells the sound woke everyone almost immediately.

Everyone knew what it meant: invasion! The use of church bells had been banned for months, so that in the event of an invasion their ringing would be the ultimate signal that the Germans had landed. Everyone pulled on the clothes that had been left folded on the bottom of their beds for precisely this moment. There was no yawning, no grumbling, as would be normal when roused from sleep. Everyone simply dressed as quickly as they could before heading for their assembly points.

In the great hall both men and women fell in under their section numbers, which were displayed on large cardboard squares pinned to various parts of the walls. Those pre-appointed to collect all files did so before joining the guardian platoon of soldiers assembled outside the front doors armed and ready, the safety catches for once already off their rifles.

'Silence!' Major Folkestone barked as he marshalled his troops. 'You know the orders! Complete and utter silence at all times!'

Kate couldn't help raising her eyes to heaven at the incongruity of their CO's commanding silence, since no one in the hall had actually uttered a sound, most of them being far too frightened to do more than stare around them, wondering if they were about to see Nazi uniforms coming through the doors. Major Folkestone and his three NCOs led their allocated sections out of the great hall and along the completely darkened passageways, the whole house observing a total blackout.

Lines of string had been fixed along the walls of the corridors to facilitate any evacuation that might take place at night, the last in line being deputed to undo the guidelines from their fixings and collect all the string up rather than leave it in place for the enemy, although why any invading army might need to be guided around a mansion by lines of string Kate was unable to imagine. None the less, orders were orders, and it being wartime no more was said. So as the lines of refugees tiptoed as silently as possible, given their heavy walking shoes and army boots, down the labyrinth of corridors and out of the house, those bringing up the rear hurriedly undid and rewound hundreds of feet of twine.

Once outside the house, everyone found themselves being ordered by signal only to proceed in various directions across the parkland. Marjorie, Kate and Billy's group headed for the dense woodland to the north side of the lake. At least half a dozen in each group had been issued with a homemade weapon before leaving the house. Marjorie found herself armed with a pike made out of a long broom handle with a sharpened blade fashioned from a cutter taken off a piece of old farm machinery, and Kate had a knobkerrie made similarly of a broomstick with a large brass bedknob at the business end. Billy now carried their trusty bread knife on loan from the cottage kitchen, and having spent some happy mornings knifing some of last season's marrows he felt that he would make a good job of despatching any Nazi that crossed his path.

Lily, meanwhile, had been armed with a stone-filled ballcock attached to a length of chain. She now stopped and started to laugh.

'Just look at us! Really. We look like something from some medieval army. Gracious heavens, Jerry is going to run when he sees us, isn't he? Bedknobs, bread knives and broom handles. They're going to take to the hills when they see us, aren't they?'

'That's enough of that, Lily Ormerod,' Kate muttered. 'You're beginning to sound like the Duke of Wellington surveying his troops before the Battle of Waterloo.'

They all turned and stared at her for a second.

'He said, *I don't know what they'll do to Napoleon, but they certainly scare me*. Or something like it anyway.'

'Humph. The Iron Duke on his dark grey horse—'

'I like men on grey horses,' Kate announced apropos of nothing in particular as she carefully avoided an overhanging branch.

Section H was signalled to a halt deep in the middle of the thick woodland.

'Dash it,' Lily moaned, as she examined her legs. 'There goes my last pair of stockings.'

'Hush!' Major Folkestone told her, having walked down the ranks to where they were standing. 'Hush. Or I'll have you up on a charge, Miss Ormerod. No one wants to know about your stockings at this moment in our island's history.'

'Don't you believe it,' Lily muttered once he had returned to the top of the waiting personnel.

300

The major, together with one of the soldiers, started to remove brushwood and several sods of thick turf from the ground in front of them, revealing a heavy trapdoor which one of the soldiers unlocked before standing aside.

Major Folkestone pointed with his swagger stick for the women to enter the pitch-dark hidey-hole.

'What is *this*?' Lily whispered to Kate. 'Not the wine cellars—*that* would be too good to be true, of course.'

'I won't tell you again!' the major warned. 'Whoever you are!'

Lily pulled a face and then put a hand to her mouth because her teeth were now chattering with the cold. Nevertheless, following hard on the major's heels, she led the way down a long flight of slippery steps, guided well below ground level by a rusty iron handrail. Finally, at the end of the descending passageway, Major Folkestone took a key from his pocket and unlocked a heavy wooden door.

Once everyone was inside, Major Folkestone struck a match and lit a succession of candles that were already in place around the cavern. As the flickering light illuminated their surroundings everyone could see that the place in which they stood had been quite obviously prepared for just such an emergency as that in which they now found themselves.

An already existing cave, the first of a succession of such places that stretched ahead and down into what seemed like the bowels of the earth, had been fashioned into a primitive security bunker. The various indentations in the natural rock formations had been fashioned into different rooms, including work and sleeping quarters as well as basic washing and sanitary facilities.

Large pipes could be seen leading upwards through holes drilled in the roof to extract the stale air and feed in the fresh, the whole bunker being furnished for every basic need including hammocks for sleeping and ranges of cabinets for the all-important filing of Top Secret documents. There was also a large supply of arms and ammunition at the entrance, the sight of which made Marjorie realise that in the event of their being found by the enemy, there would not only be no getting in, there would be no getting out.

'Blimey,' Billy whispered. 'I never seen the like.'

'Yes, well, you wouldn't, lad,' Major Folkestone replied, having now lit at least two dozen candles, most of which had been placed in niches in the walls. 'It's a pity you have to see it at all. But there you are. At least this will keep us all out of the limelight till everyone's been able to regroup.'

'What does he mean by regroup?' Lily whispered to Kate. 'We will surely have to do a lot more than regroup to survive down here for any length of time.'

'It wouldn't take a lot of finding either,' Marjorie whispered back. 'I'm surprised it hasn't got a number on it. Number 12, Dingly Dell.'

Kate and Lily giggled nervously, at which the major turned and pointed his swagger stick at them.

'I fail to understand how anyone can possibly find anything to giggle at in this sort of situation,' he snapped. 'Get a grip on yourselves, both of you. We are about to be invaded. This is no time for laughter.'

302

'They was only saying that this place would be easy to find, sir,' Billy piped up, anxious as always to be helpful. 'And you can't 'elp agreeing. I mean that trap door's pretty obvious for a start,' he added with his usual precocity.

'The trapdoor and all signs of the entrance at this very moment are being concealed by the LDV, for your information, lad—and yours too, ladies! By the time they've finished, no one will be able to tell there's anything down here, let alone anyone, I assure you. All this has been carefully worked out to the final T. I will have you know that this place is just one of many that have been got ready in case this black day ever dawned—natural caves and subterranean caverns all over England. Very useful at these times.'

'But won't Jerry look underground first off, sir?' Billy persisted. 'I mean if I was the enemy coming in and I couldn't find nobody, first place I'd have a dekko would be—'

'Thank you, Billy—that's quite enough from you.' The major stopped him. 'And luckily I doubt very much if Jerry is as bright as you, young man. Now once we've got you all settled in and organised, we're going to have to douse a few lights. We've got a fair supply of candles, but since they're going to be one of our most precious commodities if we're going to have to spend any length of time down here, as soon as we're comfortable we will snuff them.'

Ordered to fall out, the members of Section H carefully inspected their new lodgings before regrouping to sit smoking and talking in worried and anxious clusters around the now dimly lit bunker—all that is except Lily, who sat a little apart

303

from the rest smoking a leisurely cigarette and reading a very old, pre-war copy of a filmgoers' magazine.

'I know we've all talked about this sort of thing happening—'

'It's hardly a sort of thing, Kate,' Marjorie interrupted. 'It *is* happening, so it's an actual event. It isn't a *sort* of thing at all.'

'I know we've all joked about it and everything,' Kate continued, ignoring the interruption, 'but it's frightening my very expensive camisole and lace drawers off me, I do not mind telling you. I remember reading what the Germans did to women in the last war—when they took a town or a city or something like that—and they certainly didn't sit them down and offer them tea and sympathy.'

'Invading soldiers of any nation are not very nice, we all know that, Kate, and really we shouldn't be talking like this in front of Billy.' Marjorie nodded protectively towards the boy.

'What did they do in the last war, Kate?'

'They did *the* most awful things to women, *and* children,' Kate went on, in case Billy thought he was going to be let off the hook. 'You really wouldn't want to know.'

'So don't tell us then,' Marjorie suggested. 'Then we'll have one less thing to worry about.'

'No, you're right in a way. I don't think this is the best sort of talk—not under the circumstances.'

'But you must be scared, surely?' Lily said, putting down her magazine and staring round at the rest, combing her hair back out of her eyes with her fingers. 'It's only human to be scared.'

'Can I have a fag?' Billy suddenly asked. 'If we're

304

all goin' to be shot at dawn, I'd like a fag too, please.'

Lily simply smacked his hand as Billy reached towards her tin of cigarettes, closing the lid and putting the tin back in her bag.

'Marge? Tell her I can have one?'

'No, Billy. You're far too young to start smoking.'

'No I'm not. Kids much younger'n me at school smoke. And if we're all goin' to be shot at dawn—'

'That's enough, Billy. Smoking a silly cigarette's not going to get you anywhere.'

Billy sighed but fell silent, ever obedient to the beautiful Kate.

'What do you think's going to happen next?' Lily wondered out of the silence. 'We haven't much of an army left to put up any sort of a fight, and we haven't any allies either. So maybe we should just shove a few white flags up some of those holes in the ceiling and hope Jerry has the same God as us and that He's merciful like ours is meant to be.'

Marjorie, her nerves sufficiently shredded by now, was just about to try to put Lily in her place when Kate, putting a hand on her arm, diverted her.

'Perhaps we ought to start putting some of these files away,' she said, getting up from the table. 'Just because we've been evacuated doesn't mean we're off duty.'

'Guess who's Major Folkestone's favourite girl then?' Lily remarked, taking another deep draw on her cigarette. 'In more ways than one.'

'Meaning?' Marjorie said with a look as she too got up from the table.

'Pay no attention, Marjorie. She's only being

provocative.'

'If only there was someone to be provocative for,' Lily sighed. 'It was bad enough above ground. I mean I have never seen such a dearth of decent men. But now, if we're going to be holed up down here for some unspeakable length of time with only Major F for company, and having to watch him making sheep's eyes every time you-know-who walks by—*imagine*. Doesn't bear thinking about.'

'Every time who walks by?' Marjorie demanded to know, only to find herself led off by the arm by Kate.

'Leave it,' Kate told her. 'She's frightened—like us all. People say silly things when they're frightened.'

'Has Major Folkestone got a crush on you?'

'How would I know? And would you mind if he had?'

'Of course not,' Marjorie retorted. 'It's just I can't imagine you and Major Folkestone.'

'It's all right, Marjorie. Neither can I.' Kate smiled reassuringly as they braced themselves to lift a box of files and put it on top of one of the dark green metal filing cabinets.

'You're not smitten, surely?'

'Me? Don't be daft,' Marjorie replied. 'No, I like handsome men, and Major Folkestone is certainly not that.'

Kate stared at Marjorie for a few seconds, remembering how often she had caught her gazing at Robert's photograph, but Marjorie didn't look up, contenting herself with sorting through the box of files, her attention seeming to be on her work, rather than anything else.

                    *   *   *

Eugene missed the alert, but then even if he had been in the country, given his character, he would have taken no notice of it. As it was, he was on the west coast of Ireland, keeping a rendezvous.

It was a squally night, with a north-easter blowing off the Atlantic, a strong enough gale to whip the waters of the bay that lay below him into a heavy, fast-running sea. For a while, as he watched the white horses dance on the wave tops through his field glasses, Eugene wondered whether the prevailing conditions might prevent the vessel he was awaiting from coming in that close, until with a smile he remembered exactly what type of craft was due to make its appearance any moment now.

Submarines did not have to worry about such unfriendly conditions, at least not unless they were trying to get into too shallow a depth. Eugene knew the Kommandant of the incoming boat would have no such interest, preferring, as had been prearranged, to surface near the entry of the bay itself, and put out an inflatable raft to meet up with Eugene on the remote shore.

The U-boat was a mere thirty seconds late, if the shark-like shape that had risen out of the waters less than half a mile away proved to be the submarine for which he was waiting. Eugene dropped his glasses and allowed them to swing from his neck while he flashed a quick message from a signalling light. Perhaps due to the stillness of the night, the stars above bright as any diamond, the wind having dropped to a whisper, the communication appeared to have been picked up immediately and replied to in kind.

Ten minutes later a small inflatable boat swished in on the tide, finally grounding itself on the stony beach.

Eugene was there to greet it.

A tall man in a heavy black leather trench coat and captain's hat stepped ashore while two sailors secured the boat, one standing on the beach holding the painter while the other swung the stern round so that the craft lay parallel to the incoming waves.

Eugene saluted the captain and by silent consent they walked up the beach, some way from the inflatable, in order to converse in privacy, leaving the two German sailors to safeguard the tender. With only the sound of the sea ruffling the edge of the sand, the two men could be heard to be having urgent exchanges before returning to the waiting craft, the German captain now in possession of a large envelope, while Eugene slipped a smaller one into the inside pocket of his coat.

Once the captain had been returned to his submarine and the U-boat had been swallowed up by the white-topped waves, its dark, sleek shape disappearing with an ease that was almost magical, Eugene turned his back to the bay and began to scale the hills behind him to where he had left a bicycle in the hedge. He took it up and started to wheel it towards the road. In the darkness the lone cyclist, whistling quietly to himself, perhaps to keep his mind off the long journey ahead of him, began his long ride to the east coast where a boat was waiting to take him back to England.

*   *   *

308

'Right!' Major Folkestone called out, just as Section H had all finally settled into their hammocks for the night and were feeling not just safe, but almost cosy. 'Right—false alarm, everyone! False alarm! Sorry about that!'

Marjorie, who had just dropped off, woke with a start and sat up, managing to fall out of her hammock as she did so, only preventing herself from crashing to the floor by grabbing instinctively at the webbing.

'False alarm?' she cried. 'What—you mean we haven't been invaded after all?'

'No, Marjorie, I'm glad to say we have not,' Major Folkestone said as he passed by, stopping to help her on to her feet. 'Sorry and all that, but it appears some Charlie on the other side of the country thought he heard bells ringing and set off a chain reaction.'

The major had been given the message by his radio operator, who once he had got the specially installed transmitter and receiver up and running had picked up the relevant information from HQ. The whole of England had been alerted earlier that evening, only to find, as H Section was now doing, that it was a false alarm.

The panic had been brought on by the first serious air attack on London, which had left the understandably jittery watchdogs to imagine the Germans were combining the intensity of their bombing with a planned invasion.

Now the radio operator, earphones still in place, looking round in benign mood, smiled at the bevy of young women who were streaming slowly and sleepily back into the main room of the underground bunker, pulling on the few clothes they had taken off to go to bed.

'Pity about it,' the radio operator sighed to his companion. 'I wouldn't have said no to spending the rest of the war down 'ere with that lot of lovelies.'

'Me neither,' his new friend agreed, lighting up a Woodbine. 'In fact I was beginning to take a bit of a shine to Jerry for sending us down 'ere.'

'Enough of that, thank you,' Major Folkestone informed them as he strode past, swagger stick tapping one leg. 'The war's not over quite yet so I should keep listening, if I were you.'

'What now, sir?' Kate asked, pulling on her bright red cardigan over her cream blouse and tidying her mane of blonde hair with one hand. 'Do we stay here the night or return to the house?'

'I think it best to return now, so that we are all back at our desks at the usual time. Pity about losing a bit of sleep, but that can't be helped at this time.'

'A *bit* of sleep?' Lily yawned. 'We'll be lucky if we get forty winks by the time we've decamped and moved back in.'

'There is a war on, Miss Ormerod,' the major reminded her. 'This isn't a holiday—much though you seem to like to treat it as one—and we can't afford to waste valuable resources down here in case they may be needed again. So let's be moving, shall we?'

'Great,' Lily muttered as they tramped back through the pitch darkness on their return to the great house. 'My last pair of stockings gone and for what?'

'I'd have thought for quite a lot, actually,'

310

Marjorie retorted. 'Such as England not being invaded? Isn't that worth the sacrifice?'

'Oh, but definitely.' Lily stopped and considered the idea for a second. 'Brave Intelligence Girl Saves Britain by Stocking Sacrifice?' she suggested, straight-faced.

'You know what I mean,' Marjorie grumbled, her arms full of files as she struggled to avoid tripping on tree roots.

'No, as a matter of fact I don't. I only wish the Americans would join the war and bring us over some of their lovely, lovely nylons I keep reading about.'

'You're so shallow.'

'Aren't I just, and proud to be so.'

Lily was so busy being smart that, failing to watch her proper step, she promptly put one foot down a rabbit hole.

'Oh, murder!'

Marjorie turned and pulled a face at her.

'Not just your stockings now, Lily Ormerod, look—one of your peep-toe shoes has gone too!'

Marjorie walked on. Lily pulled a face behind her back after she had finally retrieved the shoe, only to find that Marjorie had walked off with the torch. She started to feel her way through the undergrowth, cursing Marjorie, Hitler, Major Folkestone, and any other person she could think of, roundly.

CHAPTER THIRTEEN

Poppy would have given anything for some company, anyone's company. Alone in the flat in which she had been installed in Grosvenor Square, she found herself whiling her time away waiting for the call from Jack Ward. Unfortunately for her the former occupant of the apartment had the strangest taste in literature, and so, for her sins, and to keep her nerves at bay, she found herself trying to read such weighty tomes as *Victorian Medical Practices* and *Melville's Riding Almanac*, all of which volumes failed, unsurprisingly, to take her mind off George's departure from her life.

'It's not for long,' Jack had tried to reassure her. 'He's going to stay with one of my people. She's a retired lady who it just so happens has recently lost her own dachshund, so she knows the breed. There's no alternative, I'm afraid,' he added, clipping on George's lead and taking him from a sad-eyed Poppy. 'We can't take the slightest chance of anyone's recognising German George, and he will be much safer away from you, for a while.' He cleared his throat and said in his usual kind way, 'Now, if you will, it would be best if you turn your back. Don't watch me go, just remember he will be coming back to you—soon.'

*   *   *

Now she sat alone in the window of her flat, trying to concentrate on an old copy of *Vanity Fair* which she'd at last discovered propping up the leg of a chair, while at the same time endeavouring to think of something other than the fact that the telephone seemed to have made up its mind never to ring, ever again. She had just begun to fantasise about Jack Ward and his contacts, imagining them all to be double agents, and wondering if, all too soon, there would be a knock at the door and she herself would be kidnapped and shot, when the telephone rang at last.

It was Jack and he was coming round to collect her that evening.

In answer to a prearranged signal, Poppy, in full evening dress, opened the door to him, and promptly poured them both a stiff gin. Outside they could both hear the sirens sounding a warning of a coming air attack but neither of them took any notice, sitting drinking their gin and smoking cigarettes in the knowledge that, even though nothing had been said, this was the last time they would be able to enjoy the pleasure of each other's company in this way for the foreseeable, and even perhaps the not so foreseeable, future.

'We're ready to move you into the limelight now,' Jack finally announced in his measured way, slowly stubbing out his untipped cigarette in a round glass ashtray. 'When you receive the next telephone call it will not be from me but from someone supposedly asking you to drinks at the Stanley Hotel. That will be your cue. You will go as asked to the hotel where you will be picked up in the bar by a young man who will claim to know you.'

At this Poppy looked mildly put out, the question being what would happen if she did not recognise him? But Jack continued in his usual airy way.

'You will of course finally recognise him, and he will introduce you to a circle of his friends who will be gathering there. After that you will be on your own except for your moments of contact back to the section. You will use a drop for written messages, a place that will be changed regularly to prevent identification, and you will receive any orders that might be necessary via a telephone call from someone pretending to be a friend of yours and inviting you to meet them. Here is a list of their names, and the meaning of their messages. I would strongly advise you to try to memorise everything on this list, rather than hide it, but if you have to put it away somewhere make sure it isn't here. Your telephone will almost certainly be tapped, and you will undoubtedly be followed. I have told you as best I can how to shake a tail, but if you have any doubts as to whether or not you have succeeded, then go through the entire process again, until you are absolutely certain you have got rid of your shadow. Remember, they are very skilled at surveillance, and will constantly switch their shadows. You will only ever call my number in the gravest emergency. If anything happens to you, as far as you go, we do not exist.'

He handed her a small revolver.

'Hide this in your gas mask case.'

'And the target?' Poppy wondered, although in her heart she felt she already knew even before he spoke.

'No one, we hope, as yet. Just a precaution, but in the event, of course, if you were in a bad situation, you might feel it better to turn it on yourself.'

314

He stood up. They looked at each other for a moment. Outside Poppy heard the crumping, muffled thud of a bomb falling, followed by the thunder of collapsing masonry. Neither of them said a word. Finally Jack Ward picked up an old brown trilby and set it carefully on his head at a rakish angle.

'I've never seen you wear a hat before.'

'I never wear a hat,' he agreed. 'Unless it is quite necessary. I am not suited to hats. Men who wear spectacles look shady in hats.' He removed his glasses, and put them in his pocket. 'But I wouldn't want to be seen coming in and out of this apartment block without some kind of thin disguise, would I?' He checked himself in the hall mirror, and satisfied by what he saw he carefully and quietly opened the front door. 'George is fine, by the way,' he added in a low voice. 'Eating up and being a thoroughly good boy in every way.' He turned at the door and nodded briefly at Poppy. 'He sends you a big wag,' he added. 'And says take care of yourself.'

Poppy shut the door, went back into her living room and stood staring at herself in the looking glass above the fireplace. She took a long hard look at Poppy Beaumont, said goodbye to her, and set her countenance for a future as Diona de Donnet.

*　　　*　　　*

It was Sunday and Marjorie and Kate did their best not to be seen to rush in an unseemly fashion out of church, yet both of them could hardly contain their excitement, Marjorie at the joy of getting not just a day pass, but an invitation to spend the day

315

with Kate's family, and Kate at the thought of seeing Robert, also home on leave from the Navy.

Marjorie was also looking forward to meeting Robert, her best friend's handsome brother, with whom she had managed to convince herself she might fall deeply in love. Not that it took much imagination, for the photograph on the table beside Kate's bed showed a tall, handsome, fair-haired young man standing between his sister and mother, tanned and healthy, every inch the hero.

Billy was Marjorie's only problem. Both of them had wanted to take Billy as well, but Major Folkestone, acting as always now *in loco parentis* for the boy, had refused Billy a pass since it had been brought to his attention that having skipped so much school Billy was falling seriously behind in his work.

'Don't mind me,' Billy grumbled as he arrived back at the cottage long after Kate and Marjorie. 'I'm going to 'ave a simply smashin' time here on me tod, doin' all me arithmetic and geography 'omework.'

'If you hadn't played hookey so much,' Marjorie reminded him as she checked the contents of her handbag, 'you could have come too. And do stop dropping your aitches, will you?'

'Certainly, miss,' Billy replied, sticking his nose in the air. 'Hi shall nevaire drop haynother haitch has long has High lives.'

'You'll be fine, Billy,' Kate assured him, kissing him chastely on the cheek. 'You'd be awfully bored with us. There'd be nothing for you to do except sit around and listen to a lot of boring small talk.'

'Kate's right,' Marjorie assured him, brushing the lipstick mark off his cheek. 'You'd be bored

316

rigid. At least here, once you've caught up on your homework—which you're going to have to do, right?'

'Right,' Billy groaned.

'Or else your friend Major F won't allow you *anywhere*. No more plane spotting, no more decoding—'

'Yeah, yeah—I get the idea,' Billy protested, wriggling his way out of Marjorie's grasp. 'Any rate, Mr 'Ackett asked me to call on 'im after I done me 'omework.'

'Mr *H*ackett, Billy. Stop pretending to be such a little oik.'

'Yeah. Well that's what I am, remember? A pesky little oik 'oo's not good enough to be asked to someone's 'ome case 'e drops 'is bloomin' aitches all over the shop.'

Marjorie eyed him, uncertain whether or not he was too old for her to clip across the back of his cheeky head.

'Oi!' Billy protested. 'Leave off, Marge! I want to live to see another day!'

Marjorie laughed, finally ruffling his hair, straightening his tie and pulling out a chair at the table for him to sit and do his work. Billy wrinkled his nose in distaste, but sat himself down nevertheless.

'Yeah,' he sniffed. 'Go on—off you go and enjoy yourselves.'

'We shall, William,' Kate assured him. 'We most surely shall.'

Kate and Marjorie had changed into what they considered to be their best—neat wool coats, hats with dashing angles to them, and thin silk stockings that Kate's mother had sent them as a present,

317

some days before.

Found these at the back of a drawer, her hastily written note had said. *They belonged to my mother, would you believe? That's why they're not a modern colour, but they are silk!*

They were a funny colour—a kind of greyish pink—but so much better than thick lisle, or, worse, bare legs, and both girls pulled them on delightedly before beginning the long train journey back to Kate's home.

*   *   *

As it turned out, from the first, the whole day was tinged with that particular shading that in retrospect makes every colour of the sky, every pattern of a leaf, every chance moment seem magical.

Kate walked up the garden path to the familiar front door feeling much as she had as a schoolgirl, half expecting to be delving into the front of her blouse to find a key on a string. Of course the house looked smaller, as it would do after Eden Park, but it also looked more welcoming, a ginger-bread of a house, and that was all before her mother opened the front door to her, and pulled both her and Marjorie indoors, laughing and talking and calling to Robert to come quickly.

'Where's Dad?' Kate asked, cautiously, after she had introduced Marjorie to her mother, and Robert to Marjorie.

Helen's eyes slid sideways as they always did when she was put on the spot.

'I don't exactly know, Kate, and nor does Robert, do you, dear?'

Robert shook his head, his bright fair hair flopping down into his eyes immediately making him look much younger, less the serious naval officer, more the boy in Kate's photograph.

In the absence of her husband, Helen's cooking seemed to take on a new lease of life, and she managed to produce a lunch of such splendour that for a while afterwards conversation steadied down to a less animated intensity as all the young people smiled happily, reluctantly refusing third helpings of apple pie and custard.

'It's not that we don't have good food where we are,' Kate told her mother, taking care not to mention Eden Park. 'It's just that we really never have much time to eat, not like now.'

'More, dear?'

'Mother!' Robert looked across at his mother affectionately. 'You want to kill us with kindness, don't you?'

Helen smiled round the table. She did really rather want to, but she knew that Robert would hate it if she became sentimental in front of Kate and her friend, so she said nothing, keeping her feelings under, as they all must.

＊　　　＊　　　＊

Finally, on Helen's orders as she cleared up, Robert, Kate and Marjorie went out for a walk after lunch, along the towpath by the river and across the fields beyond, which like fields everywhere in the country were already being intensively farmed for the quicker production of foodstuffs. But at that moment as the three of them walked deeper into the countryside they pushed all thoughts of hardship away from them, and concentrated on wartime jokes. Old chestnuts were aired and groaned at, new ones laughed at while everyone tried to memorise the good ones in order to repeat them when they went back to the war.

Kate cut a stick, and as they walked on she started to cut off the heads of the nettles that they passed.

'Killed you, Nazi, killed you, Nazi, and you, and you.'

She seemed to take great satisfaction from this activity until Robert interrupted her massacre.

'Forgot to tell you what I've just been telling Mum. I've volunteered for a shore job—so no going to sea for a while, which is good since I have only to see a rowing boat to feel queasy.'

'I say, that is good news.' Kate smiled, taking his arm, and then she stopped, her heart sinking. 'At least I *think* that's good news. Except if I heard you right and you said you *volunteered*, perhaps that isn't such good news?'

'It is as it happens, and I've got a promotion because of it.'

'Gracious, isn't that a bit quick? I mean. That is *quick*.'

'This is war, my dear sister.' Robert laughed. 'They discovered my tinkering genius.'

'Robert's always been a terrific engineer,' Kate explained to Marjorie, dropping back behind him. 'Ever since he was a boy. Could fix, build, invent anything. Drove Dad mad.'

'Not quite anything, Kate. I haven't engineered a cure for the common cold as yet.'

Marjorie laughed. She took Kate's hazel stick from her and began deadheading some nettles

320

herself.

'Hitler, done you. Goering, done you! Who else?'

'That awful Speer man, got to do him.'

Robert glanced back at them, amused. They were like two delighted schoolgirls concentrating on their self-appointed task. He walked ahead of them for a while, thinking over his new promotion. He knew exactly why he had been hauled in: first of all because he was the kind of fool that always volunteered for the most dangerous tasks, second of all because he was, as Kate had said, always and ever fascinated by taking things to pieces, and third because there was a hurry on. Or, to put it more succinctly, even more of a hurry on.

It seemed the Germans had developed a non-contact mine. Apparently it was triggered by the ship's magnetic field, which made the mines all but impossible to sweep in the conventional manner. The enemy was terrified that the British might get hold of one, so they had kitted them all out with self-destruct devices in case they failed to go off. Word had come, via an intercept from Eden Park, that they were now thinking of using them as bombs as well.

Bombs were not funny at the best of times, but it beggared the imagination to think of mines being dropped from the sky, perhaps by parachute. To say that they could do a great deal of damage was to say the least, and the long and the short of it was that Robert was now part of the Admiralty counter-measures department—based on board a ship, but ready to be called on to cope with the new devices at any time. The task, as he well knew, was not just dangerous, it was lethal, and the chances of his surviving were pretty slim. All of which, quite naturally, he was intent on not telling his mother or his sister, and since he never told his father anything he would certainly not be passing on to him this particular piece of information.

He had thought about it all a great deal, and somehow, by projecting himself into the future, he had comforted himself by reflecting that, despite being only twenty-one, he really did not think he would enjoy life after the war. It would be so different. The English, he was convinced, would never quite recover from what they were now being put through, and that being so he might find himself unable to fit in with the brand new world, whatever it might be. At least, that was what he told himself, while at the same time appreciating that crouching in some crater trying to defuse some sort of bomb was not going to be the same as being one of many on a warship.

Perhaps Kate had guessed something of the new dangers that he now faced, because she suddenly ran up behind Robert and took hold of his arm.

'My brother is completely cuckoo, as you've probably gathered,' she said to Marjorie.

'A fine thing to say to a newly promoted naval officer.'

They were nearing the house again, and Robert decided it was time to change the subject.

'Now for part two of my surprises,' he informed them, using a lofty voice as if he was an announcer on the radio.

'You've parked your warship in the garage?'

'How did you know, Kate?'

'Because I did, Bobby Maddox.'

Robert opened the garage doors to gesture

322

theatrically within. 'Ta rah!' he sang, pointing with both hands to the gleaming white sports car that was standing where Professor Maddox's car was usually parked. 'What do you think of her, then? Only got her last week.'

The two young women smiled in delight, and then sighed with admiration as Robert carefully reversed the car out of the garage for their inspection.

'It's an MG,' he said. 'Not new, of course, but hardly done any miles at all. Got her for an absolute snip from a bloke who'd just joined the Cavalry and found he'd been posted abroad. Even better news—I have scrounged enough petrol to run you girls back to your base. I'll still have plenty left to get me back to my ship.'

They were too excited over the idea of being driven back in such sporting style to linger over their goodbyes to Helen, something for which she was only too grateful.

'Bye, dears. Take care.'

She closed the front door and leaned against it, closing her eyes as she did so. What a stupid thing to say. Take care! As if it was possible to take care in a war.

*   *   *

And so they drove back to what they all laughingly referred to as 'somewhere in England', with the hood down and their spirits raised. They joked and sang most of the thirty-mile journey, Kate and Marjorie well wrapped up against the autumn chill, and Robert carefree and hatless with his blond hair standing all but upright in the wind. The car

323

seemed to sing with them as Robert speeded across country until, far too soon it seemed, the entrance to Eden Park was before them, and the car was being stopped by the two new sentries posted at the outer gates. Kate and Marjorie showed their passes, but Robert was not allowed to proceed any further.

As the three of them prepared to make their farewells, they were passed by a small party of four women returning from their own day out, waving their passes at the sentries and blowing kisses behind them as they went.

Robert, who was just about to kiss his sister goodbye, stopped and watched the girls laughing and fooling about at the gates.

'I say, Kate,' he murmured. 'Who's that rather gorgeous imp in the red coat and saucy little hat?'

'That?' Kate said, with a laugh. 'That, dear brother, is a girl called Lily. And if you ask me she is more than a little fast.'

'Really?' Robert's eyes lit up at that. 'Suits me. I don't have a lot of time. Excuse me?' he called. 'Hang on a jiffy! Wait for me!'

He hurried up to Lily, anxious to stop her before she passed through into the security area. Marjorie, seeing Kate looking at her, immediately smiled, straightened her own somewhat windswept hat on her head and swung her handbag round raffishly.

'Come on, Kate,' she said. 'Or we'll be late for check-in.'

After a few yards they caught up with Robert, who had engaged Lily in conversation. Lily smiled at the two of them, while Robert quickly broke away to run over to them.

'Cheerio, both,' he said, kissing Kate and

shaking Marjorie's hand. 'It's been an absolutely A1 day. Made A1 plus now. See you both soon! Cheerio!'

With that he hurried back to Lily, who was waiting patiently for him, smiling the smile of a girl who knows she has caught the eye of a handsome young man.

'I do love a naval uniform better than any other,' Marjorie heard her say, as she and Kate started to walk up the drive.

'Really.' Kate sighed. 'She ought to have a better line than that by now, don't you think?'

Marjorie shrugged her shoulders.

'That's Lily,' she said, staring ahead.

'It certainly is,' Kate agreed, unable to prevent her own thoughts drifting towards the horseman she had first seen cantering on the grey horse and whom she still hoped to see again, one day, with or without a tennis racket, although she would not admit as much to anyone, except of course herself.

*   *   *

The following day Kate was making her way to the tennis court to collect a cardigan she had left there when she heard the sound of tennis balls being hit at a regular fast speed. She stopped, and hid behind a tree in almost precisely the same place as Eugene had hidden to watch her.

He was practising his serve, sending the balls first to one corner of the square and then to another. Serve after serve was sent spinning down with breathtaking speed, the ball thrown high, the arm swinging the racket down towards it with an easy, athletic agility that was beautifully judged and

325

executed. Kate stood on, watching him, until the sun went behind a cloud, and she moved fractionally between trees.

'Come out of there, Kate Maddox, before I shoot you as a spy with my trusty weapon,' Eugene called to her.

Kate revealed herself.

'How did you know I was there?'

'Because, Miss Maddox, I have the ears of a fox, and the second sense of a deer. Because I am, in other words, the great, the inestimable, the fascinating Eugene Hackett.'

He turned towards her, and as he did so it seemed that he had stopped as if he had been shot by Kate, rather than the other way round. She was wearing a white smoking suit—short jacket, with wide legged sailor-style trousers—that her mother had sent her a few weeks before with a note. *Given this by Lady Daval. She thought it might suit you. She is running a second-hand clothes stall—rather good!* Kate had teamed it with a floral blouse and a single strand of pearls. It was far too dressy for life at Eden Park, but Kate took the attitude that with a war on it was a girl's duty to look as good as she could.

Eugene shook his head.

'Kate . . .'

Kate picked up her cardigan from the umpire's chair and turned back to him, making sure as she did so that she was looking vague, as if she had hardly registered his presence.

'Mmm?'

'You look—you look like something me auntie would send from Cork in a badly tied parcel,' he joked, 'as welcome as the sun coming up in the morning, or an ice cream on a hot day, or a long cold drink after coming off the tennis court.' He started putting the tennis balls back in their box, but as he did so even Kate noticed that his hands were shaking.

'And you look,' she said, staring at his hands for a second, 'you look as if you could do with that famous drink.'

'I could, I could.' He turned towards her as she walked past him, putting out a hand to catch her arm. 'Kate?'

'Yes?'

'You look like a picture, do you know that?' He ran ahead of her suddenly. 'I will carry your image before me as I go into battle.' He fell to his knees, the expression on his face once more one of mischievous humour. 'Give me at least a token to remember you by. Please?'

Kate picked up a small stone from the path that ran beside the tennis court.

'There you are, Eugene Hackett. Place that next to your heart.'

He took it, and after kissing it placed it in his pocket, by which time Kate was walking quickly back towards the house—and sanity. Was Eugene Hackett half clown, or half hero, or wholly both?

*   *   *

When it was Marjorie's turn to join her section's sitting at dinner in the former blue salon, now a canteen, a new arrival caught her eye as they queued.

'You look as though someone has taken your fancy,' Kate remarked, as she took up her food. 'I spy?'

Marjorie nodded discreetly at a tall, elegant young man who had just joined the waiting line of hungry personnel and was standing idly at the back.

'I'm trying to place the face,' she said. 'I know I know him, but I can't think from where.'

At that moment the newcomer looked in their direction, as if he had become aware of Marjorie's stare. As soon as she saw him full face, Marjorie remembered.

'The cottage, Seagull Watch,' she murmured to Kate, turning her back on the man. 'Aunt Hester's friend's cottage by the sea. We went on holiday last year. It was the first time I met Jack Ward, and he was with him.' She nodded back towards the waiting figure. 'He's French. I knew I knew him from somewhere. Except I don't remember his hair being that colour.'

'He's really quite handsome,' Kate admitted, as she managed to steal a glance at him behind Marjorie's back. 'Even if it is in a rather Gallic way. Oh dear, he's noticed us noticing him.'

'How do you know?'

'Because he just bossed his eyes at us.'

'I wonder what he's doing here?'

'If he turned up at your aunt's with Mr Ward, I don't think there's any need to ask any further.'

'True. And just when I thought it might be Fate,' Marjorie joked, collecting her food and moving off to a spare table. Having witnessed Marjorie's all too obvious disappointment when Robert had made a beeline for Lily Ormerod, Kate decided not to press the point, and instead she sat down, unloading her tray on to the table, before taking another look at the newcomer.

328

'He's too good-looking for his own good, I'd say,' she told Marjorie.

Marjorie nodded.

'He always was, even Aunt Hester was fascinated. I remember he and Mr Ward stayed until late, drinking and joking with her, and that wasn't Aunt Hester at all. Oh, for heaven's sake, don't look, he's only coming over.'

They both immediately glanced down at their plates, raising their forks to their lips, and not looking up even when the handsome newcomer placed his own tray opposite theirs.

'*Bon soir, m'selle,*' he said to Kate. '*Et m'selle*'— to Marjorie. 'May I be allowed sit with you, please? Do you think?'

'*Mais oui,*' Kate replied in her excellent French. '*Mais je regrette que nous parlons français comme tous les anglais—mal!*'

'On the contrary,' the stranger replied in impeccable English. 'I would say your French was really quite good.'

Both young women stared at him in surprise, Marjorie finally taking the initiative.

'Sorry—I thought you were French.'

'Yes?' The stranger looked at her, raising his eyebrows in astonishment. 'Why would that be?'

'When we met—because we have met, haven't we?'

'Have we?'

'Didn't you come to see my aunt? Last summer? With Mr Ward? Forgive me if I'm wrong, although as I was just saying, if it is you, your hair—at least I think it was—wasn't your hair a different colour?'

'*Mais oui, m'selle,*' he replied in perfect French once again. '*Vous avez raison—c'était brun, assez*

329

foncé, mais—plus maintenant!'

He turned his now reddish brown head round, tilting it to one side as if modelling a new hair style. Marjorie looked at Kate, widening her eyes, while Kate endeavoured to keep a straight face.

'So what brings you here, monsieur?' Kate wondered. 'You've just arrived—is that right?'

'*Absolument.*'

'You work here?' Marjorie enquired.

'No, no, *m'selle,*' the stranger replied with a worried frown. 'Work? What is this work? Is this not an hotel? For that is why I am here—*en vacances.*'

The two women stared at him in amazement, momentarily taken in by his act, until the stranger suddenly made a face.

'Of course I work here.' He laughed. 'Yes—and of course we met. You're Marjoric—if I'm not mistaken—and you are?'

'I'm Kate. Kate Maddox.'

They all shook hands solemnly.

'And you're not French really?' Marjorie asked carefully. 'Or are you?'

'Guess.'

'You're not.'

'Well done. I am utterly and entirely English. Scott Meynell.'

He smiled at them, quickly brushing his hair from his dark eyes.

'You're also right about my hair—and the fact that I was French when we first met,' he continued. 'I was working in France. I've just come back, in fact—via the beaches. Via Dunkirk.'

Marjorie looked at Kate, and Kate looked at Marjorie.

'What was it actually like?' Kate asked.

'I can only speak personally,' Scott replied. 'And what I can say is that even if we win the war—'

'When we win the war,' Marjorie corrected him.

'When we win the war—sorry. Even when we win the war I don't think I'll be going to Dunkirk for my holidays.'

'Are you going back?' Kate wondered ingenuously, before correcting herself. 'Sorry, shouldn't have asked.'

'Isn't this food terrible?' Scott sighed, ignoring her faux pas. 'The one thing about France—no, actually there are lots of things about France—many, many things about France that I love, most especially her food. One of the units blew up this chap's camembert. Do you know the sobs could be heard above the sound of the guns.'

'He probably had no option.'

'No,' Scott said with a droll look first at Kate and then at Marjorie, 'and it didn't do much for the old *entente cordiale*, as you can imagine. I mean blow up his house, blow up his motor car, but not, absolutely not, his cheese.'

'If it ever existed,' Kate remarked. 'Anyway—you were saying the one good thing about France was?'

'The food. Don't know about you, but French food . . .' Scott kissed his index finger and thumb. 'Even with the bombs dropping, the guns blazing, they carried on cooking. And now—back to this.' He sighed, staring down at his plate of stew.

'You don't think we can cook?' Marjorie asked him.

'If you want the truth, no. We have the ingredients, but we overcook them.'

'Of course the English can cook!' Marjorie

331

insisted. 'It's only because our ingredients are better we don't have to muck our food up with all those fancy sauces, and all that!'

'You've been to France, have you, Marjorie? And eaten all their terrible mucked about food, eh?'

'No-o. But I know what I like. Good English food.'

'Of course you do. And you know what they say?'

'No. But I feel you're going to tell us.'

'Kissing don't last—but cookery do.'

He looked from one to the other, and smiled his mischievous smile.

'If cookery meant that much,' Marjorie remarked, with a look at Kate, 'the French might have been able to put up a better resistance. But then perhaps their minds were on what they were going to have for dinner.'

'*Touché.*' Scott laughed. 'Perhaps that explains our two countries' histories. The reason the French have always wanted to invade us was to teach us how to cook, and the reason why we were always trying to conquer them was because we couldn't stand—er—whatever this is meant to be.'

Scott raised his eyebrows expressively and put his unfinished food to one side.

'I'd do anything for a plate of *moules marinières*,' he sighed. 'So much so I might even have to be dropped back into France.'

*   *   *

The choice, however, was not Scott's. The decision as to what his next assignment was to be had already been made. On learning of his escape from France his mentor, Jack Ward, had immediately gone after him, lobbying his superiors to assign him to work for him in London. Finally, after much political manoeuvring, Jack got his way. Scott was informed of the decision and sent to Section H at Eden Park for what he gaily called 'the briefest of briefings, so brief in fact that in future it might have to be re-named *sous-dessous*.' Part of the reason for the briefing was to show him a recent photograph of Diona de Donnet, with whom, it seemed, he was to be working.

'Can't wait,' he told Cissie Lavington, who was at Eden Park supervising training for new recruits for a few days. 'I say, though—what a stunner.'

Cissie looked over his shoulder, smiling proudly to herself as she remembered the person Poppy had once been.

'Yes, she is rather, isn't she?'

Shortly after that Scott left Section H for London, and the Stanley Hotel.

*   *   *

When Poppy walked into the bar of the Stanley Hotel at a little before noon the following day, she had no idea whom she was supposed to be meeting, except that the person in question was supposedly on her side, and had left a message in her upstairs suite. It was perhaps because of this that she found herself hesitating by the door, trying to look as confident as possible, while feeling quite the opposite.

There was a group of people, some sitting, some standing drinking and idly talking, for all the world

333

appearing to be the sort of people to be seen in any smart bar in any smart European hotel before the war. None of the men—which was almost shocking—happened to be in uniform. Instead they were sitting perfectly suited, and quite obviously rich, and equally at ease with the notion that they could indulge in cocktails and laughter; that while the world outside was one of sandbags, trenches and barbed wire, inside the reinforced-concrete walls of the grand hotel pleasure still reigned.

It made Poppy feel vaguely sick to see them all, to hear them talking and laughing as if they were entertaining each other in one of their many private houses, with a much scaled down hotel staff. Their glasses were obviously not being refilled quite as often as they might have liked, but, perhaps to make up for the slow service, there was much lighting of their expensive hand-made cigarettes, plucked at regular intervals from their gold-monogrammed cigarette cases.

Despite finding herself shocked by the scene in front of her, and instinctively loathing every one of the people she was observing at the bar, Poppy carried on walking, elegant, sophisticated, her head in its immensely chic blue hat held high, her afternoon dress and coat—one of many manifestly newly fashionable costumes provided by Cissie Lavington's people—giving her ease of movement, as well as enhancing her new, chic walk: long strides, taken easily, eyes nonchalant, gloved hands holding her bucket bag, and her embroidered velvet gas mask case.

After all, there was no going back. Forward was the only way, even if she had little idea whom she was meant to be meeting. Finally a languid hand beckoned her over, and a handsome young man stood up to greet her.

'Diona, over here, darling,' he drawled. 'Late as usual, yet even more utterly gorgeous than ever. Come and meet the folks.'

Looking as bored as she could possibly manage, Poppy drifted across the bar to his side.

'Hallo, darling.'

She kissed Scott Meynell on the cheek and as she did so, and straightened up, she realised she was kissing the cheek of someone with whom she was going to have the pleasure of working. His dark eyes gave nothing away, thank God, and his languid manner was impeccable. What he was unable to hide, however, was his huge appeal.

*   *   *

Less than ten miles away in the East End, a covered truck was hurrying to a scene of some devastation. Mines had been parachuted from German bombers. Two had exploded, causing massive damage, but happily for the surrounding neighbourhood some had failed to work, and now lay half buried in craters outside the buildings they had been intended to destroy.

In the front of the small truck, Robert Maddox was seated beside the head of his department, Lieutenant-Commander Edward Fanshaw, a large man with the beaming face of the ideal welcoming host, and as much experience as Robert in dismantling land mines. In other words, as he kept saying with a great guffaw, 'None.'

'Look—I know it's all been theory so far, Bob,' he was saying, as they went over and over their anticipated protocol. 'And granted we know about as much about the magnetic trigger as we know about knitting, but I would say we are agreed our theory's pretty sound, aren't we?'

'I would say so, sir,' Robert replied. 'Anyway, sooner or later one has to put theory to the test, otherwise it remains just that—theory.'

'Quite so,' his superior went on, lighting a cigarette while keeping an eye on the road in front and driving expertly for a few yards with only one hand. He blew out some smoke and stared at the road ahead, regaining the driving wheel with his cigarette still held expertly between his fingers. 'The first time, they always say, is the worst time, and I dare say we will both find that out very soon. You have to give it to Jerry—he's damned ingenious when it comes to inventing new ways to keep us on our toes. I only hope our boffins are working as hard for us. It's what's coming, isn't it, boffins' wars. First the cavalry goes, then it'll be the foot soldier—'

They both knew Fanshaw was waffling on in the high hope of keeping both their minds off the ordeal ahead.

'Sir.'

Robert saw they were approaching an area that had been both cleared and cordoned off. Several police had been posted on the perimeter alongside a squad of armed soldiers.

'Jolly good, everyone, stand back!' the bearded Fanshaw boomed as he jumped down from the lorry, followed at once by Robert. 'The cavalry's here!'

After an exchange of salutes, the duty officer pointed out the first mine, which was stuck at an angle with its nose well into the ground.

'The device was ticking when first discovered, so we're informed, Commander,' the officer informed Fanshaw. 'But when we got here it had gone silent.'

'Hear that, Bob?' Fanshaw called over his shoulder to Robert. 'Matches what we reckoned. The self-destruct worked on a delay clock.'

'And we won't know when it stopped until we take the thing out, I'm afraid, sir.'

'Which means we'd better get the old skates on, eh?' Fanshaw beamed.

'We'll need a wall of decent sandbags, Captain,' Robert said to the army officer. 'At a good safe distance from the device—couple of hundred feet should do it provided the wall's thick enough—and if you could possibly have your chaps dig a trench behind the bags as well?'

The officer nodded and went off to instruct his men.

'Good.' Fanshaw glanced briefly at Robert, before returning to stare at the mine. 'Now then— first thing is, make the bugger safe.'

'Without restarting the clock.'

'Without restarting the clock,' the commander reiterated, after which he cleared his throat, folded his arms and stood back to watch the soldiers preparing the defences. 'First thing?'

'Unscrew the ring closing the fuse aperture.'

'Next we find the fuse and yank it out.'

'Maybe not a yank, sir. Perhaps a little pull with a length of cord might be more the thing.'

'Figure of speech, man,' Fanshaw laughed. 'Façon de parler.'

'Yes, sir. So once the fuse is attached we then— we *yank* it out—'

337

'Good man!' Fanshaw roared with laughter. 'That's the ticket! We yank the bugger out and then explode the device from our hidey-hole! Nothing to it, eh? When you break it down like that! Nothing to it at all!'

While the soldiers dug the trench and built a solid defence of sandbags, Robert and his commander strolled the streets smoking cigarettes as if they were out on a Sunday afternoon taking the air. They talked about this and that, but no more about the mine, not until they were in place by the deadly, silent device in a crater that could in a few moments be doubling as their mutual grave.

'Who wants first in?' Fanshaw asked, smiling with assumed delight. 'Or should we toss for it? Might be more fair—although since I'm older I really think the honour should be mine!'

They both laughed over-appreciatively at Fanshaw's play on words despite the fact that it really wasn't very funny.

'I've got pretty nimble digits, sir,' Robert said. 'In fact I've always been described, in my family, as a born fiddler.'

For a second Robert's mind went to his family, to his mother and sister, sitting by the fire, listening to the radio, long before any talk of war, everyone happy and relaxed.

'Yes, but I'm older—'

'You're a family man, sir. I'm a bachelor. I believe it's my honour, really.'

'Righto, lad. Off you go then—and good luck.'

Commander Fanshaw flattened himself on the ground, watching every move as with rock steady hands Robert began work on the three-inch ring that locked the fuse aperture. It took him twenty-five minutes to get it loose and fully unscrewed.

'Aperture open, sir,' he whispered to his commander, allowing the sweat that was running off his brow to do just that.

'My turn, Maddox,' Fanshaw muttered. 'But if we've done our homework all right—'

There followed as long and as deadly a silence as Robert hoped ever to experience as his companion carefully probed for the all-important fuse.

'Which believe it or not, Bob, we bloody well have!' Fanshaw suddenly exclaimed under his breath. 'Think I might have snaffled the weasel. Give us that damn string, will you?'

Moments later Commander Fanshaw had the cord attached to the fuse. He very slowly glanced round at Robert and Robert was reassured to see his superior was also sweating.

'You're going to have to do that yanking, Bob,' he whispered. 'My hands are soaking.'

Slowly and carefully he transferred the end of the cord into Robert's fingers, taking care that neither of them jogged it, even a quarter of an inch.

Feeling the shape of the aperture with a finger of his free hand, Robert sensed that since the fuse seemed to lie at the base of a perfectly symmetrical tube its removal should be a straightforward procedure, provided his hand remained rock steady so that the fuse did not rattle or bang against the side of the holding tube.

Holding his breath he began carefully and as slowly as he could to pull the cord holding the fuse.

'It won't move, sir,' he whispered. 'It seems to be locked.'

'Can't be. Can't possibly be. They had to put the fuse in from the top of the aperture. So there's no way they could lock it in place. It would have to be locked from the bottom, unless there's another holding ring inside.'

'There isn't. I felt with a finger. The tube's completely smooth now we have the holding ring out of the way.'

'Then it can't be locked. I'll bet on it. Want me to try?'

'No sir. Thank you. No—no, I'm going to give it a much harder tug.'

'Give it a bloody good yank, Bob. It's probably just stuck.'

'I think you should go behind the barricades, sir.'

'Wouldn't hear of it. Now get on, man, I'm dying for a drink.'

'Me too,' Robert smiled. 'I can just see that first pint.'

'Pint be blowed. Mine's a very large pink 'un. Off you go.'

Robert, still holding the cord, managed with one finger of his free hand to wipe away the river of sweat that was blinding him. Then, taking another deep breath and half closing his eyes in anticipation of the explosion, he pulled twice as hard as he had been pulling before.

In a second there it was, lying on the ground at the end of the length of cord, looking as innocent as a cigar on a dinner table—the fuse.

'Good show, Bob,' Fanshaw whispered. 'Except that means I'm paying.'

'I suppose we should really have done the yanking from back there,' Robert remarked, nodding backwards to the sandbagged trench. 'Except I don't think we'd have got it to move from there.'

'Certainly not. In circs like these, one has to live over the shop. Now then—we need to plant some explosive here—get back—and blow Jerry's little present to pieces.'

Having made sure everyone was well out of the danger zone, Robert and Fanshaw drew the fuse wire back to the trench and taking full cover fired the detonator. There was a massive explosion as the mine burst into a hundred thousand fragments, causing a rain of metal to fall about the site.

'Rather be here than there,' Fanshaw laughed as he and Robert scrambled out of the trench covered in dust and dry mud. 'That would have given us a bit of a headache all right.'

*　　　*　　　*

Later, as they sat enjoying their well-earned drinks, Robert remarked that he had never tasted beer so good.

'Good for you, Bob,' Fanshaw replied, as usual wreathed in smiles. 'But to hell with tasting it. I just swallowed mine!'

*　　　*　　　*

First thing Robert did when he was finally off duty, in other words when Fanshaw and he had finished their mutual congratulations not to mention celebrations, was to telephone the switchboard at Eden Park and leave a message for Lily to call him.

Half an hour later he received a return call to his temporary lodgings.

'Robert? How lovely to hear you,' Lily tried to keep the delight out of her voice, and knew instantly that she had failed. 'How are you?'

'Oh, I'm fine,' Robert said, trying to block the knowledge that the pain in his head from his recent celebrations was beginning to make itself felt. 'I was wondering . . .' He paused before going on, not wanting to be turned down. 'I was wondering if you would like to come out, some time. You know, dinner or something like that.'

In fact making a date wasn't easy for either of them since Robert at that moment was never not on duty, and leave was a matter of hours rather than days, while Lily hardly left Eden Park.

'If I can call you when I think I've got an evening off and if you can get a pass—we could at least go out for a drink or something. The thing is . . .'

Robert petered out, once again wondering, given the nature of his work, whether it was fair to rush in as headlong as he was doing.

'The thing is what, Bobby?' Lily prompted him.

'The thing is I simply have to see you, Lily,' Robert replied. 'That's the thing. I'm afraid I haven't stopped thinking about you since we met. And not just because you're so pretty, but because you're so—sassy.'

Lily laughed.

'That's a new word.'

'I heard it the other day, and I thought it was you. Sassy.'

'Look—I can't really talk here or now—not the way I'd like to,' Lily half whispered into the phone. 'It's a public box in the hall here and other girls are waiting to use it. So let's just hope we get a chance to meet again *very* soon—when we can *really* talk.'

'Absolutely,' Robert agreed, captivated by Lily's wonderfully emphatic way of talking, and consequently finding himself even more smitten than he thought possible. Imagining her just as she had been when he had first caught sight of the lively, effervescent young woman skipping up to the gates at Eden Park. 'I can't wait, Lily. I won't pretend. I can't.'

'Here's a kiss in the meantime,' Lily whispered close to the receiver, and blowing a kiss down the line despite the fact that the girl behind her was starting to groan loudly and mutter, 'Hurry up, would you, dear!'

'Keep you going till we do meet, Bobby, will it?'

'Heck,' Robert laughed. 'That could keep a chap going for ever.'

*   *   *

The Irish Sea had been at its roughest as the first gales of early autumn whipped the sea into a foaming storm. Eugene could not have cared less; he had sailed this sea so many times since boyhood he found it dull when the wind failed to get up, so he was one of the few up on deck that night, storm watching and smoking his usual cheroot while the salt spray stung his face and matted his thick hair.

The waters calmed as the ship approached the Welsh coast, so that as she berthed it was as if there had never been a gale blowing and they had crossed in a summer calm. The only tell-tale sign of the rough passage was the pale green look to the countenances of all his fellow passengers.

Eugene was naturally one of the first ashore, striding down the gangway whistling merrily to himself as he looked forward to tucking in to breakfast at the first opportunity.

343

The customs officer who greeted him knew him well by now and the two men exchanged pleasantries while the officer searched Eugene's holdall.

'This is very disappointing, sir,' the officer said. 'No bacon and not the one slab of butter.'

'Ate it all on the boat,' Eugene told him, relighting his cigar. 'Storms always make me ravenous.'

The customs officer smiled back and nodded to Eugene to indicate that he could proceed.

'See you again!' Eugene called.

'No doubt of it!' the officer called back.

Eugene was all but clear of the customs shed and about to head for the waiting train when a short burly figure in a plain raincoat and battered trilby hat stepped out from the shadows.

'Mr Hackett?' a mellifluous voice asked quietly. 'Would you mind coming with me?'

*   *   *

Poppy and Scott were soon drawn into the group at the bar. It was in Scott's upbringing to be able to ski the slopes of Society, particularly the sort of inbred Society to which the supercilious, languid group in the bar of the Stanley Hotel that afternoon belonged, so he was at ease at once.

Within no time at all connections were readily established between both the men and the women of the group and Scott, as recognisable names were bandied back and forth, together with the mention of pre-war parties and dances. In her new disguise, her eyebrows thinned, her makeup changed— bright red lips, face heavily powdered, hair colour

344

now pale, pale blonde—Poppy felt so relaxed that she immediately recognised the identities of some of the people that were being discussed. It was difficult not to join in the stories connected with balls and dinners that Poppy Beaumont had attended, but to which Diona de Donnet would never have been invited, so she merely smiled, and smoked and drank, and listened, an expression of boredom fixed as firmly on her face as her mask had been all that time ago when she had made Basil laugh by putting her glasses over the top.

For a second she thought back to that time, amazed by one thing and one thing alone—that Basil had laughed. Was it possible?

Now, having perfected her air of disdain, she went on to cultivate it, looking bored and tired by turns, allowing everyone to try to entertain her, and making sure they realised that they were failing miserably. Cissie Lavington had advised her that this was not just the best way, but the only way in which she could work her way into the inner circle of company such as this.

'The only way with arrogant persons, d'you see, is to become more arrogant than they are. I do assure you, my dear, it is the only way. It's a very false way of conducting oneself, but it has to be done. Even though it leads to countless social impasses, nevertheless it does take effect. This way they find out nothing about you, but are impressed that you are, if anything, better at the game than they are. Because that is all it is. A game. Believe me, all social life is a game.'

At first Poppy had found it difficult, but once Section H had managed to turn the plain little mouse into a sophisticated butterfly, she found it actually became second nature. It went with the person she was meant to be, and to judge by the amount of attention she was receiving it brought men of all ages to heel, and in no time at all. As she more than happily maintained her air of boredom and contempt, treating all who flirted with her as if they were badly behaved schoolboys, it seemed they found it impossible to leave her side.

Noting her immediate success with everyone, Scott affected social dyspepsia and tried to insist on removing Poppy from their clutches, much to the loudly voiced dismay of all.

'You can't remove this beauty, not possible. We're going to make her the bar mascot, aren't we, chaps?'

'Don't be dull,' Poppy remonstrated. 'There is a war on, you know. Besides, I have no wish to be a flying lady at this moment in time.'

'Wouldn't mind you on the front of my motor, Miss de Donnet—'

'Go away, dull little man.'

The dull little man turned out to be someone Poppy had never met before but who she swiftly realised had been at one of Basil's shooting weekends, and of course the ruder she was to him the more the look in his eyes became one of adoration.

'We're all going to dine at the Rat Trap Club. Will you come?' he begged Poppy.

'I don't really think so, actually,' she said coldly. 'I have an important dinner engagement tonight that I imagine will look after my needs for the rest of the day.'

'Anyone we know, Diona?' one of her new admirers wondered. 'Because if it is, I shall go round and bloody well fill him in.'

'Where in God's name did you pick up an oiky expression like that, Michael?' a long-faced woman with thick straight eyebrows enquired casually.

'Scott?' Poppy enquired, turning to him at last. 'It's been quite fun seeing you again. I'm staying here if you want to get in touch—sometime. You at least are not quite as dull as the rest, although that is not saying too much.'

Hearing this, a tall, beautifully dressed man, with dark hair creamed flat to his head, a fashionably thin moustache and an eyeglass, let his monocle fall from his eye as he turned his attention on Poppy. So far he had been the only man to ignore her charms, perhaps anxious to preserve the social niceties while engaging himself in conversation with a perfectly dressed older woman who Poppy had learned was the Duchess of Dunedin.

'One must have just taken up residence then, Miss de Donnet,' the man, whom she understood to be Lord Lypton, said, cleaning his monocle on a silk handkerchief. 'I make it a habit to know everyone of interest who is living within these portals. One has so very little else to do of any worth.'

'I took up residence yesterday as it happens,' Poppy replied. 'One understood with its specially reinforced concrete this was a safe haven.'

'Quite correct, Miss de Donnet. Although there are even better places to be.'

'Such as, Lord Lypton?'

'Such as, Miss de Donnet. Well, quite. In the meantime, one is assured of more than adequate protection here. How strange to be grateful to concrete, of all things.'

347

'I meant to go to my place in the country, but the country at any time of year is just *too* safe, don't you find?' Poppy asked, casually checking her looks in a mirror taken from her handbag.

'Far too safe. Bombs are infinitely preferable to bumpkins.'

'And country people are so frightened, don't you find? I mean to say, the least sound and they throw themselves into hedges and howl like banshees. It's pathetic, really it is, to see them hiding themselves in the hedgerows every time they hear an engine noise.'

'Just so. Everyone says the same. The cockneys are incorrigible and the bumpkins are pusillanimous . . . I imagine we shall be seeing quite a lot of each other then, Miss de Donnet.'

'I imagine so too, Lord Lypton.'

'I shall look forward to it. One gets so bored with the same old faces. And in many cases, one means *old. A bientôt.*'

'Perhaps.'

'I do hope you have an enjoyable dinner,' Lord Lypton added, now slipping a black cigarette into a long white ivory holder. 'It must be an important one.'

'I never have unimportant dinners, Lord Lypton.'

'Connections are everything, would you not say?'

'Gracious, you sound like someone working at a telephone exchange.' Poppy shut her handbag decisively and decided to bestow on the serpent-eyed aristocrat her most insouciant smile. 'Nevertheless you are right. Connections are everything, most especially in these critical times.'

'Another time then, perhaps.' Lord Lypton

348

nodded. 'The boys here can be quite fun. Last night, soon as the sirens went, they decided to dance a conga round the swimming pool. It was quite amusing, really.'

Poppy nodded without smiling, as if she herself did not think much of such a prank, then she was gone.

*   *   *

Dinner of course was a necessity, since, as Jack had warned her, Poppy would have already been marked out. She found it interesting how quickly she knew she was being watched, hoping that it was a sure instinct, and if so that it would stand her in good stead.

It seemed that Jack had managed to persuade a member of the government to include Miss Diona de Donnet in his list of guests invited for a dinner that evening at his private house. The Cabinet minister was of sufficient interest to impress Poppy's new admirers, and if she reported back in the ambiguous manner suggested in her briefings, then the dinner date would certainly add the right sort of gravitas to her curriculum vitae.

Henry, the Cabinet minister, happily was more than just a good social and political connection for someone with Diona de Donnet's aspirations. He was also a lifelong friend of Jack Ward's, and although Jack had not of course told him anything more about his unknown dinner guest than that the young woman was a friend of his who was just recovering from a great unhappiness and needed cheering up, Henry knew Jack well enough to appreciate that the reason for having to include the unknown woman was nothing to do with anything Jack had told him.

*　　　*　　　*

Down at Eden Park, like everywhere else in the country, all eyes were on the September skies where the battle for supremacy was reaching its crucial stage. Ever since Dunkirk the country had been steeling itself to try to repel the invasion they knew was about to be launched, and yet with every day the task seemed more hopeless. So much invaluable equipment had been left behind on those French beaches that the newly formed and named defence force, the Home Guard—moulded out of the old Volunteer Defence Corps—had few if any modern armaments, most of its soldiers being equipped with scmi-antique weaponry from the previous world war or makeshift weapons along the lines of those the women of Eden Park had fashioned to defend themselves with. Generally speaking there was no ammunition for any of the working rifles they had been given, and even less of an idea as to how exactly to repel the hundreds of thousands of Germans expected to be landing at any minute on their precious beaches.

The RAF, the force that was to be the first to be engaged, was also in a parlous condition. Air Chief Marshal Sir Hugh Dowding was said to need 120 squadrons for the forthcoming task. He had sixty. Nor was there any chance of making the numbers up in time for the operation now dubbed Sea Lion.

*　　　*　　　*

On the other side of the park, from the window in his flat at the top of the Home Farmhouse, Eugene Hackett also watched the sky filling with aircraft heading for the City. He watched them through his binoculars without emotion, leaning his top half out of the attic window and steadying himself with one hand on the windowsill as the sinister pageant passed by overhead.

Finally, when the last fighters had flown past, protecting the rear of the vast squadron, Eugene threw his now finished cheroot out of the window, his relaxed expression changing almost immediately as he turned his thoughts to his duties.

Once he had closed the old sash window and pulled the blackout blind down into place, he opened the panelled oak cupboard in one corner of the room, and deftly removed part of the back before finally producing a transmitter, a Morse tapper and a pair of earphones. Lighting a fresh cheroot he pulled a chair up to a table in one corner of the room, set up his wireless set and began to transmit a series of signals.

*   *   *

Unfortunately the news reached Bomber Command too late to scramble the necessary fighters. As a consequence German bombers were able to fly unopposed up the Thames and dropped hundreds of thousands of pounds of high explosive on a City with little or no air defence.

London was taken by surprise, and not just London. Poppy found herself being ushered down by her new friends to the basement of the Stanley to seek protection in the swimming pool complex,

351

where the cubicles provided makeshift bedrooms as the bombs dropped, seemingly without cessation, above them.

'We go here,' the Duchess explained, 'because of the concrete, you see, it's the concrete, modern concrete of the hotel that provides such an excellent shelter from the bombs.'

'This is all so totally unnecessary,' Scott drawled as he lit a cigarette and produced a hip flask full of gin. 'There is absolutely no reason for us to have to scurry down here, really there isn't.'

'You think not, Scott,' Alfred Lypton said, accepting a cigarette. 'You think perhaps Chamberlain was right in the first place. And that this isn't really our scrap.'

'Course I do,' Scott sighed deeply, raising his eyes upwards. 'It most certainly is not our scrap. And it certainly isn't too late to sign on the dotted line right now and stop any further misery. If this war goes on it's going to ruin this country.'

'I think I'm inclined to agree with that,' Lypton replied. 'What say you, Lizard?'

The Duchess, who was busy playing Patience on top of one of the lockers, accepted Scott's offer of a shot from his hip flask and glanced at Lypton.

'You know perfectly well what I feel, Toots,' she said. 'And I certainly agree with this young fellow— any more of this and it will be the ruination of this country. We simply can't afford a war—and even if we do endure it and come up trumps, it'll be the end for the likes of us—you mark my words.'

'I always do, Lizard—always do,' Lypton replied slowly. 'One would be a complete ass not to.'

'I can't imagine you feel differently,' Scott said casually to Poppy, offering her the hip flask, which

352

she declined with a brief shake of her now blonde head.

'Absolutely not,' she said. 'I also understood from certain conversations of late with certain parties in certain places that one is not alone in one's desire to see this fracas concluded as soon as poss.'

'Conversations, eh?' Lypton eyed her the way Poppy imagined a toad eyes a tasty insect. 'Dinner party talk perhaps.'

'Perhaps.' Poppy lit a cigarette and held the look between them, much as it upset her to do so.

'Interesting,' Lypton remarked. 'Wouldn't you say, Lizard?'

Elizabeth, Duchess of Dunedin, looked over the top of the locker, tapped her cards on top of it, smiled briefly and dealt herself a fresh hand.

'You must come and have dinner,' she said to Poppy. 'One's always looking for new faces, particularly young ones. Or perhaps you might like to come down to the country this weekend, get out of the bombing for a bit. We have some home produce, and even a cook to cope with it. Not like the Duchess of Somerset who is doing all her own cooking, poor dear.'

'Why not?' Poppy replied without displaying much enthusiasm. 'I might like that. What fun.'

'Good. Put it in the book then,' the Duchess replied. 'I'll let you know chapter and verse later.'

'Absolutely,' Poppy agreed flatly, being careful not to look at Scott. 'Why not?'

*   *   *

The first intense blitz by the Luftwaffe on the

353

capital resulted inevitably in a number of bombs failing to explode when falling on their targets, which in turn led to a flurry of activity among the bomb disposal experts. Because of their growing reputation, due to further successful disarming of another half a dozen lethal mines that had fallen near important targets in Deptford and Chatham, Commander Fanshaw and 2nd Lieutenant Maddox therefore found themselves being invited by the army to use their newfound expertise to help detonate bombs whose apparatus, like the mines', was also of unknown construction. The bombs had all fallen in a normally busy part of the City, and as a consequence had brought life in that part of London to a standstill.

This particular morning Commander Fanshaw and 2nd Lieutenant Maddox, together with two petty officers they had seconded to help them deal with their increasing workload, were all relaxing over a pot of tea after a splendid breakfast cooked for them by a local café owner when they received a call to go to the City where three more unexploded bombs had been located in the area of Moorgate.

Fanshaw and his squad hurried to the scene where they found the first bomb lying in only a shallow crater in the middle of the street, the other two having both penetrated the roofs of their intended targets to lie unexploded within the buildings.

'Can you deal with this one, Bob?' Fanshaw asked Robert after their initial inspection of the first bomb. 'Looks a fairly alfresco job!'

'Alfresco it certainly is, sir,' Robert replied, having knelt down carefully to get a closer look at the bombshell. 'But not entirely straightforward I'd say. The casing's taken a bit of a belt from striking the road surface, and I've a feeling the ring round the fuse casing might be damaged. Which might mean we won't be able to unscrew it.'

'Hmm,' Commander Fanshaw said, leaning forward and putting his hands on the fronts of his knees while he also took a closer look. 'Then you're going to have to try drilling it out—way you did with that mine in Chatham. What do you think?'

'I'll give it a go, sir, certainly,' Robert agreed, standing up slowly and carefully before turning to the army experts. 'Either of you chaps got a drill?'

While Commander Fanshaw and Petty Officer Watkins hurried off to inspect the bombs lying inside two buildings no more than three hundred yards away, with the aid of a drill purloined from a small back-street factory Robert slowly and carefully drilled out four holes around the damaged holding ring causing it to splinter, and then fracture, which in turn allowed him to extract the fuse by his now well tried and proved method.

'Not sure what we look for now,' Robert whispered to the soldier helping him. 'We don't know whether these things have magnetic triggers, do we, now?'

'So far not,' the other man replied, hardly able to breathe for the thumping of his heart. 'We should be home and dry now we got the fuse out.'

Both men eased themselves back from the bomb, as confident as they could be in the circumstances that the device had been made safe. Just as they were getting to their feet they were knocked to the ground by a huge explosion.

In his confusion for a moment Robert thought he had been blown to pieces. It was only when he was sitting up and looking around him, as he saw his companion in arms was now doing, that he realised that the cloud of thick stone dust was actually rising from buildings not connected to them. There could be no doubt as to what had caused the explosion, just as there could be no doubt that anyone nearer to the blast could not be expected to have survived.

*   *   *

Lily was in the middle of typing a Top Secret report. It was actually more than Top Secret. It was the highest grade—and it was of a dullness that couldn't be believed. She threw herself forward over her typewriter. Her war was going to be tip, tap, tip, tap, that was all her war was going to be, and what was more and what was worse, it was also going to be claustrophobia. Nothing but women, a sea of women, swarming all over Eden Park, and only a few ordinary soldiers, and poor Major Folkestone, to represent the all too divine opposite sex.

'I feel like dancing a wild fandango, or singing "Love For Sale" at the top of my voice,' she told Kate who, seated at the next-door desk, was frowning at her shorthand notebook as if it was an importunate suitor whom she had come across in a dark alley.

'Why don't you do both, Lily dear?' asked Kate. 'It might make you feel less fractious.'

They both stiffened as the section door opened yet again, for despite the fact that dusk was falling they knew only too well that they would be lucky to be free by dinner time, such was the hurry on at that moment, what with the London bombing, the intercepts to type up, and the memos of the endless meetings held at Eden Park. Then Major Folkestone spoke.

'Miss Ormerod here?'

Every head turned at that. To be called by name out of the section by the major meant bad news, everyone knew that. Only last week the girl on the other side of Kate had hurried out to find that most of her family were missing in an air raid. She had not yet returned.

Lily lost colour as she rose reluctantly to her feet.

'Follow me, Miss Ormerod, would you?'

Seeing Major Folkestone's expression Lily at once hurried after him, realising now that he did indeed want to speak to her, rather than send her to take yet more dictation from yet another security officer.

'Miss Ormerod.' The major, tall, respectable and wildly in love, as Lily well knew, with Kate, not to mention several other girls in the section, looked down at her with less of his usual authority. 'The thing is, Miss Ormerod, there's been a bad accident, I'm afraid, in the City, one of several, I gather. Bomb disposal's taken a bit of a lashing, and Kate's brother, young Robert—'

Lily stared up at him, knowing at once that she wasn't going to be able to concentrate on the next few words he was going to speak, because that was what always happened to her in moments of crisis. She found that what was actually said did not penetrate her waking consciousness; rather the words seemed to pass her as if they were unidentified birds flying silently by.

'He just rang from London. From what I gather, he's had a bit of a tough time of it. Just lost his commander. I think he's rather in need of company. Brave chaps these bomb disposal people, you know. Well, of course you do. At any rate he asked me to give you a late pass, which I willingly do. Six hours' compassionate leave do? He'll be ringing back early evening.'

He handed Lily a late pass.

'But see here, best probably if we don't tell Miss Maddox. I can't lose two of you out of the section at this moment in time, and, you know, no matter how much a young man loves his sister, at these times he needs a pretty girl, which is probably why he rang up, because if you ain't pretty, Miss Ormerod,' despite himself the major's eyes ran appreciatively over Lily for a few seconds before finishing, 'then no one is, you know. No one.'

He turned on his heel and walked off, swagger stick under his arm, ready to do battle with the night's problems.

CHAPTER FOURTEEN

As he went about the City at first trying to help not just to defuse several more bombs, but to restore order, Robert finally gave in, and went into the nearest pub and drank two large quick whiskies, but even as he did he could not get it out of his mind that Fanshaw was still with him, as he had been up until now, laughing, holding up his glass,

358

toasting the next 'big so-and-so that Jerry sends us, God rot him'.

He knew Fanshaw had a wife and two children, he knew he lived in Sussex, somewhere near the sea, and that before the war he had liked to sail a boat that he kept at Itchenor harbour, but that was all he did know, because that was war, most especially their war. The people who did his kind of work, his and Fanshaw's kind of work, they couldn't expect to live long; to do so, he had known from the first, would be ridiculous. In which case why was he so surprised that Fanshaw was dead, that Petty Officer Watkins was dead, that, inevitably, he too would be dead soon. Why was he so shocked?

'Another?' The publican looked at the glass that Robert had handed him.

'Make it two, would you? In the same glass.'

It was only after the whisky started to do its work, at what seemed to be too slow a rate to be possible, that Robert came to and realised that there was only one thing he needed now, and that was a woman. And not just any woman. He needed Lily. He went to the pub telephone, raised the receiver and then thought better of it. Lily worked with Kate. He didn't want Kate, he wanted Lily. He replaced the telephone. It was damned embarrassing, but there it was. The wise thing to do was to explain to their Head of Section first. That way he would be able to see Lily, without Kate.

*   *   *

Robert drove faster out of town than he would have imagined possible a few hours earlier. He had more than enough petrol coupons to last the journey, so he did not care how much fuel the MG was using. It was only when he nearly lost control going round a bad S-bend as he sped down a deserted country road that he came to his senses and slowed to a stop, realising that there was a flaw in his plan. He had forgotten to ask Lily's Head of Section, Major Folkestone, to get Lily to telephone him. He stared out of the car window at the sky, hearing the sound of aircraft long before he saw them. He stared up at the fighters, soon to be followed by bombers. More, and more, and more bombers, all heading for London, more bombs, more devices to stare at while sweat dropped into his eyes, more magnetic triggers, more and more, and more. He should have stayed where he was. He should be helping, not driving down to see Lily Ormerod, not running away. He should be like the young men overhead, preparing for battle, not longing for love.

*   *   *

When he at last reached her on the public telephone, she seemed to know at once what was wanted because she merely said, 'I've got an evening pass. See you in the Three Horseshoes.'

In the event he was there long before she arrived, waiting with growing impatience for over an hour, whiling away the time by drinking more doubles, so that when the door of the bar swung open and Lily finally walked in in her best green coat and with her fair hair swinging loose, Robert was only able to rise painfully slowly to his feet.

'I can't tell you how much I've been looking forward to this, Lily,' he mumbled. 'The thought of this—of seeing you again—it's been keeping me going.'

Lily stared up at him. He looked awful. He had grey lines of fatigue under eyes that mirrored the crushing despair the day's tragedy had brought upon his spirit. She took his hand, kissed his cheek and pushed him gently back down into his seat.

'I'm so glad you came down, Robert,' she said gaily. 'But I'm not sure that you should have, really I'm not.' She looked at him. 'Not seeing that you're seven sheets to the wind, and about fifteen drinks ahead of me!'

'Nonsense, Lily,' Robert tried to say as coherently as possible while realising that his speech lacked the clarity that might be considered normal. 'This is what matters. This is all that matters, finally. Me, here, with you. Now let me get you a drink. What is it to be? Gin and something? If they've got any gin, that is.'

'Funnily enough they've always got lots of booze.' Lily smiled. 'Something to do with this place being Eden Park's watering hole we reckon. I'll have a gin and orange, please.'

While he stood at the bar waiting to be served, for the first time since it had happened Robert's mind became filled with the terrible devastation he had witnessed that morning. He closed his eyes as the whole bar seemed to rock and reverberate around him, but all he could see was bright flame and brilliant lightning. The reflected brilliance was such that he became certain that his head must be exploding. He gripped the bar with both hands and slowly opened his eyes, half expecting to find himself standing among ruins like those he had seen earlier, hearing screaming such as he had heard earlier, observing despair such as he had witnessed earlier. But all was normal. There was no dust, no destruction, nothing but people talking and laughing, the gentle light of an old English inn, the rows of bottles behind the bar all painted into his vision with a warmth that had nothing to do with flames and lightning, so that eventually he found himself staring into a pair of concerned eyes belonging to the kindly landlord.

'You all right, sir?' he asked, setting the drinks down in front of him. 'You gone quite white, so you have. Quite white. Like you've seen someone walk across your grave, if you don't mind me saying so, sir.'

'It's nothing.' Robert tried to smile, waiting for the trembling in his hands to quieten before he picked up the drinks. 'It's nothing. Nothing at all. Just a bit tired, that's all.'

'Just come ashore, have you?' the landlord went on, noting Robert's naval uniform, while he wiped the bar dry with his tea towel. 'Seen a bit of action, have you?'

'That's the ticket,' Robert said, picking up the drinks and grinning suddenly and fatuously while swaying slightly. 'I joined the Navy to see the world. And what did I see?'

'You saw the sea,' the landlord filled in for him tonelessly. 'Glad to see a naval uniform in my pub, I tell you. I was in the Navy, but I was wounded out, I'm sorry to say, sir. Oh yes, wounded out of the Senior Service. That was not a good day. Still. We can still show 'em, can't we, sir?'

Robert nodded to him, not really knowing what to say next. Who was it they were meant to be showing? Oh yes, of course. The enemy. He

362

returned to his table.

Lily looked at him, swaying gently above her.

'I should try sitting down, before you spill any more,' she told him with a wry smile. 'I like my gin in a glass, Lieutenant.'

Robert sat down and lay back against the pub bench with his eyes closed for a few seconds.

'What do you want to do, Bob?' Lily wondered. 'How long have you got? Leave, that is.'

'What do I want to do, Lily? First things first,' Robert replied, offering her a Senior Service cigarette. 'What I want to do is sit here with you and tell you what a beautiful girl you are. That's the first thing I want to do. In fact I don't mind sitting here just telling you that for the rest of the night, do you know that?'

Robert stopped. Everything was so easy just thinking about it; it always was so easy as long as it remained in your head—but soon as you came to say it you were a boy again. The tongue-tied schoolboy handing a flower to the girl with all the freckles and the pigtail who had smiled at you in assembly that morning. And you found that all those words you had so carefully practised saying to her in front of your looking glass stuck to your tongue, just as they were sticking to his tongue at that moment.

'Oh, Lord,' he sighed quietly, raising his eyebrows. 'I sound a complete idiot.'

'You sound nothing of the sort,' Lily said, putting her hand on his. 'And as for holding my hand, there's nothing I'd like more. Well. . . ' She paused. 'On the other hand, thinking about it—there might be.'

'I've only got until midnight. I have to drive back

tonight. I'm on duty first thing in the morning. They thought I—they thought I—I should have twenty-four hours' leave, but we can't leave the things, the bombs, littering the streets. Can you imagine? People have to get on with their lives, but you can't hide from these darned things, all lying unexploded in the street. Just can't.'

He could feel the warmth of Lily's body through her skirt on the back of the hand she was holding. All he wanted to do was fall against her and hold her to him. He wasn't going to let the side down. Fanshaw, good old Fanshaw, wouldn't have wanted that.

It's just a job, Bob, he'd have said. *Others have got worse jobs, others not so bad. But it doesn't matter. It's just a job. Just something that has to be done.*

'There's a war on, that's the point, Lily,' Robert continued, even more slowly. 'When I was driving down, at one point I could see them up in the sky. Right above me. I could see a dogfight going on right above me while I was driving along. I'd nearly gone off the road, and when I pulled over I heard the planes. When I looked up there were these two Spitfires taking on four or five Messerschmitts. Just two of them. They shot down two Jerries while I was looking—one of them crashed in flames about a couple of miles from where I was parked. Then the others hightailed out of it—I mean they were running for home—and our boys went after them—two after three and before I lost sight of them they'd got another. They're bringing in pilots with less than ten hours' training, you know. They're getting bomber pilots to fly fighters to fill the gap—that's how tough it is up there. So I can't just sit around feeling sorry for myself. Just because—just because. I can't do that.' Robert shrugged. 'It wouldn't be fair.'

'They have rooms here.' She squeezed his hand now in both of hers, moving her hands up so they now pressed his against her stomach. 'You could spend a few hours here, leave at dawn, that way it won't take you much time to drive back.'

Robert frowned at her.

'Lily.'

'Robert?'

He was going to tell her then. He was just about to say it, but once more the words stuck—not just to his tongue, but all round his mouth—to his cheeks, the roof of his mouth, his lips, everywhere. He was speechless. All he could do was smile.

*   *   *

Marjorie saw Lily the following lunchtime. She was just leaving the canteen as Kate and Marjorie were coming into it. Lily failed to see them, wandering out calling back happily to some friend.

'I wonder what she's got to smile about?' Marjorie said, watching her go.

'I think she was probably born with a smile was our Lily,' Kate replied. 'A smile for the doctor who delivered her. She always seems so carefree. So happy-go-lucky. Some people are like that.'

Marjorie nodded.

'And not only that,' she said, sounding sadder than she wanted to. 'She is very, very pretty.'

'That does help,' Kate agreed, remembering Robert's reaction to seeing Lily. 'She is very pretty—well, beautiful really.'

Marjorie nodded sadly. It was true. Lily

365

was beautiful.

*　　*　　*

'Your bed is now ready, madame.'

The maid led the way to the bed. Poppy nodded to her.

'I think it is as madame would like it—no?' the maid asked anxiously.

'It is not quite as madame likes it.' Poppy frowned. 'I prefer the sheet to be folded lower—'

She was going to say 'please' and then remembered her role. The maid did as she was told, and Poppy nodded nonchalantly.

'Better.'

She slipped off her dressing gown so that it fell to the floor and the maid stooped to pick it up, and then began to withdraw.

'Goodnight, madame.'

'Goodnight.'

Poppy switched off the light, and lay gazing into the darkness. The dinner party had been fascinating, and sheltering in the swimming pool with all those Society types too. She had learned so much, but she had finally found the last few days exhausting, as if she had been required for the first time to be really tested, to be both on the alert as Poppy and a Fascist pain in the neck as Diona. She closed her eyes, suddenly wishing for her old life, whatever that had been, before the war, walking George to the Park, sitting listening to records on her gramophone. So long ago, such a quiet time, she longed for it, wished for it to come back, and in doing so fell asleep at last.

Billy seemed to have made it his duty to keep everyone informed about the depressing state of the national supplies, and gave it as his opinion that the task was impossible.

'You in line for taking over from Lord Haw Haw's broadcasts on the wireless, then?' Mrs Alderman demanded as she set a plate of porridge in front of him. 'Because if so, I can have you shipped out of here and over to Germany before you can say Hitler.'

'We haven't got enough ack-ack guns neither, Sergeant Briggs upstairs told me,' Billy added informatively, as Kate and Marjorie, having been up all night typing up intercepts, collapsed on the kitchen bench beside him.

'By ack-ack I take it you mean anti-aircraft?' Marjorie demanded, trying to smother a yawn. 'And you'll get had up if you spread propaganda and rumours, you will. It's prison for you, my boy, if that goes on.'

'I'm only being honest,' Billy protested.

'You know such an awful lot, Billy,' Kate told him. 'I hope Jerry doesn't capture you because you'll have to spill all the beans.'

'I wouldn't tell 'em a thing, Kate. They could do what they liked. But I'd never squawk.'

'Squeal?'

'I'd never say a dicky's. Not a dicky's.'

'I don't think we've done badly so far,' Kate announced, collecting her things together. 'When you realise they're chalking up the scores on the news boards in London—like cricket scores. We're not doing badly. If what they say is true, we might even be pushing ahead.'

'Yeah, but Sergeant Briggs upstairs, he says how long can we hold out, what with them having thousands of fighters where we've hardly any.'

Marjorie and Kate looked at each other but said nothing. They knew Billy's friend Sergeant Briggs was right. Even Major Folkestone, when the battle for supremacy in the air had begun after Dunkirk, had inadvertently admitted that the RAF had only six hundred aircraft while the general opinion was that the Luftwaffe might have thousands.

'Yeah, but things 'aven't worked out that bad considering,' Billy went on, inexorably, while they all three now tucked into Mrs Alderman's delicious food. 'Mr Hackett was telling me—'

'Oh yes, and since when was Mr Hackett back, may I ask?' Kate asked in a cold voice.

'He came back the other day.' Marjorie turned and looked at Kate briefly, surprised by her tone, since she was normally the most easy-going of characters. Hail-fellow-well-met wasn't in it, really, as far as Kate went.

'Do you know—his uncle owns the place.'

'No he does not, clever clogs, and if he tells you he does, he's not telling you the truth,' Kate growled. 'At least not according to Major Folkestone. He let it slip one night when Cissie Lavington was in our office and going on about some piece of furniture that had been damaged, and he said that he had to have details because he had a duty to inform the owners of Eden Park, Lord and Lady Dunne.'

'Maybe Lord Whatsisname's Mr Hackett's uncle?' Billy suggested. 'He could be.'

'I don't think so, Billy. I think Mr Hackett was

368

possibly having another of his little jokes.'

Kate turned away from him to pick up a greatly reduced newspaper and stare at the headlines. Mr Hackett might well be turning into something of an accomplished liar, if that was what he had maintained.

'Well anyway,' Billy continued, handing back his porridge plate to Mrs Alderman in return for a soft-boiled egg. 'Mr Hackett, he told Sergeant Briggs that the Messerschmitt 110s can't 'andle our Hurricanes and Spitfires 'cos they aren't manoeuvrable enough.' Billy expertly chopped the top off his boiled egg with a swift movement of his butter knife. 'There goes Adolf Hitler's head,' he added with some satisfaction.

'You see?' Marjorie interrupted. 'You *can* say your aitches when you *have* to.'

'Sergeant Briggs says Jerry didn't reckon on *how* tough our boys are,' Billy continued. 'And *how* determined. They chase their bombers right out to sea—did you know that, Kate?'

'Not far enough, Billy,' Kate said as they all watched Mrs Alderman taking a freshly baked loaf from the oven. 'To judge from what they're doing to London.'

'Blimey!' Billy said, half rising in his seat. Returning his egg spoon to his saucer he started up from his chair and went to the window. 'Blimey, listen to that.'

'Billy,' Marjorie groaned. 'What have I told you about saying—'

'No! Blimey! Listen!' Billy cried, now running to the side door and pushing it open. 'Listen to that!'

Reluctantly they all followed him, and stood outside in the courtyard looking up at the cause of the noise, as all over Eden Park windows were being opened and people were peering up at the skies as the rumble of heavy aircraft grew louder and louder.

'Blimey!' Billy cried. 'Look, everyone! Jerry!'

He didn't need to point. Everyone could see well enough. Everyone could see that the sky above them was full of aeroplanes, hundreds and hundreds of heavy bombers and their escorting aircraft coming from due south and headed north for London.

'Do you think this is it?' Marjorie said to Kate, shielding her eyes with one hand against the sun for a better sight of the invaders. 'I suppose this has to be it.'

'I suppose it does,' Kate agreed, shading her eyes and frowning anxiously. 'I don't see any of our lot.'

'They'll be back defending their airfields! They got to!' Billy cried. 'They got to! Sergeant Briggs says Jerry bombs 'em to smithers whenever they go on sorties!'

'Well, if we're going to stand a chance,' Marjorie said quietly, 'they're going to have to chance it and go after Jerry. Or there won't be any London left.'

'Sergeant Briggs says—'

Mrs Alderman turned on Billy.

'Will you hush your mouth about Sergeant Briggs, Billy Hendry. Much he knows. He only stands about the front door earwigging, that's all he does.'

She went back to her kitchen range in high dudgeon, while Marjorie and Kate, with sinking feelings, stood staring up at the crowded skies above them.

*   *   *

From his office window Major Folkestone too watched the skies. Up there somewhere would be his youngest brother, all of nineteen years old, and his brother's best friend—the Little Chaps, the family had always called them. Now the little chaps were fighting for this other Eden, this jewel set in the silver sea, this England. If he was truthful he knew that he had little hope that either of them would come through, and yet because he loved them he had so much hope for them too. Since he was a praying man, he prayed, and yet somehow too, because he was also rational, he could not help wondering who might be listening.

*   *   *

That weekend, as previously arranged, Poppy was due to attend the house party being thrown by the Duchess of Dunedin in one of the several houses she had scattered around the British Isles. Mercifully as far as Poppy was concerned this was not the one in Scotland or, even more mercifully, the large estate she had in Yorkshire not far distant from Poppy's short-lived marital home of Mellerfont. The estate to which they had all apparently been invited was in Gloucestershire, but even so in these days of restricted travel it still meant a long and possibly difficult journey for Poppy, seeing as she neither had a car of her own nor indeed drove. Elizabeth Dunedin had originally arranged a lift down for Poppy, but at the last moment this fell through, leaving Poppy no

371

choice but to travel down by train on the Friday.

'Don't worry, my dear,' her hostess had reassured her in a final telephone call before she left for Paddington Station. 'I've deputised a chum to travel with you. Great friend of mine—Elsie Lightwater—she's great fun and you two will have no end of a hoot travelling by PT.'

'PT?' Poppy had enquired.

'Public Transportation, duck. Quite a real experience nowadays, one hears. We'll have great big drinkies waiting for one on arrival, never fear!'

The journey was every bit as difficult and uncomfortable as Poppy had been led to expect, the train leaving over an hour late and packed to the corridors with soldiers and airmen returning to their bases. Poppy and her travelling companion, a tall extremely elegant woman who was already fairly drunk by the time they boarded the train, were unable to find a seat anywhere and became crushed against each other and several strangers in the corridor of what should have been a First Class coach, but due to the increasingly difficult travel conditions was now an unrestricted zone.

Poppy resigned herself to a long and uncomfortable journey, but not her companion, who finally elbowed her way to the door of the nearest compartment and stood glaring at the male occupants until two of the older men felt compelled to offer her and Poppy their seats.

'Thank you!' Elsie Lightwater said loudly without a trace of gratitude as she quickly took her seat, indicating for Poppy to do likewise. 'I really thought good manners had died with peace. Didn't you?'

Poppy as Poppy would of course have been

happier to remain standing in order to rest vital troops, but as Diona de Donnet she had a different role to play so sank into her vacated seat with a loud sigh and round agreement with the atrocious woman with whom she had been lumbered. Elsie Lightwater, imbued with that peculiar sense of utter insularity which denotes either the highly insecure or the furiously foolish, continued to hold a loud and totally inane conversation with Poppy at the top of her strident voice until finally and mercifully as far as everyone else was concerned— including Poppy—she suddenly fell into a stupor.

'Blimey,' a young soldier in one of the corner seats sighed. 'If that's what we're bloody fighting for, I'm desertin'.'

The carriage exploded with suppressed laughter, leaving Poppy feeling ever more isolated.

*　　　*　　　*

The house party was not at all as Poppy would have imagined, for although the other guests were standard house party fare the rest of the residents of the large, Regency house were certainly not.

'We're chock a block with expectant mothers from cockneyland,' Elizabeth Dunedin explained with a laugh as she welcomed her guests into her estate manager's exquisite little eighteenth-century house half a mile from the main house. 'At least we ain't got the army in as yet—we're doing all we can to stop that little one. Far too much of value in the house to have Tommy vandalising it, so Henry's pulling every string available to get our parturient guests removed as soon as poss, so one can move back in. As if a war's not dreary enough, but to be

373

without everything is too bad. Not a stick of furniture that isn't stored, or a painting that isn't the same.'

Given the precarious times, Poppy was amazed to find that there were half a dozen other guests staying, not to mention her loud-voiced travelling companion. The list was much as if the regulars of the Stanley had been plucked out of the bar and set down in the wartime countryside. Lord Lypton was there, predictably enough; John Basnett, a singularly tall and languid gentleman who talked, drank and smoked non-stop, together with his all but silent and vastly overweight wife, and Scott Meynell.

'If I'd known you were here I wouldn't have come,' Poppy murmured to him, which made Scott quickly turn away, whether to smother a smile or to look furious she wasn't sure.

The initial talk at dinner that night was of the victory the RAF had won against all odds over the Luftwaffe, the climax having come a few days earlier when the vast armada of German bombers that had finally taken to the air to strike what had been hoped to be the decisive blow against the capital were all but knocked out of the skies by seventeen squadrons of the Royal Air Force.

But far from there being any sense of celebration at the dining table, there was an air of unease, as the Dunedins' house guests aired their opinions about the progress of the war.

'Not going to please the Führer much,' Lord Basnett scoffed. 'Operation Sea Lion was meant to pave the way for the invasion, don't you know.'

'Didn't even know such a thing had such a name,' Poppy droned. 'You *are* clever.'

374

'Johnny here has friends in all sorts of very high places,' Elizabeth Dunedin informed her. 'Johnny here is a much travelled fellow.'

'Some might even say a *fellow* traveller,' Lord Lypton said, hooding his eyes at Poppy in what she thought he must imagine to be a sexy fashion as he looked at her. 'Although which carriage he's in is sometimes debatable.'

'Come off it, Lyppy,' Basnett laughed. 'I'm not the only fellow here who knows the man. You met him too.'

'Not as often as thou, Johnny. Three times now, is it not? Or maybe four?'

'One's been mighty fortunate to have been invited, that's all,' Basnett replied, having drained a whole glass of wine in one draught. 'Not sure the housepainter's quite as honest as he makes out—you know, one wouldn't feel *quite* at ease turning one's back—while Goering—different fish altogether. Goering's a gent, do you see. Goering would fit in perfectly well and happily here—different sort of chap altogether. Ribbentrop—well, not quite so sure, but Goering—got a lot of time for our Hermann.'

'Got a lot of time for a lot of people, our Johnny,' Lypton said generally, drumming the table in front of him rhythmically with his fingers. 'Had a lot of time for our Neville, right? Great admirer of NC, our Johnny.'

'So are you, Lyppy,' Basnett replied, piqued. 'Can't say he isn't a friend of your family too.'

'Chamberlain never spent quite as much time *chez moi* as he did *chez toi*, old lad. But then there's no accounting for taste, is there?' He smiled and looked at Poppy. 'No accounting for people's

375

tastes—particularly the taste of politicians.'

'Chamberpot just liked what Johnny laid on for him, that's what,' Elizabeth Dunedin remarked. 'You're just jel-jel, Lyppy. Always prone to attacks of green eye, our Lyppy.'

'I just cannot understand, Lizard, why Neville and Halifax of all people should use Johnny here as the means of communicating to Hitler the views of the government.'

'The government that *was*, Lyppy,' Elizabeth reminded him. 'We have a new boy at the helm, remember?'

'Let me put it this way, Lizard. The views that matter. If things go the way they should we should still be able to get the peace we all want very soon. New boy or no new boy.'

'No new boy hopefully,' Basnett said without thinking, earning himself looks of reproof from both Lypton and his hostess. 'Sorry!' he said gaily, as if he had just given away a small surprise instead of something important, particularly bearing in mind the gist of the secret message that had been placed in Poppy's tin of Black and White cigarettes.

Basnett continued to regale the dinner party with an account of how the democratic press was a constant thorn in Hitler's side and how the Führer had told him that Chamberlain should throw journalists into a concentration camp.

'Only if you put all your press chappies likewise, I told him.' Basnett laughed. 'Fair's only fair, dash it. Put your chaps in a camp and we'll all be the merrier for it. Know what he said? Know what Hitler said to me? *I vill put zem in ze zame camp! I vill put zem in ze zame camp!* How about that, eh? How about that?'

This anecdote re-established Basnett's credibility until, overcome by drink, he gradually disappeared under the table. His outsize wife had already retired.

'Good riddance,' Lypton said, lighting a cigarette and staring with contempt at where Basnett had been seated. 'Don't know why you tolerate the idiot, Lizard. I really don't.'

'Because, Lyppy, he has oodles of dough,' his hostess replied in a tired voice. 'Remember?'

'I was quite interested in what he said about Hitler though,' Poppy drawled. 'About Hitler getting shirty about what the press says about him over here.'

'You think he has a bit of a raw deal, do you?' Lypton wondered idly.

'He's done wonders for the German economy already, so one's told,' Poppy replied. 'And for their employment. Pity the same can't be said for this lot over here.'

'Singing our song, my dear,' Elizabeth said with a glance to Lypton. 'Isn't she, Lyppy? Told you she was one of us.'

*   *   *

After the gentlemen had rejoined the ladies and a few idle hands of cards had been played, Lypton sat down at the piano and revealed himself to be a surprisingly adequate musician. Poppy came over and watched him.

'Well done,' she said, clapping almost silently after Lypton had finished playing a Schubert impromptu. 'That was rather good.'

'Do you play, Diona?' Lypton enquired.

'Not as well as you, no.'

'Can you read?'

'A bit.' Poppy shrugged, as if it was of no real consequence.

'Try this then.' Lypton produced a Chopin nocturne and set it open on the piano music stand. 'You take the right hand.'

It was a piece Poppy knew, but even so she played well enough to have been able to sight read it. By now, a lovely young woman and a handsome man playing beautifully at the piano had the attention of everyone in the room, not least Scott, who was the first to lead the applause when they had finished playing.

'Good,' Lypton said, turning to look at Poppy. 'You played that very well.'

'Ta muchly,' Poppy said in her best mock cockney.

'In fact I'd say we make rather a good duo.'

'Would you?'

'Wouldn't you?'

'Who knows?'

Poppy smiled briefly, and got up from the piano, happy that she now had the man she had marked eating out of her hand. She was also happy when on returning to her room to go to bed she discovered when checking the contents of her handbag that her membership card of a certain international Fascist party, so kindly supplied to her by Jack Ward, had been put back in its holder.

*   *   *

When Marjorie returned after her lunchtime break she found Jack Ward in Major Folkestone's office,

378

together with a short, wire-haired and bespectacled man she recognised as Nigel Greene from C Section. Seeing there was some sort of conference in progress Marjorie excused herself and went to leave the men alone, only to be summoned back immediately by Major Folkestone.

'It's all right, Marjorie,' he said. 'We're nearly finished. Not that there's any cause for privacy, because we seem to have drawn a bit of a blank here.'

Marjorie glanced at Jack Ward who was too busy to take any notice of her since he was carefully studying a leather-bound journal he had in his hand, turning over page after page as if in search of some solution.

'As I said'—Nigel Greene took off his glasses and cleaned them on the end of his tie—'I thought it was some really, really smart code—that he'd invented some sort of impenetrable screen through which we couldn't pass. At least I must say I did hope so.'

Jack frowned, looking up now first at Nigel Greene then round at Major Folkestone.

'No,' he said after a thoughtful silence. 'No, I don't think lightning ever strikes the same tree twice, as the old saw has it.'

'You see all these strokes, do you?' Nigel continued, pointing out the markings on the page that Jack Ward had been examining. 'They all go in slightly different directions, which made us think that it had to be coded—and that all these various strokes at their various angles represented the next layer, the first level of the code if you like. But they don't. It's a red herring. Devised to put us off—or waste our time.'

379

'Or both,' Jack added, looking up at him briefly. 'But then why go to all that trouble? To fill a journal—what is it? Two hundred odd pages? With thousands and thousands of these lines—all painstakingly done. No fudged work this—it would have taken Tetherington hours and hours. Yet you say it's a marsh light. A device to throw us—or whoever got hold of this journal when they shouldn't have done—but why? If the book contains nothing of any sense at all, if it is just a mass of meaningless hieroglyphics, what's the point? Why lock it away in a safe—and why should all hell break loose when it was nicked? Tell me that, somebody, if you will.'

Major Folkestone frowned deeply, thought for a long time then raised his eyebrows and shrugged hopelessly.

'Haven't the faintest, sir,' he said. 'Not a clue.'

'Maybe there was something else in the safe, sir,' Greene suggested. 'And when this book was stolen they thought the real prize had gone.'

'No,' Jack Ward replied immediately. 'Before they set off after us they had time to look into the safe and see what was gone. If there had been anything else there they'd have seen it then. But since this was *all* that was taken—and since all hell followed on hard—we have to assume this book was and still is the real prize.'

'Yes, I think you have to be right, sir,' Marjorie ventured carefully, earning a look of slow surprise from Jack who had barely been aware of her presence.

'Marjorie?' he wondered. 'You have something to say on the matter?'

'Don't think this absurd—'

380

'We won't,' Jack interrupted. 'In this job the absurd is more often than not the answer. So go on.'

'It's just I remember reading a story to Billy once, when he was a bit younger—it was in one of his comics, as I remember it.'

'A comic?' Major Folkestone snorted lightly.

'It was a Sexton Blake adventure, as I also remember it,' Marjorie went on with her usual stubbornness, because when it came to theories she was a dog with a bone, and would never let go.

'As a matter of fact I like Sexton Blake,' Jack admitted, staring with sudden interest at Marjorie. 'Good stuff, actually.'

'Well, in this story, they were looking for some vital clue—or evidence, I can't remember what precisely, and I don't suppose it matters. The point is there was this old volume—a large heavily bound book—it played some vital role or other, and Sexton Blake I think it was—or it might have been his assistant . . .'

'Go on,' Jack encouraged her, as she tailed off, feeling suddenly embarrassed as she realised everyone was staring at her. 'The point being?'

'Whoever it was had this idea that what they were looking for might not be in the book but in the—um—cover. And that is rather thick, sir. Bit like me, eh?'

She had hardly finished before Jack had started to search his pockets for his precious penknife.

'It was actually a priceless drawing, which they'd concealed in between the front board and the binding, but you know a lot of these tales are based on real facts,' Marjorie finished lamely.

'Always worth a try,' Jack nodded, sticking his

pipe back in one corner of his mouth. He glanced at Nigel as much as to indicate that it might have been a good idea if his section could have come up with the same sort of solution, while Major Folkestone fingered his dapper moustache in hope of concealing his own embarrassment.

'It was just a thought.'

'Might even prove to be more than that,' Jack replied, as, penknife in hand, he began to cut the leather cover.

It took some time, during which they all stared at the hands that were carrying out the painstaking task, until finally the front and back board of the journal had come free. Between the hide and the board was a piece of white paper, which Jack now carefully removed.

'Film, by George,' Major Folkestone exclaimed as he leaned over to take a closer look.

'In miniature—' Jack smiled fleetingly, before wandering out of the room at his usual unhurried pace followed closely by a sheepish Nigel Greene.

'As a matter of fact,' Major Folkestone nodded after them as they left, 'I don't mind admitting I'm a bit of a Sexton Blake fan myself. Well done, Marjorie.'

He smiled at Marjorie, who turned away. Poor old Major Folkestone. He really was no hero, not like Robert Maddox.

*   *   *

Billy was late home. Marjorie went in search of him as she had often to do, finally finding him sitting on one of his favourite perches, a length of the park railings that ran around the home paddocks. From there he had a clear view of the skies, and more interestingly the seemingly endless battle being carried on above them. Even as Marjorie arrived by Billy's side there was the buzz and throb of aeroplanes overhead, and looking up to where Billy was pointing she could see a stream of incoming enemy bombers being attacked by a wing of RAF fighters.

'Hurricanes,' Billy said. 'Even better than Spitfires, I think. They're getting cleverer too—see? They're coming in over Jerry now—usually out of the sun and coming down bang! on his tail. See?'

Marjorie watched as the planes sparred as if in some make-believe airborne ballet. They looked for all the world like some sort of graceful birds, swooping down on to each other, except for the deadly streams of lead that poured from the guns in their wings.

Marjorie could see it was somehow magical to Billy.

'Billy—time to come in.'

'Not just yet, Marge—look—fantastic!'

Marjorie looked up at the sky feeling more than a sense of dread as she fell silent, watching this time in pity. Despite the fact that the men in the dark planes with Swastikas painted on their sides were the enemy, as she saw one diving to earth before finally bursting immediately into flames she felt a sense of utter desolation, and it seemed to her that she could hear Aunt Hester's voice murmuring, 'There is nothing worse than losing one's son, do you know that, Marjorie?'

Now, suddenly, thousands of feet above them another Messerschmitt exploded, turning from a plane into a fireball in a second, a huge orange and red and yellow ball that spun in the sky before falling in hundreds of fragments on the countryside of Kent far below.

'Yeah!' Billy cheered, jumping down off his railing and raising both fists in the air. 'Yeah! Yeah!'

'Don't, Billy, don't!' Marjorie pulled him by the arm. 'That wasn't a nothing—that was somebody. A human being.'

'That was Jerry, Marge! That was our enemy!'

'One of them. It was also someone's son.'

'Don't be so soppy, Marge!' Billy called back over his shoulder as he ran off down the edge of the paddocks. 'We've got to kill them before they kill us.'

Marjorie followed him down the fields, looking around her at the great park with its myriad fine trees, some of which had been planted many hundreds of years before. Now it seemed somehow that they appeared to be reproaching the mayhem in the skies above them, as if all the leaves were turning brown in protest at the death and destruction they could sense.

She knew from Aunt Hester that an early autumn was meant to presage a hard winter, and despite the earlier success in finding the film, something which must have cheered up Major Folkestone's section no end, Marjorie felt low, as if there was nothing much to look forward to now, as if she had realised, too late, that really killing the enemy was no solution, only an admission of some kind of past failure, that something which should have been stopped years before had finally blown up in their faces.

And that was it really, she realised slowly, that was what was making her feel low, something Aunt Hester had always been on about, way back when, something which Marjorie had never really understood at the time.

'By applying the principles of hygiene, disinfection, and so on, and so on,' she used to say proudly of her heroine Florence Nightingale, 'which now seems such a basic nursing principle, but which was certainly not then, Florence Nightingale proved that you not only saved the necessity for amputations, you saved lives. Same with politics. Clean out the political wounds, make sure your disinfectant is working, and you won't have to amputate the limbs.'

Nevertheless, on their way back to the cottage, as much to cheer herself up as to encourage Billy, and despite the fact that she knew she was breaking all the rules, she told Billy about finding the true content of the mysterious journal.

'I say, not bad, Marge.'

Billy shook his head in admiration, not of her, but of Sexton Blake.

'Funny though, don't you think, Billy? Getting a solution out of a comic. I mean that is funny.'

'Yeah,' Billy agreed. 'But then whoever wrote the story in the first place—I would say he could well have been a spy himself, because a lot of those writers were, Aunt Hester said. Remember that story when he caught the bloke who was dressed up as a woman?'

'I don't think so, Billy. Remind me.'

'You remember. They were in this railway carriage, and Sexton Blake suspects this woman of not being a woman, so he throws him–her a box of matches?'

'Yes, of course. And the woman puts her knees together and catches them like a man,' Marjorie finished for him.

'Yeah. 'Cos if he'd been a woman she'd have opened her knees and caught them in her skirt. It was brilliant. So the bloke what wrote Sexton Blake—'

'Who wrote Sexton Blake,' Marjorie corrected him.

'Yeah. I don't know,' Billy replied in all innocence. 'Anyhow—he must know a thing or two. See what I mean? I say, I wonder what's in the films, Marge? Could be something vital. Could save England. Imagine.'

Overcome with excitement, Billy turned a cartwheel in front of Marjorie.

'German War Secrets Cracked By Top British Agent!' he cried like a news-vendor. 'Read All About It! Read All About It! German War Secrets Cracked By Top British Agent!'

Marjorie laughed, and, lifting her hand as if to give Billy a smack, gave chase. But Billy had got too quick for her now, and easily out-sprinted her back to the cottage, while overhead the now victorious Hurricane fighters dipped their wings and wheeled down out of the blue skies to head for home.

*   *   *

Locked away in his attic flat at Home Farmhouse, Eugene Hackett sat waiting for the call that for once was late in coming. They were usually so punctilious in calling. He glanced at his watch, worried that the deadline was now five minutes old.

386

He waited another thirty seconds then tried once again to establish contact. This time he was successful.

He listened to everything that was said intently, noting down certain important details in a language few could read or understand. Even so, once the call was ended and he had digested all the salient facts, he carefully burned the piece of paper containing his notes, lighting a fresh cheroot with the end of the taper before watching it annihilate itself finally in a curl of blackening ashes that rose and fluttered out of the ashtray in which he had ignited it.

So it was definitely on.

He sat back smoking his thin black cigar. *After all the initial difficulties and setbacks the game was finally afoot.* He smiled, sitting back in his wooden rocking chair at the window and watching the first of the leaves fluttering from a giant chestnut tree that stood at the end of the garden path. He couldn't help feeling excited at the daring of the plan, the madness of it, let alone at what might be achieved if they pulled it off. It could be perfect. It could be more than perfect. It could be just what was needed.

*　　　*　　　*

Less than half a mile away one of the girls listening in Section H suddenly stiffened, sitting up straighter than usual. Adjusting her earphones more from force of habit than necessity, she quickly and accurately took down everything she had heard in shorthand, hurrying off to quickly translate her words into longhand once the air had

387

gone dead again.

'Sir?' she said, after she had finished and been admitted to Major Folkestone's office. 'A fresh intercept into the section, sir, and judging from the content I thought you should see it at once, sir.'

*   *   *

Since it was such a fine, warm evening, Eugene decided on a stroll, knowing that provided he kept to his side of the park the chances of bumping into anyone who knew him would be remote. Not that he needed to worry about his presence there; he had a perfectly good and valid reason to be living where he was. It was just that he didn't want any interruption to his train of thought. He wanted to concentrate his mind and all his mental energies on the task ahead.

Yet there was a distraction, and one to which Eugene found he could not finally object. As he strolled the far side of the small copse that lay on the north side of the lake, in the quiet of the evening, beneath the higher sounds of the birdsong around him, he could hear the unmistakable sound of someone playing tennis.

At first he stopped, sensing that it would not be a good idea to even glimpse the person he thought it might be on the court, but finally the temptation became irresistible, and he found himself pushing his way carefully, lightly, through the woods until he reached the other side, where he was afforded a perfect view of the court below, and, more important, the person practising.

Eugene hadn't seen or spoken to Kate since she had given him his precious stone. He had been away, and now that he had returned he had been keeping out of sight of the other sections. But he was a man and whenever he had an idle moment he found his thoughts invariably straying to her whom he now thought of as his heroine.

He would have given anything not to have done what he had done when they first met on the tennis court, but given the fact that he had an allotted task he knew he must stay emotionally unencumbered. There was no other way. Besides, there was the undeniable fact that men like himself were not supposed to fall in love. It was just a fact. Of course, they could have affairs, many of them did, some in the course of duty, some for other reasons, but none of them were meant to fall in love. It was just not done—just in case. Those were the three words that mattered most. Just. In. Case. You never knew. That was why you didn't fall in love, because you just never knew, ever, if you might have fallen in love with that most deadly of the enemy's secret weapons—the double agent.

Yet here he was, drawn back to watching Kate, unable to resist the siren call, standing watching the figure below him on the court striking perfect serve after perfect serve and flashing forehand after flashing forehand.

She was practising with a dark-haired young woman he had seen with her before, the one he assumed to be young Billy Hendry's sister. She was throwing balls over the net for Kate to hit, exactly on the spots Kate was indicating while Kate was hitting the balls back to her. Finally, as the other girl stopped, tapping her watch to indicate that she had to go, Eugene found himself walking forward, when he really meant to walk backwards. He meant to, but he didn't, for the truth of the matter was that she was alone, and Kate alone was irresistible. He knew he was doing the wrong thing, and yet he continued on, even as he told himself that by doing so he was blowing his cover, he was breaking the rules, he was doing something that he himself would find infuriating in another agent. You did not break the rules, you did not reveal yourself unnecessarily.

But. She was looking so beautiful, so gazelle-like, so artless, swinging her racket to and fro in the air, high above her head, talking to herself as she did so.

'That's better, you silly ass, that's much more the thing,' he heard her murmuring. And then again, 'Why do you do that?'

Of course he told himself that it didn't matter, that she was not going to become suspicious, that he had as good a reason to be where he was as she had, arguing with himself so that by the time he had walked quietly from his woodland hiding place and got to the court, Kate had already gone to the chair to collect her things, having obviously decided she had practised enough.

'No!' he called from just behind her. 'Don't go.'

She wheeled round in surprise, and looked genuinely astounded when she saw who it was.

'Do you actually live in the woods?' she asked, after a short pause during which she stared at him, a wary look in her eyes.

'Why do you ask?' Eugene was suddenly well aware that his heart was beating faster not because he had been walking, but because he had heard Kate's voice.

'Why I ask is because you're forever popping out

of there like an overlarge leprechaun.'

'I live in a tree with a large hole in it.' Eugene nodded. 'It's full of gold and broken promises.'

'Blarney,' Kate said, picking up her things. 'I bet you kissed that wretched stone the day you were born.' She rolled her eyes expressively, making sure to walk away from him.

He took the lucky stone she had given him at their previous meeting from his breast pocket. 'This is the only stone I've kissed,' he said quietly. 'Don't go,' he heard himself pleading again.

'Why not? I've finished practising,' she called back, hoping her voice sounded indifferent.

'Who are you practising to play? I've never seen such practice. Have you a match?'

'There's only one person I'm practising to play,' Kate replied, eyeing him hard. 'Guess who.'

'Any time you say.'

'No time like the present.'

'Sure I don't have my togs,' Eugene protested. 'I'm not the same player without my togs.'

'You didn't play in *togs* before, I seem to remember.'

'I did indeed. I had my tennis shoes for a start.'

'Well seeing how easily you won, I'm sure you wouldn't mind giving me a small advantage.'

'You serious?'

'Perfectly,' Kate replied. 'After all, you didn't exactly play fair before.'

'You're on,' Eugene said after a moment, sitting down at once and taking off his shoes.

'Barefoot?' Kate queried.

'I was brought up on shingle beaches. It won't inconvenience me,' Eugene replied, pulling off his second shoe. 'Not in the slightest bit. You have a

391

spare racket? I'm not so good with my hand.'

'Oh dear. You should be writing for *Comic Cuts*, you should.'

'When this lousy war is over maybe I will.'

*   *   *

They knocked up, and even as they did so it was obvious this was not going to be any light-hearted return game. As she warmed to her task, Kate was hitting the ball with even greater strength and speed than Eugene had witnessed from his hiding place in the woods.

For his part he tried not to show that he was finding a lot more difficulty returning even her practice shots, so in order to cover this he rushed her into playing the first game, hoping that once they were playing competitively he would be able to re-establish his former supremacy. After all, whatever his private feelings about the beautiful young woman the other side of thc net, Eugene was damned if he was going to allow himself to be walloped by a girl.

But Kate had been practising hard. She hadn't taken her first defeat well—her loss hurting not because it was a defeat but because she thought she had been tricked, and because she had been tricked she had foundered, and the moment she had foundered she had lost her confidence, so that inevitably he had triumphed. Just as inevitably, that had irked Kate. More than that, it had rankled and continued to do so, so much so that every free moment she had she was out on the court practising, trying to regain the confidence she had lost, so that she could get back her self-belief.

392

As for Eugene, he might melt at the sight of beautiful Kate, but romantic feelings would never rob him of his determination to show no mercy and give no quarter. Whatever his feelings might be for the beautiful, athletic young woman facing him across the net, he was damned if he was going to play the gentleman, and he was double damned if he was going to allow himself to be beaten by a slip of a girl, even if he was obliged to play in his bare feet. It would never do to let her triumph. He had to win. That way she would surely hate him more? He served and won the first game after three deuces. It was the only game Eugene took off Kate in the first set.

He fared a little better in the second, winning three games against her six, but he still walked off the court a loser, going down 1–6, 3–6. Neither of them said a word as they sat down to cool off, Eugene choosing to direct his gaze between his two bare feet while Kate carefully and slowly towelled herself off with a white towel, slowly extending one arm after the other in front of her to wipe them dry before turning her attention to her long sunburned legs and finally the back of her neck.

Eugene refused to look, staring instead at the ground, aware of what she was doing and longing more than anything at that moment for a sight of his young goddess towelling herself dry, but denying himself the delight.

'Could I have my racket back, please?'

Kate was standing in front of him, one hand out, having pulled on two extra sweaters to protect herself from the autumnal chill that was now in the late evening air.

Eugene said nothing. He just got to his feet and

393

handed her back her tennis racket. Kate was about to thank him and wish him goodnight, but before she could draw breath she found herself being kissed.

'There was no need for you to do that!' she heard herself exclaiming as she pulled herself clear.

'*Au contraire*, princess,' Eugene replied with a poker face. 'There was absolutely every reason to do so, for I am leaving you for a long time.'

Without another look at her he turned on his bare heels, shoes in hand, and wandered off the way he had originally come, whistling one of his favourite Gaelic airs to himself as if he hadn't a care in the world, which of course was the very opposite of the truth.

For a second Kate was seriously tempted to hit him, so curmudgeonly did she feel he was being, so all male, but she resisted the urge, preferring instead to poke her tongue out at his retreating figure before collecting the rest of her belongings, and hurrying back to the place Eugene mockingly called the Fortress. She now felt she knew considerably less about Eugene Hackett than ever, and before she even reached the main house she herself had reached the conclusion that, all in all, it was most probably a very good thing.

*   *   *

Poppy walked casually over to the tobacco kiosk in the hotel foyer as the rest of the party with whom she had been drinking began to disperse behind her.

'A box of Du Maurier Red, please,' she ordered from the tall, dark-haired girl in attendance.

394

'I'm sorry, madam,' the girl replied. 'We're out of Du Maurier. I could offer you a tin of Markowitch Black and White.'

'Oh, very well,' Poppy sighed ungraciously. 'How very tedious.'

'They're a very good cigarette, madam.'

'I know, I know.'

'I particularly like the design of the packet,' the girl continued, taking Poppy's money. 'The black and white stripes. And the little picture of the man in his top hat lighting his cigarette from cupped hands.'

'Yes,' Poppy returned curtly. 'Isn't it just so charming, if you like that sort of thing.'

She looked at the girl handing her the cigarettes just once and very briefly, but it was enough, quite enough for each of them to register that they were both singing the same tune.

*   *   *

Upstairs in what she hoped was the relative security of the living room of her suite, Poppy carefully unsealed the Black and White tin, tipping the contents out on to the glass table in front of her. Then she took out the wrapping that protected the cigarettes and with the aid of a nail file eased the paper off the back of the silver foil. Inside, as expected, was another sheet of paper, a very thin one made of rice paper.

Separating this slowly from both the foil and its protective paper Poppy smoothed it out on the table and then held it up close to read the message written in a beautiful clear hand. When she had digested the information it contained she set fire to

395

it with a match.

It ignited instantly, curling to nothing in a second. Poppy then took one of the cigarettes from the table and lit it with the same match she had used to ignite the message. She leaned back, enjoying her smoke, staring up at the ceiling as she thought of what lay ahead. She was glad they now had the information, since it meant that it would at least spell an end to the waiting. Now they could move forward in the hope of preventing a catastrophe.

CHAPTER FIFTEEN

Major Folkestone was happy, too. That had not been the case when they had first got wind that something serious was afoot, but now that not only significant but rapid progress had been made his mood had become much more optimistic. He knew there was still an enormous amount of work to be done, but, unusually for him, he was sure that they had everything under control, that the hidden enemy would not win. His pre-war reading might have been more than a little narrow, confining itself as it had to the *Wide World* magazine and Agatha Christie, but he now needed little convincing that a side to life with which, he thanked God, he himself had never been acquainted was not just still present in England, but active. It was shocking. It was, in many cases, blatant. Worse than that, it was against everything for which he believed his country and its ancient history stood.

'You'd be surprised, Tony, at the hold they have here,' Jack had told the major during their many meetings over the plot that was slowly being uncovered. 'I'm forever telling my people the same thing, that one must not be shocked at what one discovers. People like this are everywhere in Europe at the moment. There is strong evidence to prove that there are other countries besides Germany, Italy and Spain that have a very strong allegiance to the Führer and his politics. We're now adding a growing number of Englishmen to the list, but what is even more startling is that countries such as Ireland, Sweden—yes, Sweden and Denmark—and even more surprisingly Norway have a quite considerable number of Fascists who have pledged their allegiance to Germany, and who are more than willing to fight alongside her. The object in this country, as in some of the others, is to come to an early agreement with Hitler, although of course the neutrals have no such ambition since they consider themselves free to do as they choose. But here—and this is what is important—here there is a growing feeling among the Fascists that we must sign a truce now with Hitler and pull out of the conflict altogether.'

Jack had paused, knowing how much he must have shocked his colleague, allowing time for this information to sink in.

'Are you sure about all this? I mean, the names I have in the files on my desk, some of them are influential people, many of them are. Some of them are MPs, one or two in this area, as I remember it.'

Jack looked momentarily sombre, a rare moment.

'Oh yes, Tony, you're quite right. And I'm afraid our information is absolutely on the Gold Standard. They voice their opinions quite openly, too. They go about London, in the clubs, everywhere, deploring the war. They think it should be stopped, and we should shake hands with the Führer, and apply the same principles to England as he has been applying to Germany. Lock up the dissidents, persecute the Jews and the gypsies, burn the books, and so on, and so on.'

Major Folkestone had been shocked to his foundations, and had he not had proof positive on his desk now he might have continued to feel the same. The idea that he might go to London and pass such blighters in the street, that he might sit down in a restaurant and they might be eating at the next table, was truly insupportable. He had allowed himself to think that while there indeed were a growing number of people sympathetic to Germany and its despotic leader, they were few and far between, a bunch of extremists, not representative, and no real threat to the security of the nation. But now that Section C had the details of not just how they thought, but what they were planning, not to mention a more than adequate indication of their actual strength and capability, he had been forced to rethink his attitudes.

The conclusion that had to be arrived at, and not fudged, was that there were English people, living and breathing in their own country, who would be happy to bring about its downfall.

This was why he felt happy the evening Kate slammed Eugene into defeat on the tennis court. He was happy because now, with an uncluttered mind and he hoped an unblinkered vision, he felt stronger and even more prepared to take the fight to those whom he knew to be treacherous. Being a soldier, he felt exhilarated at the idea of the battle ahead, particularly when he realised that he was to be among the few privileged enough to be picked for the task. Major Anthony Folkestone was all too ready for action. Perhaps this confidence translated itself into every area of his life, for he finally found himself brave enough to ask the young woman about whom he had been nursing romantic thoughts out for a drink.

Kate, fresh from her match with Eugene, tried not to look too surprised. Poor old Folkestone asking her out for a drink—what a thing!

'I was going out to the village with some friends, actually, Major,' she explained, looking round her as if for help. 'We're all going for a drink at the Masons Arms, as a matter of fact, so why don't you come and join us? If you want to come out for a drink.'

'I was actually thinking of you and me going out for a drink, Kate,' he replied. 'There's another extremely nice pub in the next village, in Finton. I happen to know they still have plenty of supplies there. Plenty of good beer. And plenty of gin.'

He smiled at her, hoping that a plentiful supply of gin would do the trick, but since Kate hardly ever drank alcohol in any amount the suggestion fell on unreceptive ground.

'I really have made an arrangement with Marjorie and some of the other girls from the section. Thanks all the same. Perhaps another time?'

'Understood,' Major Folkestone replied, brushing down the ends of his neat moustache with thumb and forefinger. 'Understood. Try again next week, shall we say? Jolly good. Really, jolly good. I—um—quite understand. Must get on, however.'

He nodded at her and marched off over-smartly, as if to take a parade, instead of which he found himself returning to his section to stare at the walls and wonder what it was about him that failed to attract not just a pretty girl but any girl.

Kate looked after him and pulled a glum face, feeling suddenly sorry for the forlorn young man inside the crisply pressed uniform, because when all was said and done, although everyone in Section H thought of Anthony Folkestone as being about a hundred, he was probably only all of thirty years old.

'Oh, dear,' Kate murmured out loud, and then turned away feeling miserable as she realised that she had been less than tactful.

Poor old Major Folkestone. But he had after all caught her at a quite inopportune moment, fresh from her victory against the elusive Eugene Hackett. She started to run down the corridor towards the exit, towards the courtyard and the cottage she still shared with Marjorie and Billy. If she'd had the energy, which she certainly didn't, she would have done as she had seen Billy so often do, and turned a cartwheel at the memory of her tennis match. She had after all beaten Eugene Hackett. She had exacted her revenge. What could be better than that?

Nothing it seemed could destroy her good mood until Lily bounced up to her in the pub and embraced her.

'Kate, dear Kate—I wanted you to be the first to know. Robert and I are going to be married.'

400

Kate stared from Lily to Marjorie, and from them to the rest of Section H who had all been standing around enjoying themselves until that moment.

Wartime marriages were ten a penny, of course. People were marrying after knowing each other a matter of days, perhaps hours for all Kate knew, but for Robert to fall for Lily of all people, and then propose. It didn't seem possible.

'Does Robert know about this?' Kate joked to Lily, earning herself a huge laugh from the rest of the section, only for her eyes to catch Marjorie's and see in them a look of matching hurt despair.

*   *   *

The happy-go-lucky atmosphere in Section H was bound to change the moment one of them became engaged, but as soon as Lily announced her engagement to Robert Maddox it changed so quickly it was breathtaking.

It was inevitable of course that the longer the war went on, the longer they were all cloistered up in the great house together, the more the place would finally remind Lily of her boarding school, where the girls spent the whole time either hanging pathetically on to the barred windows to ogle the day boys at the neighbouring state school or writing overheated love letters to themselves in carefully disguised handwriting, which deceived no one at all.

It was that, perhaps more than anything, that had made her accept Robert's proposal, that and the fact that she feared being left at Eden Park, stuck among all the other women of varying ages, all of whom were longing for romance of some sort or another. So when Robert Maddox proposed marriage to her, even though they barely knew each other and even though Lily knew she felt nothing deeper for him than a marvellously intense physical passion, she was only too happy to agree, since she, more than any of her colleagues, wanted to be free from the constraints of Eden Park, from the intensity of the atmosphere, from the inevitable routine of the work.

*   *   *

Two days later, having been warned by letter that he was coming to take her out, Lily found herself sitting on the low part of the boundary wall of the park, smoking a cigarette and dreaming of what she might soon bc wearing on her finger.

'I am so shallow,' she had told a privately appalled Kate. 'The first thing I want to see, besides your darling brother, of course, is that ring on my finger. And I can't say I'm not hoping for a diamond, because I am.'

The longer she sat waiting, the more determined Lily became that she would persuade Robert to buy her a beautiful ring. She tried to imagine wearing it, tilting her head from one side to the other as if she could actually see it, while holding her hand out at full stretch in front of her. She also imagined the looks on the faces of the women in her section as she showed it off to them. They would be pea green with jealousy, and justifiably so.

'Daydreaming?' Robert called out cheerily from the cockpit of his car, having silently freewheeled up to where Lily was perched.

'As a matter of fact I was,' Lily agreed, straightening her hat after he had kissed her in greeting. 'I was dreaming of coming down the aisle on your arm and walking out under a guard of honour with their crossed swords.'

'You'll be lucky.' Robert laughed. 'The amount of weaponry we have in this country at the moment it's more likely to be crossed broom handles. Even so, I can hardly wait. Just have to introduce you to the parents, but their reaction is a foregone conclusion, because I know they will love you as much as I do.'

Lily glanced at him as they drove off. This was the first time Robert had actually professed his real feelings for her and to her embarrassment she found herself oddly disconcerted, because much as she wanted to return the compliment, somehow she found herself unable to do so.

She put her hand on his knee instead, hoping that the intimate gesture would distract from her lack of reciprocation. Robert turned and smiled at her, and picked up her hand to kiss it quickly before returning his own to the steering wheel.

'It's all right,' he assured her. 'You don't have to go making any soppy statements back. Just the fact that you've agreed to marry me's enough. I'm the luckiest man in the world, and I know it, don't you worry!'

All the way into Bendon she helped him change gear, Robert having placed her hand on the gear stick so that he could touch her every time he had to shift a gear. It was still warm enough to drive with the hood down, although Lily knew without asking that Robert was undoubtedly the type to drive with the hood down even in winter, always provided the sun was still shining. Not that she minded; she tied a scarf over her precious little hat so that it wouldn't blow off, and also to protect her ears. Lily couldn't bear getting her ears cold because, as she had explained to Robert, cold ears killed romance, instantly. They were worse than cold feet.

'Can't have that!' Robert had laughed. 'When we're married I'd best get you some ear muffs!'

On the outskirts of Bendon they heard a siren sounding an air raid warning. Immediately scanning the skies above them and cutting the car engine, Robert and Lily listened for the tell-tale drone of incoming bombers. Shortly after they heard the dreaded sound of heavy airborne engines and at once dived out of the car and took to the nearest cover, a semi-underground water conduit running under the edge of the road. They sheltered here while they heard the thud and boom of bombs falling and exploding somewhere in their vicinity, Robert holding Lily tightly in his arms while Lily, simply to take her mind off the air raid, allowed her thoughts to stray to the all-important engagement ring.

At last the siren sounded again, this time proclaiming the All-Clear. Robert and Lily emerged and looked towards the town of Bendon. On the far side they could see plumes of smoke and dust rising from what were obviously bombed buildings.

'I think we ought to turn back, Bobby, don't you?' Lily said, dusting down her coat and dress. 'I think it's only sensible.'

'No, I'll tell you what,' Robert replied after thinking for a moment. 'They could be needing help—you never know. So why don't I drive us to the outskirts and you stay in the car while I go and see what exactly's going on?'

'I'm sure they've got plenty of people to help. It is a town, after all.'

'I know, Lily—but one never knows. They might need help. You'll be all right, I promise. I'll find somewhere safe for you while I just have a look to see if they need an extra pair of hands.'

Ignoring any further protests, Robert drove them quickly to the outskirts of the town. Although the side from which they were approaching hadn't suffered any hits, there was already an outbreak of panic, people running, people shouting, police blowing whistles. Parking the car well away from any buildings, Robert searched for somewhere to shelter Lily, and found a bunker a couple of hundred yards away from the MG. Then he kissed her briefly, touched her cheek, and was gone.

On an impulse Lily ran out of the doorway after him but he was soon lost to her in the rush of people and the ever-increasing clouds of dust and smoke. Retiring to the bunker, she pulled her coat round her and sat on a bench next to a shivering and shaking young woman clutching a baby.

'Why us?' the young woman kept asking. 'Why here? We haven't done nothing. We haven't done nothing—and there's nothing here to bomb. So why us? Why us?'

'It's all right, duck,' a moon-faced woman in WVS uniform comforted her, bringing a tray of tea round the shelter. 'They were probably just unloading their bombs on the way home. The way they do. We just got in the line of fire, that's all.'

'I just hope our boys do the same to them, that's

405

all I hope,' the woman replied, rocking her now bawling baby. 'The swine. I hope we give 'em a taste of their own filthy tactics.'

Lily took the mug of tea offered to her, feeling touched and grateful for such immediate help and already more than a little shaken by the raid. It wasn't like being at Eden Park at all. At Eden somehow it all seemed to happen in the distance, but here it was all too real. She even forgot to think about her engagement ring.

*　　　*　　　*

In the centre of the small town there were bodies everywhere. Two of the offloaded bombs had fallen directly on the market place as at least a dozen or so of the inhabitants were still running for cover, blowing them to pieces. Another bomb had hit the town hall where the staff and their visitors had been still trying to make their way down the crowded stairwells to shelter below ground.

'We just weren't prepared for it,' one of the volunteer wardens muttered to Robert as a party was being quickly organised to search the ruins. 'We done all our drills, but what's drills when you get a shock raid like this? You just don't take that into account, know what I mean?'

'Inevitable,' Robert agreed. 'But no one must blame themselves. You simply can't be prepared for this sort of thing. No one can.'

Stretcher parties materialised through the thick pall of smoke and began to remove the living and the dead from the rubble. An eerie silence had now fallen, broken only by cries and moans from the injured and the still-buried survivors. Fire was now

406

raging where the bombs had fallen, adding to the confusion and creating a thick black and suffocating smoke that hindered rescue operations even more. Standing on a pile of shattered masonry, Robert shielded his eyes as he tried to get a visual purchase on the scene of devastation, but all he could see was a fog of smoke and dust.

A wind got up as if from nowhere, created by the acute difference between the chilly temperature of the day and the fierce blaze of the blitz. However, it cleared the smoke in front of where Robert was standing, revealing a street of shops half of which were either fully on fire or smouldering. He could see people running from doorways to escape the flames and crashing masonry, and as he jumped down and ran in their direction he could hear pitiful cries for help coming from inside the buildings.

The first shop he passed was already completely gutted, as was most of the second one. But the third was still standing, although fire had broken out in the second floor window. To his disgust Robert saw two loutish-looking young men running from the shop stuffing looted goods into their pockets as they fled. He was about to go after them when he realised that it was ridiculous. Human life was infinitely more important than the rescue of property, so wrapping his scarf tightly round his mouth and nose to protect his throat and lungs from fire and shielding his eyes with one raised arm he looked into the shop to see if there was anyone left alive inside.

On the floor lay a dead body, its head crushed by a beam from the floor above which had collapsed into the shop, scattering the merchandise from broken glass cases everywhere. The flickering light of the flames was being reflected by what the cases had contained: watches and necklaces, bracelets—and rings. Jewellery lay everywhere, most of it still miraculously intact. For a second, seeing it, he remembered why he had come to town. For Lily's ring, her engagement ring, to buy her a sapphire perhaps, like his mother's, a dark blue stone set in diamonds. His mother always took it off when she washed up, hanging it on a cup hook above the kitchen sink. He wanted Lily to have one just like it.

Seconds later he found himself distracted by the sound of a whimpering cry.

Above him, suspended somehow in a gaping hole in the ceiling, was a child, a little girl no more than three years old, Robert thought as he stood below her staring up. She was alive because he could see her moving, and because now that she saw him below her she was holding one hand out to him to be rescued. There seemed to be nothing trapping her, no beams, or boards or masonry—she was simply lying in a hole without any support yet somehow not falling, miraculously held in place by some invisible device.

If she fell from that height on to the masonry below, at the very least she would be badly injured. Robert looked slowly and carefully about him for something on which to stand or climb.

'It's all right, sweetie!' he called up to the child. 'Just don't move! Don't move anything just in case! Don't move because I don't want to have to catch you! What I'm going to do—what I'm going to do is climb up and get you—so just—don't—move!'

The child lay as still as could be, hardly

breathing while Robert pulled what remained of one of the shop's counters below the hole in the ceiling. But even if he stood on it he realised he was going to be a good two or three feet short, and if the child was actually trapped there would be no way he could reach her.

He found a chair upside down in a corner of the ruined room, still with all four legs intact. By standing on that he knew he could reach the child. All he needed after that was luck—the luck to find the little girl wasn't trapped and could be freed from below. He would need that luck, as now he saw that the fire that had broken out on the floor above was creeping down into the room where the little girl lay trapped.

'Quickly!' he called from the shop doorway. 'Help needed! Quickly!'

He saw two figures running towards him at once, a warden in a tin hat and a woman in a torn and burned WVS uniform. He directed the woman to stand by to take the child and run once he had her freed and the warden to hold the chair on top of the half-broken showcase while he climbed up on it.

Holding on to the round back of the shop chair with one hand, Robert slowly and carefully got his balance and stood right up to his full extent. The child's face was opposite his own now, and as he appeared in front of her the little girl instinctively reached out for him. As soon as she did she dislodged a considerable amount of small masonry fragments and a lot of dust.

'No, sweetie! No!' he whispered. 'Don't move till I tell you!'

He didn't say that he couldn't even see her

now—he just steadied himself on the rickety chair and slowly raised both his hands, hoping he could keep his balance. As the dust cleared behind the child he could see flames billowing ever nearer, and as they did so the child began to scream from the pain of being scorched. Slipping both his hands through the hole in the ceiling, Robert tried to feel if the child was trapped, and found to his vast relief that as far as he could ascertain she was simply lying stunned all but in space, just as he thought.

Taking hold of her as gently and as slowly as he could he tried to ease her to him, but as soon as he did so he felt resistance. It was not as if there was any great weight behind it, just as though something was holding the child in place. He pulled harder, and heard the faintest rending of what sounded like material, and the next thing he knew he was holding the child free in his hands above his head. He guessed what had been holding her in place and saving her from probable death was nothing more than her clothing.

Now he felt her weight. She might only be a toddler, but that amount of weight above his head was almost too much to bear. It was certainly too much for him to maintain his balance.

'I'm going to drop you, sweetie,' he whispered to the whimpering child. 'Not far—I'm just going to let you fall—very gently—into the arms of this kind lady who's just below me—you'll be perfectly safe—but you're just going to take a little drop— here goes.'

With a nod to the woman who was standing with upstretched hands and arms, Robert swung the child round and let her go. As he did, he began to lose his balance, so to save himself from falling on the child and injuring her he grabbed a portion of one of the floor beams sticking out of the gap in the ceiling. Fortunately it held.

'Quickly!' he shouted to the woman. 'Out! Run! Go on! Quickly!'

But the woman was already gone, darting as fast as she could into the safety of the streets outside.

'You too!' Robert yelled to the warden. 'In case the wretched ceiling falls in!'

'What about you, sir?' the warden called back. 'Let me give you a hand down!'

At that moment the chair beneath Robert gave, leaving him swinging in space still holding on to the beam. He was just about to drop when the beam moved violently, jumping upwards as something heavy crashed from above onto the other end of it, causing Robert to all but disappear into the remains of the room above. He let go at once, hoping to fall, but whatever had caused the beam to upend so suddenly had also caused more masonry and timber to cascade from the floors above, all but filling in the hole where the child had hung suspended and now completely trapping Robert.

Below him through what was left of the hole he could just see the terrified face of the warden staring up at him.

'Get out, man!' he called. 'This whole damn ceiling could collapse! Get out! And be quick about it!'

The face remained looking up at him aghast for a moment and then, as some more masonry collapsed, was gone. Robert struggled, carefully at first lest he should trigger another avalanche of masonry and timber, and then, when he realised he

411

was completely caught, more violently. Both his arms were free, but it felt as if one of his legs was now well and truly stuck between boards and beams. Turning his body round as far as he could, he began to scrabble at the junk trapping his leg, clawing his way down to a heavy beam that was lying across his knee. After two or three good pushes and pulls, he felt the timber move, falling off his leg, and then he heard it crashing through what was left of the ceiling to fall far below on the floor.

He was free. Gently easing his leg back under him, he realised both legs now hung uninjured below him on the other side of the hole. All he had to do now was work the top half of his body free and then wriggle through and drop down. But he would have to hurry. The flames that had threatened the child were now only a matter of yards from his head.

He could feel the heat becoming more and more intense as he struggled harder and harder to free himself. If only someone would jump up and pull his legs from below he would probably just pop out like a cork from a bottle, but there was no one in the shop below.

Except there was. Now he could see two anxious faces peering up at him through the smoke and dust.

'Jump!' he yelled at them. 'Jump up and catch hold of my legs! Quickly! Jump!'

The tallest of them jumped. Robert could feel his hands brush the bottom of his feet. Pushing himself down with all his might he tried to force his body nearer to his rescuers but he couldn't move himself an inch let alone six.

'Hold on!' he heard one of them shout up to him. 'Pete's gone to fetch a ladder!'

Pete would have to be quick, Robert realised, as with a loud *whoosh!* a ball of flame exploded on the other side of the room in which his top half was stuck, scorching his face like the sun even from that distance. Now he could barely breathe, so little oxygen was there left in the air—so closing his eyes as tightly as he could, he breathed in slowly and deeply through his nose, held the breath and gave one last mighty push downwards.

He felt the floor give way and sensed he was beginning to fall—but even as he did there was a huge explosion above him.

Meanwhile Lily sat on in the shelter. It was only when she realised that she was by now quite alone that it came to her that something must have happened.

*   *   *

Gas, they said later. It had to be one of the gas ovens in one of the flats above the shop, to go off like that. Or it could just have been combustion, one of the firemen reckoned, as they sorted through the rubble.

Whatever it was was of no consequence to Robert, who was killed instantly by the blast even as he fell through the hole from which he had rescued the jeweller's little girl.

When they finally disinterred him from the massive pile of rubble that had collapsed on top of him, they found his tall, handsome body face down, arms spread out, barely covering, among many other pieces, a cluster of rings.

413

Kate stood staring at the dark rectangle in the ground. The nightmare was still running. She tried hurting herself again, surreptitiously bending her little finger back as far as she could until she could practically bear the pain no longer but refusing to cry out, hoping only that the self-inflicted agony would shake her sleeping mind into consciousness, and when it did she would be lying in her bed in the cottage at Eden Park looking out on the glorious landscape that lay beyond her window, with Marjorie asleep in her bed beside her, and Billy in the room next door—instead of standing at Robert's grave. But the terrible event was not a nightmare. Robert was dead, tragedy had triumphed and grief was exultant.

She turned to Marjorie, putting out a hand to place it on her arm, as Billy stood a little way behind her, hands folded in front of him, head tilted upwards, staring at the sky above him as if unable to face the reality of death. Robert's father and mother stood at the head of the grave. Helen's face was immobile, still as a statue, while at her side Harold stood in a black overcoat holding his homburg hat in front of him, seeming to glare down into the hole in the ground where his son's coffin rested, its shining brass plaque now all but obscured by a handful of the earth thrown by the vicar. At the other end of the grave Lily stood apart from the family, a small, slender figure, her face concealed by the veil on her hat.

The ceremony ended, Kate turned to look at Lily, about to go and ask her to come back to the

414

house with the family and closest friends and relatives, but Lily seemed unaware of Kate. Instead she took a step nearer the grave, dropped a white lily on the coffin, turned and stumbled hurriedly out of the graveyard.

'Arc you going to be all right?' Kate asked Marjorie. 'I'm just going after Lily.'

'Lily?' Marjorie said, staring at Kate. 'What for? Why do you want to go after Lily?'

'I think I ought to invite her back to the house.'

'Why? Why should you think that?'

'Marjorie.' Kate took her friend aside. 'Marjorie—Lily and Robert were *engaged*.'

'Not officially.'

'That doesn't matter, Marjorie. Robert was mad about her and they were going to get married. So I think it's only proper that I should ask her back.'

'They weren't engaged. Not officially.'

'It really doesn't matter, Marjorie. Really it doesn't.'

But by the time Kate made it out into the lane by the church, Lily appeared to have vanished. Thinking she couldn't have got very far, Kate began to hurry towards where the lane met the road, but as she reached the junction she heard the throaty roar of a car driving away. Looking to her left she saw Robert's MG fast disappearing in a cloud of dust as Lily fled the burial ground.

*   *   *

'You'll be giving up that secretary stuff now I take it,' Harold Maddox said to his daughter after the last of the guests had left the house. 'You'll be coming home to look after your mother.'

415

'She'll be doing no such thing,' Helen replied, helping Kate and Marjorie begin to clear away.

'Leave this please, Mum,' Kate insisted. 'We can manage this perfectly well.'

'Just as I can manage perfectly well here on my own,' Helen replied. 'I'm not helpless. I can manage perfectly well on my own.'

'Katherine will have to give up her work for a while, that's all there is to it,' Harold insisted. 'I am not having you moping around the place on your own without any company.'

'You can insist till you're blue in the face, Harold,' Helen replied. 'Kate is not giving up her work.'

'I can if you want me to, Mum. It's all right.'

'It is not all right. And I do not want you to. Robert wouldn't have wanted you to—it's no good looking like that, Harold. He told me several times how much Kate was enjoying her work, and more important how good she was at it.'

'How on earth could he know?' Harold snapped. 'Her work's meant to be hush-hush.'

'Lily told him, if you want to know. They work in the same section and she told Robert how highly they thought of Kate. And what important work she's doing, so I'm certainly not having her giving it up on my account, particularly since it is quite unnecessary.'

'Well I say she does,' Harold insisted. 'And that is an end to it. Kate has not achieved the age of majority, so what I say still goes.'

'Oh, for God's sake!' Helen turned round and confronted her husband face to face. 'There's a war on, Harold! We all have to do what we can to help fight it—as well as win it, please God! It's bad

416

enough fighting one dictator without having to take on another one in one's household!'

'I'm afraid I insist, Helen. Do you understand? These are my wishes.'

'Then you know what you can do with your wishes, Harold! You insist once more and I shall walk out that front door! I mean it! And you can bet your last penny no one's going to give up anything to stay at home looking after you!'

Her husband had no idea at all how to cope with this sudden display of emotion, with the fact that his wife was, for once, showing her feelings. Looking first to his daughter and then equally hopelessly to her friend, he was unable to do anything except shake his head and begin to hurry out of the room.

'You haven't heard the last of this, Katherine,' he muttered as he reached the door.

'Oh—oh, go to *hell*, Harold, will you!' Helen cried at him from behind her hands. 'Just *go to hell*!'

Kate sat comforting her mother while Marjorie and Billy continued to clear up the funeral tea with the aid of Helen's daily help.

'As if it's not enough to have lost Robert,' Helen said quietly, twisting her handkerchief round her fingers. 'God knows it's bad enough losing our son—but then to have him trying to wreck your life.'

'It's all right, Mum,' Kate comforted her. 'He's not going to wreck my life on top of it all. And, you know, if you want me here, there's no problem in me getting some compassionate leave, really there isn't.'

'I don't want you to, Kate—and for two good

417

reasons. First of all, I don't need it. I am working twenty-four hours a day with the WVS, and heaven only knows what else.' Helen patted Kate's hand and smiled bravely at her. 'And secondly I don't think you should leave your post at a time like this. And anyway, if you did come home to help out, I'd only get so used to you being here again I wouldn't want you to go back. Particularly now.'

'That's three things, Mum,' Kate tried to joke. 'Not two.'

'Me all over,' Helen said, wiping her eyes with her hankie. 'I was never any good at maths. Now don't you worry about a thing—I can take care of your father, believe me.'

'You sure?'

'I'm sure. Now if you'll excuse me, I think I'm going to go and try to make myself look a bit more presentable.' She got up, kissed Kate and left to go upstairs.

'You can stay here tonight, Marjorie,' Kate said as finally all the clearing up was done. 'You don't have to go back tonight. Mum said it would be fine and it really is a bit of a trek back to Eden Park.'

'I don't know that we should,' Marjorie demurred. 'I mean, where would we sleep?'

'There's a spare bed in my room,' Kate replied, knowing Robert's room was strictly off limits. 'And perhaps Billy wouldn't mind sleeping on the sofa?'

'Course not,' Billy replied gruffly. 'I don't mind where I sleep, Kate.'

No one had any appetite for supper, so everyone retired to bed early. Having settled Billy down on the sofa, Kate and Marjorie took themselves off upstairs. As she got into bed Kate dreaded the night, thinking she would never fall asleep, but due

418

no doubt to the terrible strains and the emotion of the day she soon and suddenly fell into a deep, dreamless sleep, only to find herself being awoken in the smallest of the hours by the sound of terrible sobbing.

'Marjorie?' she said quietly. 'Marjorie, what is it?'

Kate knew perfectly well.

'I feel bereft. I loved your brother so much.'

'You were not alone, Marjorie,' Kate whispered, and she pulled the bedclothes over her head in order to prevent herself from saying, 'You only met him *once*. I knew him all my life.'

Downstairs her mother stared into the lifeless sitting room fire, as if willing it to spring once more into a blaze. Meanwhile, outside, walking the now silent, dark streets, while fires from another town lit up the skies, and not knowing quite where he was headed, Robert's father started to face bitter despair.

CHAPTER SIXTEEN

Any sense of shame Poppy might have felt she had buried the day Jack Ward commissioned her to see her first task through to the end. She knew she was going to be asked to do things she would never before have imagined doing, to be a person she could never have imagined being, and to make intimate friends of people she despised. Of course she had suffered many moments of doubt at the thought of what might lie in store for her, but the moment she had to resume her dreadful new

419

persona publicly Poppy found she was able to forget all about her old self.

So far at least she had been successful. The new set seemed to harbour no suspicions about her, taking her into their outer circle almost at once and very shortly into their inner one. Scott had been a great help, since he sowed all the correct sort of propaganda about Poppy to her newfound admirers, tempering his information with the impression that he himself was none too keen on her as a woman since she had not only turned him down, not once but twice, but was if anything too extreme in her views.

'And that is saying something. I mean even the Führer's talent scouts thought I was ideal material until they met Miss de Donnet. Just imagine, if Miss de Donnet played the right sort of cards in the right sort of order, she could well be the next Mrs Hitler.'

Remarks like this, designed to raise an easy laugh at cocktail hour, also more than served their purpose, since Poppy then had to do or say very little more to convince her new circle of friends that she was the sort of woman all the men admired and all the women feared—apparently devoid of warmth, displaying emotion only when something unfortunate or untoward happened, when she would be seen to smile to herself in private satisfaction.

'Hard as nails,' Elizabeth would mutter behind her back. 'No, harder actually. But you have to give it to her, she is not just frightening, she is fascinating too.'

Far from frightening Henry Lypton, however, the more disdainful and uninterested Poppy appeared to be in his company the more he pursued her. Having decided that she was not only indispensable company at the piano, he now determined she was to be his constant social companion for as many hours per day as he could persuade her to be, with an eye obviously on extending their friendship well into the hours of the night.

The moment Poppy realised that this was his all too obvious design was the closest she found herself coming to running away to ring Jack Ward from the nearest telephone and telling him that becoming Lord Lypton's mistress was taking everything a step too far.

They lunched or dined together at least once every two or three days, as their so-called friendship developed. Despite wartime restrictions Henry Lypton seemed to know any number of places where they could eat and drink quite adequately. They would also dine at friends' houses where again the war seemed to be taking place elsewhere. The more houses Poppy was invited to the more well-known and influential people she met, the more she heard, and the more she was able to carefully jot down in the privacy of her hotel bedroom to pass on to HQ via her usual post box, the cigarette kiosk in the hotel foyer.

One evening when she and Henry were dining in a private room in a small, extremely exclusive restaurant in Mayfair, Poppy decided to take the initiative a little more than usual, having been advised by her masters that they were getting every indication that whatever was being planned was now imminent, and therefore it was essential that as much information as possible should be collected quickly but still as discreetly as ever if a successful counter-strike was going to be organised in time.

'Sometimes one wonders, you know,' she drawled, sipping her gin and It, 'whether everyone one knows is just perfectly content to sit on their more than ample British backside hoping for the best—which is to say that someone else manages to knock a few heads together—or whether anyone one knows is actually going to have the spunk to *do* something. Frankly, Henry, I don't know about you, but I am getting most *dreadfully* bored waiting.'

'*Moi aussi*, my pet,' Henry replied, hooding his reptile eyes at her. 'Being bored is dull enough, but being dreadfully bored is positively narcotic.'

'I am trying to be serious, Henry.'

'The *on dit*—for what it is worth—is that the fat is in the fire.'

'The fat has been in the fire, Henry, for *years*. First of all everyone went around saying Neville C was going to come up trumps—then it was Halifax—then it was that funny little mob of muddleheaded aristos who thought all they had to do was have a word in the right ear and everything would be hunky-doo. Then there were all the rumours that Herr H was doing all sorts of stuff backstage so that we could sign a quick and sure-thing treaty with him that would protect our interests after he'd finished sticking Swastikas all over Europe—yet here we are at the end of year one *still at war*. It's all the little Fat Man's fault, I do swear. If the Fat Man hadn't barged his way into office and started banging on about how great we are and how we'll fight everywhere to the last drop of blood et cetera et-boring-blasted-cetera we would *not* be having to endure this dreadful bombardment that is simply wrecking one's social life.'

Henry smiled slowly, amused as always at his Diona's cold-blooded egoism and her utter contempt for what the British public considered the rights and wrongs of this particular war, warming to her more than ever. Lord Lypton was absolutely on the side of Hitler and the Third Reich. He belived in everything the Führer said, thought and wrote, and was at a complete loss when it came to understanding how anyone of any proper education could not see the brilliance of the Nazi political values, military ambition and ethnic ideals. But most of all he smiled because he knew what was in hand, just as he knew that if they were able to pull off the coup that was planned, then one enormous obstacle would be removed from their path at one fell swoop, leaving the way to an early truce with Germany considerably clearer.

'You realise that there are those who wish to drag America into this dogfight, don't you, Diona?' Henry enquired, pouring them both some more brandy. 'And if that's the case, our cause will be lost, I would say. There is no way we are going to be able to take on Uncle Sam. But while the Yanks are still dragging their feet, we still have a chance. That is why—and this is for your ears only, my duck—that is why we are coming to what could be the moment we have all been waiting for. Won't that be good? Will madame not be pleased with monsieur if this is so?'

'I do so hate it when people talk in riddles,' Poppy replied, taking care to look as though she was drinking when in fact she was getting rid of as much as possible in a convenient plant pot placed in the middle of the table. 'How can madame say whether she will be pleased or not when she hasn't the slightest idea what monsieur is talking about?'

'I like it when you are cross with me, madame,' Henry replied quietly.

'I shall be even crosser if you don't tell me.'

'Ah.' Henry smiled, a smile that Poppy found singularly unamusing.

'In that case, madame, I shall not tell you.'

For a moment Poppy failed to read the game— then suddenly she cottoned on.

'In that case I shall not be cross, monsieur,' she replied, eyeing him coldly, an expression which she had no difficulty at all in mustering.

'Oh, please,' Henry mock pleaded. 'Please be cruel and cross.'

'So tell me everything—and I mean everything.' Poppy sighed, closing her eyes and then opening them very wide for effect. 'And when and *if* you do—then, and only then.'

There was a silence at the dining table. Henry steadily regarded the beautiful woman opposite him, whom he now considered to be far and away the most exciting and attractive woman he could ever remember meeting.

'Diona—madame,' he smiled, lapsing into a French accent. 'What would you say to monsieur— or what would you do for monsieur—if he told you that the little Fat Man is soon to be just a memory?'

'The little Fat Man?' Poppy stared at Henry as coolly as she could while realising at once who their target must be. She lit a fresh cigarette.

424

'I don't honestly think you have the ability to carry out what you're hinting at,' she said, blowing a thin plume of smoke upwards. 'I think the trouble with half the people I have met with you is that they are—as the saying has it—full of wind and a certain amount of fury and signifying damn' all.'

'You would be surprised, madame,' Henry replied, a flicker of anger appearing in his cold eyes. 'We are really rather well organised, as it happens. If our *coup* succeeds, we have people in place to step into certain shoes. As you may imagine, there would be a certain amount of chaos if the Fat Man goes. Ally this to the somewhat parlous state of our present defences, and the well-known depletion of our armed forces—the air force particularly needing to recoup—and you will soon see that, with the sudden loss of its head, this country will be running around like the famous headless chicken.'

'I understood we had plenty of reserves left after the last air battle,' Poppy said casually. 'That the air force repulsed the so-called enemy with plenty to spare.'

'Not what our spies told us, madame. The Fat Man was actually at Uxbridge at 11 Group's HQ during what turned out to be the last day of the battle—and when he asked at a very crucial stage how many reserves there were, Vice-Marshal Park had to tell him none.'

'That's how close it was?'

'Last gasp stuff. The Germans have plenty of air strength left when they care to use it. We have sweet Fanny. So it is time to strike, wouldn't you agree?'

'It would seem so.'

'It will be no cakewalk, madame, most certainly not, but it will be successful, believe me. Now I'm bored. I want a little entertainment. Are you in the mood for a little entertainment?'

'Later.' Poppy handed him her cigarette to extinguish for her. 'If it is of any interest, it is well known that the Fat Man travels everywhere in a bullet-proof car with a Tommy gun on the seat beside him.'

Henry Lypton opened his eyes wider than normal, generally a sign of slight amusement. To underwrite this the corners of his thin-lipped mouth curled upwards almost into a smile while he clapped his long-fingered, lilywhite hands slowly twice.

'That is well known. But we have other plans. Once inside the houses of friends he is notoriously careless. Sits up drinking at dinner for hours on end, starts work late in the night, when everyone else has retired. Quite a soft target for us, really, when you think of it.'

Poppy nodded. All this was well noted in patrician circles. More than that it was all too true. The Fat Man could be said to be quite an easy target, if, that is, they had infiltrated his inner circle, which judging from Lypton's expression would seem to be the case.

'Your suite or mine?' Henry Lypton wondered aloud after he had paid the cab off and they were strolling towards their hotel entrance.

'Neither, Henry,' Poppy replied with a tired sigh. 'You really haven't been anywhere near bad enough for me to allow you to visit, and I certainly am not going to call on you.'

'Oh, but madame?' Henry wheedled, taking one

of Poppy's arms just above the elbow. Had he been directly wired to the mains Poppy reckoned she could not have felt a more uncomfortable and unpleasant *frisson*. 'I have been *very* bad, I assure you. If the Lizard and the others—if they knew how dreadfully indiscreet I have been, I shudder to think what they would do to me.'

'Then surely your greatest final pleasure, Henry Lypton, would be for me to tell them what a bad boy you really are?'

Poppy shook herself free and turned to stare at him as they stood in the hotel foyer.

'I think—that is one doubtful pleasure I would rather forgo, madame,' Henry replied smoothly.

'So long as we understand each other.'

Lypton swallowed and nodded.

Poppy gave him one last look of contempt, turned on her high heels and took the elevator to her floor, shutting the lift door over on him and refusing to let him accompany her as his final humiliation. Lypton turned away looking strangely satisfied.

*   *   *

After making sure she was alone, Poppy sat down at her desk and wrote the all-important information she had on a note to her Head of Section. She then transcribed it into code and folded it into as small a note as she could, sliding it in the bottom of a specially prepared matchbox that she then placed not in her gas mask case with her gun, as she had been taught, but in a pocket of the coat and skirt she intended to wear the following day.

Preparing for bed she recapped what was required of her over the next week. She had managed to sidestep lunch the following day with Henry Lypton, pleading a previous lunch engagement with a non-existent relative whom she was relying on Jack Ward to conjure up, since she knew she would as always be shadowed everywhere she went.

In the evening she had a dinner engagement with Elizabeth Dunedin, who was throwing a party especially for Ambeline Melford, freshly returned from Germany where she had been the Führer's house guest in his mountain retreat. Finally on Friday morning Henry had arranged to pick her up in his Bentley and drive them both to what he had promised would be a mighty celebration—rumour being that there would even be a firework display.

Poppy had protested lightly that she understood fireworks were now proscribed, to which Henry had winked and said she was to think beyond just ordinary fireworks. Now, having dined with the hateful man and learned what was more than possibly afoot, Poppy had a very good idea exactly what Henry Lypton had meant by his remark.

That left Poppy enough time to make her drop in the morning. But remembering Jack Ward's instructions, and mindful of quite how vigilant the most dedicated of her set of newfound friends were, Poppy knew she had to stick to the protocol, or risk failure.

She had changed for bed when there was a knock on the outer door of her suite.

'Hotel security, madam,' a voice called. 'Would you please be kind enough to open this door?'

'I don't wish to.'

428

'I don't know why you shouldn't.'

'Because it's ten to midnight and I don't know who the devil you are.'

'I understand perfectly, madam. But all you have to do is ring down to the desk and check that the manager has instructed a Mr George Bulstrode to call on you.'

'At this hour of the night?'

'This is an emergency, madam. I would not be troubling you otherwise.' The man on the other side of the door paused, then lowered his voice. 'You are in a little bit of danger, madam. You really must open the door.'

'And if I refuse?' Poppy said in her haughtiest tones.

'I shall have to use my master key.'

Poppy hesitated, and then, pulling her silk wrap around her, she opened the door and admitted her visitor.

He looked every inch a hotel private detective, with his clean but shabby dark suit, his large cheap shoes, his somewhat sad drooping moustache and his reddened nose.

'Sit down, Mr Bulstrode,' Poppy said brusquely, indicating a straight-backed chair. 'I just want to put on some clothes. I really am not in the habit of receiving callers at this time of night. I must cover myself.'

Bulstrode acknowledged his thanks with a brief nod of his head and moved towards the chair while Poppy, keeping an eye on him, headed for her bedroom to pull a sweater and pair of slacks over her silk pyjamas. When she returned to the sitting room, Scott was sitting on the sofa smoking a Black Russian cigarette.

'Scott,' Poppy said, factually, determined not to give him the pleasure of hearing her surprise.

Scott grinned.

'Heil Hitler.'

'Scott!' Poppy said, dropping her voice. *'There could be microphones.'*

'There are no microphones,' Scott assured her. 'I should know. I was there at the discussion as to whether or not you should be bugged. I was all for it—but they decided against it, purely because they didn't know anyone who could do it. Honestly. That lot. When they're not being vile they're being stupid.'

'That lot, as you call them,' Poppy remarked tersely, 'are about to try to assassinate the Prime Minister.'

Scott stared at Poppy, then lit a fresh cigarette.

'We knew they had a VIP target,' he nodded. 'But the money was on this American billionaire staying just up the road. One of Roosevelt's top buddies—and more important one of his top investors. He's all for America coming into the war and the word was that if they could take him out of the equation, Roosevelt would feel less sympathetic to Britain.'

'It's not him,' Poppy replied. 'I have it from the—I was about to say the horse's mouth but that would demean the horse. I have it from the Reptile. The Fat Man, as they call Churchill, is an easy target once inside one of these country house parties. Loves to sit up and drink, stays awake all night with minimum security dictating to hapless secretaries, that sort of thing.'

'You're certain?'

'Quite.'

'Have you informed the office?'

'Can't. Not until tomorrow.'

'Any idea of the date for this?'

'Mention of fireworks makes me think it just might be on Saturday night.'

Scott looked at his watch.

'Can't get to a public phone box now, not without rousing suspicion, and can't use a telephone from here, so I dare say it'll have to wait until dawn.'

'I'd say.'

Scott smiled at her and began to tidy up his disguise.

'This wasn't just fun and games,' he told her. 'This was *très* necessary, my friend. You have no idea how much trouble I went to just to call on you.'

Poppy shook her head at that, not believing him.

'Your fun and games will land you in trouble one day.'

'Then I'll be perfectly poised to say it was fun while it lasted. Anyway—I'd go to even more trouble than this to see you.'

Now Poppy stopped, momentarily thrown off balance.

'Me?' she echoed. 'Why on earth?'

'Because I admire you.'

'You don't know anything about me.'

'So tell me.' Scott sat back in his chair and smiled at her, flicking his long hair back from his bright eyes.

'I'm not anything. I mean—not anything very much, truly I am not. The real me is not at all interesting.'

'Oh yes you are. *Oh yes you are.*'

431

'I'm not. I'm really dreadfully ordinary, really quite plain—I wear glasses most of the time—and I read an awful lot. And I only really like dogs.'

'I don't believe a word of it.'

'It's entirely true.'

'What I see is a beautiful, elegant and poised young woman—'

'That's just make-up.'

'You wear elegant and poised make-up?'

'I meant the beautiful bit. I really am quite dreadfully plain. I've been told so from birth.'

'And now I'm telling you differently,' Scott replied. 'You are one of the most beautiful women I've met.'

'What are you trying to do?' Poppy asked him. 'Are you trying to do what I think you're trying to do?'

'I wouldn't know how to answer that.' Scott looked quizzical. 'I really wouldn't.'

'Are you trying to—' Poppy tried again, before frowning and running aground. 'Are you—er—flirting with me?'

'*Flirting* with you? I hope not. I really hate flirts.'

'So then what are you doing?'

'Telling you the truth. I think you're perfectly beautiful—perfectly gorgeous, extremely clever—and above all remarkably brave.'

'No more than you, Scott.'

'That goes without saying,' Scott replied, poker-faced. 'Including the extremely clever bit. Everyone knows I am Jack Ward's favourite boy. I am H Section's perfect master of disguise, will o' the wisp, not to mention Secret Weapon.'

'I don't think you're ever serious,' Poppy said, sinking down into the chair opposite. 'Not ever. So please, don't joke. It can be a little tiring.'

'I'm being perfectly serious now, Poppy. I've never been more serious. I think you're what my grandfather would call a "stunner". In fact if you really must know I wish to God you weren't on this shoot. I wish to God you were safe home in some lovely bed in some lovely big comfortable house somewhere out of bombing range and with nothing to do with this wretched business you've got yourself involved in.'

'Any particular reason?'

'A very good reason. I have fallen madly, head over heels, in love with you.'

There was a small, stunned silence while Poppy looked at Scott as though he were mad.

'No you haven't,' she said. 'Of course you haven't.'

'Come on.' Scott laughed. 'Let me be the best judge of that.'

'You are flirting. I knew it.'

'I am *not* flirting. I am telling you the truth. I. Am. Crazy. About. You.'

'I think you ought to go to bed.'

'I think you ought to as well.'

'I was just about to. Why did you come here anyway? Just to tell me what you've just told me?'

It was Scott's turn to stare, which he did, for quite a while. Then he burst out laughing.

'What I've just told you—Poppy—people would cross continents, frozen seas, universes to tell someone they were in love with them.'

'Some people might.'

'I'm one of them.'

'Thank you—but you can't be serious. Now go to bed.'

433

'On one condition.'

'No.'

'On one condition.'

'Oh very well.' Poppy looked at him, trying her best to appear glum.

'You at least let me kiss you.'

'You want to *kiss* me?'

Poppy managed to make it sound as if what Scott was requesting was supernatural.

'Yes. I want to kiss you.'

'That's ridiculous, Scott.'

'Why?'

'People don't *announce* they want to kiss someone. They just—they just kiss someone.'

'You have a lot of experience in this field?'

'Enough,' Poppy lied. Suddenly wishing she was still Diona she switched to her character, and using the change in voice and manner she said, 'Besides, I don't kiss house detectives.'

'Fair enough.'

Scott got to his feet, put out his cigarette, smiled at Poppy and moved towards the door as if to leave. Poppy followed on behind him, now feeling somewhat glum.

'Right,' Scott said by the door, turning back to her. 'Goodnight, Poppy.'

'Goodnight, Scott.'

He kissed her then, taking her by complete surprise. Nor was it a sweet or chaste goodnight kiss. It was a real kiss, a proper kiss, a kiss of love. Poppy was astounded.

'I don't think I should have done that. I really don't think I should have done that,' he said.

'You shouldn't.'

'I'd better go.'

'Yes, you'd better,' Poppy agreed.

'I really had,' Scott repeated.

'Yes you had,' Poppy agreed again. 'Goodnight.'

'Goodnight, Poppy.'

And of course he kissed her again, and then again.

'You really should go,' Poppy whispered, barely audibly.

'I know,' Scott whispered back. 'I'm trying to. But I'm finding it rather difficult.'

'Me, too.'

'I could stay.'

'What?'

'I said—I could stay.'

Poppy moved herself slightly away from him and looked up into his eyes. He was looking down at her intently.

'Scott,' she said. 'Supposing something happened to you.'

'Yes. I'm supposing.'

'I don't think I'd be very good at getting over it.'

'I'd be hopeless. If something happened to you.'

'So we shouldn't. We're just storing up trouble, Scott.'

'And if we don't—and if something happens to one of us?'

'Scott. If you stay—if you do, we could betray each other by a look, a tone of voice—anything. You know what they say—things like that get written all over people's faces. We can't take that risk. You're sure to be there at this wretched weekend.'

'Look, it can't be that much of a risk. I mean—I might be terrible. I might be the most awful lover in the world. You might hate me. In fact it might be

435

the best thing we could possibly do—for King and for Country—'

'Scott—you have to be *serious*! Just for *once.*'

'I have to make love to you, Poppy. If I die without making love to you, I shall—I shall shoot myself!'

'*Will you be serious!*'

'I meant to be.' Scott stroked the side of her hair, then, frowning, gently kissed her cheek. 'I really love you, Poppy. And if I'm going to die, I would face it so much better if you let me make love to you. If we became lovers.'

'But what about what I feel about you? Or don't? Don't you think that should come into consideration?'

'So what do you think about me, Poppy? No— no, better—what do you *feel* for me?'

'I don't know. I've never been in love before, you see, so I don't know how it should feel.'

'Roughly.'

Poppy looked up at him and smiled so sweetly Scott's head spun.

'Roughly? Well, roughly, roughly I think I might just have fallen in love.'

'That makes two of us. And as they say, it only takes two. Come on, we could be dead tomorrow.'

Seconds later he had hold of her hand and was headed for the bedroom, where they quietly closed the door for a few hours on the rest of the world.

CHAPTER SEVENTEEN

Scott, once more a house detective, left Poppy at dawn. Later, Poppy, immaculate in a silk dress and coat, descended to the hotel foyer, making her way as usual to the tobacco kiosk where she bought a box of Du Maurier Red and a box of matches, at the same time discreetly leaving her own box of matches on the counter. By the time she picked up her change, as always her box had disappeared. She was about to turn when she sensed someone behind her.

'Good morning to you.'

'Greeting people in the morning is not a habit I find endearing, Henry. Particularly early in the morning.'

'It is eleven o'clock, Diona, although I dare say you may be feeling a little tired after sitting up with your nocturnal visitor, are you not?' Henry enquired. 'Do join me. I'm having a little pick-me-up.'

He nodded towards the bar and started to guide her towards it.

'Visitor?' Poppy said in a bored voice. 'And it's just a little early for me to have a pick-me-up, as you call it, Henry.'

'I understand you had a late night caller,' Henry stated, pulling a bar stool out for Poppy to sit down. 'Barman? Two Bloody Marys.'

'I had no such thing,' Poppy protested. 'Oh—unless you are referring to the little house detective not very *extraordinaire*.'

'I caught sight of the fellow as I was lighting up

my late night cigarette.' Henry sighed. 'I had taken to mooching about the place, having been rejected by madame.'

'As it happens, the silly little man thought he saw someone trying to get into my room.' Poppy gazed purposefully past Henry, her expression one of supreme indifference. 'Perhaps it was you, Henry?' She turned her large eyes on Lypton. 'I hate people who spy, do you know that?'

'*Moi aussi.* I just happened to take a stroll up and down your corridor—wondering whether I dare perhaps invite myself into madame's boudoir—then, having decided against it, took myself off—which was when I noticed the arrival of madame's night visitor.'

'Absolutely, I did, Henry,' Poppy said coldly, looking at the long sallow-skinned face staring at her without expression. 'We spent the night together. He was an absolute gem.'

Henry Lypton allowed himself to give a small, quasi-amused smile.

'Jolly good,' he said. 'Glad you had some fun.'

Poppy raised the drink the barman had placed before her and took a sip, putting it down immediately.

'I thought I told you,' she scolded the barman. 'Very little Worcester sauce, but a generous squeeze of lemon. Make me another.'

The barman nodded his apology and hurried off to remake the cocktail.

'If you must know, Henry, although it's absolutely none of your business, Mr Whatever, house detective un-*extraordinaire*, thought it best to check the neighbouring suite as well—in case someone had got into my room and taken refuge

438

next door. I imagine he then did as he said he would, and left through the service door in the side passage.'

'What a shame,' Henry sighed. 'I was rather enjoying my flight of fantasy—with you and the house detective un-*extraordinaire*.'

Drinking half her cocktail and smoking half a cigarette, Poppy engaged Henry in desultory chatter about their weekend plans before excusing herself to leave for her midday appointment.

'May I escort you there?' Henry enquired, also getting up to leave. 'If it is nearby, I should be so delighted.'

'Thank you but I am being collected,' Poppy told him, hoping that Jack Ward had managed to supply her with a chauffeur-driven motor to whisk her away to what anyone following her would assume to be an important lunch appointment in a heavily sandbagged private house in Knightsbridge.

In fact had anyone been able to follow Poppy up the steps into the house and into the dining room at the back of the building where lunch for two had been laid, they would have found the person sitting smoking a cigarette through a long white ivory holder as she awaited the arrival of her lunch companion to be Cissie Lavington. Jack Ward had arranged the meeting in order that Poppy could be properly briefed.

*   *   *

Two days later Marjorie placed a file in front of Major Folkestone, who was sitting at his desk reading the day's reports. Attached to the buff cover of the file was a paper-clipped label

439

announcing the contents to be *Top Secret*. As soon as the major opened it he saw another note clipped to the first page, urging that the file be read at once and acted upon immediately. It was signed JW.

Removing all the contents from the folder Major Folkestone extracted a large brown envelope containing a series of photographic enlargements, finding them to be blow-ups of the microscopic film found within the binding of Tetherington's so-called journal. Accompanying them were pages of typescript, either describing the relevance of certain of the photographs or decoding pages of hieroglyphics that had been photographed along with the rest of this vital information. He was about to close the file over when the telephone on his scrambled line rang.

'Folkestone.'

'The Colonel here,' Jack Ward said quietly. 'Interesting post, I'd say.'

'I would agree.'

'A little bit more news. They've named the star player. Flower Girl has been detailed to cover the event.'

The line went dead. Major Folkestone took one last look at the information in front of him, as if to make sure he hadn't been seeing things, then, having despatched Marjorie to summon all the various Heads of Section for a briefing, began the first stages of a strategy that had been in place since May 1940.

*   *   *

Although Poppy was not to know it, the name of the girl who worked in the tobacco kiosk in the foyer of the hotel was Angela Plum. She was a sensible, reliable sort of the kind that Jack Ward liked to choose to push out into the field. Not easily disquieted she had nevertheless been puzzled by the instruction she had received the previous day, namely that she was not to collect her merchandise from the supplier as usual, but wait until first thing the following morning. She was to go for an early morning coffee instead of a late afternoon tea. Her training forbade her to ask the reason, but being a diligent soul she left herself more than enough time to make her journey from Swiss Cottage to Mayfair with plenty of time to spare. At the café she had a cup of tea and a slice of toast and margarine with a thin spread of jam, before beginning the pantomime of searching for some matches to light her cigarette. Seeing this the waitress wandered over, wiped the table half-heartedly with the tea cloth she was carrying, fished in the pocket of her apron to light Angela's cigarette while idly gossiping to her, then leaning over to reach for the full ashtray on the table allowed the day's delivery to drop neatly into Angela's open handbag. Only the keenest-eyed observer could have spotted the transfer.

When Angela left the café the sirens started to sound. Everyone began moving quickly, almost routinely, to their nearest shelter. So intense had been the city's bombardment that the reflexes of the inhabitants as soon as they heard the siren wail its quick up and down strident warning were becoming automatic. Angela on the other hand ran in the opposite direction, having decided that she had sufficient time to make it to the hotel and then straight downstairs to the reinforced safety of the underground swimming pool complex.

She had done this run several times before. Dashing at full pelt up Curzon Street, at the last minute she suddenly decided to cut the corner from north to south side to save precious seconds, and as she did so a car being driven far too fast careered into the street from Park Lane. Its left front wheel hit the kerb, spun the steering wheel out of the driver's grasp and slewed the car across the road before Angela—who in one terrible split second saw it coming for her—could get out of its way. She was still moving when it hit her, tossing her six or eight feet up into the air before throwing her back against the body of the car, knocking her unconscious and her handbag out of her hand and into the nearby gutter where it lay undisturbed, its vital message still lying carefully folded in the relevant matchbox.

*   *   *

In the foyer of the Stanley the Flower Girl sat staring at the still closed tobacco kiosk from behind her copy of the *Tatler and Bystander*. It was now well after ten o'clock, by which time the kiosk should have been open for over an hour and a half, yet the place was still firmly shuttered and locked. A small bunch of hotel employees had gathered round it by now and were standing in conference, while Poppy feigned disinterest. She had heard sirens sounding, and then stopping as suddenly, while she tried to concentrate on her magazine in the hope that it was a false alarm.

'You didn't bother to go to the shelter?'

Henry stood in front of her.

'No, none of us do much any more. The siren going off—it's so often nothing to do with where one is. They don't even sound the clackers in here,' she added, referring to the wooden clappers that were used everywhere to alert people to a coming bombing raid.

'We have to leave,' he reminded her, but she ignored him, disappearing up to her suite, accusing the maid of having forgotten to pack an extra pair of her evening gloves.

On her way down she chose to descend by the stairs as she knew this would bring her out to one side of the kiosk, allowing her a chance of a quick word with the hotel staff out of sight of the ever-watchful Henry.

'Miss Plum is always the soul of punctuality.' The man she had addressed shook his head. 'Merchant, the hall porter, thought he heard an ambulance, and someone *was* taken off from outside the hotel, but we couldn't be sure who it was.'

'I suppose she might have slept in, perhaps? Whoever she is.'

The man looked shocked.

'Not our Miss Plum. You could always set a clock by her.'

Poppy could well believe that to be true, so utterly reliable a contact had the young woman proved to be; yet she had to keep up the pretence of disapproval and dissatisfaction. One of the staff offered to open the kiosk up, and seeing Henry strolling across the foyer with a look of growing impatience on his shiny, smooth countenance Poppy quickly agreed.

'I have plenty of cigarettes,' he complained when

443

at last he managed to lead her out of the hotel to his waiting car, already packed up with their luggage.

'I only smoke Black and White.'

'I thought Du Maurier was your brand.'

'Only when I can't get Black and White.'

Nothing in Poppy's training was able to provide her with the necessary sequence of actions when an agent did not receive her drop. She must have fallen silent a little too often, because Henry suddenly sighed.

'I hope to God you're going to prove to be a little bit more amusing over the next few days. It's like taking a journey with a Cistercian monk.'

'I hope to God I don't have to prove to be any such thing,' Poppy replied, turning to look at him. 'I understood the entertainment was going to be first class this weekend. The little Fat Man coming down to entertain us, and all sorts of other fascinations.'

'Well, no, on that front, I don't think you're going to be disappointed. In fact I don't think any of us are.'

Henry smiled meaningfully at her. Poppy shrugged idly, half closed her eyes and settled down for what she intended to look like a good snooze. Taking his cue from her, Henry did the same, pulling his travel rug well up to his waist and settling down under it. In a matter of minutes he was fast asleep.

Poppy eyed him, then used the valuable time she had to herself to work out what she might have to do if things turned against her and she was faced with the choice of flying—or dying.

Jack Ward was driven back to his office under police escort. Major Folkestone, with Marjorie accompanying him as his personal assistant, was waiting for him when he finally arrived back, having travelled post haste to London by car in response to a summons by Jack.

'It's not just for me—Mr Ward needs a secretary to be present at all times during this crisis,' Major Folkestone had explained. 'He needs someone whom he can trust.'

Marjorie couldn't tell Billy exactly where she was going or precisely why, but Billy was now wise enough in the ways of Eden Park to understand that when someone wouldn't tell him anything, then that person was off on a Top Mission. So when Marjorie said goodbye that morning, he gave her a quick but unusually strong bear-hug, even managing to pluck up the gum—as he and Marjorie always called an attack of the braves—to give her a peck on one cheek.

' 'Ere!' he called after her as she hurried to the staff car that was waiting to take them to London. 'Good luck, Marge. Keep your 'ead down—and bring us back somethin'!'

'Like a whole new batch of aitches for you—Billy *Hen*dry?' Marjorie called back.

*   *   *

'He didn't actually turn a hair when I told him,' Jack explained to Major Folkestone as Marjorie sat taking everything down in longhand in his office that evening. 'Typical of the man, I suppose. He

445

just lit another cigar, poured himself—and me—quite a large whisky, and immediately launched into his idea of how we should play it.'

'Which was?' Folkestone wondered, accepting a cigarette from Jack.

'His first idea was to brazen it out.'

'Also typical of the man you could say, sir.'

'It was difficult to dissuade him from driving down to his friends as arranged.' Jack held up his hands hopelessly and shook his head, cigarette in one corner of his mouth, a glass of whisky in the other. ' "I have a bullet-proof car," he said. "I have my Tommy gun. More than that I have prior knowledge," he said.' Jack leaned over Marjorie's notebook. He gave her a boyish smile. 'One of my hobbies, reading longhand upside down. So. To continue. All we know is that explosive has been mentioned, but not whether they intend to use it.

'The route is only known to the driver, and then only at the last minute, and he does sometimes change cars, so the likelihood of where they will try to strike is as near to the final location as possible. Either in the final stretch of road leading to the house, perhaps the drive, or maybe even the house itself.'

'The Prime Minister is never more in danger than when he travels.'

'Correct. However. This whole thing could be a red herring for all we know—to distract us from the real objective. We have to consider that too.'

'So what's the plan, sir?' Folkestone asked. 'It is now 2100 hours on Friday the eighth of November, rumour has it the strike is for tomorrow—so how far advanced are we?'

Jack looked at them both slowly over the top of

his spectacles. Then he took his all but smoked cigarette from the corner of his mouth and drew on it one last time before crushing it to death slowly and methodically with two or three pushes from one strong solid hand.

'The PM wants them all. As he said he takes it very badly when persons from his own class want to kill him, very badly indeed. Remember the suffragette who tried to push him under the train? He was never the same about women's rights after that.'

'I don't suppose you would be,' Marjorie, who had always secretly admired the suffragettes, murmured.

'Very well. We have all the facts now.'

'And we seem to know where they all are, sir,' Folkestone said. 'So, would it not be possible just to nab 'em?'

'It would be nice, but not possible,' Jack said. 'The point being, at the moment any attempt on the PM's life is still only hearsay. And secondly, they could well get wind of what we are up to and simply vanish into the night. I'm referring to the ringleaders here, the big boys—not the pansy boudoir Fascists who sit in the clubs boasting about how they're all going to have positions of power in Hitler's Britain. Thirdly, we have two operatives working from inside. If their cover is still intact— which we all hope it is—they may get out intact. If on the other hand our enemies see the game is up, they will also see they have been betrayed—and they will begin to look closely for the traitor or traitors in their midst, which is grim stuff,' he added, lighting a fresh cigarette. 'Believe you me, as far as our agents are concerned, the chances are

447

they're already on to them. So I'm told.'

Marjorie's insides trembled at the thought of someone within the organisation working as a double agent. There were always rumours circulating at Eden, naturally enough. The first worry for anyone working in a place dedicated to Security and Intelligence, most particularly in a time of war, was betrayal, which was why there was such strict protocol in place. It wasn't only in public places that loose talk cost lives. Within the secure fortress that was Eden Park, Marjorie knew that to exchange information of a classified nature even with one's closest friends was to run a risk.

'So we're to take it the PM's private trip to the countryside is now cancelled,' Major Folkestone surmised. 'And if everything's in place, we're to move in and arrest these johnnies.'

'Not a bit of it, Major,' Jack replied, referring to a file on the desk in front of him. 'The PM insists we round 'em all up and put 'em all behind bars—'

'With their chum Mosley,' Folkestone chipped in.

'That's the idea. And the only way we're going to do that is to carry on as if we know nothing.'

Both Marjorie and Major Folkestone stared disbelievingly at Jack, who paid no attention, simply continuing to consult the file and make some notes.

'The PM still intends to honour his invitation?' Folkestone asked carefully.

'Put it this way, we will make sure his host and hostess—who by the way are one hundred per cent on the Gold Standard—we will make sure that they, and everyone else concerned, are convinced that he is coming to stay. The PM's armoured car will definitely drive up to the house.' Jack tapped the papers in his hands together before putting them away in the file that he then closed. 'More than that I can't tell you.'

*   *   *

The house to which Poppy had been invited was a long drive from the centre of London. Since all the signs for towns and villages through which they were driven had either been painted over or removed she had no idea of its exact location, although she hoped to God that Jack Ward did. While Henry Lypton slept beside her, Poppy stared out at the landscape hoping to spot something that would help her identify where they were headed. By the time they had been travelling for over an hour she became convinced they were heading for Kent. Certainly the direction in which they had been driven out of town had told her they were going south. Henry had been vague about the details of where the house party was to be held and who exactly was hosting it, referring to the host and hostess by nickname only.

Poppy knew that she had to identify the place to which they were headed. It was vital. Jack Ward had always impressed on her the need to think not just ahead, but well ahead, and, if necessary, around every corner. But as the car turned into a drive guarded not by one but by two gate lodges and swept up a long straight drive to a tall, square and perfectly magnificent William and Mary manor house, Poppy knew exactly where she was, because she had seen the house in pictures. She also knew who the owners were: Ralph, sixth Baron

449

Kilmington and his French wife Veronique, an enormously wealthy couple who, before the war, had lived a famously extravagant lifestyle, and whose parties and weekends had always been attended by those with political influence.

Henry awoke as the car pulled up in front of the steps leading to the main doors. Poppy glanced at him briefly.

'Such a heavenly colour, this stone, I always think, don't you?'

She turned and smiled brilliantly at Henry who looked for a second as if he had been blinded before following her up the steps to the house.

*   *   *

When she came down dressed for dinner that night, all the guests had arrived, so that by the time Poppy wandered in her now usual desultory way into the main salon it seemed that most of them were also assembled. Despite the war the women were all wearing evening dress, and few of the men were in uniform, so that far from finding the scene fascinating or glamorous Poppy found it nauseating. She thought of all the fine young men and women fighting not just for their country, but for the freedom of the world, and it seemed to her to be almost horrifying. It was as if this spoilt international set had simply turned their backs on the events outside the huge windows—which had been most efficiently blacked out—deciding to enjoy themselves in as lavish a manner as they possibly could, without a thought to rationing, necessity, common sense or indeed the future. Champagne was being served and there was even a band playing down the far end of the gilt-decorated salon, while above the music rose the ever increasing noise of the guests' laughter.

She knew Henry would pick her up sooner or later, that she would be able to set her watch by him, and sure enough, just as she was about to be engaged in conversation by a young, handsome Scandinavian, she felt a long thin hand clasp one of her elbows to turn her round to him.

'Good evening, madame,' he said unsmilingly, just tilting his long thin head to one side to stare at her quizzically. 'Quite a gathering, isn't it?' Henry went on ignoring the other man so pointedly that he finally moved away.

'People *will* shout at parties. I wish they wouldn't. So tiring.'

'Perhaps they'll soon have something to shout about.' Henry smiled, taking a drink from the tray proffered by a waiter. 'Why aren't you off fighting somewhere, boy?' Henry asked the lad, with a sideways look at Poppy to make sure she was listening. 'Shouldn't you be off poking that head of yours over some barricade or other?'

'I got a heart condition, sir,' the waiter replied, colouring. 'Failed me Grade Three.'

'Sure it wasn't jaundice that you had?' Henry stuck his tongue in one cheek this time as he raised his eyebrows at Poppy.

'No, sir. It was definitely my heart, sir, the doctor said.'

'Thing about jaundice is—it turns you yellow.'

Henry laughed at his own joke as he led an unsmiling Poppy all the way across the room.

'By the way, should you too not be poking that head of yours over some barricade or other,

Henry?'

'Not my fight. Besides, I have this frightful ingrowing toenail. Now—time for you to meet our guests of honour.'

They had arrived at a small group that contained their host and hostess, another couple unknown to Poppy and two unusually tall men, one of slender and elegant build, the other taller and very broad-shouldered. Both were standing with their backs to Poppy and Henry.

'Ralph,' Henry said, to excuse his interruption. 'Veronique. If you'll excuse me, I should very much like to introduce Diona here to our special guests.'

'But of course,' their host agreed, with a polite smile. 'Please.'

'Diona,' Henry said. 'Allow me to introduce Mr Eugene Hackett to you.'

Eugene had already turned round to bestow his best and most charming smile on the beautiful young woman being presented to him.

'And Diona,' Henry continued, 'may I now introduce Signor Ponterino. Signor—Miss Diona de Donnet.'

As the second man turned to greet her, Poppy found herself looking into a pair of eyes that not so very long ago she had come to thankfully believe were closed for ever.

CHAPTER EIGHTEEN

Basil bowed briefly in the diplomatic manner over Poppy's gloved hand, and having exchanged the briefest of niceties returned to the conversation he

452

had been conducting in fluent Italian with his host, the pair moving apart from the rest of the group.

Poppy stared after them, hardly believing what she saw. Basil, for it was certainly he, had clearly not recognised 'Diona de Donnet'.

'You must excuse both my husband and Signor Ponterino,' Veronique Kilmington drawled, taking Poppy aside. 'They are both concerned about the future of so many of the great Italian art works that are going to be jeopardised by this *wretched* war. The two of them are *scheming* for all their worth as to how best to remove as much as they can before the peasant Mussolini gets his hands on them.'

She smiled at Poppy without any warmth, putting one hand on Eugene's forearm.

'So what I am going to do now—because I have to whisk dear Henry here off to meet an old friend,' she continued, 'is to leave you in the charming company of gorgeous Eugene here—who will tell you everything you want to know about anything and not one word of it will be true.'

'I've never been to Ireland,' Poppy said, still trying to steady herself from the shock of seeing Basil, while carefully turning her back on him.

'It hasn't missed you,' Eugene replied. 'The grass still grows, the rain still falls and the tide still comes in and out.'

'I hear some of it is quite pretty.'

'None of it is quite pretty. Most of it is extraordinarily beautiful.'

'What fun,' Poppy sighed, eyeing him. 'Must give it a shot sometime.'

'Don't hurry,' Eugene said, preparing to move off. 'She can wait.'

For a second Poppy felt lost, as well she might

453

since she had no instructions as to what the plan for the night might be. She looked around, and seeing Scott she tossed her hair slightly to one side, pinning it behind her ear, a previously arranged signal that they had used before, and which meant 'follow me'. She slipped from the room into the main hall where she knew the placement would be laid out, every guest's name carefully written in beautiful Italianate writing on tiny crested cards.

'You're sure Basil Tetherington didn't recognise you?' Scott asked, smiling quite falsely while trying not to sound anxious, as he joined her. 'Oh dear, I'm sitting next to that boring old cod from Denbighshire yet again. Is our hostess trying to make a match of it, do you think?' He paused. 'Do you think he recognised you?'

'No, at least I don't think so. Oh, how marvellous, I'm placed next to the Duke of Bruton. Adorable.' Poppy smiled back, trying, like Scott, to pass their conversation off as party small talk. 'No, I can't be sure,' she went on. 'But then as far as Basil is concerned there is no such thing as sure.'

'I won't be far away from you at any point,' Scott said, giving a loud party laugh. 'So just make sure to indicate to me if anyone we know goes too far!'

Poppy shrugged in the way Diona would in such a pretend situation, relieved to see from the table plan that she could not have been sitting further away from her supposedly dead husband. The problem therefore was clearly not going to be the dinner, but the rest of the weekend.

For once she was grateful for the little revolver that lay at the bottom of her gas mask case, well wrapped up in two silk handkerchiefs. As they all began to move into the dining room, she wondered idly whether she might at last have occasion to use it. If so she only hoped she would not, as Cissie would say, 'make a bish'.

*   *   *

'Is there no other way we can get a message to her, sir?' Marjorie asked Jack when she and Major Folkestone were called into conference the following morning to learn of the accident that had befallen Miss Plum.

'Miss Plum was carrying the information that the Flower Girl's husband was far from dead. Always so reliable, our Miss Plum. It was my fault that she didn't collect at the usual time. I felt it was such a vital piece of information I should delay it to the last minute, to protect it from leaking.'

'You can't legislate for these things, sir. If I may say so.'

'Hmm,' Jack grunted, lighting his pipe. 'You may say so, Marjorie. But it's not going to get us out of this dilemma. If Tetherington spots our ringer, we're cooked.'

'The Flower Girl has the advantage, sir,' Marjorie continued. 'She can recognise him, but he won't necessarily recognise her. That gives her the edge, sir. If she can just keep one step ahead—'

'Which I'm sure she will,' Jack grunted. 'She's a first class operative. A natural for the job. So let's just keep our fingers crossed—we only need— what?' He looked at the clock on the wall. 'We've got eight hours almost precisely. So I had better trundlc on and get myself ready.'

'Anything I can do to help, sir?'

Jack turned back and stared at Marjorie.

'Depends how good you are at dressing up,' he replied. 'Or rather at dressing other people up.'

'I'm not bad, sir. I used to turn young Billy into a most convincing wood nymph.'

'Hmm,' Jack pondered. 'I should say that took a bit of doing. In that case, come along. And hurry. We haven't got all day.'

*   *   *

Even before she began to help put the final touches to his appearance, Marjorie saw that her mentor was an ideal build to be passed off as the PM, being of stocky stature and with a heavily jowled face. Of course Jack Ward was considerably younger than Churchill, but once the make-up artists and the costume people had finished with him Marjorie was astonished how close the resemblance was between the two men. Once he was seated behind the bullet-proof windows of the official car wearing the hallmark hat, and smoking the even more famous cigar, everyone concerned felt justifiably proud.

'You'd never know it wasn't the great man himself,' Marjorie told him.

'They will as soon as I have to say anything,' Jack grunted, positioning himself beside the loaded Tommy gun that had been placed on the back seat.

'I don't think so, sir,' Marjorie assured him. 'Every time you growl at me I could swear it's the PM.'

'Never in the field of human conflict—' Jack practised.

'No, sir, I don't think so.' Major Folkestone smiled. 'I don't think you'll be called on to make

456

any speeches. At least we hope not.'

'Hear, hear,' Jack agreed. 'If forced, I shall just grunt. That should do it.'

One of the War Office boffins came up to give Jack a final briefing.

'Doors and windows—all triple reinforced. They'll stand any calibre of small arms fire—in fact they'll take most damage up to a tank if you ask me. All the upholstery and fittings are fireproofed, and what we've done—in the time allowed—is put another skin on the floor and the roof, just in case things go wrong.'

'I'm sure you did splendidly,' Jack replied, extending a hand. 'Thank you.'

'Good luck, sir,' the captain said, standing back. 'God speed.'

'Thank you, Captain.'

'Take care,' Marjorie added, giving him a shy smile. 'We'll be thinking of you.'

Major Folkestone added his good wishes, and a moment later the driver fired the engine of the large black car and prepared to drive off. As it eased out of the underground garage, Jack raised his left hand and rewarded his small crowd of well-wishers by giving them Churchill's famous V for Victory sign.

*   *   *

It was now five o'clock in the afternoon of 9 November. Poppy sat in a window seat of the ladies' drawing room in the great house where she was still a guest, playing Patience. Several other female guests were in the room, either reading magazines or dozing in front of a well-stocked log fire, while most of their menfolk were having an early drink, having just returned from an afternoon's shooting.

Fortunately, Poppy had neither seen nor heard anything more of her supposedly late husband. She knew that he had not gone on the shoot, as she had watched those who had decided on a bit of sport climb into the trucks that were to carry them off into some distant part of the estate. She had also noted that another absentee was the tall, handsome Irishman who had so enjoyed insulting her before dinner. She had fully expected him to be one of the party. She therefore concluded that he had to be part of whatever it was that was going on—and if her so-called late husband was implicated then what better accomplice? Hearing her name called from the door, she looked round and saw Henry beckoning to her. Putting her cards down in obvious irritation Poppy wandered as slowly as she could over to the door.

'Thought you might like to know everything's going to plan,' Henry murmured as he strolled her down the corridor, one hand on one of her elbows as always, as if she was never going to escape him.

'If one knew what everything was,' she grumbled in return, 'and what the plan was, I suppose one might just be jumping for joy?'

'Success is expected at any time,' Henry grinned, managing to look even more skeletal than ever. 'The big banger is due to go off any moment.'

Poppy turned her face to him and raised her eyebrows in a deliberately childish manner.

'Jolly good,' she said. 'But let's just wait until it does actually go off, shall we? Before we start patting ourselves on the back.'

The car and its outriders were now less than five miles from their destination. So far the journey had passed without incident, the driver having followed a long and complicated series of diversions that were designed to bring him and his passenger to their destination via a set of very different routes. But now that they were close to their final goal, the choice of roads quickly dwindled down to the usual now unmarked lanes that meandered apparently aimlessly around the landscape.

Jack had studied the map very closely before leaving on the journey, noting that as a vehicle approached the old estate access became reduced to only two roads, a minor road that ran around the village and halfway up the hill behind the house and its grounds to drop down to the trade entrance at the rear, and a better surfaced but still minor highway that led in almost a straight line to the front gates. He had guessed the plan might be to try to block off access to the front road under some pretext or other, forcing the car to make its approach to the house via the more obscure route, a way that would take the car all but unobserved right up to the back walls of the estate, a course that would be easier to booby trap and perfect for such an ambush.

So it was with some surprise that Jack found the car and its outriders being flagged down by the police while still on the main road and some four miles or so from its destination. There was very little traffic due to petrol rationing, the time of day and the remoteness of the location, but the one or two cars that were out and about Jack could see were being turned back by an officer who was standing on duty in the middle of the road. Behind him, parked across the highway, was a police car with another policeman sitting in it apparently communicating on his two-way radio.

'Well, sir?' Jack's driver enquired, looking at his passenger in the mirror.

'Must obey the law of the land, my dear fellow,' Jack growled, practising his Churchillian tones. 'Let us see what they have to say for themselves.'

Jack sat watching as ahead his own two police outriders stopped their bikes to listen to what the traffic policeman had to say to them.

A moment later one of them, having parked his bike, tapped on Jack's driver's window. Jack nodded for him to wind the reinforced window down and leaned forward to hear the news.

'Road's flooded ahead, sir,' the outrider told them. 'Hence the diversion.'

'Sure of that, are you? Has there been that much rain?' Jack wondered in return.

'There's been a fair bit, sir, when you think of it. Heavy down here in fact, so we've just been told. There's some tributary or other over the hill ahead down in the valley that's burst its banks and the road's impassable.'

Jack nodded. The weather had been foul.

'Go up and turn about,' he instructed the driver. 'And take whatever diversion they recommend.'

The driver did as he was told, with Jack sitting as far back as he could in the car so as not to draw undue attention to himself. As the driver began to manoeuvre the car across the road, Jack took out his pocket torch to examine the map that was lying ready by his side, folded it open at the exact area where they were at the moment. Spotting the road they were on Jack traced a line ahead, through the copse on the top of the hill and down the other side.

As far as he could see there was no river within miles, let alone any tributary. The land ahead was all farmland and large estates, the nearest river being actually one mile behind them, to the north.

'Call that policeman over,' Jack ordered his driver. 'I want him to run an errand for me.'

'Sir.' The driver wound down his window and called to the policeman, who after a moment's consideration walked over to the driver's open window.

'I want you to run an important errand for me, Constable,' a deep voice growled from the shadows of the back seat.

The constable peered into the car and then promptly stood to attention.

'Sir. I had no idea. Sorry, sir.'

'Why should you?' Jack growled. 'Now I need you to take a message to your station. It's urgent, man, so look sharp. That understood?'

'Sir.'

'You're Kent Constabulary, and we're near Little Folding, yes? A neck of the woods very familiar to me. So at a guess I'd say your station's Goodhurst, yes?'

'Yes sir.'

'Should know it, dammit. I opened it meself— after it had been burned down and rebuilt. Before your time, probably.'

'No, sir. Not at all. I remember the fire very well, sir. What message do you want me to take, sir?'

'I want you to tell them the game's up,' Jack replied, picking up his loaded Tommy gun. 'Because it is. There is no police station at Goodhurst. Now call your accomplice over here— don't try to be smart—then get in the car, both of you. If you don't, I'll shoot you both.'

The policeman looked at him slowly, one hand slipping behind his back.

'I don't advise that either,' Jack said quickly. 'If you look down you'll see my driver has a revolver pointed straight at your throat. Now do as you're told and call your friend over. Now. Voice only.'

The policeman looked down and saw the glint of the driver's small arms pointed straight up at his face. After a moment he called to his companion to come over. As he did, Jack's driver pushed his door open, keeping his gun trained on the nearest policeman, and waited. As soon as the second bogus policeman arrived alongside he moved quickly behind him, put a gun in his back, frisked him efficiently and swiftly, found his Luger revolver and disarmed him, chucking the weapon to Jack who still had the first policeman covered with his Tommy gun. The driver then disarmed the first policeman, pulling his revolver from under his belt at the back of his trousers, opened the back door of the car and pushed first one man then the next in and on to the floor with a large heavily booted foot so that they lay on top of one another.

'Faces down, and keep 'em down,' Jack ordered, directing them with the point of the Tommy gun. 'Hands on back of head. And not a squeak.'

The driver got back into his seat, turned the car round and headed back up the road. Half a mile further on there was another policeman on duty, directing with his torch that the car was to leave the highway and take the country lane that ran off sharply to the driver's left.

'Sir?' Jack's driver asked, looking in the driving mirror.

'Do as the man says,' Jack replied, keeping both feet in the small of the back of the man on top of the pile of two.

The car swung off the road and began to descend a steep hill.

'No!' one of the men suddenly cried from the floor. 'No—no! No, stop the car! For God's sake stop the car at once!'

The driver stopped the car.

Jack switched on his powerful torch and shone it on his two prisoners.

'Any particular reason we should stop this car?'

'Landmines. At the bottom of the hill.'

'Good. Now the names of everyone involved, please.'

'Can't—'

'Don't see why not,' Jack said, chewing the end of his cigar.

'We've got our families, that's why,' one of them muttered with his face still on the floor of the car.

'Either you tell us everything you know—'

'We can't—'

'Well, we're going to blow the car up anyway. It's up to you, my dear fellows, whether or not you want to go up with it, that's what I'm saying.'

*   *   *

Lord Kilmington's butler apologised for interrupting him before informing him there was

463

an urgent telephone call for him.

Ralph Kilmington detached himself from the group standing round the fireplace in the drawing room and went to his telephone room, into which he shut himself for only a matter of about a minute. When he re-emerged he was beaming, and having first dismissed his servants from the room he tapped on a nearby table for silence.

'My friends,' he said. 'I have the most excellent piece of news—news that I know will please and excite you as much as it does me, since we are all of the same political and philosophical complexion. The surprise we had planned has been successful.'

At once around the room there was a babble of excited conversation. Kilmington waited a moment then tapped on the table again, this time much louder in order to be heard over the noise.

'Yes, my friends,' he continued. 'This is indeed a momentous moment. So please—please raise your glasses to our success and to the future of our country. Ladies and gentlemen—to a new England.'

Later Kilmington found Basil staring across the room at Poppy, and drew him aside.

'Is something the matter, Basil?'

'Yes, I'm very much afraid there is.' Basil glanced sideways at his regular companion, a small, cherubic-looking Italian, and taking Kilmington aside he said in a low voice, 'I think I know that woman over there.'

Kilmington, looking relaxed and happy, shook his head. 'Surely you would remember?'

'No, because she's so changed her looks.'

Ralph came round to stare at Poppy full face. 'Henry had her checked out. She is a stunner, do admit.'

'Yes, that is what I mean, Ralphie. I am sure I have known her, in the biblical sense. Had an affair with her once, years ago. In Cheshire, I think it was.'

Ralph Kilmington laughed.

'Very unusual for you, dear boy, very unusual, to find yourself in Cheshire, and with a woman.'

Basil nodded, moving back to his regular companion.

'I know,' he agreed. 'Wasn't it?'

A few minutes later he was once more drawn aside, this time by Eugene.

'I think you had better come outside with me. I don't want to spoil the party, but—'

'Please, my dear fellow, I am just beginning to relax. I've had the most terrible shock.' He nodded towards Poppy. 'That woman over there—'

Eugene stared across at Poppy.

'Yes? That woman over there? What, you mean the redhead?'

'No, the blonde.'

'Stunning, isn't she?'

'If you like that sort of thing, yes. But I've just realised that I think I had an affair with her, and it wasn't even after hunting. Do you think she will know me? I am sorely tempted to go over and tease her, really I am.'

'Well, don't,' Eugene said shortly. 'Come outside. I have to explain something.'

'Explain what?' Basil wondered, picking up Eugene's obvious tension, but nevertheless following him out of the room. 'Has something gone wrong?'

Eugene, only too relieved to have taken the pressure off Poppy, turned to face Basil.

465

'We have to get the hell out of here and fast,' he replied. 'The fresh news is that the keg exploded all right—but there was no one sitting on the bloody thing.'

'What are you talking about?' Basil said coldly. 'Ralph had a first-hand report.'

'But a second-hand result. I vote we get the hell out of here, before Ralph and the rest of them find out we've failed.'

'I am not fleeing before I have confirmation.'

'If you know what's good for you, signor, you'll follow me into the car and vanish into the night. As soon as the authorities have been warned they'll be round here like flies round a dungheap.'

As previously arranged through underground sources, the egregious Leon was waiting to drive them to a private airstrip.

'You up front, Basil!'

Eugene climbed into the back of the car. Slamming the door he yelled at Leon to get going, and Leon did so at once, firing the engine immediately and roaring off down the drive.

'How much time have we got?' Basil enquired, as Leon braked hard at the bottom of the drive, unsure which way to go.

'How in hell should I know, man?' Eugene roared back. 'Not right! Left! Turn left, you eejit! Left and left again at the top!'

'Where are we going, Eugene?' Basil asked calmly. 'We're not driving all the way to the Emerald Isle, I take it?'

'We're driving to an airfield, about twenty miles north of here—and with a bit of luck we'll be on the west coast in about another two or three hours, where we'll hole up till the boat comes in, as they say!'

'How long do you think before your famous boat comes in, Eugene?' Basil idly wondered, lighting a cigarette. 'According to our discussions, collection was to be arranged for tomorrow night.'

'And so it shall be,' Eugene replied. 'Weather and water permitting. Now take a right here, Leon, on to a minor road—which fortunately is a straight one so you can drive like hell. Something I strongly recommend.'

Eugene sat back and began to whistle his favourite Gaelic ballad.

'Drive with your headlights on, Leon,' Basil ordered. 'If anyone tries to stop you, run them over.'

Leon turned the car's headlamps on full and accelerated as hard as he could along the narrow but straight country road. He drove as fast as he dared while his passengers sat in silence.

'Pity,' Basil said finally, sighing. 'Such a pity. We have been so near and yet it seems now it is all too far. And we won't get another shot at it for some while, I don't suppose.'

'Had we succeeded, you were going to be our new Prime Minister, weren't you, Basil?'

Basil smiled wryly.

'Not quite, but with Churchill out of the way and a treaty already drafted for an early truce with Germany, we were certainly going to be in a very strong position to help save our country from ruin. But there you are—the best laid plans, as they say.'

'They haven't yet gone awry, old bean,' Eugene stated grimly. 'If we can get you out of this country in one piece, we truly live to fight another day.'

'True enough, Paddy.' Basil sighed again. 'True

467

enough. Where exactly are you taking us, Eugene? I don't know this part of England that well, but I do know one private airfield in this neck and it certainly isn't in this direction. It's the other side of the hills, a couple of miles beyond Great Stedford.'

'Ah bedad, but you're wrong there, Tommy,' Eugene said, in a complete change of tone. 'De strip dis Paddy uses—well very few folks know about it. Sure it lies well hidden in a little valley, and beautifully maintained by de pixies and de elves.'

'What are you talking about, you idiot?' Basil said tightly. 'Have you lost your reason or something?'

'Ah no, sir,' Eugene shook his head. ' 'Tis just a little Paddy joke so it is. Knowing how Tommy likes to laugh at us Paddies, I taught I'd have a little joke, dat's all, sur. Now turn in right here, Leon, would yous ever? In about a hundred yards. T'rough dem great big gates.'

As the car slowed down to make the turn, 'See dem lodges ahead?' Eugene asked Leon. 'Dat's the entrance.'

'For God's sake talk normally, will you?' Basil said irritably. 'Joke well and truly over.'

'You're absolutely right, old boy,' Eugene said in his normal voice. 'The joke is well and truly over. And the game is well and truly up.'

From out of the shadows of the gate lodges two armed sentries appeared, rifles cocked and aimed directly at the windscreen of the car.

'Halt!' one shouted. 'Who goes there!'

Leon quickly changed gear. He turned round to look over his shoulder as he was about to reverse as fast as he could out of the gateway, but found himself staring down the barrel of Eugene's large service revolver.

'First gear, Leon,' Eugene said. 'And slowly.'

Basil then whipped round, but he too found himself with a gun to his head.

'Surprise!' Eugene asked. 'Isn't life just full of the most surprising old surprises?' One of the sentries was now at the driver's window, rifle pointed directly at Leon's head.

'I should get out, Fritz, if I were you,' Eugene advised. 'Before he blows what passes for your brains out the other side of your head. Nasty thought.'

Leon opened the door, put his hands on his head and climbed out, as the other sentry opened the back door and Eugene leaned across and grinned at him.

'Evening, Percy,' he said. 'How are the rabbits? Got them under control?'

The sentry grinned back and lowered his rifle.

'I'm glad to say, sir, the rabbits have stopped eating the lettuce.'

'Good show,' Eugene said, sitting back. 'Dashed good show all round in fact. Just hope the Flower Girl and the House Detective surface all right.'

*   *   *

As it happened, in the ensuing panic, Scott and Poppy were quite able to vanish into the grounds of the great house without anyone noticing. Unfortunately for Poppy their method of escape was on foot.

'I don't know what it is,' she moaned to Scott as they walked along side by side in the darkness. 'But

469

every time I have to escape from anywhere it's always in something long—nightdress, stupid evening dress, nothing suitable.' She sighed. 'Must make a note to pack better in future.'

Scott laughed. 'It's all right, we're nearly there.'

'Where?'

'At the safe house, Lady Tetherington. Where we can bide awhile. And don't worry about your evening dress—' He looked at her appreciatively. 'I can help you take care of it. Really.'

'Cheek,' Poppy replied, but in Diona de Donnet's voice.

*   *   *

Naturally the incident never made the nationals, and only the local newspaper noted the landmine going off in a country lane. So, besides the formal congratulations within the various sections and to the staff at Eden as a whole, and a long personal note of thanks from the Prime Minister who regretted he was unable to visit Eden because of— as he put it—pressure of work, the whole affair was hushed up.

There were private parties, of course. Scott and Poppy continued to celebrate their success in the luxurious comfort of Diona de Donnet's suite of rooms in the Stanley before she finally had to vacate them, while Marjorie returned to Eden in quiet triumph with a delighted Major Folkestone who immediately granted her a twenty-four-hour pass to go where she liked and do what she pleased with Billy. They both chose to remain at Eden and start preparing for Christmas. Meanwhile Kate had a pleasant if embarrassing surprise, when she learned from the security files of the role Eugene Hackett had played.

'He's been gone so long, to tell you the truth I—I thought he might be a double agent.' She laughed.

'Shows what a good chap in the field he is,' Folkestone told her. 'I tell you, Kate—he is so good at what he does that sometimes I begin to worry about him. I began to worry in case he was truly double crossing us. That's how very good he is.'

'Where is he now?'

'Gone for a hack on his horse. Says it was the only thing that got him through. No—no that isn't quite right,' Major Folkestone corrected himself, turning red and looking at the toecaps of his highly polished shoes. 'No, he said there was something else he had to get back for. You probably know what he was talking about. In fact if anyone does, it's you.'

Without even looking at her, the major turned on his heel and walked quickly away, on parade as ever. Kate, her shift for the day now finished, fetched her overcoat from the cottage and took herself off to wander the parkland in the hope that she might catch sight of Eugene and his grey horse.

The cloud had thickened and lowered all day, resulting in a fine steady drizzle that was almost as impenetrable as a mist, and the landscape, normally so fine even in winter, was reduced to a grey murky haze, making it difficult even to pick out the great trees and the splendid follies that decorated the park. But as she continued her walk the wind changed direction and turned the drizzle to a vicious sleeting rain that stung Kate's face and made the visibility worse.

471

She stopped by a small stone building, not at all sure which folly it was until a sharp gust of wind swept the rain away, allowing her to identify what they all called the Picnic House, since the little temple-like building was obviously designed for alfresco meals, having a covered terrace at the front with a room within behind a pair of elegant French doors, allowing guests to eat inside if the elements became inclement.

Half frozen and thoroughly soaked, Kate tried the doors and happily found them to be unlocked. She let herself in, shutting the doors behind her, and taking off her coat shook as much rain as she could from it. But there was no chance of getting it dry, so heavy had been the downpour. The rain had even penetrated her tightly buttoned up collar, soaking the neck of her polo-necked sweater as well as the ends of its sleeves. Thoroughly soaked and really rather miserable, she was about to throw her wet coat on again and make a dash back to the main house, now that she had her bearings, when she noticed that the fine iron fireplace in the middle of the back wall was stacked with dry firewood, as was the practice in all the follies around the estate, just in case anyone like herself should get caught out by a sudden and vicious change in the weather.

The only problem was that being a non-smoker she had nothing with which to light the fire. Hoping against hope that some other refugee might by chance have left some on the fireplace she hurried to look, to her amazement finding a half-open box of Swan Vestas on the mantel. Unfortunately they were too damp to light. She was just about to give up when a hand appeared from behind her bearing

472

a well-lit match with which to light the paper under the firewood.

Kate turned at once, somehow knowing who it was before she even saw his face.

'You're a bit of a Red Indian, aren't you? Stalking up on a girl like that?'

'Irish man wears boots made from moss,' Eugene replied, widening his eyes at her. 'Pitter-patter, pitter-patter—hallo my darling Katie.'

She was in his arms before she knew, just putting up her hands to his chest in time to prevent him from kissing her—until she got a few things straight.

'Does your horse wear shoes made from moss too?' she wondered. 'I didn't hear a sound. Not even the doors being opened.'

'I wouldn't take the boy out on a day like this. He hates the rain, you know. Hates what it does to his mane. He's a bit of a dandy, is the boy.'

'So you were just out for a stroll, were you? Picked a good day.'

'Like yourself. You obviously don't mind what the rain does to your mane.'

'I most certainly do. But I wouldn't be seen dead in one of those awful rain hats.'

'You look like the most gorgeous drowned rat I've ever seen.'

'Thank you very much. And you look like some great Irish retriever that's just splashed out of a river.'

Eugene held her all the tighter.

'God, but I missed you,' he sighed finally. 'I thought about you all the time.'

'Liar.'

'Of course. But a nice lie all the same. The truth

is I did think about you whenever possible. When the light turned dark, you were always on my mind.'

'I thought you hated me for beating you at tennis.'

'That's what I wanted you to think. I have this thing, you see—not to mix work and pleasure. Particularly not to mix work with love.'

She shivered.

'You're cold,' he said quietly. 'Let me get that fire going properly.'

'That wasn't why I shivered.'

'Then let me get the fire going really properly. Did you know these doors have shutters? On the inside?'

Taking his heavy Aran sweater off and wrapping it round Kate's shoulders, Eugene got to work on the fire.

'First we dry our coats out thoroughly,' he said, sitting cross-legged on the floor and holding his heavy overcoat up to dry. 'Likewise, princess.' He nodded to her. 'Get to your work.'

Kate held her coat up in front of the dancing, cheek-reddening flames. In no time at all both garments began to steam.

'Then what?' she asked.

'Then when they are utterly and completely as well as quite, quite dry,' Eugene replied, 'we dry the rest of our damp clothes. I don't know about you but that rain penetrated practically everywhere.'

'Right down my neck.'

'Right down mine too.'

'But this fire's too hot to stand in front of and dry out.'

'I hadn't thought of that,' Eugene said carefully.

'Any suggestions?'

'Not really,' Kate said, refusing to catch the look he was giving her.

'We could always peel off the old togs now, couldn't we,' Eugene suggested, as if the thought had just occurred to him. 'And hold them up to toast.'

'And then?'

'Optional really. I had this idea we could spread the coats out on the floor—'

'On the floor? Why?'

'Katie—it's a marble floor. Marble is not the warmest of surfaces, Katie.'

'Depends what you want to use it as a surface for.'

'It might be fine for chopping meat, and for dicing the old vegetables.' Eugene sighed. 'But not for other things. I thought what we might do is lay the lovely warm dry coats out as a kind of—a kind of bed if you like.'

'Sounds cosy—'

'Roll the toasted sweaters up as lovely warm pillows, you see—'

'And then?'

'Then we could hug each other until we got warm and dry. Really hug I mean. We could hug and hug and hug.'

'A very new way of getting dry.'

Eugene padded barefoot over to the doors and closed the tall, ancient shutters, dropping the iron latch across to lock them from inside.

The weather outside had further worsened, blowing a gale now that thrashed a furious rain against the Georgian glasses in the shuttered windows. The fire, still blazing, billowed as a fierce

475

gust fanned down the flue, making the flames dance higher and the old burning timbers crackle even louder. Kate wrapped her slender arms around her tingling flesh, pulled her knees up and rested her chin on them, staring into the blaze to try to read her future.

Eugene was beside her, half behind her, one arm round her waist.

'My. Silk. We shall have to turn you into a parachute.'

'Only if it's you I can drop to safety.'

'Turn to me, and kiss me, and I shall show you stars shaped as you have never seen them.'

Outside the temple the rain grew harder. Inside, the flames in the fireplace grew stronger, as for a while two people were able to turn to each other, and away from war.

*   *   *

In one way Poppy realised she was reluctant to say goodbye to all of Diona de Donnet. Not to her personality—most certainly not. She was only too glad to shake herself free of the haughty, disdainful racist with her unpalatable political views and her overweening snobbery. But her feminine side hated saying goodbye to the exquisite clothes and beautiful accessories she had so enjoyed wearing during her masquerade. Yet she found when she had finally packed them away in the white and gold tissue paper and carefully labelled boxes Section H had supplied for their storage, that not all of Diona went into storage.

So well trained had she been in that brief but intense period of her education, that the poise and the grace with which she had been imbued remained long after the haute couture had been carefully folded up and packed away. Poppy was no longer the socially awkward and timid bespectacled bookworm.

'Everything changes you,' Kate confided to her, on one of their lunchtime walks around the park. 'But nothing surely more than war? I keep wondering if we're going to win, and then I think what does it matter—better to die, as Robert did, doing something that you believe in, or in his case saving a life, than to live in a grey and loveless world. Besides, I think Robert would always have died young, war or no war. He believed in living every minute, not minding about his own life, because he loved life itself so much. That was Robert.'

Poppy, who had only just begun to know Kate and the rest of H Section, was quietened by this, sensing as she did that part of Kate would always be in mourning for her beloved brother, that she would always miss him.

'How are your parents?'

'Leading separate lives. It's their way of coping. Everyone has to find their way, and they've found theirs.'

Kate looked away. There was no point in saying more.

*   *   *

Nowadays poor Billy found himself hopelessly in love not with one but with two beautiful women and refusing to find a life of his own, hanging around both Kate and Poppy, not to mention

Marjorie, doing his once loved but now discarded pet act.

'I know this is hard for you, Billy,' Marjorie kept telling him. 'But you know—you do have to have a life of your own.'

'That's right, Billy.' Mrs Alderman backed her up. 'Hanging round older women isn't healthy, really it's not.'

Marjorie looked across at her, grateful for her intervention.

'Girls,' Billy had sniffed. 'They make me sick.'

'So get some friends of your own, Billy. It doesn't mean we all won't go on being friends, but you're growing up, and you need friends of your own.'

'You're right, Marge. But till I do, can I hang around with you lot?'

But it was Billy who spotted the bracelet.

*　　　*　　　*

The three girls were getting ready to go out for a drink one evening in the local, Kate with Eugene, Poppy with Scott, and poor Marjorie, since there was no one else, with Major Folkestone. Poppy had come across to the cottage to pick up Marjorie and Kate, all dressed up and ready to leave, but since Kate wasn't quite happy with what she had chosen to wear and Marjorie with the way she had done her hair, inevitably Billy was left to entertain Poppy while they set about doing a last-minute change.

'Fancy a game of cards, Pop?' he asked her, producing a pack out of his pocket, Eugene having managed among other things to turn Billy into a proper card sharp. 'Fancy a game of Brag?'

478

'You know I don't have a clue how to play cards, Billy.' Poppy laughed. 'Not to your level, that is, and particularly not Brag. Last time I played you, I lost nearly two shillings.'

'Pontoon for matches?'

'Very well.'

Poppy dealt, but as she did so she realised that Billy's attention was not on the cards she was giving him, but on the bracelet she was wearing round her wrist.

'Where did you get that, Pop?' he asked. 'Where, Pop? Someone give it you, did they?'

'As a matter of fact they did, Billy,' Poppy replied.

'Marge!' Billy called up to her. 'Marge, come and look at this! You won't Christmas Eve it! Pop's wearing a bracelet just like that one what we gave Aunt Hester!'

Marjorie came downstairs, feeling happier with her restyled hair.

'What is it now, Billy?'

'Look, in't that just like the bracelet what we gave Aunt Hester that time?'

Marjorie stared down at the bracelet which Poppy was now holding out for her inspection.

'It's very like it, Billy.'

There was a short silence during which Billy, obviously thinking that some sort of explanation was needed, turned back to Poppy.

'See, our Aunt Hester, she had this bracelet that Marge and I gave her for Christmas, and you know she really liked it. Well, it was more from Marge than me actually, but anyway, she died while she was out practising for the war in the forest, and we never did find that bracelet that Marge and I gave

479

her, and we never did find who done her in neither. But it was our first Christmas, see?' He looked across at Marjorie. 'Our first Christmas together, wasn't it, Marge?'

Marjorie nodded. 'Yes, Billy, quite right, it was our first Christmas.'

Billy's eyes clouded for a while, and he still did not look inclined to pick up his cards.

'Come on, muggins,' Poppy finally chivvied him. 'If you don't hurry up I'll be taking more than my two shillings back off you.'

Marjorie went to the mirror to check her hair one more time. Her new hairstyle was more flattering, she thought, more feminine, caught up into her neck in a soft figure of eight. As she checked it she found herself remembering that first Christmas, Aunt Hester bringing Billy from the school as a present for her, Mr Arnold and Mavis. It all seemed like a century ago, but now it was Christmas again it seemed to her that she could stretch out her hand and touch it, and by doing so it gave her heart. After all, if Billy and she could come through together, anything could happen, and still might. They could even win the war.

*   *   *

Given the worsening situation with the all night raids continuing on London and now even extending to other cities, not to mention the intensifying of the U-boat attacks on merchant convoys, and despite the ever increasing shortages of food and other vital commodities, the Nosy Parkers had done wonders in decorating the great hall where their Christmas party was to be thrown,

480

festooning it with yards and yards of home-made paper decorations that the more artistic girls had fashioned into highly colourful chains, bells and streamers as well as making huge wreaths from braids of holly and ivy garnered from the parkland. An enormous yule log had been cut and was finally creeping into life in the vast ancient stone fireplace, while in one corner a rostrum had been constructed for a band that had been formed by a quintet of in-house musicians, two soldiers supplying the rhythm section of bass and drums, the drum set having been begged and borrowed from the local brass band and the double bass from a classical orchestral musician whose daughter was one of the Nosy Parkers.

The pianist was an over-tall and extremely serious decoding genius from Section C, the guitarist was a jazz fiend from Section H, and the clarinettist was a small, dark-haired young Jewish refugee who had been semi-adopted by Jack Ward and given a job at Eden Park after Jack had helped organise the young man's escape from Germany. It was this young man's idea to form a band since the only thing that had kept him sane through this terrible period of his life was his music, playing his clarinet every evening after he had finished work, usually closeted away in one of the most distant follies in the park so that he would not get on the nerves of his colleagues.

By the time the trio of young women and one young man had made it across from their cottage to the main house, the band was in full swing and the hall was already full of people dancing. And not just boys and girls, girls and girls, since because there was still a far greater number of young women than there were men a lot of the girls danced quite happily together.

Scott spotted Poppy the moment she came into the hall, although he could hardly miss her, as she was in a bright yellow dress with her mane of still blonded hair piled high. However, he barely even managed a greeting to her, let alone to her friends, before whisking her off to dance.

'*Jeepers creepers*,' he began to sing lustily as he danced her round the floor. 'I just love this tune! And the way you look! You are just purely *ravishing!*'

Poppy laughed. The terror of the last few weeks evaporated as couple after couple passed them, everyone suddenly in explosively carefree mood.

'Will you teach me to dance, Marge?' Billy asked, as Kate, Marjorie and he wandered over to a bar set out on a long trestle table to get some refreshment. 'I really think I should learn how to dance.'

'Knowing you, Mr Pick it up Quick,' Marjorie replied, 'one lesson and you'll be treading the light fantastic as if born to it.'

'I don't think so,' Billy said gloomily, watching Scott and Poppy float by. 'Looks too bloomin' difficult to me. Think I'll learn the drums instead.'

Taking a bottle of Mrs Alderman's home-made pop he wandered off to the bandstand where he stood earnestly studying the soldier drummer's great expertise.

'Wonder how many more Christmases the war will last?' Marjorie said, as she and Kate sat down at one of the tables that had been set around the dance floor, lit by a candle in a jam jar.

'No, Marjorie,' Kate scolded her. 'We agreed—

482

no talk of war. It's the party rule.'

'I don't remember agreeing to that, Kate.'

'You do now,' Kate smiled, then raised her glass. 'Happy Christmas. And an even better New Year.'

As they toasted each other, Major Folkestone appeared, almost unrecognisable out of uniform, immaculate in black tie, and with his hair even more carefully creamed and parted than ever.

'If you ladies will excuse me, I wonder if I could have the pleasure of this dance?'

Marjorie nodded to Kate that it would be perfectly all right for her to go and dance, only to find Kate smiling back at her.

'I'm sorry, Marjorie,' Major Folkestone said. 'I meant you. I'm sorry. I should have said. Please forgive me.'

Marjorie frowned and then stood up.

'Yes, of course. I was day-dreaming. So sorry.'

'If you'll excuse us, Kate,' the major said, before dancing away with Marjorie in strictly orthodox fashion.

The band was now playing 'A Foggy Day In London Town', a slow foxtrot, rather than the hectic quickstep of 'Jeepers Creepers'.

'I'm not too bad at the slower ones,' Major Folkestone told Marjorie, trying to sound chatty. 'But do for heaven's sake, if you suffer any toe injuries, remember no radio silence.'

'You dance very nicely, Major,' Marjorie replied. 'If anyone's toes are in danger it could well be yours.'

They danced a full circuit of the floor in silence.

'I find it tricky talking while I dance.'

'I find it practically impossible, Major.'

'So why don't we just dance, Marjorie? And

483

perhaps talk later?'

'That would suit me really well, Major,' Marjorie said, a vague look of cheek in her eyes. 'That way I can keep count of the steps.'

*   *   *

Kate had slipped out on to the front steps of the house. It was a bitterly cold night with a frost already forming and she hadn't been out there longer than a minute when she began to regret her excursion. But rather than lose face by returning straightway through the very doors she had just come out of, she took herself round the front of the house and let herself in through the Orangery.

As soon as she was safely inside the superb glasshouse she stood rubbing the tops of her bare arms to get warm. She stopped as she smelt a familiar aroma, turning to see a curl of blue smoke rising from behind a magnificent tropical-looking plant with huge shining leaves.

'Eugene?'

'The very same. Is that you, Kate?'

'Are you drunk? You sound drunk.'

'I don't think I remember ever being quite sober. Thank the Lord.'

Kate stopped, wondering whether to go and confront him, or simply sneak away and hope that he was drunk enough not to remember having seen her. But that would look as if she was afraid of him, which she most definitely was not. Which was probably why she found herself standing in front of Eugene, who was sitting slouched in an old cane armchair, cheroot clamped between his teeth and a glass of whisky in one hand.

484

'Where have you been, Eugene?'

He stopped her, raising his hand.

'Why didn't you tell me about your brother?' he demanded, looking up at her with a slow sad shake of his head.

Kate stared at him.

'Why should I?' she finally replied, shaking her own head back at him. 'Why should I have told you?'

'Because you should have, that's why.'

'You never met Robert. You didn't know him.'

'I have met you, Kate. I know you.'

'You didn't know how I felt about my brother.'

'I should have treated you differently, had I known.'

Realising what he meant, Kate sat down opposite him and put one hand on his knee.

'Are you trying to say—'

'I'm not trying to say anything, Katie,' he interrupted. 'I *am* saying. I feel, I feel—I have taken advantage of your plight.'

'You can't take advantage of someone if you don't know the state they are in.'

'Which is why I *should* have known.'

'Actually, if you really want to know, if anyone took advantage of anyone, then it would have been me.'

'Are you sure?'

'Quite sure. Now, come on, let's join the party. No more getting lachrymose—this little lady wants to dance.'

Eugene stood up slowly, put his glass down on the table by his chair, looked at Kate carefully and tenderly put his arms about her.

'Can't I have a go?' Billy asked the drummer yet again.

'No, kid,' the soldier replied firmly. 'Sorry.'

'But why not?'

'Because you can't play.'

'How do you know?' Billy protested. 'You haven't given me a go.'

'Afterwards perhaps,' the soldier said with a grin. 'OK. At the end. Afterwards. Maybe.'

'After what?' Billy demanded. 'The set? The party?'

'The war,' the soldier laughed, crashing his cymbal. 'And then only maybe.'

Marjorie came to the rescue. The soldier gave her the eye.

'I'm almost tempted to let him have a go, so that I can dance with you.'

'Oh please?' Billy cried, hopping on the spot. 'Please dance with him, Marge! Then he'll let me play.'

'Trouble is the other guys will kill me!' the soldier called, as the music grew louder. 'Maybe later? One of the slower numbers? That don't need me.'

'Maybe!' Marjorie called back. 'And then maybe not!'

Scott and Poppy stopped by Marjorie, no longer dancing.

'Look after Poppy?' Scott asked, on the move. 'I have to fetch something!'

'Billy wants to learn how to dance,' Marjorie told Poppy with a hidden wink.

'I don't,' Billy grumbled. 'I want to have a go on

486

the drums.'

'Tell you what,' Poppy suggested. 'To see if you have rhythm or not, why don't you dance with me? Then if you have got rhythm, perhaps Marjorie and I will be able to persuade this nice man here to let you have a go.'

Poppy bestowed her best smile on the soldier, who was busy signing triplets on his side cymbal. He was so overcome he missed the next beat. By now Poppy had hold of Billy and was showing him the basic dancing position before carefully and skilfully dancing him off round the floor.

Someone tapped Marjorie on the shoulder. Still with half an eye on Poppy and Billy, who had his head down to watch where he was putting his feet, she looked round and saw it was Lily.

'Have you got a moment?' she wondered. 'I'd like a word.'

Marjorie eyed her. They had hardly exchanged a word since Robert's funeral, preserving only the niceties when their paths crossed, but avoiding contact of any deeper significance.

'I had promised the next dance to Major Folkestone,' Marjorie replied, after what she hoped was a telling pause.

'Please?' Lily said. 'It won't take a moment.'

*   *   *

Overhead, thousands of feet up, the stricken Dornier DO17, nick-named the Flying Pencil because of its long slender fuselage, was limping its way back to base after yet another night raid. The crew were flying their seventh mission, the lucky mission their captain had called it—number 7 would bring them all home safely. They were a crack bomber crew, singled out by Goering himself for their accuracy and for their unblemished record.

But number 7 wasn't so lucky for them after all— not that night. Their run of luck ran out on the approach to their target. As their squadron entered the mouth of the Thames to home in on London they were attacked by a flight of high-flying Hurricanes, under the command of the famous daredevil Jimmy Richardson, who, although severely wounded by cannon shells that had ripped into his cockpit, stayed at his controls long enough to hit and take out one of the Dornier's twin engines before finally bailing out, landing in the seas far below which at once and mercifully put out the fire that had all but burned up his flying suit.

Aware of the seriousness of the damage to his craft, the Dornier's captain at once ordered a return to base, knowing that to continue would be to sign his crew's death sentence. Stabilising the aircraft as best he could once he had turned tail, he realised that if the benign flying conditions prevailed, then they should just about be able to make it home . . . just about.

And before the worst came to the worst they always had the option of lightening their aircraft up by dumping their bomb load.

The only problem was that the shortest but not the safest way home was over land, not sea. In this instance the shortest distance between two points was very definitely a straight line—a straight line that was going to head the Dornier DO17 right over Eden Park.

*   *   *

488

The two young women sat at a table at the back of the hall, as far away as possible from the band so they could speak to each other more easily.

'I don't expect us to be friends,' Lily was saying. 'That is, I don't expect you to like me, Marjorie. So that's not what I wanted to talk to you about.'

'It's not impossible,' Marjorie replied. 'We could still be friends.'

'That would be rather up to you,' Lily replied, lighting up a cigarette. 'But I know you've got a thing about me, because of—because of Robert. And because I've always been a bit of a pain anyway. That's just me. Sorry. I don't mean any harm by it. Honestly.'

Marjorie looked at her, but said nothing.

'If it hadn't been for Robert,' Lily continued, 'I think we might have been friends. But because—well. Because he asked me out, and because he wanted to marry me—'

'It doesn't matter,' Marjorie said quickly. 'I'd really rather not talk about this if you don't mind. Especially not at a Christmas party.'

She went to stand up.

'I have to talk about it,' Lily insisted, putting a hand on her arm. 'We have to talk about it. To clear the air. You're choked with me because Robert asked me out—because he chose me, if you like.'

'No I don't like actually. Not much.'

'Yes, I know, Marjorie, but these things happen. At least that was how this thing happened. It wasn't as if I pinched him from you.'

Lily looked at Marjorie expecting some sort of answer, but Marjorie didn't reply. She just looked

489

past Lily as if something totally riveting was happening behind her on the dance floor.

'Well, was it?' Lily demanded. 'It wasn't as if you'd been out with him.'

'I spent a whole Sunday with him, if you must know,' Marjorie said defensively. 'The Sunday you eyed him up.'

'I didn't *eye him up*, Marjorie. And as far as I understood it from Robert, you'd gone to his home with Kate. It wasn't as if he'd asked you.'

Again Marjorie refused to reply, for the very good reason that she knew that Lily was right.

'Look,' Lily continued, keeping hold of Marjorie's hand. 'I don't want to sound sorry for myself, and I don't expect you to feel sorry for me. But I can't tell you what this has been like. These last few weeks—ever since Robert was killed. I'm not saying it's been worse for me than for Kate say—I can't say that. All I *can* say is that I have been to hell and back every single damned day. I know now it was all my fault Robert was killed. But for me and the wretched ring he would be alive tonight. We'd be dancing here, tonight.'

'It was an accident.'

'Robert wouldn't have been anywhere near that shop let alone that town if it hadn't been for *me*, Marjorie. He'd asked me to marry him—and I'd seen this ring in Bendon . . .' Her voice tailed off, and she quickly lit a cigarette.

Marjorie stared at her. 'Once,' she began, in a different voice, 'once I was moaning to my Aunt Hester about how something I'd done was all my fault, and she said no—no, it was an *accident*, Marjorie. That's why we have the word—that's why things like that are called accidents. Because they happen by accident—accidentally—not on purpose. They're awfully hard to come to terms with, she said, because we're always trying to come to terms with things. To tidy everything up and give a reason for everything, particularly when it comes to pinning the blame. But it isn't always someone's fault. Often it's exactly what the word says it is—an accident. You and Robert being in Bendon that day—that was a perfect example. You wanted to get an engagement ring, you went to a town, it got bombed. There was an accident—and Robert—Robert got killed. But you might have gone to another town and there might have been a different accident and he might still have got killed. Or he might not. But whatever happened, it was not your fault. You didn't kill him. It was an accident.'

'If you knew how I felt—'

'Feelings won't bring Robert back. What we have to do is harness all that—all those feelings—into making everything whole again. That's what.'

Lily nodded, silent, still smoking. Kate had said the same thing to her, in different words, but it still made no difference, for the truth that she was facing was that she loved Robert now more than she had loved him when he was alive. She had wanted to be married to get away. He had wanted to marry her because he loved her. Now she realised how much she had loved him—and he was gone.

*   *   *

High above, although not as high as they had been when they had turned for home, the Dornier

491

continued its slow but still steady flight.

'We have sufficient fuel?' the captain asked. He had hoped it was a rhetorical question since one of the many strengths of the Dornier was its long-range ability.

'We had enough fuel, sir,' his second in command replied. 'We seemed to be containing the leak we sustained as a result of the hit to the starboard engine—but now we're losing it from somewhere else.'

'Have we enough to get home?'

'Not with what we're carrying, sir. We're going to have to jettison our bomb load.'

'Reichsmarschall Goering won't like it! We waste not and we want not!'

'Reichsmarschall Goering won't need to know about it!' his subordinate grinned back.

'With him on board?' the captain nodded back at their bomb-aimer, their unfriendly Fascist as they called him, the only card-bearing Party member in the crew. 'Fat chance.'

'We're going to have to jettison, sir, come what may.'

'Then we'd better find a safe place to do so.'

They were fast approaching the place that was going to be selected by their bombardier as safe—or certainly as far as he was privately concerned suitable.

That target lay only twenty miles south of them, half hidden in a fold of frost-covered hills.

*   *   *

Jack Ward arrived late for the Eden Park party, detained on business concerning the arrest of the other leading players in Basil Tetherington's dangerous drama, which happily for everyone had

492

failed to unfold. Once inside the great hall of the house, he was delighted to see the extent of the Christmas decoration, including a huge tree that had been felled on the estate and beautifully decorated by the most artistic members of the Nosy Parkers.

He had with him a small box that he carried most carefully, leaving it with his coat and hat in the nearest cloakroom while he went to look for the person to whom he wished to present it. On his way across the crowded room he was greeted by Major Folkestone who was sitting at a table on the edge of the dance floor talking to Lily.

'Happy Christmas, everyone,' Jack called as he walked by.

'Thank you, sir,' Lily replied.

Major Folkestone excused himself for a moment.

'A thoroughly satisfactory result all round I'd say, wouldn't you, sir?' the major said, as they walked along the side of the dance floor.

'Not bad at all, Major,' Jack replied. 'The Old Man's certainly pleased. As he should be, by God.'

'I've got something I need to discuss with you when you have a moment.'

'Will it keep till tomorrow, Major? This looks like a good party.'

'Certainly, sir. I wasn't going to discuss it tonight. No fear. It can most certainly wait. It only concerns young Lily back there.'

'She was engaged to Kate's brother if I'm not mistaken,' Jack said with a discreet backward glance. 'The poor chap who was killed rescuing that child.'

'That's the girl. She wants to volunteer for SOE.

493

She can speak French, and German, to a degree.'

Jack stopped and frowned at Major Folkestone, then looked back at Lily who was sitting smoking a cigarette and swinging one long elegant leg in time to the band.

'Interesting. I wouldn't have said she was the type.'

'My thoughts precisely, sir. Funny thing is, they were also hers.'

Jack frowned at the major again, awaiting an explanation.

'I said the same to her, said, "I didn't think you were the type." And she said, "No sir, no neither did I. Until now."'

Jack thought about what the major had just told him, looked back at Lily once more, who was still smoking her cigarette and watching the dancers, and then nodded.

'Knows what she could be letting herself in for, does she?'

'Should do by now.'

Jack thought a moment more then nodded again, this time finally.

'Very well. We'd better go into it in a bit more detail with her, wouldn't you say? Bring her in to my office tomorrow afternoon around tea time. We should have all recovered from the party by then.'

Jack wandered on, scouring the room for his target. Finally he saw her, being returned to her table by Scott who had just finished dancing with her yet again. Poppy seemed to sense his presence because although she was looking in the opposite direction entirely, she suddenly turned round and met his eye. Jack smiled, nodded and crooked his little finger for her to come over. Poppy promptly

494

excused herself.

Jack signalled to her to go round the dance floor on the opposite side to him and meet him over by the Christmas tree.

'I have something for you,' he said. 'I was going to hang it on the tree, but then when I saw you, I thought I might as well give it to you in person.'

'That's very kind of you,' Poppy replied. 'I'm afraid I haven't had time to do my Christmas shopping yet.'

'Perfectly understandable—I didn't have to shop for this. Come along.'

Poppy followed Jack out of the great hall and into one of the side passages that led to the cloakrooms, thinking of that night not so long ago when she had been in a similar position in a large house, but that time she had been in grave danger and Jack had been her rescuer. She was able to smile at the memory as she followed Jack once more to the gentlemen's cloaks into which he now disappeared, thinking of the strange and odd and completely unpredictable way her life had been turned quite upside down by that chance meeting.

Jack now re-emerged and handed her the carrier box with which he had arrived.

'I haven't even wrapped it,' he grunted. 'But I don't think you'll mind.'

Poppy knew before she opened the top of the box that she had now placed carefully on the floor. She looked up at Jack, who was frowning back down at her.

'Open it, for goodness' sake,' he muttered. 'Get a move on.'

Poppy folded back the two flaps of the strong cardboard box and saw the nose at the end of the beautiful long doleful face she had missed so dreadfully.

'George!'

His long tail wagged furiously now as he recognised his mistress.

'He's put on a bit of weight, I'm afraid. He's a bit of a doer, your George.'

'We'll soon walk that off.' Poppy laughed. 'We'll walk that off in no time at all.'

'He's put something else on, too. You won't be able to see if you're holding him.'

Putting the dog at her feet, Poppy stood back to take a good look. George yawned in excitement then shook himself, and as he did so Poppy could see that Jack had taken off his old collar and replaced it with a brand new thick leather one resplendently coloured in vibrant red, white and blue, with a decorative bulldog's head hanging from its identity ring.

'Oh, Jack!' Poppy laughed. 'Jack, that really is most elegant. Thank you. Thank you very much.'

'No, Poppy, not at all,' Jack growled, sticking his pipe in his mouth. 'Thank you. Now I'm going to rejoin the party, and if you know what's good for you you will too.'

*   *   *

The Dornier, still weighed down by its unused high explosive bombs, was now no more than one dance away, no more than a tune. But far below the Flying Pencil there were others who were not at play but at work—a new unit, working a brand new installation not more than a mile from Eden. And it was a local man on watch who first heard the drone, who sounded the alarm to his unit and who finally pinpointed a raider homeward bound.

*　　*　　*

Actually it was Scott who was the surprise hit of the party, most especially after he had reappeared with a large cloth bag tied tightly at the neck with a coloured cord, which he produced at the table at which now sat Poppy, Kate, Eugene, Marjorie and Billy. The bag immediately aroused Billy's interest. Scott had hardly sat down before Billy grabbed it and tried to undo it.

'Time they altered the call-up age,' Scott told him, narrowing his eyes in mock anger at Billy. 'High time they reduced it to *fourteen*.'

'But what's in it?' Billy demanded. 'Is it a present for someone?'

'That depends on how people see it,' Scott replied. 'It also depends a lot on my lip.'

'Your lip?' Billy frowned deeply. 'What's it got to do with your lip?'

'Everything,' Scott said, having undone the cord and produced from the cloth bag a shimmering highly polished silver cornet.

'Wow!' Billy gasped. 'Can you play that?'

Scott certainly could. He introduced himself to the band, talked through a few numbers, jotted down some chord sequences for the pianist, guitarist and bass player, and blew a few perfect and clear notes by himself to make sure his lip was in, as he had explained to Billy—then tapped the band in to 'Falling In Love With Love'.

One chorus in and everyone who hadn't danced before now got up and danced. By the time Scott's cornet was soaring over the band with a slow and heartbreaking version of 'September Song', the great hall was a mass of people dancing, and those who weren't dancing stood at the foot of the bandstand just to listen to the wonderful music.

' "I Can't Get Started"!' someone called.

' "Pennies From Heaven"!' someone else suggested.

' "I Can't Get Started"!' the first voice insisted.

'The man's right,' Eugene agreed, getting up on the rostrum and taking hold of the microphone. 'Play it like Bunny. Play it like Berigan and I'll croon it like Crosby.'

All over the hall the candles in their jars sputtered and danced and flickered, as Eugene sang and Scott played.

*   *   *

'I have the area, Captain,' the bombardier's voice came through the captain's headset. 'I have found a good place for us to drop.'

'It needs to be soon and it needs to be now,' the captain replied. 'You are quite certain this is just land? No buildings? No houses, no village?'

'Just land, captain. What they call downland I believe.'

'Are we over it now?'

'One minute to target, sir,' the bombardier replied, looking through his sights, hoping to get some sort of image of the huge grand house he believed now lay almost directly below them. But just as he was taking perfect aim, something hit the tail plane of the Dornier, tearing half of it away. The plane shook violently, shuddered and started to tilt alarmingly.

498

'Flak!' the captain called as he looked out of his side window. 'Anti-aircraft battery ten degrees west! Seems to have taken out our rudder! Losing control fast!'

More shells hit the already stricken craft, knocking it first sideways and then upwards as a shell exploded directly under the left wing, holing the fuselage and letting a sudden great gale of air into the cabin.

'Prepare to bail out!' the captain called. 'Prepare to jump! Go on! Jump! Jump everyone! Everyone jump!'

But not until he had opened his bomb doors, the bombardier crouched over his sights decided. If they were going down then let them feel the full and mighty force of his bombs. Let them be blown to the next life by the might of the great Reichsmarschall's air force.

'Bombs away!' he called, but no one was listening. No one heard his cry because they were already earthbound, floating down on umbrellas of silk. The bombs had plunged past them in the dark, but they had fallen straight down, while the airmen who had already bailed out were being gently blown southwards, away from the targeted house far below.

'Bombs away!' the bombardier called again joyously, as he too prepared to bail out. But it was too late for him. Another shell smashed into the aircraft directly below his position, killing him instantly and causing the plane to explode seconds later. The sky was filled with a huge orange fireball that seemed to hang in the air before fragmenting to fall in myriad pieces on to the downland below.

*   *   *

The band had just finished playing. Scott was swinging his cornet on one hand while wrapping his

499

free arm round Eugene's shoulder, who was taking an extravagant bow to wild and happy applause, when everyone stopped still as they heard the unmistakable crump of a bomb exploding somewhere nearby. Everyone either threw themselves to the floor, to take cover under the tables, or ran to the huge double staircase to shelter under the overhang. One or two even made it down to the cellars. There was silence everywhere.

There had been no siren, at least not one anyone in the hall had heard, yet that was definitely the sound of a bomb they had heard exploding.

Everyone waited, hands over heads or ears, many people embracing whoever it was that lay nearest to them. The absolute silence continued and because it was absolute one or two people began slowly to look about and wonder. There was no damage to the house, at least none that was visible.

Eugene, Scott and Major Folkestone were the three who had refused to take cover, running instead to the great front doors that they had flung open to see what if any the damage was. In the clear frosty moonlit night they could quite clearly see where the bomb had fallen, down by the lake where it had destroyed many of the ancient oak trees, leaving a huge crater in the ground. The fact that the waters of the lake were still greatly disturbed on a windless night suggested that if any other bombs had fallen, that was where they now lay—at the bottom of the ornamental water.

Eugene saw them first—pointing up to the sky where, illuminated in the bright whiteness of moonlight, three parachutists could be seen descending, the remains of their aircraft having already preceded them to earth beyond the line of hills that sheltered Eden.

Major Folkestone, once more on duty, ran up the steps to the house snapping out orders. Almost immediately the resident platoon of soldiers ran out of the hall, pulling on jackets and tin hats and slinging loaded rifles over their shoulders as they rushed off to capture the falling airmen. They were followed by the rest of the party.

Everyone began to hurry towards the home paddock, so that by the time the three men landed in the frozen grass there were a dozen soldiers bearing down on them, followed by at least three dozen more civilians, armed with sticks, boulders and an assortment of home-made weaponry. As the rest of the party began to arrive they found Billy was already at the paddock fence, prevented from hopping over and taking the first German prisoner by Major Folkestone.

As the three German airmen picked themselves slowly up off the ground, and stepped out of the parachute harness, the soldiers under Major Folkestone's command dropped to one knee and took aim. The major barked an order in German, aiming his own pistol at the nearest airman, the captain of the Dornier. Everyone fell to silence.

The captain of the stricken aircraft called to Major Folkestone, in perfect English, that they were going to reach for their pistols and throw them to the ground. Major Folkestone thanked him but called back that if anyone tried to shoot they would be killed immediately. The captain responded that he understood perfectly and then surrendered his weapons to the frosted grass in front of him. His two fellow crew members did the

501

same and then they all three put their hands on their heads.

Marjorie left her group of friends and walked down to the paddocks, not noticing the bitter cold, intent only on getting sight of the enemy. Billy was standing by the paddock gate that one of the soldiers had swung open, hands straight down by his sides, head unmoving as he watched.

The soldiers now surrounded the three airmen, outnumbering them to an almost absurd degree. With rifles at the ready, some still aimed and trained, they steered the airmen out of the field ahead of them. The captain, a short, handsome man, with blond hair cropped close and eyes that seemed to be more humorous than serious, walked alongside his two airmen with a nonchalance that must have belied his feelings. He must have hurt himself on landing, because he limped, and so eventually was helped by one of the soldiers, who finally lit a cigarette and put it between his lips.

As they approached the crowd of people waiting, some of whom drew instinctively back, the captain nodded and raised one hand in salute. Everyone stared at him, except Billy who now detached himself from the gate and carefully approached the airmen in order to get a better look.

'Ah, hallo,' the captain said, seeing the boy. 'And how old are you?'

'Me?' Billy wondered. 'Me, I'm fourteen.'

'What is your name?'

'Billy. My name's Billy.'

'Good.' The captain smiled and tilted his head to get a better look at the boy who was now walking alongside him. 'You're a good-looking chap, Billy,' he said. 'And you know what? I have a young brother at home just the same age as you are.'

He ruffled Billy's hair and walked on with a smile. Billy frowned, stroked his hair back into place, then hurried on to catch up so that he could walk alongside the captain all the way back to the house where a number of the partygoers were still waiting. Poppy watched intently as the figure of Major Folkestone in his evening dress, still carrying his pistol in hand, approached the front steps of the great house. To the major's right were the three captured airmen, and to their right young Billy, with Marjorie walking by his side. Behind were the armed soldiers, outnumbering their prisoners by at least four to one, while behind them were the men and women of Eden Park. No one talked. All that could be heard was the sound of many footfalls on the frozen gravel. Until another sound was heard, the silver sound of a cornet, clear as a clarion on the winter night air. When the playing started, everyone stopped, staring at the silhouetted figure of Scott as he played 'Silent Night'. The three airmen stood looking up at him from the foot of the steps, none of them moving as the notes fled across the frosty ground, to finally bury themselves in the English countryside.